MESOPOTAMIA//TIAMAT

The Shadow of Asgard

Ashley Wrigley

To Mom, the most beautiful woman in the world,
and Dad, my very own John Wayne

It was in the darkness where no innocent tread.

The run down service tunnels stretched for miles above the coal pockets and under the slate ridges. The electrical system buzzed in a sort of haywire cluster-fuck of loose and snapped wires where static flashes and fleuro-neurescents flickered in the dense air. Old train cars littered the railways; some were still on the magnetic hinge but most were tipped over and propped in unnatural positions by gangers, rastas, hack-jobs, and skinheads.

The filth that wandered the subway, so affectionately called the Mine by its inhabitants, included rodents, mites, spiders, stray dogs, hairless cats, 15-year-old punk jobs, a-heads, Tamden mutations, new viral strains, subterranean needlers a.k.a. ass-fucks, and any other half-a-brain-and-drugged-up criminal still calling himself human.

The Mine was the breeding and resting ground of the criminal, the pervert, the reject, the exiled, the druggy, the hopeless, the spiritual, the wicked, and the damned. A scum-scutter network, quite literally, as sewers and transit tunnels connected caverns, blow-out pockets, and scatter towns. It even had a name—Kishar—which encompassed the whole of the underground nation. It was its own civilization beneath the wonder-world of shining white hope in the form of steel towers that reflected the green haze of lipilus gases and micro-toxins of the Vexender Age.

That wonder-world was Anshar—surface realm and shining white hope, where the exiles, cast down criminals, druggies—and the list goes on—descended from. It was the place of prosperity, even as the scorched sky churned above. Thriving cities of varying cultural significances and monetary extremes bloomed over the surface, gaps filled by industrial wastelands and scrap parks.

Finally, there was the Grey, the last piece of the territorial puzzle that made up the grand nation called Lotus Maze. It was the middle-ground between surface and subterranean, the old pipelines, sewage and electrical system, and grid stations. It was a twisting path going up or down between the worlds, a refuge, a hiding place—and only the truly insane actually stayed for any length of time. It was ruled—term used loosely—by the Krueh-jin, though the gypsy-nomads held no sway in the Paragon.

The Paragon of Power was made up of three authorities that held sway over the common people—those independent of an agency. The three supremacies waged constant war.

Mirax Augmentation and Aero-cognition Research was a monolith and megacorporation of the Sykolictic Age with hands in every aspect of street and cyberwire on the virtual and physical grid. Their white hand symbol was plastered on every product pumped out of the factories and sewn onto the flags that waved in the winds of the hierarchy.

They ruled the surface world of their borders—Anshar.

Their agents were called angels and they moved out of the White Tower into and through every layer of the city's civilized world above ground where those with a heartbeat possessed identification to prove their existence, unlike those of the Mine. The angels wore suits with bald heads. On their right hand, angel wings were tattooed in silver ink. Their ears were in every wall and their eyes could be found down every street. There was no place the angels could not and did not go, even when their bodies were not present.

MAAR—often dubbed Mirax—controlled the city-nation and branched out to those beyond its borders into all societies except for the subterranean city beneath its monumental belly—the Mine—where the archenemy of Mirax held sway.

They were called occultists and radicals by some. Others referred to them as prophets. Still, their names ranged from Mafioso thugs to the divine engineers of the coming apocalypse. The corporate union knew them for what they really were: thugs and mercenaries united under black market merchants. They were corporates of the black world with rumors to cover their dirty hands with grimy gloves just as their twins in the white towers had hands powder puffed to hide the dirt they excavated under the labor of the citizens of Anshar.

The corporation was called Black Tuesday and they mimicked Mirax in their defiance of corporate control—a mercantile band of freedom fighters transformed into a power-hungry commercial and communal rebellion designed to aid the scum-scutters in wrecking their lives and fight the oppression of the White Tower's will. Their symbol was a black hand and their agents were the terrors of the tunnels, spewed forth from that dark and terrible agency often called

The Black Hand.

They were cogwheelers, recognizable only by two defining features: the cogwheel tattoo on the back of the left hand and the copper pocket watch frequently checked. They pushed every inch of the Mine so that no corner was safe from feeling the fear of their step-above-thug power principle.

There was something more human about the cogwheelers than their angel counterparts. Perhaps, it was their upbringing: the liberation from white plastic walls and starch-smelling teachers that schooled their students in addition and subtraction, the ABCs, geography, biology, and, oh yeah, how to stealth-kill a civy at 1000 yards with a paper air plane and an environmentally safe styro-fork. No questions asked.

No, the cogwheelers were street meat. Some were shock troops—shot up with adrenaline coming out of an alley, roped up, mind-grafted, and rolled onto the back truck for deployment. Some were recruited out of the womb from mother's who couldn't afford to feed themselves, much less a baby. Others joined the cause because smoking green, chasing hackers, and fighting off needlers was a wasted existence. They weren't smart, but instinct made up for their enemies' intelligence. They were able to replace the million dollar education with the pressure of being born into a world that threatened to take their lives at every corner they crossed since they could say, "Tit for tat, fuck you Redge Millers", and those were practically their first words.

The two powers had only one common enemy: the Keepers.

The Keepers were the secret society of harpers whose name broadcasted their purpose in beautiful, bold navy blue letters written in archaic script: Keepers of the Balance. They were the silent saviors of the people, invisible, moving unrecognized through the throngs amassed. Their towers were unmarked, erected all over the city, opened by a glyph only Keepers could see. The angels and the cogwheelers did not know how to find them. MAAR and Black Tuesday had never done business with them. The Keepers were all but ghosts, locked in their hidden sanctuaries, watching the world and the madness unfold.

Whenever the angels took precedence on the battlefield, the Keepers were there to cut them down and even out the score. If the cogwheelers were pushing the angels back into the city, the Keepers pounced upon them, breaking the force and returning balance to the scale. If either authority sought machinations of power to aid them in their quest for supremacy, the Keepers joined the race for such an artifact or relic to maintain equilibrium.

The Keepers could not be recognized by a tattoo or a form of dress. The Keepers were unmarked. The Keepers were everywhere.

The agents of the Keepers came in darkness where no innocent tread.

Part One

"He cannot complain of a hard sentence, who is made master of his own fate."

Johann Friedrich Von Schiller

Ralph Gobol was dusting the Seer's Cell, the chamber of the Oracle. Though the collective were still under Elysium, Ralph saw no reason why they shouldn't keep the Oracle's room tidy. After all, it was one of their most important artifacts, revered in Keeper society. The Oracle was a core of their power, he thought to himself, as though imagining the excuse he would give were he caught disobeying orders. It was a core of their power, near god-like, and deserved to exist in clean conditions.

So he had snuck in after hours and kept the room dark so as not to disturb the others. The eerie, blue glow of the scrying pool cast dancing reflections and light onto the walls and Ralph used the bit of luminosity to clean the chamber.

He was dusting around the far wall, cleaning beneath one of the relics when he heard a strange sound. Ralph stopped and turned around.

The pool was gurgling.

He dropped his feather duster and braced himself against the table, swallowing a squeak of surprise. A light shot up from the pool and a wraith-like whisper hissed, echoing around the circular chamber.

The words were prophecy.

Ralph ran to the pool and stared down into the depths. A blue flame streaked across the water's surface, tracing exact lines to form a glyph. It continued to burn over the gurgling liquid as the hissing voice repeated the prophecy over and over again

Ralph flung himself from the chamber and raced down the halls toward the library.

"Elysium's broken!" he screamed. "Prophecy! Prophecy! Elysium has been broken!"

"Tad, hur'yup!" Bit yelled to the rafters bellow as he ran along the station platforms, watching his dread-head friend race the magnet charge along the transit railway from L-Pole to South Crossing.

"Just gettada bridge!" Tad told him, jumping every other

rung as the EM pulses nipped at his heels.

"You ain't gonna make it! Jump th' deck!"

"Fuck no! I'm gon'make it!"

"I sed jump th' fuckin' deck, asshole!"

"Fuck you, bibby-bitch! I'm gon'make it!" Tad screamed, feeling the charge on his ass. He jumped across three rungs and did a roll, barely missing the flack-trap along the track. He was on his feet faster than a sprinter in a two-yard needler chase and running once more. South Crossing was just up ahead and he could see Bit headed for the bridge.

Bit's sneakers hit the cement and cracked tiles hard, crunching everything under the soft soles of his shoes as he raced for the wooden bridge between Newyard and Kettle Kot. He jumped the junk rolls and dodged some Rastafarians as he neared the outskirts of town.

"Slow it down, little mon," one of the Rastas said as Bit barreled by him. The Rasta had to flick his lighter three times before finding a flame to catch fire at the end of his joint. "Kids d'ese days," he muttered with the fix between his lips. "Always in-a hurry."

Bit took a wide turn, unable to slow his momentum, and rounded into a right onto the bridge. He flung himself at the railing, unconcerned by the shudder of the wood under his weight, and lowered the rubber line.

Tad hauled ass down the train-way with the electro-magnetic charges popping under his feet. He could see the rubber line dangling up ahead and knew that freedom lay in twenty yards in the form of stripped tires knotted together. It was so close…

Then he felt it. The wind was on his back.

Tad risked a glance back and saw a surge of air funneling toward him out of the blackness of the tunnel behind him.

"Whadda fuck?!" he screeched, tripping over his own shoes. He would've fallen onto electric charges and been rail-cooked had the wind not pushed him a bit further. Tad felt the rubber rope scratch his face and he grabbed with all of his might, scurrying up onto the tether as fast as he could climb, whimpering and cussing and praying that he hadn't shit himself.

Bit pulled him onto the bridge and the two friends looked up just in time to feel the gust of wind on their faces and see the dark shape cut through the blackness at the roof of the cavern. They jumped to their feet and ran to the other end of the bridge, seeing the wake of the whatever-the-hell-that-was moving deeper into the Mine.

"Whatever itus, itsa headin' ferda cogwheels'rs," Bit muttered. He then scrunched up his nose and glanced over at Tad. "You'da shit yerself, didn'cha?"

"What'sit to ya, chicken shit? I had some flying freak sneak up on my ass while EM charges is threatenin' ta light it up!" Tad argued, hiding his embarrassment. Bit waved his hand, dismissing his friend's excuses.

"Yeah, whatever, just go change 'fore Nissy sees. We don'need bitchy-Nissy gettin' us'n more trouble."

"Damn sure. We'll be shovelin' pacers for the next two weeks, she catch us runnin' railings like Charlie and Sampson," Tad muttered, patting the back of his pants in disgust. He pulled his sweater over his head and tied it around his waist to hide the stain then he and Bit moved along the bridge down the makeshift path toward Newyard.

The cogwheelers pulled crates of micron-semicilin off of trucks and loaded them onto jerry carts to be pushed down the boardwalk toward Black Tuesday's warehouse location in Bilf, one of hundreds of underground towns in the Mine. The micron that was being herded was one of the Luna-II strings, rare and invaluable on the Lotus Maze market.

"Careful with this next shipment, boys. Boss'll freak if anything happens to it. It's supposed to be high-crime and worth its weight in gold and all our heads if we let it go missing or break it," the head cogwheeler told his contingent.

"Another relic snuck out from under the White Tower's big, fat nose?" one of them asked, snickering behind crooked teeth and a rather large nose himself. A fellow cogwheeler sneered in glee, hoisting a crate from the truck and sliding his squatted self to the jerry cart.

"They don't need no relic, the pansy pushers. They gots the light while they stuff us down here in the dingy, dirty, mother-fuckin' depths of oblivion, the sods," he muttered. As if on cue, all ten cogwheelers spit at the ground in near perfect unison.

"Doesn't matta! The Black Hand will fix 'em soon

enough."

"We all will."

"Alright, alright, get movin'!" the head cogwheeler barked, curling his left hand into a fist where veins protruded beneath the cog tattoo.

A ball of black smoke hit the ground where the cogwheelers were working and seemed to explode in all directions. Commotion reared up around the small space as the Black Hand's agents drew their guns and sick-sticks, ready to pounce upon the intruder.

The coal-like cloud sucked into nothingness and left a body in its wake.

A woman stood amid the cogwheelers, wrapped head to toe in leather the color of pitch and silver ringlets where slips were knotted to hold the uniform to her frame. Long, ebony strips of cloth hung off of the outfit like ribbons, spiraling in circles on the ground. The same material was wrapped around her mouth, hiding the lower half of her face.

The cogwheelers stared in shock and wonderment, watching the wannabe-ninja bitch standing perfectly still amid their circle. The head cogwheeler peered at her more intently and his eyes caught a glimpse of something unusual. A flicker, a sparkle. He focused harder and then finally understood what we was looking at.

In the center of her forehead, a blue glyph was glowing.

"Fuck!" he screamed, lifting his shotgun to the ready. "Keeper!"

The fellow cogwheelers didn't wait to figure out the big revelation for themselves; they lifted their weapons and took aim or charged.

The Keeper drew her sword in seconds, darting around the small space at unreal speeds. Shotguns and pistols were popping off in chaotic intervals as the gurgling sound of dying screams and choked coughs accompanied the swings of the Keeper's sword amid the black shadow that followed her. Those ribbons danced in wide arcs and graceful, fluid motions as her blade ripped through each tender throat and pierced each sturdy chest.

Before long, the only sound that could be heard was the sound of the silver bells jingling around the Keeper's right wrist.

The cogwheelers lay dead around her.

She moved to the crate rumored to carry the relic. In one swift movement, she sheathed her sword onto her left side and knelt at the box. Quickly prying the wooden crate open, the Keeper lifted the top off and glanced inside.

Empty.

She slammed the top back on the crate as she stood. Turning on an angry step, the Keeper disappeared in a burst of soot-like wind and shot off down the tunnel like a shadow racing away from the light.

"There's nothin' out here," Charlie muttered. "For the last time, you kids'is been sniffin' too much coal-crack."

"Charlie, theres'wa weird winds a-blowin'. I swearit," Bit argued. Tad jogged alongside the platform, looking down into the tunnels he was racing along only an hour before. He'd changed his pants and Bit had gotten his older brother Charlie to come investigate the happenings.

"He ain't lyin', Charlie," Tad told the twenty-year-old. "It lit up my ass! Tripped me over th' five-run stretch an'ran me right in'ta th' rubber."

"There ain't no wind down here, guys," Charlie explained, hands on his hips. "There ain't no wind down here 'cept during winter, an-it's the middle-a summer."

"Duuuuuuh!" Tad sang, throwing his voice in a low, droll pitch.

"No shit, Charlie!" Bit said over Tad's hum. "That's why it's-a weird."

"Stop playin' near the coal chutes. The soot is gettin' in yer brains." Charlie smacked both Bit and Tad on the side of the head as he walked passed them. "Now leave me alone."

"You ass, Charlie!" Bit yelled after his brother.

Just then, a gust of wind blew past them, going the opposite direction than before. It knocked Bit and Tad off of their feet and caused Charlie to stumble backward.

Silence.

"Told ya, dumb-head," Tad muttered. Charlie stared wide-eyed down the tunnel and only one word found his vocal chords.

"Whoa…"

Jeebo James-Jameson was walking across Black Tuesday's guild hall fortress in Thebes, grand city of the Mine. Other cogwheelers and Black Hand operatives and merchants rushed here and there on errands and tasks, shuffling about their daily business as the previous week rolled into the next and so forth.

Jeebo reminded himself that it was just another day in the struggle for dominance against the White Tower. He folded his thick, stubby fingers across his wide belly and thumbed the thick gold rings on his fat phalanges. *Ah, it's a good day to be a mercantile madman,* he thought. He'd thought the same thing the day before, and the day before that. He thought the same thing every day and it had yet to ring false to his money-grubbing mind.

"Boss!" a cogwheeler exclaimed, bursting through the front doors and spilling onto the main floor. Jeebo slowly turned his heavy body to face Jilk as he slid up to him.

"What is it?" Jeebo asked cheerily, ignoring Jilk's lack of propriety as he thought to himself that nothing would ruin such a fine, money-making day. He could practically hear the sound of coins tinkering with one another.

"The cogs were attacked outside Bilf. The special delivery was opened and the relic is gone!" he explained. To Jilk's horror, Jeebo's face went from high-cholesterol red to blood vessel's bursting purple in three seconds flat.

"What?!" Jeebo screamed, spitting thick saliva all over Jilk's new vest.

"The entire team was slaughtered, boss," he continued. "Knife wounds to the throat and chest. Precision moves. The boys fired, but they didn't hit their target once. Looks professional, boss."

Jeebo was not feeling any better. The ruffles around his neck looked as though they might snap as he strained, muscles tense, blood boiling, eyes about to pop out of his head.

"Reinhardt?" Jeebo bellowed. Jilk shook his head.

"We think it was a Keeper," he said quietly.

"Keepers strike in groups, you idiot!" Jeebo yelled, smacking the cogwheeler upside the head. "There's no way they would've gotten to Bilf without bloodshed!"

"We checked the Mine," Jilk protested. "There were no reports of anything unusual. We think it—"

"I don't care what you *think*!" Jeebo exclaimed, foaming at the mouth. "Find me that relic!"

"Yes, boss," Jilk said crisply, turning on his heels and racing out of the guild hall.

"The crate was empty," a woman said as a breeze gently carried her long dark hair past her face.

"I know. Before we could reach you, you'd gone into the Mine. We discovered the relic had been intercepted by the white hands," a male explained.

The Keeper from the Mine was standing on the edge of a gargoyle's dais at the top of a tower where the wind blew the ponytail on the top of her head around her face. The wrapped leather now hung loose as a dress around her body, revealing long and pale legs and sturdy, bare feet keeping perfect balance.

The man stood across from her and was dressed in formal fashions from head to toe, complete with a cravat tied around his neck. His hair was loose curls of jet black that contrasted his pale skin. Blue orbs defined sharp eyes.

"Where is the relic now?" she asked calmly, eyes closed in a meditative way. The man spoke as gently as she had in his reply.

"It is being moved through Saigon and into Rome toward the White Tower."

"And the guardrium?"

"Thirty angels move the relic," he replied.

"I understand. I will retrieve the relic."

"Shade, hold a moment. There's more," he said, gently touching her arm.

"More, Eros?"

"The Enoch has been restless. A glyph was discovered and the collective have broken another prophecy," Eros explained.

"What does the Regent have to say about this? I thought the collective were under Elysium and no longer allowed to break prophesy until the awakening."

"There was some unrest among the delegates, but the Regent sanctioned the act when the collective became aware of the relic the Hands have discovered."

Shade took hold of her hair at the base of her ponytail and slipped the long strands to her other shoulder, allowing them to blow in the wind from a different side. Eros watched her affectionately, gently gliding his fingers through her hair as it blew in his direction. He let his gaze linger on the glyph softly glowing on her forehead and made a silent acknowledgement of the glyph on his own forehead.

"Shade," he continued. "The relic is a sight stone. Fortunately, the Hands are not aware of its power. Yet. You must move quickly to prevent such power being obtained by either corporation. However, your task goes beyond this assignment. There is a man by the name of Knick Coltin. We believe him to be in the Mine."

"What is his significance?" Shade asked.

"He is the prophecy. It is foreseen by the collective that he will one day bring a great advantage to the Black Hand. He must be eliminated before he can become a threat to the Balance—a threat we may not be able to contend with."

"I understand, Eros. I will retrieve the relic and remove the potential threat. For the Balance…"

"For the Balance."

Shade stood with Eros for a moment longer before willing her thoughts. The leather coiled up around her body, fastening with the rivets to form the body suit once more. Before she left, she turned to her fellow Keeper.

"Eros," she began, "you say another glyph was discovered. Was it identified?"

"No," he replied. "Not yet."

Shade nodded and slipped the silk over her mouth. She pushed off of the ledge and swan dived off of the tower, free-falling into the fog of the city where Eros watched her burst into a wisp of black and fade into the depths below.

He smiled gently.

The angels were moving the relic in a vacuum-sealed hover bin through the port city of Saigon, moving beneath plastic tents that cut through the bazaar.

Sol's light was boosted in the sky by giant solar bulbs and reflector panels that dotted Lotus Maze, seeking to capture the limited sunlight and use that to energize the power plants. The radiation was down and the novum gas clouds were diaphanous so the sun shined brighter than usual.

The angels were quiet, blending into the hum of the

merchants around them. No citizen messed with them and no child had the audacity to interfere with their business. The cobblestone streets cleared as the angels moved through them in their starchy, white suits, eyes hidden by silver glasses.

One of the angels tilted his head up toward the tower known as Heaven—the headquarters of the angels. His bald brow was creased as he stared into the distance, perfectly still and concentrated like an invisible person was whispering some invaluable secret to him. After a moment, he touched the wire in his right ear and walked to his closest comrade.

"The hive mind has detected an assault," the angel said. His comrade turned his silver gaze upon him, stopping the caravan transporting the relic. One by one, each angel stopped, hearing the high-pitched frequency in their right ears transferring the messages of a possible code yellow threat.

The black shadow dropped onto the mob, causing them to scatter. As the cogwheelers had before them, the angels stood perfectly still, staring through silver lenses at the Keeper woman, sword drawn.

"Identify yourself," the angel in charge commanded the Keeper. She said nothing, eyes closed. "Identify yourself!" Still, nothing. "Identify yourself!"

The Keeper opened her violet eyes, the glyph on her forehead pulsing invisibly. The angel growled.

"Kill her," he ordered his units. All thirty agents lifted foot-long sticks called Nightwalkers, products of polyspace technology. The sticks unscrewed in the center, producing morning stars, maces, quarterstaffs, katanas, and other miscellaneous weapons from the open-space film inside.

Shade lifted her sword, braced in her right hand, and the tiny bells jingled around her wrist.

The first three angels charged and Shade easily parried their attacks, making swift cuts along their wrists, unarming them and going straight for their throats. They dropped to her feet, squirming and choking on their own blood.

Five angels rushed after their fallen companions, spinning their weapons expertly in their hands. They moved in on Shade at once, attempting to overcome her at every angle. No agent could combat their expert battle skills in such numbers.

The Keeper lifted her sword and the bells around her wrist jingled. A spear of dark energy shot up the length of the

14

blade from the hilt, swirling in a dragon-like curl and exploding in a plasma pulse.

"Specter Rising!" Shade yelled, voice riding the vibrations climbing through her body. Columns of green-black energy shot out of the ground and speared the angels that charged her. Violent screams of unearthly caliber echoed around the bazaar as the mystical attack sucked the life-force from the angels until they slumped to the ground as shriveled, stiff, gray corpses.

Shade lowered the sword, eyeing the next set of agents that brandished their weapons, circling her. Her feet left the ground in a flip, body spinning sideways in the air. The sword arced with her ponytail, leaving a wispy trail of ethereal smoke. The bells jingled with every move.

Her feet touched the ground, pulling her into another turn. She fought as many as could crowd around her until she became overwhelmed by their numbers advancing on her. A vicious serpent of jade-black smoke exploded from the ground, rising up into the sky and dropping down on top of an angel, sinking fast into the ground, leaving a bloody body behind, and rising up again, swimming in a destructive rage. Angels rolled and jumped out of the summoned beast's angry path.

The head angel touched the scrambler in his ear.

"Operations," he said. A screech shot through the coiled wire and his brain translated the message.

"Angel Agent 10-41-36. What is your request?"

"A Keeper has attacked us at Saigon West Edge Ridge."

"Coordinates?"

"3653.123.093," he told the unit on the other end of the communication device.

"Number of enemy units?"

"One."

"Agent 10-41-36, what is your disposition?"

"Operations. The Keeper is wielding a high-vitae emitting blade with some sort of battle-ether. We think it may be a Dionysian Artifact."

"Agent 10-41-36, angel status?"

"11 dead, 19 capable," he replied. There was a moment of silence.

The angel looked up, watching the Keeper's sword clash with an angel's blade, quickly parrying the attack and rebounding to the next swing from a morning star. She ducked and rolled around the ground, fending off every attack and doling out some of her own. His angels managed to defend against her attacks as well, but neither warrior broke any ground.

"Operations," the angel persisted. Silence. "Operations?"

"Agent 10-41-36, three back-up units are being deployed to your position. Your objective is to disarm the Keeper and secure the Dionysian weapon. Are your objectives clear?"

The angel grinned.

"Clear."

Scholar Marcus Nico gasped, hoisting the large book in his arms. He rushed pass fellow scholars, racing from one platform to the next.

The tower was comprised of layers upon layers of tiers that were small libraries where the collective spent day after day researching the old and ancient tomes and texts by candlelight, scrounging for hidden messages and information about the world, the past, the future, and all existing creatures and objects.

Nico was a scholar among the collective who had been busier than usual researching the new glyph Ralph Gobol discovered.

"Move, move! Neevo!" Nico hissed as he pushed through the brown-robed collective and down the winding stone staircase. "Move, I said! Neevo, neevo!"

The monks moved to the side slowly, shaking their heads in disapproval as Nico rushed past them. He took the steps by two, nearly tripping over his own robe and falling the rest of the way down. At the bottom, he raced down the stone corridors, dipping in and out of torch light as he shuffled toward the High Study.

The wooden door flung open on iron hinges and Nico hurled himself into the room.

"High Counselor!" he exclaimed, holding the heavy book high, eyes wide and mouth gaping in anticipation.

The High Counselor stood on a dais behind his desk, surrounded by stacks of books, shelves overflowing with tomes and scrolls, and papers strewn everywhere. He peered over wire-rimmed glasses from the tome he was exploring and his consultants turned their aged gazes upon the scholar. They stared down at him, waiting for his explanation, but Nico was so wired with his discovery that he merely stood there, shaking in silence.

"Well…what is it?" the High Counselor asked. Nico stumbled over to him and threw the weighty book onto the Counselor's large, wooden desk over piles of other books and papers. The High Counselor scrunched his face in annoyance, but Nico did not give the Counselor enough time to chastise him for his lack of manners.

"Slow down, son," was all he managed to say before Nico interrupted him, jabbing an old, frail finger to a picture on the page.

"The glyph," Nico stammered, "is inscribed on the shield of the Fourth Century Deigno Knight, Maximus Marius Malentos, who later discovered the Rumble Relic."

The High Counselor adjusted his glasses on his tall, pointed nose and bent over his long, gray beard to get a closer look at the picture Nico was pointing to. The rest of his consultants bent over after him, following his direction to see the source of commotion.

"I see," the High Counselor said, lifting his gaze eye-level with Nico. "You are, indeed, correct."

"High Counselor," Nico began, "we may be approaching the awakening of a new road…"

The High Counselor pursed his lips, causing the shorter whiskers around his mouth to fan out in small, fuzzy spikes. He clicked his tongue thoughtfully as he stood up straight and stroked his beard, keeping his gaze locked on Nico's.

"Send word to the collective," the High Counselor began in his brittle voice. "Tell them to change objectives. Tell them to find out all they can on this Maximus Marius Malentos character and the rumble relic."

Nico nodded once and turned, jack-rabbiting out of the office and slamming the door shut behind him, kicking loose papers into the air. The High Counselor glanced to his consultants on either side in wonderment of the energetic monk as papers drifted from side-to-side down to the floor.

White suits charged the Keeper from every direction, falling under cold steel and primordial powers. Shade fought them as back-up angels spilled from every alley, filling up the space where a dead comrade lay.

I cannot hold out much longer against this assault, she thought.

"The Keepers have interfered for the last time," the ranked angel told her, bringing his mace down in a crushing blow aimed at her shoulder. Shade caught the head of the weapon with her blade, meeting his silver-lens stare.

The bells around her wrist jingled.

The angel cocked his head as he held down her attack, imagining some spell to be at work, but nothing seemed to happen.

A plasma explosion from the weapon knocked the surrounding agents back, but the ranked angel was locked in his position, mace to sword. Smoke began to seep off of the blade and take the form of skeletal hands that snaked toward him. He tried to fight, but some invisible force was holding him fast. The skeletal hands clutched his throat, choking him in a violent manner. His face ripped open in several places and his blood curdled and dissipated against the nethergy like paper burned by fire. He tried to scream but his throat was filled to the brim with his own bile, bubbling and boiling open. With one last vicious tremor, his body slumped to the ground and all of his organic essence flowed into the blade. He hit the cobblestone street as nothing more than a jade-blue skeleton, darkened by the nethergy.

Shade turned to look at all of the angels staring at her. She could not combat the one-hundred soldiers that were closing in on her.

Shade dropped to her knees, bursting into a cloud of smoke. The dark ball of wispy energy shot into the sky and off into the distance.

The angels stared dumbfounded at the soot stain on the ground that was the wake of the Keeper.

"There were too many of them," Shade explained, feeling the wind whip about her face. Eros stood behind her, looking out of the tower window to the city beyond.

"I understand," Eros said, "and so does the Regent."

"I used the blade's power too much."

"There's nothing we can do about that now. It was sooner

or later before the Hands found out what we're capable of."

"Still, it's cost us the hunt," she said, fingertips drifting over the glyph on her forehead. She pushed her hair back.

"We still have time to recover the relic. The delegates are still deciding how they want to handle it. First, you must find Knick Coltin."

Shade turned to look at Eros.

"Any news on the identity of the glyph?" she asked. Eros smiled.

"You're awfully curious about this glyph," he remarked. She shrugged.

"It's just that…" Shade trailed off. His smile faded and he looked upon her with a sympathetic gaze.

"The last glyph that was discovered was—"

"It doesn't matter," Shade interrupted. "I'm just curious. That's all."

"Right," Eros whispered in that quiet, gentle voice. Shade willed the leather from a dress into the bodysuit and wrapped the silk around her mouth.

"I'm going to find the prophecy," she said. Before Eros could say anything, Shade hopped up onto the window's ledge and pushed herself out.

Eros sighed.

"Do you think we should have told her about the rest of the prophecy?" a voice asked him from the shadows. Eros glanced back at his hidden companion before dropping a sad gaze to the floor. He sighed gently and shook his head.

"There's no point. The delegates decided the fate of this prophecy. Shade needs know only that to enact the will of the Regent."

"But Eros—"

"We are not Keepers of morality, Daelus. We are Keepers of the Balance. They are nothing alike. The Regent and the delegates decided that this is the best way to keep the Balance. We, the Interim, need know only what must be done to maintain the Balance, and do it."

Daelus said nothing in reply.

Eros walked to the window and stared out at the dim sky, feeling a sense of desolation and despondency that he could not explain.

"Angel Agent 4-56-29."

"Yes, Operations," the angel replied, touching his right ear. The angel wings rippled with the veins in his hand.

"Status on the relic, captain."

"Entering Rome as we speak," he told his mysterious commander. "It will be entering the capital by nightfall."

"Your objectives remain the same. Protect the relic at all costs. Should the Keeper attack again…do not fail to secure her—dead or alive—and obtain the Dionysian Artifact."

"Affirmative, Operations," 4-56-29 said.

"Update on the fallen angel."

4-56-29 glanced around through silver-lens glasses, watching his fellow agents moving in a caravan fashion, escorting the hoverbox through the city like a damn Mirax CEO-sultan. Licking his lips, the agent turned away from his compatriots.

"Nothing to report…yet, Operations," he said, jaw tight in irritation. The subject seemed to be the largest thorn in his side and one of great distaste. The voice in his ear was silent for a moment. The agent licked his lips again, nearly holding his breath. The voice gave its final command.

"Find him."

"Affirmative, Operations," 4-56-29 said, lowering his hand as the voice fell silent. He faced the caravan once more and motioned to them to keep moving forward before he joined the ranks, easily disappearing into the crowd of bald-headed, white-suit-wearing agents of the White Tower.

Knick Coltin pushed open the swinging door to the bar, crossing the western-style threshold of a canteen just outside of Britz. The bar was called the *Toxic Ox*—some post-cyberpunk style joint with an old-world western theme. It was an eyesore, but the only place in town that anyone wanted to go. The T, C, and I in the green neon glowing sign were out, so the name read ox Ox.

Britz was a back-lot town on the edge of the Cradle—the inter-perimeter of underground civilization where the mercantile populous reigned. Everything outside of the Cradle was border territory originally referred to as the Outer-Perimeter Sub-Terranean Settlements. However, the boys in the bureau kept referring to is as "over there", so the OPSTS was shortened to OT, or simply the Over There.

Knick paused inside the door and glanced around. His hair was long, dark, messy tendrils long enough to cover his eyes. He wore a worn leather jacket with a faded red racing stripe down each sleeve and dingy cowboy jeans over street boots. Old, sock gloves covered his palms; the fingertips chopped off at the knuckles for easier maneuvering.

The *Toxic Ox* was pretty empty. There were a few skinheads and adrenaline junkies at the booths along the walls. Knick spotted a couple of sub-runners stopped in for a quick meal before getting back on the track.

He walked to the bar and knocked on the surface. The bar tender was an old, tired-looking refugee—a top-world escapist. He was a thief or con that got caught on a job or a murderer faced with two options: plastic prison walls with death by sanitized injection or the Mine. Some people thought the odds were the same.

"What d'ya want?" he asked, cleaning out a styrosteel tumbler with a stained rag. His voice was exhausted, as if he'd lived all the life he could handle and was now just riding the waves to the grave.

"What's the strongest in the house?" Knick asked, eyeing the liquor bottles on the back shelf.

"We got some Ajeena in the back," he replied. Knick twisted his mouth, sighing out the word 'eh' as he eyed the tender hesitantly. The man took the hint. "Well, I got a bottle of absinthe-sky in the back, as well."

"There you go, that's more like it. I'll take some of that," Knick said.

The bar tender set the tumbler down and flung the rag over his shoulder as he moved to the door in the back corner. He disappeared inside for nearly two minutes, reemerging with a bottle of what was practically glowing, green liquid.

"Shot or shake?" the tender asked.

"Uh, shot," Knick replied.

The tender pulled a shot glass from under the bar and filled it to the brim with the green liquor. Knick took the drink tenderly between his fingertips and lifted it to his lips. He knocked the shot back in one gulp and nearly dropped the glass as he lurched in a coughing fit. A few people in the bar glanced back at him but quickly lost interest, going back to whatever it was that occupied their attention.

The bar tender laughed.

"That strong enough for you, kid?" he asked. Knick nodded, still coughing and pounding on his chest.

"Shit, yeah," he replied. "Got a whole new pair of lungs. If I keep drinking, maybe I'll raze out my burner habit."

"Ha ha ha, now that's the truth. Th' name's Duke, kid," the tender said, pouring him another shot.

"Coltin," Knick replied, taking the drink. He knocked it back, coughing less the second time around. "Think it's safe to light up?"

Duke chuckled, corking the bottle of absinthe-sky.

"You might wanna wait a few minutes," he said, placing the bottle on the shelf behind him.

Knick grinned, sliding the crinkled pack of Jacks from his back pocket. He slipped one of the filterless cigarettes from inside and placed it between his lips, dropping the pack on the bar counter. Patting himself down, he went searching for his matches; they were in his right inner jacket pocket. Knick pulled them out and slid open the box, grabbing a tiny matchstick.

"You catch my bar on fire, you pay for it," Duke told him, still smiling. Knick grunted, smirking.

He lit the match and transferred the flame to his cigarette then shook out the fire. Thick, gray smoke blew from Knick's lips and nostrils, dissipating in the hazy bar atmosphere.

"What brings you to Britz?" the tender asked him. Knick took another fast drag on his cigarette, burning the ends in bright red.

"Work," he replied on tendrils of smoke.

"Shit, there's nothing out here but sub-runners passing through and druggies pushin' A."

"Yeah, but boss said go so I said where, you know? He say, Britz; I say, no. He say, fired; I say, just kidding." Knick sucked on his cigarette, already halfway through it. Duke just laughed.

"Yeah, right," he replied. "I know how it goes. Well, good luck. This is the shit-town, edge of nothing. Beyond this, there ain't anything. You got the drops to the coal mines. The end. Know what I'm sayin', kid?"

"End of the world?" he asked, exhaling gray through his

nose.

"Hell yes. God's shithole."

"Everyone's gotta do it, man," Knick replied. "Just like drinkin' Jack and eatin' too many pretzels—it's bound to happen."

Duke laughed again, throwing his rag on the bar.

"You're a character, that's for sure. Stick around a bit."

"Stickin' around as long as boss-man says," Knick explained, motioning for the bottle of absinthe-sky.

"Well gimme his name. I'll make a recommendation," Duke said, grabbing the bottle and popping the cork. He poured another shot and Knick tipped it back.

"Damn, that's rough," he muttered, feeling like he might breathe fire with the cigarette smoke and alcoholic fumes mixing in his body. Something was bound to spark a fire.

The swinging doors pushed open again. Duke glanced back and made a face, dropping a soft whistle. Knick took a quick look over his shoulder. The newest patron was a tall woman with long, black hair that fell down the length of her back, tied back with a blue bandana.

Shade was out of her leather bodysuit. She now wore black pants and a matching sleeveless sweater. Beneath the sweater came long, white sleeves that were tied to her arms by black ribbons extended off of lion-face shoulder mounts that belted across her chest.

"Is that a pretty picture or what?" Duke whispered. Knick kept his gaze locked on Shade, taking a deep drag on his cigarette.

"It's an attention getter, that's for sure," he replied on a breath of smoke. He couldn't help but notice the tip of a sword sheath on her left side.

"Knick Coltin?" Shade asked the establishment, narrowing her gaze on the bar tender. The place was silent. Shade grunted. Another dead end, but she really was surprised this time. Rumor told her that he'd headed for Britz and her gut told her she was on the right track.

She moved to the bar and unknowingly stood next to her target.

"Has anyone by the name of Knick Coltin come through here?" she asked Duke. He shook his head, pouring Knick another shot of absinthe-sky.

"Not by that name, if he has," Duke replied. Shade sighed, turning around and leaning against the bar. She felt a pair of eyes on her and glanced to her right. Knick was staring up at her with a grin on his lips as he lifted the shot of green to his mouth.

"What are you drinkin'?" he asked behind the glass. Shade narrowed her gaze on him.

"What can I do you out of?" she retorted.

"These pants, for starters," he replied, not skipping a beat.

"Excuse me?" she said, a bit startled by his response. Knick shook his head.

"Uh-uhn. A better question is: what will you do for me?" he asked, taking the shot. He coughed once and set the glass back on the counter. "Cause, baby, I can think of a ton of things you can do for me."

"Keep drinking. You're losing your charm," she told him, pushing off of the bar. Knick stood up, blocking her path.

"I'd like to lose a lot more than that with you," he told her. She said nothing. Knick reached into his jacket and pulled out a few bills. Without checking their value, he tossed them on the counter and grabbed his cigarette pack. "Be seeing you, Duke."

Duke gave him a half-assed salute. Knick grinned at Shade one more time, kissing in her direction, before he went for the exit. Shade turned back to the bar, ignoring him, wondering if she should contact Eros.

"He-hey, Coltin! There you are!" someone yelled from outside. Shade spun on her heels, glaring at the doorway. Knick shook his head.

"Fuck!" he yelled, sprinting through the swinging doors. "Reemer, you idiot!"

"What?" Reemer exclaimed, confused as Knick sprinted past him, moving fast for the tunnels. The thug turned back toward the *Toxic Ox* just in time to see Shade burst from the building, racing after Coltin. "Hey! Hey, you! Stop!" Reemer shouted. "Stop her!"

The posse with Reemer immediately took action, running up to Shade. She jumped into the air and flipped over the three that came at her from the front. Before the thugs realized what was happening, Shade had pulled her sword.

She sliced the throat closest to her before dropping. She

swept her leg around, knocking one of the thugs to his ass. As she came to her feet, she was nearly tackled. Hooking her arm under the attacker, she sent her sword through his chest, flipping him over her head and onto the thug who was trying to get back on his feet.

Knick had paused to watch the battle, wondering if running was really necessary. As the woman fighter ended the brief tussle, he realized that running was still in his best interest.

Shade noticed a tattoo on the left hand of one of the men she'd disposed of.

"You're cogwheelers," she said, lifting her gaze to Reemer. He stared wide-eyed, standing perfectly still. She didn't have time to ask questions. Turning, Shade sprinted after Knick, who was moving fast for the tunnels.

Knick jumped down into the ditch onto the train tracks and ran full speed down the stretch. Shade jumped in after him, moving just as fast as he was. The pulse charge was coming up behind them in its ten minute interval but neither seemed to care.

"You know this is really dangerous!" Knick yelled back to her. "Someone could get killed!"

Nethergy burst forth from the sword and the Dragon Esper rose up from the ground, racing for Knick.

"Shit!" he cried, dodging to the side. He almost lost his footing.

The dragon came up at him again and he jumped to the side, running in a zigzag motion to avoid the attack. The dragon pursued him for only a few moments before crashing down to the ground and fading into the tracks.

"I guess that's the plan!" he yelled back to her. "You wouldn't want to let me die a virgin, would you?"

The wall exploded on his right and he dipped to the side.

"C'mon!" he exclaimed. "Do me before you do me in!"

Another explosion.

"We can talk about this, can't we?" he shouted.

Up ahead, Knick could see another body running on the tracks.

"Tad! Hur'yup! You ain't gonna make it!" Bit screamed.

"Stop sayin' that!" Tad shouted, racing down the tracks.

"Hey! Hey! Jump th' deck!" Knick yelled.

"Shut th' fuck up!" Tad told him.

"No, seriously! There's an evil witch back here shooting dragon spells and shit!"

"Stop takin' drugs, man!" Tad replied.

"Seriously!" Knick exclaimed.

A second Dragon Esper exploded behind him. He dodged it like last time, almost losing his footing. The nethergy kept going. Tad risked a glance behind him, wondering what the commotion was about.

"Shiiiiiiit!" he yelled, seeing a gaping, fang-filled mouth flying toward him. He veered to the side and jumped for the platform, barely catching the edge and pulling himself to safety. Bit tripped over him and landed on his ass, watching in shock as Knick went sprinting past, dragon nethergy chasing him, and Shade following up the line with an electro-charge heading up the rear.

"Fuck... Whatta hell was that?" Bit muttered.

Tad heaved breaths. "I donno," he replied.

Bit sniffed the air. "Aw, man! You shit yourself again?" he exclaimed.

"Oh, fuck you!" Tad retorted.

"Boss?" Jilk began as he paced the sidewalk outside of the temple in Genie.

"What is it?" Jeebo muttered. Jilk switched the ear comm from one side to the next and then dabbed his sweaty forehead.

"We finally got the info on that relic..." he explained.

"Well, where is it? Do you have it? Is it safe? Are you bringing it to—"

"Sir... It entered Rashrima Haan two days ago. Mirax has it..."

The angry words that came through the other line were indecipherable. Jilk grimaced and pulled the comm away from his ear, worrying about whether this slip-up would cost him his job.

"Solo! Slot!" Jilk barked. The two, scruffy cogwheelers jumped off of the boxes they were sitting on.

"Yeah, Jilk?" Solo replied, folding his arms over his thin chest. His sister, Slot, looked just as rough as he did.

"What'cha need, boss?" she asked. Jilk rubbed his thumb

across his nose and sniffed.

"Time to get back to Romulus," he told them.

"We ain't going back to Thebes?" Slot asked.

He shook his head.

"Uh...no," he responded, twiddling his fingertips. "Not yet." He cleared his throat and popped the collar on his old jacket, strutting off in a nervous way. Solo and Slot exchanged glances and shrugged, imitating their boss's strut in a mocking way as they marched after him.

Knick knew he wasn't getting anywhere on the tracks. There was no where he could hide and he was getting tired of running. The next platform that came up, he dove for it. He pulled himself onto the ledge in one swift motion and raced into the small town just off of the station.

Shade jumped into the air and landed on the platform. She recovered in a second and continued the chase, winding through the crowds of diggers and dregs and through the alleys. She was losing her patience.

The sword pulsed and the bells around her wrist jingled. She could feel the ethergy throbbing within her, connecting with her psyche. Her mind willed her next step and she disappeared in a cloud of smoke, reappearing in front of Knick.

"Whoa!" he exclaimed, stumbling back.

Shade grabbed him by the scruff of his jacket and threw him against one of the buildings in the alley. He regained his footing just as she came upon him. She sheathed her sword and took hold of his jacket again, slamming him against the wall and pinning him to it.

"Auh, baby, you play so rough," he muttered, biting back his pain. He tried to grab for her throat but she secured his wrist, forcing it to the wall. "I've never done 'force' before, but it's not rape if you like it, right? And I'm liking you all up on me like this," he said as he shifted to find an opening to free himself.

Shade glanced at his wrist, noting how the glove had been pushed up. There was the marking of a tattoo on his right hand.

"Oh my god," she whispered.

"Fuck..." he groaned. Shade yanked his wrist down and

ripped the glove off of his hand.

The angel wing tattoo.

"You're an angel," she said, meeting his gaze.

"Fallen," he explained. "My sins caught up with me."

Shade was not amused. She grabbed his left hand and pulled the glove off.

Cogwheel.

"And a cogwheeler," she whispered, remembering the prophecy.

"Latest trade," he admitted. "The boss is a bit cracked out, but the guys are nice. Pay's not too shabby. Nice Christmas bonus if you shine your shoes and hold your tongue. If you're sweet, I could put in a good word for you."

Shade took a few steps away from him, staring at the ground, running Eros's words over and over in her mind: He will bring a great advantage to the Black Hand. *That's it*, she thought. *He's an ex-angel. That's the advantage.*

"It's happening just as the prophecy said it would," she said, meeting his gaze. He offered a cheesy smile. Shade drew her sword, expression darkening. "And it ends here."

Knick's smile dropped when he saw her pull her sword. Lifting his fists, he prepared for the battle. When she charged, he was ready.

He countered her attack as quick as she had launched it.

Nico sat on a stack of books, flipping through page after page of History of the Deigno Era, eagerly seeking engravings with the new glyph or paragraphs that might mention Maximus Marius Malentos or the rumble relic.

His fellow collective were doing just as he—sitting on books, the floor, shelves, tables, anywhere they found a space while they ravaged scroll after scroll, tome after tome, and volumes upon volumes of history in the off-chance the new glyph might be mentioned.

Suddenly, Nico jumped. The monks all looked up, staring in anticipation at him.

"What happened?" one of them asked. Nico glanced up with his round, owl eyes and then dropped his gaze back to the page.

"What is it? What did you see?" another monk asked. Nico looked as pale as death.

"The glyph!" he exclaimed. "It appeared on this page and then disappeared. Look! Look there!" Nico was now pointing across the room at a book on the same shelf one of the monks was sitting on. "I saw it on that one just now. And there!" He pointed to another book.

The collective was following the directions he was pointing in, wondering what in the hell was happening.

"Check those books!" Antion, Nico's apprentice, exclaimed. The monks nearest the volumes Nico had pointed to dropped what they were reading and quickly grabbed the new material, frantically searching through them.

"Curious..." Nico muttered as he glanced over the page in his book where he had seen the glyph appear.

"What does this mean?" Antion asked him.

"Something is happening with the glyph," Nico guessed.

"What's happening to it?"

"Not *it*," Nico corrected his fellow monk. "*Who*."

Shade was extremely frustrated that Knick was able to match her combat prowess. Though he was unable to attack her, she was unable to get past his defense. He was able to get around her sword, regardless of being weaponless, and did not allow her even a moment to use the power behind the weapon.

"What is it with you?" Knick asked, dodging her thrust. He chopped at her arm but she bent with the attack, flipping backward. "You a bounty hunter? An assassin? A merc? What?"

"Just shut up and hold still," she hissed, spinning in a circular strike. He ducked and moved to kick her feet out beneath her. She jumped the attack.

"Did Mirax send you?"

"No," she replied.

"Then what the fuck do you want with me?"

"I want you to die," she said, swinging the sword in a downward arch. Knick pulled away, rolling backward.

"What the hell for?" he asked, kicking at her wrist. She spun with the movement, missing his foot. When she came back around, she dropped to her knee, bringing the sword down. Knick rolled out of the way just as the tip struck the ground.

"For the Balance," she explained, standing up and stalking

after him.

"Shit, you're a Keeper. Now it makes sense," he muttered, using the wall for support as he stood. He turned to face her, flicking his hair out of his eyes with a jerk of his head.

Shade's eyes widened.

A glyph was suddenly shimmering on his forehead.

"What...?" he asked, feeling a little awkward with her staring at him like that.

"Can't be," she whispered. The shimmering faded and the glyph was gone. Knick waved his hands and whistled.

"Hey, you, what's the deal, huh? One minute you're trying to kill me, the next you're ogling me like I'm a piece of meat. Which is it, cause this bipolar, chase-stare-kill-stare thing isn't working for me," he said. "And just so we're on the same page, I'm hoping it's the second one."

Shade wasn't listening. She was thinking. A glyph had appeared on his forehead...a glyph she didn't recognize. If he was the new glyph, she couldn't kill him. Knick used the opportunity to sneak up to her; when he was close enough, he lunged for her wrists, pinning them at her back so she couldn't suddenly spring at him again.

Shade's gaze was stuck on Knick's, deadlocked in uncomfortable silence and proximity.

"Don't look so conflicted, Keeper," Knick whispered, a tinge of disdain in his voice. "You seem like you already know what you believe in."

Suddenly, his glyph glowed brightly, and she felt hers light up in response. The blue and purple light that shimmered between them reflected on both their cheeks and Shade was just as surprised as Knick was. The light grew until the glyphs were no longer pulsing, but solid and bright. Then, the power dimmed and they were returned to shadow.

"What *was* that?" he asked, taking deep and uncertain breaths.

"I..." Shade didn't know what to say.

Suddenly she felt her cheeks burning bright red. Knick furrowed one brow when he noticed. The awkwardness shared between their eyes resonated and he felt his grip loosen. She jerked away from him and immediately looked at the ground.

"I have to talk to Eros. I have to find out what this means," she said. Knick rolled his eyes, wondering what kind of psycho he'd attracted.

"You what?" he mumbled, unsure why he was even bothering asking. Shade sheathed her sword and met his gaze.

"I think you might be the One," she told him. Knick lifted his hands in surrender.

"Not that I'm not flattered, but that's moving a little fast, don't you think? We just met this morning, I'm not ready to be tied down—unless you mean literally. I—"

Shade burst into a ball of shadows and hovered there for only a moment before vanishing, racing down a tunnel and disappearing into the darkness. Knick dropped his hands, looking in the direction she'd gone.

"I don't even know your name," he mumbled, finishing his joke to himself. "And I have a commitment problem. It'll never work."

Knick shook his head resignedly and lit a cigarette.

The stones on the seemingly entrance-less tower rumbled, moving away to create a door. The glyph marking could only be seen by Keepers, and Shade knew exactly where to go to enter the tower. She moved inside and ignored the grumble as the stones returned to their natural place, sealing the door behind her. She was used to the magic of the Keeper's edifices.

She climbed the tower, racing for the Interim levels, and flung open the first study chamber.

"Eros!" she exclaimed, moving into the room. It was empty at first glance. A voice behind her startled her.

"He's with the consular," Daelus said, closing the book he was reading by the fire's light.

"I need Eros," she said. "I need to speak with him. It's more important than whatever Beonan has to say."

"He'll be back soon," Daelus told her, standing up and moving to place a comforting hand on her shoulder. "What's wrong?"

"The glyph," Shade whispered. "I need to see it."

"Which glyph?"

"The new one."

"Oh…" he muttered. "Why?"

"Does it matter?" Shade asked, ripping from his grasp.

She moved to the window and stared out at the sky.

"I guess not," Daelus said softly. He looked up, almost going to her but deciding not to. He clutched his book tightly, trying to think of something to say.

"I saw it," she began. Daelus looked up hopefully. "I've never seen this glyph before. I think it may be the collective's latest discovery. I need to know if it is what I think it is."

There was a moment of silence between the two Keepers. A distant rumble in the sky enveloped them.

"Where did you see it?" Daelus asked. Shade hesitated, lifting her violet eyes to the dark, stormy sky covered by rain clouds and metrin gases that created a deep, blue haze against the gray. "Shade?"

"I need to speak with Eros."

"About what?" Eros asked, coming through the door. Daelus and Shade spun around to face their companion. "Shade, I thought you'd be in the Mine—"

"Eros," she interrupted, racing up to him. "I think the new glyph the collective discovered is actually the birth of a new road."

Eros and Daelus exchanged glances.

"Why would you think that?" Eros asked.

"Because I saw it," she replied. "It appeared on Coltin's forehead." After a split second's thought, she decided to leave out the part about her glyph reacting to his.

"You don't even know what this glyph looks like."

"Then there are two new glyphs, Eros, because I did not know the glyph I saw. It didn't even resemble our founded sigils."

"It doesn't matter, Shade," he said, reaching out to brush her hair with his fingers. "He is dead by order of the delegates and the Regent. The prophecy states—"

"The prophecy is incomplete!" Shade exclaimed. Eros and Daelus froze in shock, wondering how she could possibly know that. "You or the collective or the Regent and his delegates are withholding pieces of this prophecy. I won't—I can't believe that from those ancient murmurs, they have deduced only that Coltin will bring a great advantage to the Black Hand. There is more. There has to be."

Eros was silent for a long time, staring her in the eyes for what seemed like eternity. He was running her words over and over again in this head. On one hand, he had orders from the Regent—orders that were infallible. The Regent and the delegates knew what was best to obtain balance. They had no reason not to trust them. The system had yet to fail them. On the other hand, Eros could not justify the murder of a potential Keeper. He trusted Shade; he believed in her judgment. If she saw the glyph on Coltin's forehead, then he believed her.

"Show me," Eros said. "Show me the glyph you saw."

Shade studied his gaze, trying to find out where he stood.

"Fine," she uttered.

Shade went to the hearth and pulled a glowing limb from the fire. She didn't bother to wait for the end to cool. Using it as a writing utensil, she traced the lines of the glyph into the wall, ignoring the glowing embers that flew from the burnt end.

Eros and Daelus stared at the ash and cinder drawing, stunned by what they saw. The glyph shimmered unnaturally for a moment, lighting up blue. The Keepers tensed as the glyph pulsed in blue light and then faded back to the dull charcoal writing.

"I'm going to see the Regent," Eros said. "I'm sure he'll want to know of this development."

Daelus watched Eros exit and turned his attention on Shade. He had no idea what to say.

Agent 4-56-29 stood at the sewer's edge, staring down at the manhole cover, watching the steam and fumes rising up through the holes in the metal plate. The angels around him were examining every inch of ground around the Mine entrance #157 in the D-Water Industrial Sector near Holdum.

All evidence pointed to Knick Coltin fleeing to this district and the research team was confident in their theory that he'd gone into the sewer system.

4-56-29 knew he wouldn't stop in the sewers. He'd fled to the Mine, no doubt about it.

"What's your order, sir?" one of the angels said. 4-56-29 glanced at his companion and then looked back at the manhole cover.

His jaw tightened in agitation.

Night had fallen and Shade had retreated to her room

in the Keeper Hold. She sat on the ground by the floor window, watching the rain fall in torrents from the fractured sky to the synthetic city below, sliding over slick and reflective surfaces.

The blending of old and new architecture was a burden to look at and Shade hated seeing the stone structures standing next to the white towers and reinforced steel.

She remembered the glyph appearing on Coltin's forehead. She remembered the Regent's words when the last glyph was discovered. If fate was falling into place, the future was about to be shaped. Shade always proclaimed to be a believer in the prophecies, but seeing them unfold, watching them manifest themselves before her was both terrifying and exciting.

The winds of change were always daunting, facing the foundations it shook with an unsure future. She didn't know what was happening. She only knew something deep within was motivating her and she couldn't ignore the internal, unseen force that was so greatly influencing her actions and her mind.

Coltin's eyes pierced her. She couldn't get them out of her mind. She felt the heat from his body so close to hers and his breath on her face. In that moment, she felt truly shut out from the entire universe. *Why?* she thought. *Why do you seem so important?* Something in his eyes told her there was more but left no clue as to what.

The door flung open and Shade spun around. Daelus was next to her in an instant, dropping to his knees to be level with her.

"Shade," he began, clearly rushed. "Eros is still in council with the delegates. The collective is all astir. I don't know what's happening, but the entire Keeper faction seems to be alive with this news you've brought us."

"What's going to happen?" Shade asked.

"I don't know," Daelus confessed. "But you were right…there is more to the prophecy. I…" he trailed off. Daelus studied her, reluctant, wondering what his words would mean for the future. "I can't tell you how to act, Shade. I can only tell you—"

"Tell me the prophecy, Daelus. Tell me what you know," she implored him. Daelus swallowed hard and nodded.

"He shall be born with wings of heaven's light and in secret sins will uncover the truth of the pale hands. Marked a beast, the fallen angel will seek the darkness, and be welcomed into their selfish arms. He will hate the blackened palms that feed him for they love him only for his tainted wings, but his knowledge of the white will aid the shadows in the fight. His blackened wings will spread so far they change the stars of both light and dark."

Shade's brow was creased as she listened to the words that Daelus spoke. Every utterance seemed to awaken a truth inside her.

"Daelus—" she began, but he silenced her with his hand to her lips.

"Regardless of his fate, he will soon be a dead man. Angels have been dispatched to end him. If you have any faith in this man, you must find him and save him."

Shade did not think twice.

She stood up and sprinted out of the room, grabbing her sword from her bed as she passed. Daelus watched her go and sighed. He had a terrible feeling that he'd done the right thing…and that it would cost him dearly.

Knick had just finished a plate of pul potatoes and razer steak and was pushing the dish away from him, head surrounded by a cloud of cigarette smoke.

He'd stumbled into The Rotten Log somewhere in Turin; it was the town's central tavern, but it was rather empty for being so principle. Knick noticed that all the towns in the Over There tended to be thin in population.

Knick clenched his hands into fists, feeling his gloves over his palms once again. He kept running the incident with the Keeper over in his mind, chain-smoking more than he had since he first ditched the White Tower. Kicking Operations from his head and disconnecting from the hive mind had been hell; learning to exist without them was like learning to walk, talk, and write your name in your own piss all over again.

Knick took the last drag on his cigarette and ground out the butt on the clay ashtray on his table. Enough was enough. He stood up and dropped some bills for the meal, and then headed for the door. Outside, he lit up again, watching the rain cascade from the cavern ceiling.

The water systems of the Mine were activated whenever there was a heavy concentration of water on the surface. Essentially, the reserves emptied in on the Mine whenever the sky emptied its bladder on the earth. Equal opportunity for both depths of the world was the achieved goal.

"Balance," Knick muttered, thinking about the Keeper again, puffing on his cigarette. "More like interference."

The ground exploded on his right and a chain shot out of it. Knick ducked instinctively, nearly dropping his cigarette. He rolled to the side, pausing in a ready crouch.

The chain rose higher and higher into the air and then dropped fast, hitting the ground where he had been standing, tearing up the terrain. It slithered back into the ground. Knick's jaw dropped and the cigarette hit the concrete.

Another explosion near him caused him to jump, moving fast.

"What the hell is going on?" he yelled. "This just isn't my fucking day!"

White suits appeared out of no where, blocking his escape. There was something unusual about these angels: they were wearing white hoods to hide their faces.

Knick slid to a stop and tried to turn around, but the white suits closed in on him from behind. As he turned, he found a fist flying for his face. He slipped back, dodging the punch, and braced his knuckles. His fist connected with the angel's jaw, sending him flying backward. He ducked another swing and side-kicked his attacker in the gut.

They were everywhere.

He kept up his martial arts, fighting the angels as they came at him, but there were just too many to deal with. Something was different about them...something more vicious and precise than even the carbon clone servants of the White Hand.

Knick spun around to see a blade glisten in the neurocandescent spill from the street lights above. His eyes widened, watching the razorblade edge flying for his face.

A black blur dropped down in front of him and he stumbled back.

When he looked up, he saw Shade poised, blade under blade in a perfect block. She was drenched from the rain. When her violet eyes looked back at him, he knew she wasn't there to help the assassins.

Shade was fighting angrier than before, attacking the angels with intensity Knick hadn't seen in their spar. She was fighting almost like they were.

She executed a few skilled moves and disarmed the sword-wielder, sending her blade through his chest and across his throat. Shade reached her next target before the body hit the floor.

Knick found that fighting was a lot easier with Shade behind him, keeping his back protected. Not only could he hold defense, but he could push offense as long as she was guarding his ass.

"Why are you doing this?" he yelled back to her, throwing a punch at the nearest angel. He flicked his hair from his eyes and kneed the man in the gut, elbowing his back. The man crumbled to the ground in pain.

"Long story!" she replied, not really sure how to answer his question with any ounce of honesty.

"Gimme the short version!"

"The prophecy!" she explained, bearing down on her blade and side-stepping, slapping the edge across the small of a man's back.

Too short, he thought then yelled, "What prophecy?"

"Regardless of the destiny you choose, I can't let you die here!"

Knick shrugged before he grabbed the wrist of the arm that came at him. He pulled the attacker forward and his knee connected with the man's face.

"I knew you'd warm up to me!" he exclaimed. Shade pretended not to acknowledge his comment.

She twisted her sword, growling, and speared the nearest angel through the chest, sliding the sword all the way through him. He lifted his face, mouth gaping as he clutched at her shoulders. He jerked only twice and his head fell back on his neck, hood falling off.

Shade's face fell as the body slid out of her arms, slipping off of her sword.

"Are you sure we shouldn't go after him?" an angel asked as 4-56-29 ordered the team back to headquarters. The head angel nodded.

"The Mine is not our playing ground. We'd be slaughtered if we moved in on Black Hand territory. I won't lead this team to a suicide mission." 4-56-29 glanced back at the manhole briefly and kept moving. "We'll let Operations know the circumstances and wait for their plans on how to proceed."

"Yes sir," the angel said.

"Alright, let's move out!" 4-56-29 yelled, evacuating his team from D-Water.

"You're a Keeper," Shade whispered, staring at the glowing glyph on the assassin's forehead. "I don't under-stand..."

"Behind you!" Knick yelled. Shade gasped and turned around. Knick tackled her to the ground before the enemy's blade could touch her. The bells jingled around her wrist and the Wraith Wind whipped up from the menacing fang of her sword, grabbing the assassin by the throat and sucking him of his life-force.

When the body hit the ground, withered and dry from the spell as a jade-blue skeleton, the sounds of battle died with the rain. Knick lifted his head, staring Shade in her violet eyes. Rain dripped off of his face onto hers. He slowly lifted his arm, brushing his thumb over the glowing glyph on her forehead, and then he stood up, offering her his hand. She took it and he pulled her to her feet.

One of the bodies on the ground stirred, lifting the chain-claw weapon for one final attack. The claw retracted and the chain shot out, racing for Knick and Shade.

A great swell of electricity rocked the ground, riding like a wave across the pavement. The chain was ripped in half, stopped midflight. Shade cut her gaze to where the electrical attack had originated.

"What happened here?" Eros exclaimed, standing on the tin roof of an auto-knot shop. Daelus was beside him, clutching his weapon.

"Eros," Shade began, moving to meet him. The two Keepers jumped down and ran to her.

"You've killed Keepers," he said.

"They were disguised as angels," she explained.

"You've killed them for what?" he asked. "To save this

abomination?"

"Hey…" Knick muttered, knowing the stranger was talking about him.

"He's the new glyph!" Shade argued.

"He's not the savior!" Eros retorted. "He's a traitor! He betrayed Mirax for Black Tuesday. You'd have him betray them for us. And then he will betray you!"

"You can't know that!" Shade exclaimed.

"Even still, how will you explain this to the Regent? You defied his orders to kill a potentially large threat to the Balance and killed our own kind to save him. I can't protect you from this type of retribution."

"I will deal with the repercussions on my own, Eros," Shade replied. "I do not deny my actions, nor can I justify them to the Regent. I will face the consequences."

"You could die for this," Eros whispered, pleading with her.

"Then I die for this," she affirmed.

"Whoa, whoa, whoa…die?" Knick asked. "That's just a bit dramatic…isn't it?"

Eros stared at Shade a long time, trying to find some sort of hope in the situation. Daelus came forward.

"Run," he said.

"What?"

"Run," he repeated. "Run until we know what is to become of you."

"Yeah!" Knick piped in from behind. "Good plan!"

Shade half-smiled and shook her head.

"No, Daelus. I will not run. I take full responsibility for what has transpired."

"Why?" Eros snapped. She turned a gentle gaze on him.

"I don't know," she replied. "I guess I just followed what my instinct told me…and I realized that I believe in this more than I thought I did. You know what it's like, Eros…to believe in something so much that you act to near insanity on its behalf…"

Eros felt a pang of guilt rip through him and remembered the past. His so-strong faith…had been in her.

"I'll do what I can for you," Eros told her. Shade only smiled. "Let's go."

Eros and Daelus turned and began walking away. Shade

glanced back at Knick, who was already shaking his head in protest.

"Wait, that's it? You just drop in on me, try to kill me, molest me in an alley, save my life, and leave? I'm not a piece of meat, you know," he said. Shade faced him. "You owe me some answers, Keeper."

"I'm sorry, I can't answer all of your questions," she said quietly.

"Then just answer one."

"Alright," she agreed. "Go ahead."

"Who are you?" he asked.

She smiled at him for the first time. "My fate is unknown... My identity is forfeit."

Knick watched the three Keepers walk away, transforming into blurs of that mysterious, unknown power.

They disappeared into the rain as shimmering flashes, like shooting stars into the black universe.

Knick Coltin was standing under a wooden overhang, watching the cogwheelers loading the truck by the hollow bay. He was smoking a cigarette as usual, one hand stuffed in his jacket pocket while the other held the roll of tobacco.

Solo and Slot were poking fun at Jilk as he ordered them about. The hum of conversation by the shipment drowned into ambient sound in Knick's head.

It had been two months since the incident with the Keepers and he hadn't seen or heard from anyone belonging to the mysterious group.

He pushed off of the wall he was leaning on and took a walk down the road, moving away from the cogwheelers. He puffed on his cigarette, creating a gray halo around his head as he walked.

It was hot out. All the rain had brought humid temperatures, pissing off the coal mine's below. The Mine was already closer to the core than the surface was. The steam generated after the rainy season made living underground nearly unbearable. The weather wouldn't clear up for another month.

He was thankful that it would, at the very least.

He stopped on the other side of the street and stared out at the introverted, wooden shacks that sprinkled the cavern, twisted and collapsing in on one another to make up a town that looked like the reflection of a trick mirror. It was a gloomy looking place, but the people seemed to like it just fine.

"Sad, huh?" a voice said from somewhere behind him. Knick spun around, recognizing the voice.

Shade was standing a few yards away, healthy as ever. Oddly, he felt relieved.

"It's sad how no matter where you go, the view is always so dreary," she said gently. Her gaze drifted from the town's expanse beyond him and moved to meet his eyes.

"I thought you might be dead," Knick said. She shook her head.

"By the time we returned to the Order, the Regent and some of the delegates had fled. The rest were put on trial and an investigation of council corruption is still underway. A new Regent is being sought. The collective is quite upset, but things are slowly beginning to calm down."

"I don't know what that means," Knick began, walking toward her. "But I'm gonna guess it means you're off the hook."

Shade nodded. When he was close enough, she reached up and brushed the hair away from his forehead. The glyph had not yet reappeared, but she was confident that it would one day. Her thumb caressed the skin there for just a moment before she dropped her arm back to her side.

"I'm convinced you're one of us," she said.

"Sorry, baby, but your friend was right... I'm a traitor. I can't be trusted," he told her, exhaling a cloud of smoke. With a grin, he added, "But I can be had." His words didn't seem to deter her.

"You may not realize it now, but you will one day."

"God, I hope not," he muttered. "I'm not really the hero type."

"No, you aren't," she agreed. "But I...believe in you."

Knick was silent, staring her down. For the first time in his life, he wasn't sure how to respond. Shade cleared her throat.

"I fear the Regent's retribution is not over. His intentions, his intimate knowledge, his purposes—we don't know them.

Whatever the reason he sought your death so intensely was, we know it was not for the Balance. His assassins will, most likely, still come for you."

The end of Knick's cigarette glowed as he took a drag.

"At least I've been warned," he mumbled. More silence. Shade cleared her throat again.

"About that attack on you before, back in the alley—"

"Yeah, about that—"

"I didn't mean to—"

"Maybe you did a little—"

"I didn't mean to hurt you if I did—"

"You didn't—"

"I was following orders—"

"Who isn't—?"

"It was before I knew who you were—"

"Let's figure me out some more on a mattress some-where—"

"Right, then I guess that's settled—"

"Yeah, yeah. It's settled," he finished. She almost cracked a smile.

"Yeah..." she mumbled. Knick smirked behind his cigarette, reveling in the awkwardness.

"If you ever find yourself between heaven and hell with nowhere to go...give me a call," she said, dropping a black leather bracelet into his hands. Tiny, silver bells were braided into it. "Those bells match the frequency my bells emit. If you will your mind to mine, these bells will reach me...regardless of how far apart we are."

"How?" he asked. She drew her sword and ran her finger along the edge.

"The sword will know...and so will I," was all she said in reply. She gave him one last attempt at a smile. Knick clutched the bracelet tightly as she sheathed her weapon and turned to go.

"Who am I summoning exactly?" he asked. She glanced back at him.

"Summon Shade, Sovereign of the Sword of Shadows, Keeper of the Balance, and Interim of the Order."

Knick smiled as the Keeper disappeared in a ball of shadowy fury, flying off into the distance. He turned back to survey the town, taking a deep breath. He opened his palm and studied the bracelet before he shoved it in his jacket pocket.

Solo wiped the sweat from his brow and looked up, seeing Knick reemerge from the alley. For a moment he thought he saw something blue shimmer across his forehead. He squinted and checked again.

Nothing.

"Man, it's so hot out here, I'm seeing things," he muttered.

"What's that?" Slot asked, dropping a crate onto the truck.

"Nothing," he replied.

"Coltin!" Jilk exclaimed, checking his pocket watch. "You ready to get out of here?"

Knick took one last drag on his cigarette and tossed it to the ground.

"Yeah," he said on tendrils of gray, pushing off of the wall. "I really am."

Part Two

"Never let the future disturb you. You will meet it, if you have to, with the same weapons of reason which today arm you against the present."
Marcus Aurelius Antonius

The same scene again.

It was somehow different than the others; it was softer, warmer—not crisp and cold and detached. Normally, This One's mind's eye saw visions of the future, the present, and sometimes the past. This One did not know of the outside world. This One did not even know of This One's self. This One saw the world and the people in it with second sight; This One's first sight—This One's eyes—saw nothing.

Moving forward through white light. The same tunnel. Through the mouth. A bright, wide world. A tug? On…a face? Near the mouth. A smile? Moving through this city, praying the other visions don't come. Don't interrupt again. Don't know what this place is— why being seen. It's exciting. Don't want to lose the scene again.

This One explored deeper into the dream.

New things. New things not here before. Going further than before. Ah! A face! Face—an entire body. Move closer. Closer. This face. A man. People! People everywhere, walking past, walking in and out of sight. He's smiling. Staring at Sight. He lifts his arm. Waves. Waving at Sight? Why can he see Sight? What is this place? What is this being seen? What is this? What is this? Never seen anything like this. Never seen this boy.

The scene had no purpose.

No! Not supposed to see. Not supposed to see. Running, moving, out of this scene. Get out of this scene. Don't belong. Don't know what this is. Are you there? Why is Sight seeing such? That man! Reaching! Reaching for Sight! Tender face! What does that mean? No purpose to this scene!

Something was rising within This One's unconscious state, spreading across This One's body. This One's brain waves were going crazy, and the liquid around This One began to resonate with strange, foreign waves.

There was no one in the dark room with This One.

This One was alone.

Running, fleeing! Not this scene! Dangerous! Dangerous! Turning! No! What…is that? A girl? A girl… A mirror? Girl… lying down. Girl…surrounded by water. Darkness. "Help me!"

This One's brain activity spiked.

Girl reaches. A touch. Not Sight. Sight…is girl. Girl…is me.

This One saw This One's self for the first time. This One became aware that This One existed—a body, not just sight. This One achieved the impossible.

This One became aware of herself.

Knick Coltin took deep breaths, inhaling and exhaling through O-shaped lips as he sprinted down the alley and turned the corner. Another body dropped from the rooftops and he skidded on the cement and turned the corner, throwing his power into the right-hand move. His boots were hitting the pavement hard, snaps and buckles on his jacket jingling as he ran full speed.

The fleuro-neurescents were pale, flickering or burned out, and Knick hoped they would conceal him. *Yeah right,* he thought. They would find him; their ways were unnatural. *Fucking Keepers.* No, not Keepers. Shade had told him that much. They were runaways or something. But how long had it been since this mess started? Seven months? He'd found life much more difficult since she'd shown up on the scene; now, he was constantly alert for ex-Keeper assassins, paranoid that they were around every corner, or actually running from them. To make it worse, he hadn't seen Shade since that day she gave him the bells.

Knick rammed his shoulder into the next door he came upon, splintering it from the hinges. He ran into the darkness and cut through the warehouse, trying not to run into anything and too afraid to stop. A light on the other side gleamed and he ran for it, breaking through that door as well.

The warehouse opened up to an alley and a rusted railing with a fifteen foot drop into a drainage ditch. He didn't even think; he just grabbed the piping and jumped, flipping over the bars and hitting the ground hard. His knees buckled and he rolled, but he found his footing and sprinted as he stood. He couldn't stop; he knew they were right behind him.

A network of tunnels branched off of the ditch and he crawled into one, scurrying through until he found a metal grate. His fingers slipped across the grime as he sought an opening. He heard shoes all around him, hitting the ground, running.

"Come on, piece of shit," he spat, trying not to give in to

panic. The grate gave way and he slipped inside then closed it over his head. The rungs in the wall weren't very safe—loose to the touch, rusted—but he used them and the intimacy of the small space to support himself, suspended in the tunnel. He didn't know how far the drop was or where it led, and he didn't want to find out.

Black soles scurried around the grate, sliding over it. He tried to slow down his breathing, unable to tear his eyes away from the body standing over his head. The man looked around and moved on. Knick held his breath a bit longer, listening to every drop of condensation on the mucky ground. He listened until he thought it was safe and he sighed out his fear, wondering how long would be long enough to wait for them to be gone.

"I'll bet you seventy rials and a pack of Jacks," Slot said, staring straight ahead. Solo sucked on his teeth, starting to shake his head.

"I donno," he replied, lifting the cigarette to his lips and sucking in. He exhaled, gray smoke blending in with his visible breath. "That's a bit risky."

It was cold, middle of October. The Mine was just like a slushy during the winter season—the ice from the surface and sub-temperatures was melted by the heat from the coal mines. It was one of the suck seasons for Kishar; hell, every season seemed to suck when one lived underground.

"Alright, sixty," Slot said, licking the paper end as she rolled her cigarette. Solo didn't seem to want to give in.

"Fifty," he said. "Fifty and a pack of Jacks and you got a deal."

"You drive a hard bargain," Slot mumbled, cigarette between her lips as she lit it. "I can respect that," she continued, exhaling. "Deal."

Slot held out her hand, palm up, and Solo slapped it twice before their fingertips danced together for a couple of seconds and they both snapped simultaneously. It was a sort of ritualistic handshake that sealed every bet they ever made. A well-practiced handshake.

They both took a drag on their cigarettes, eyes fixed across the street where their boss, Jilk, was arguing with his boss, Jeebo James-Jameson. They were having a heated discussion and Jeebo was flinging his arms. Jilk flinched when Jeebo's arm came too close.

"Oh, oh!" Slot began, getting anxious.

"That doesn't count. No contact," Solo quickly said. They continued to watch and smoke, looking like a pair of druggies to anyone else on the street. Then it happened. Jeebo hit Jilk upside the head.

"Yes!" Slot exclaimed, throwing her hands into the air. Solo shook his head, tapping her shoulder.

"Man... Double or nothing?" he asked. She couldn't resist a bet.

"Sure, why not," she said, looking cocky as she readjusted her jacket with a shrug-n-tug maneuver. They went back to their stoner poses, staring and smoking and waiting for the next slap if it was going to happen.

Nothing. Jeebo stormed off without doling out anymore beatings. Slot groaned and Solo touched his fingertip to his forehead and moved it up, acknowledging the Divine for his win.

"Doesn't count," Slot said.

"What?" Solo exclaimed, turning to face his sister. She took a drag on her cigarette and shook her head.

"We didn't shake on it. Doesn't count."

"Man, you're a—"

"A what?" she asked as he forked over the cash.

"You're a—"

"Alright, time to go," Jilk interrupted the argument, unaware of what he walked into. He snatched the cigarette from Slot and took a drag, rubbing his hands together. She didn't argue, knowing he was in a bad mood.

Jilk hated the cold; no skullcap could save his bald head from the icy temperatures. Not only that, but all of his face metal seemed to be in freeze mode during the winter season. Plus, he hated dealing with Jeebo; getting smacked around 'cause the boss-man was feeling bitchy that day wasn't his favorite pastime.

They moved down the street, wandering through Thebes like a couple of schoolyard rebels. Practically everyone in Thebes was a cogwheeler and so no one even took notice, knowing the three clowns were part of the same, black circle.

"So what's the job?" Solo asked, eyeing his boss. Jilk

scratched his neck, squinting against the cool air.

"We're moving russells outta Mike through Buschers," he told them.

"Which side of Buschers?" Slot asked. "Bacon or paper?"

"Paper," he replied. "We're going to Knox."

"Auh, gross," Slot muttered, wrinkling her nose. Solo grimaced.

"Shit," he said. "Why do we get the shit jobs?"

Jilk shrugged. "Better than runnin' needlers outta OT subways for cargo trains."

"True," Solo agreed, lighting up another cigarette.

Buschers was known for two factories: a paper mill and a ham plant. One side of town smelled like ass crack and the other smelled like breakfast. It was no mystery which side of Buschers was the better side.

"Tell Coltin to get over to the docks. We're pullin' out in an hour."

"Don't know where he is," Solo said. Jilk glanced at him, eyes demanding for him to explain. "Haven't seen him since he left Oolong's last night."

"Man, that dude is a lot of trouble," Jilk muttered. "Ex-angel my ass. Who cares what he used to be?"

"Boss-man," Slot replied, throwing her cigarette to the street. Jilk looked ready to fume.

"Whatever," he grumbled. "Just find him and tell him to get to the docks."

Slot and Solo nodded and stopped, watching Jilk walk off toward Moss Street.

"Bet you twenty rials he gets knocked the fuck out by Old Man Byrd comin' outta the butcher shop," Solo said to his sister.

"Fifteen," she snapped.

"Deal."

The handshake ensued. They watched intently again, Solo puffing on his cigarette. Forty-five seconds later, Byrd bumbled out of the butcher shop and slammed right into Jilk, knocking him into a sign pole that gave his head a nasty thunk and dropped him flat on his ass.

Slot shook her head, recognizing defeat, and handed her brother a few bills.

"You still owe me a pack of Jacks," she said as they turned

to go find their friend.

Eros was standing in front of a fireplace, staring down at the flames as they danced upward as if trying to escape. It was somehow eccentrically fitting with how he felt. The fire only burned because the logs were there to be burned, and without the wood in place, the flames would die; yet, the wood was an anchor, keeping the fire from reaching the sky, from going anywhere.

He gently touched the fireplace mantle, silence invaded by the popping of the logs in the heat.

"You wanted to see me?" a familiar voice said from somewhere behind him. He slowly turned around and smiled when his eyes fell on the beautiful woman before him.

"Shade," he began. He bowed his head. "For the Balance," he said.

"For the Balance," she replied.

"Things are getting progressively worse."

"What do you mean?" she asked, moving closer to him. He reached out and touched her hair, eyes glassy in the dim light.

"Another Keeper was caught sending coded messages to *him*," he told her. Shade frowned, knowing who he meant: the ex-Regent, the traitor.

"Have we discerned the messages?" she asked. He shook his head. "Who was it this time?"

"Elfonne."

"I see..."

"There's more. Another delegate committed suicide."

"I thought Rank was watching them."

"He is."

"How could this keep happening?" she asked.

"Methaletamine," he replied. "That was the cause this time. We think it was delivered by an insider. We're going through all visitors to the delegates, trying to weed out the rat. We have no real way to tell who is a Keeper and who is a follower of Muriel."

Shade reached up and let loose her hair, shaking out the silky, black tresses, and used her fingers to comb out the tangles. Eros started to reach for her hair but stopped, with-drawing his hand. Shade draped herself on the old, leather couch and propped her head up on her hand, eyeing Eros as he went back to watching the fire on the hearth.

"Eros," she said and he looked to her. "What do you think we should do?"

He was silent for a long time, staring intently into the fire, feeling the heat, feeling the flames riding up through his soul, wondering how long he could last this way.

"The traitor Muriel fled with thirteen of the twenty-six delegates, and six of those remaining thirteen have committed suicide. We are doing the best we can to guard the lives of the remaining seven. No one but Rank, Nigel, the High Counselor, and myself are allowed to see them unsupervised. Consular Beonan was found dead in his chamber with cause-of-death unknown; we're no closer to discovering how he died, why he died, or how involved he was with *his* deceit."

"What about Muriel? Any news on him?"

"Daelus, Rexis, and Vox are still scouring Anshar for traces of his flight. Dimitri, Bartimaeus and Sonia move through Kishar, but neither group has had any luck finding him, or anything of any help. What about your team?"

Shade shook her head. "We've been tearing up the Keeper channels, but we've found nothing."

"I suspected as much. He's covered his tracks well. Seven months and we can't find him. The trail is cold…and it's beginning to be too troublesome to have the Interim split between the streets looking for Muriel and handling problems created by the Hands."

"We're doing our best, Eros," Shade reminded him and he nodded. "The Kur are working just as hard."

"It's not just that, Shade. Things are in a total state of unrest here."

She knew that. She remembered their conversation just after they'd found out Muriel had fled with some of the delegates and the Keepers broke out in panic. Never before had a regent betrayed the Order. Trust had been severed, and finding Muriel's replacement was difficult, to say the least.

"How are the elections coming along?" she wanted to know.

"Sometimes, it seems hopeless. We've been astir for months, but little progress has been made narrowing down the candidates."

"There are that many?"

"Not really," he admitted. "We've never done this before. Naming a candidate is sometimes done out of sheer panic, I think. The collective are starting to feel that support toward a strong candidate is like taking sides and they're afraid to divide the Order." He sighed.

The Order was already split, but for different reasons. The Interim was working hard to find Muriel or any of the runaway delegates as well as combat machinations of the Hands. The Kur was split into a three-way: searching with the Interim, helping the Interim handle the Hands, and going about their own daily jobs. The Keepers were stretched thin. An internal divide could cause their house to crumble.

Not to mention...Shade still hadn't heard from Knick. She wondered if he was dead; she wondered if the ex-Regent had finally caught up with him. Shade had wanted to watch him from the shadows but, between her duties as a Keeper, she found it near impossible. He hadn't called her, and she wasn't sure that he ever would.

"And the Oracle?" Shade asked. Eros shook his head.

"No."

"The Enoch?"

"Restless. More so than ever. The naga are having immense difficulty sorting through the information."

Shade studied her companion and, when she saw his glassy, blue eyes, she felt completely hopeless; her sinking heart was more for Eros than for the true state of things. He was trying desperately to hold everyone together and find the answers, but she knew it was tearing him apart.

"Eros," she began. "What do you want me to do?"

"Keep searching," he replied. "I will let you know if anything develops here."

Eros felt her slender hand on his back and was comforted by her touch.

"Something will turn up," Shade told him. "Something is going to happen, and our steps will be guided. All is not lost. The Keepers, though crumbling, have not fallen. The Balance will be maintained as long as there are those of us who believe in it."

Eros stiffened his muscles to keep himself braced against the mantle. He nodded at her words. She pulled the silk mask over her mouth.

"For the Balance," she said and departed. Once she had gone, Eros let out a heavy sigh.

"For the Balance…"

"Welcome to Mirax Augmentation and Aero-Cognition Research," the woman said, firmly shaking the hand of Dr. Robert Basset. He noted how the skirt suit was starched over her body as if they'd ironed it on her; her hair was pulled tight on her scalp and wound into a bun, pulling her brow back and giving her a surprised expression.

"Thank you, Ms. Mulley," Basset said, clutching his briefcase. "Is he ready?"

"Yes," she replied. "Feel free to go on up. Take the third elevator on your left; the guard will send you to the appropriate floor."

Basset nodded and motioned to his associates to follow him. Three men and one woman crossed the white marble floor and stairs to the elevator landing where six elevators—three on the left and three on the right—stretched down the hall before them. A guard was stationed behind a desk at the end of the row.

"My name is Robert Basset," he began. "I'm here to see—"

"He's expecting you," the guard said curtly, motioning to the opening elevator doors. Basset smiled politely and stepped inside the white leather and glass box. He wasn't sure how many floors they went up; there were no dings to signal a checkpoint and it moved so fast that it seemed like they'd only gone up a few.

The doors opened to a stylishly sterile office. Floor-to-ceiling glass panes stretched across three walls; a white tiled ceiling and floor gave the room no sense of definition. The serbo-steel furniture made the room seem cold.

"Welcome, Dr. Basset," the man said, standing behind his desk. He motioned to the sitting area on the right. "My name is Amil Hosef. Join me."

The group sat down on the white, leather cushions and waited until the attendant had served the coffee and left.

"You've been informed of why you're here?" Hosef began, watching them pour cream and sugar into their coffee.

"You're in need of a specialist," Basset said, stating the

obvious, "but that's all I was told."

"We need your expertise on a certain artifact," Hosef explained, watching Basset's movements.

"What kind of artifact?" he asked. "I'm a geologist, not an archaeologist."

"I'm well aware of your profession, Dr. Basset. We would not have called you had we felt you didn't meet this study's requirements. The artifact is a stone and our scientists are at a loss."

"What kind of stone? Can you describe it for me?"

"Smooth, spherical, polished—exactly thirty-one centimeters in diameter—tiger-eye, jade, and onyx in coloring. It's been crafted, but we can't tell how long ago or by whom. It's emitting strange psywaves, similar to the ether substance."

Basset had a very bad feeling about this. He had been praying that Mirax had wanted him to glance at a stone and tell them some specs, not undergo a several weeks research project.

"I see," Basset replied, keeping the disappointment from his voice. He cleared his throat and creased his brow to seem curious and deep in thought.

"We would like you to stay on here, working with the best in archaeology, gemology, lithology, and any other relevant ology you can think of. You'll be working with the best team of scientists Lotus Maze has to offer, and you'll be working in a top-of-the-line lab. All your needs will be met, and anything you require will be supplied."

Basset set his coffee down, trying not to show the concern in his face. He ran his rough hand over his mouth and jaw, feeling the stubble hiding in his skin. His fingers pushed back into his thinning, mousy-brown hair and then drifted back down the wrinkles in his forehead. Having stalled enough, he laced his voice with the disregard of a businessman.

"I have a company to run," he said. Hosef smiled politely.

"You will be compensated for your time away from the office, Doctor. I'm sure they'll manage without you for a few weeks."

Basset knew what that meant. They weren't asking him for his help; they were telling him he was going to help them. He knew how Mirax worked.

"Well, then I'll be going. I'll need to arrange for my leave of absence," Basset began, standing. His associates stood with him. Hosef motioned for him to wait.

"No need," he said, holding his sickly sweet smile. "It's already been done. Drink your coffee. There will be attendants to escort you to the labs once you're finished."

Basset returned the smile as he sat down, playing the role of the eager geologist. He was not stupid enough to let Mirax know he was displeased by their methods; nor was he insane enough to refuse them.

When Mirax needed someone to do something, that person had two options: one—they could do it without delay and hope the results didn't cost them their life, or two—they could refuse, risk their business, risk their life, risk their family's lives, and risk the lives of everyone they'd ever been involved with.

Basset had a wife and two daughters. He had a healthy and successful company. He was forty-eight. He knew the system, he knew his options, and he knew he had to do this research project if he wanted to resume his likeable and comfortable lifestyle. He knew he had to do this research project if he wanted his business, his family, and his own life to be ensured.

Knick came sauntering up to the docks late, as usual. The train had been due to leave two hours before he'd shown up. No matter how much Jilk threatened to leave him, he didn't.

"Where've you been?" Jilk exclaimed, spitting angrily. "We were supposed to leave two fuckin' hours ago!"

"Business, man. Business," Knick replied, still feeling cold and clammy from hiding out in the drainage ditch for the whole night.

"What kind of business?" Jilk wanted to know; Slot and Solo were looming behind by the cargo car, smoking, not trying especially hard to keep their eavesdropping a secret.

"Uh, about 5'8", pale skin with long, black hair and violet eyes," he told him, describing the Keeper he hadn't seen or heard from for four months.

"Sounds gothic," Jilk muttered distastefully. "Sounds like a push-over, I-wish-I-was-dead gothic kid." Jilk grimaced at the mental picture and Knick as the two made their way to the cargo car.

"No one's asking you to do her," he retorted casually.

"Everything ready?" the conductor yelled. Jilk's hand motion signaled things were green.

Knick was the last to hop the train, piling in the car with Jilk, Slot, Solo, and a couple other cogwheelers already asleep in the back of the car. Everyone was packing some kind of weapon. The two in the back had a couple AR15 rifles, some grenades, and possibly a .45 or two; Jilk was sporting a sawed off 12-gauge shot gun with both slugs and widespread ammo, and a .38. Solo had two .44 Desert Eagles and a couple of grenades; his sister, Slot, had at least three 9mms on her—most likely four—and some dynamite and matches. Knick was the least packin' of the trigger-happy troupe weighing in at nil. He'd been hiding out so long after he left Oolong's that he went straight to the train yard when he got back in town and heard he was lined up on a job; he didn't have time to go get geared up.

Jilk passed him the .38 and leaned back on the open door to the train as it crept out of the station. "I doubt we'll need it," he said. "Who really cares about russells, anyway? Still, better safe than sorry."

Knick leaned on the opposite side of the door, feet hanging over the edge. He studied Jilk for a moment, watching the bald-headed weirdo stare out at Thebes passing by. He was a pretty young guy. He was nice. He didn't look too great, with all those rings, spikes, and balls in his eyebrows, nose, and ears, but he was a nice guy; he cared about his team, even if he had a hard time showing it. Knick felt like Jilk would've done something honest with his life if he'd been born into an honest world. Hell, Knick probably would have, too.

Too bad.

Otto Ferés hoisted the canister up and tossed it into the street-cleaner. It was a bright, white day as the white alloy of the truck reflected the solar bulbs' and reflector panels' broadcasted light.

Anshar's skies were mostly gray and black, sometimes green, and rarely blue, so MAAR did all in its power to magnify the sunlight hidden by the wasted sky. That included white and alloy walls. Because the light was so artificial, the metal never got hot, just bright. Sand-colored buildings and off-white structures were packed tightly together in the big cities, like Saigon and Rome and, of course, Rashrima Haan—the capital. The further outside a major city one went, the dingier the buildings became, the darker the streets were. The solar bulbs couldn't reflect off of gray stone and warped, wooden beams.

Otto heaved the next canister and tossed it in the truck. He would've wiped the sweat off his brow, but there was none. It wasn't hot out; it was dry, which was just less than unusual. He hopped the back of the truck and whistled. The street-cleaner rolled on, power-vacuuming the cobblestone roads in the front and giving a final scatter-sweep in the back. He watched the black needles all bunched together, swaying left and right beneath the ass of the truck, doing their best to clean the road.

He sighed and leaned back. The complimentary refreshener puffed twice and the familiar scent of tangerine over waste filled his nostrils and made him feel sick. He leaned as far away from the truck as he could, trying to suck in some fresh air, trying to make it to his lunch break.

Otto was pale, clammy. He wasn't sick; he hadn't been sleeping well. It'd been this way for about a year. At first, it was minor; he had a few restless nights where he remembered waking up feeling disturbed, unwell. As time went on, the night's got worse. He woke up feeling anything but rested, feeling his muscles sore from tension; he thought his brow might be permanently creased. Still, it got worse. His dreams grew more and more vivid until he began to dream of this woman. She was beautiful—not with any specific details, more like a feeling, like her presence was beautiful. She was an angel. She was in trouble. He couldn't stop thinking about her, even when he was awake.

Every morning he woke up, he felt worse. The guys at work thought he was shooting herp or snorting ash. Someone once asked if he was hooked on A. *Stupid son of a bitch,* he thought. *You can't get adrenaline out here. I'm a garbage guy. Where am I gonna get the money to get adrenaline in Tirmaline?* He had to give the guy credit, though. His symptoms did seem classic to a junkie too gone on adrenaline and about to collapse from a body run too hard. Still, it wasn't easy to get drugs in

Anshar, much less the big cities. The druggies lived in the Mine for a good reason: Mirax pushed them out.

But no drugs. Otto just couldn't sleep. He'd gone to the doctor a couple of times, but he was diagnosed with too much stress and inhaling too much sarpis gas from the waste he picked up, which was caused by the new drug recently added to the vegetable supply, particularly the lettuce. *What a crock,* he remembered thinking. *None of the other guys got this fever.*

When he and Larry finally finished their rounds in Sector IV, they stopped outside the forum and split ways for lunch. Otto went to a hole-in-the-wall deli that had a large tent roof in front of the ordering window with stone tables underneath where the patrons could eat. He ordered up a chafkin sandwich with two sides: salad and flats. 3, 291 forints. *What a rip-off.*

Choosing a seat at the end of the tent, Otto planted his ass on top of the table, feet propped on the bench where his butt should be and he squinted into the light while he ate the chopped up nuts, berries, greens, and an assortment of dairy products mixed into some tasteless condiment. He didn't feel any better, really, but at least the urge to hurl had mostly gone.

As he was finishing up his food, he spied a woman out of the ordinary. She was walking through the crowd, standing out in his mind. He wasn't sure why exactly; probably the colors she wore.

Her hair was orange, short, thick. Her clothes were shades of burnt red and poppy seed. They were flowing into what seemed like hundreds of sheer layers that, at any given moment, could fall off of her and leave her standing just as she was when she came into this world. To his relief, that didn't happen; he would've been embarrassed for the poor girl.

Otto was only twenty-five years old, but he was a gentleman. He believed in modesty and fidelity and loyalty. He only ever slept with a woman while he dated her and he never raised a hand to strike her if she made him angry.

Well, that's how it was normally, anyway. He was currently single. Otto wasn't a bad looker. He was 5'10'' with short, curly brown hair and a fair face. He wasn't overweight, but he had a hard time turning his 155 pounds into muscle. It was like he never lost all of his baby fat. But that wasn't the problem. The problem all of his exes had was his lack of backbone.

Otto Ferés was a coward.

He didn't want to start a fight if some jerk bumped into him. He didn't make a fuss when he was overcharged. He liked moving through life void of confrontation, quiet and peaceful. 10 out of 10 times it got him dumped. Otto's manhood had been too crushed when even the pacifist had had enough, which cut him out of the dating scene for awhile.

He came out of his inner thoughts and watched the orange-haired woman move through the streets, eventually disappearing in the crowd. He finished his meal and grabbed a few drinks of water at the public hydration station. Back to work.

Dr. Basset was frowning at the relic. He'd never seen anything like it. He pulled on his coat and face mask and moved through the vacuum-sealed door into the sanitation chamber. Once the pale gases passed over his body, he walked through the other door and pulled off the mask. A fellow ologist, though he had no idea which kind, passed him a pair of gloves and he snapped them on.

"Dr. Basset," one of them said. "I'm Dr. Denise Rattelade, resident gemologist. You must be our geologist."

"Pleased to meet you," Basset said, shaking her extended hand. He shook three more hands.

"Ellis Woodard, lithologist," one of the men said.

"Mark Guerre, archaeologist," the other man said.

"Mara Favre, parapsychologist," the other female told him. No one introduced their assistants looming behind them.

"What have we discovered so far?" Basset asked, moving toward the stone.

It was just how Hosef had described it—smooth, spherical, and polished. He didn't have to take a measurement to guess that it was thirty-one centimeters in diameter. The coloring was, indeed, peculiar. The outside seemed to have an almost transparent onyx color with a middle layer of jade. The tiger-eye was in the center. The colors seemed to swirl together, but Basset knew that was a trick of the eye. Many gems and stones presented the illusion that their colors or markings were moving; a fault of human optics—easily deceived.

"It's emitting psywaves in a rather peculiar manner,"

Favre explained, approaching the stone. "Human psywaves work like SONAR. A telepathic signal, if you will, is sent from the brain and it bounces off of everything around it, forming a picture in the mind of the organic emitter. Psywaves are not limited by the physical plane. They operate on a much higher level of the brain that most people cannot tap into or, even more rarely, control.

"Inorganic psywaves are completely different. They are emitted and are passively absorbed by whatever they run into. Ether works in a similar manner, but is actively absorbed by whatever it comes in contact with. Unlike inorganic psywaves, ether has a specific pattern recognition process like SONAR and organic psywaves that allows it to distinguish one thing from another."

"Hosef said that this relic is emitting psywaves similar to the ether substance," Basset said aloud.

"Hosef has misunderstood. This isn't emitting waves similar to ether. It functions like ether, an enhancement to other objects or beings."

"What does all this mean?"Basset asked, finding the idea of the stone being ether both alarming and intriguing. "How are the psywaves peculiar?"

Favre smiled as if she were both incredibly proud of herself and excited with the verge of scientific breakthrough.

"This object is emitting organic psywaves...as if it had a brain. It's reaching out and bouncing off of everything, recording pictures."

Dr. Basset cut his eyes to his female associate. "That's not possible," he told her.

"Or so we thought," she said. "Dr. Rattelade, Dr. Woodard, and Dr. Guerre have been working hard to deter-mine how old it is, how it was crafted, and who might have crafted it."

"So far, we haven't discovered much," Guerre told him. "It's a complete mystery."

"Your focus was geochemistry, was it not?" Woodard began. "Perhaps you can shed some light on this discovery."

Dr. Basset glanced around at his associates; they were all excited about this enigmatic rock dropped into the hands of Mirax. He could tell they were thrilled about what they might learn. He felt that excited tingle in the pit of his stomach right next to the gut instinct to pack up and walk away as quickly as possible.

He bent down to examine the stone.

He was first and foremost a scientist and that meant taking risks to better understand the world. So, he did what every curious creature did when faced with an enigma; he reached out and touched it.

The train rolled into Mike by nightfall and the cogwheelers forced themselves alert. They slowed into the cargo yard where the russell packers were standing by large crates and drums, ready to load the shipment onto the train. The cogwheelers jumped the train before it even stopped, fanning out to create a perimeter around the tracks. Militia attacks were rare, but one too many hits to business and the clientele start forking over extra for insurance. Jilk and his crew were there to make sure no crazed independents, like Reinhardt's inspired, thought it would be a good idea to try to steal from Black Tuesday.

The motto was: don't steal, Black Tuesday hates competition. And it was the truth. But to steal from the biggest thief of all? Only Reinhardt's flunkies or those idolizing his bravado would dream up something so dim.

The packers hoisted the drums and crates onto the train as fast as possible, dying to end their shift, and finished the job in less than an hour. Incident free.

Jilk lit up a cigarette.

"I love it when things run smoothly."

And they were back on the train, crowded by night and smog, powering through the Mine with Buschers not far in the distance. They made the city near lunch time and the overwhelming smell of ass-sweat invaded everyone's nostrils, and no one wanted to breathe, afraid the taint was glued to every particle in the area and they'd be stuck with it all the way to Knox.

Knick threw up two minutes in the town, and Jilk patted his shoulder.

"Happens to everyone their first time," he said, but Knick wasn't comforted.

The train was refueling and the cogwheelers took lunch breaks in shifts. Jilk, Knick, Slot, Solo, and a few others were near the last to eat, and they made it count by picking the best joint they could find not too far from the yard.

Buschers ham really was the best pork in the Mine and they ordered more than enough to pack their guts. As they shoveled food in, Jilk noticed Slot's fingers rolled in band aids again. She was like a walking wound, with scrapes and cuts all over. She had more stitches and thread than the most hardcore cogwheeler the rumors whispered into legend and yet she was a beacon of health.

"What's with the—" Jilk began, motioning to her fingers, "—this time?"

Slot glanced down at her fingers, a wad of bread and meat in her cheek and she made a sound something like "mm" behind all of that food.

"Wonothuh packers had-a split inis crate so I picked the russells-he dropped up an' tossed 'em back in the bay. Cut mah fingers-up pretty 'n red," she explained with a full mouth, taking another bite of her sandwich before she swallowed her current mass. Jilk made a face, thinking of the razorblade-like animals not yet skinned.

"What the hell you pick 'em up for?" he asked, feeling a bit ill. "The packers are supposed to do that shit. That's why they wear those reinforced gloves and aprons."

Slot shrugged. She never had much of a reason for doing careless things.

"I've never seen a russell up close like that with its skin still on," she said after she swallowed her food. "Reminded me of too much skin bubbled up and blistered and sprouting saw blades. Fuckin' weird."

Jilk's face expressed disgust.

"You're ruining my food," he said. "It's not tasting good anymore, talking to you."

But Slot only shrugged, attention focusing on Solo's food art. He made a high-looking angel out of straws, bread crust, and an inappropriate use of boiled eggs.

Knick could only eat half of his food before the smell of Buschers to his virgin nose forced him to leave. "I'll meet you back at the train," he said, barely managing to keep his food in.

"It's not any better out there," Jilk told him. Knick just kept going, almost falling through the door and back into ass-crack central. He stumbled by the storefront window and they all heard their comrade vomiting in the alley next to them.

Slot and Solo glanced at their boss and Jilk shrugged one shoulder.

"Ain't never been through Buschers before," he said. "He'll get used to it."

"Pfft," Solo snorted. "I've been through loads of times, and I've never gotten used to it. Immune reflux, maybe, but not used to."

Jilk and Slot had to agree.

Outside, Knick pushed his hair from his face and tried to hold his breath. The vomit mixed with the paper plant potpourri was more than he could handle. He shut his eyes tight, trying to slow the sickness.

Shade's face—or what he remembered it looking like— popped up behind his eyes and he zeroed in on that one, genuine smile she'd given him. For some reason, he always went back to that image; he couldn't shake the thought.

Another wave of nausea hit him as a fresh whiff of ass-crack blew up his nostrils. He decided to attempt to make it back to the train without vomiting, so he splashed his face with old water dripping from open pipes hanging off the sandwich shop and ambled toward the train yard.

The Keepers came out of nowhere, dressed like any professional assassin: that of their surroundings. Knick felt something connect with the back of his head and he fell to the ground, disoriented from the blow and the nauseating environment. He tried to push himself up and took another blow to his back.

The commotion of Jilk and fellow cogwheelers rushing into the fray gave him the moment he needed to get to his feet.

"Run!" Knick yelled, stumbling backward with his hand on his head. He could feel the warm, slick texture of blood matted in his hair. "Run!" he yelled again, knowing the cogwheelers—as they were then—were no match for the Keeper assassins.

.44 and 9mm shells hit the ground like metal rain and the attention was taken off of him for a minute. Knick threw himself at the nearest baddie and wrapped his arms around the guy's neck, taking the guy's head with him as he dodged the elbows angled for his gut; the Keeper went to kick, caught by surprise from the sudden assault. His neck snapped a split second later, and the commotion raged around the corpse.

The shotgun explosions that blew two Keepers across the street focused attention on Jilk, sawed off in both hands and a clear path between him and the Keepers. The heavy cracks like deadly thunderclaps shuddered through everyone's body as, one after the other, Jilk cut down the assassins. For a moment, Knick thought Jilk looked like a real badass, walking in to save the day; maybe the cogwheeler firepower would be enough.

Reinforcements were close by and once the Keepers had assessed the situation, they turned on their attackers. Knick had a horrible feeling tremble through his gut when one of them raised his arm toward Jilk and he found himself yelling before his brain processed his words.

"Run!"

The Keeper Channels were dark, damp, narrow corridors of stone bricked in enclosing cylinders; tunnels branched off of each other in such a fashion that one wouldn't even see an opening until they were right up on it. Near three inches of water ran along the bottom and dripping noises echoed from everywhere. It was a living, breathing stomach of Anshar with a bladder problem.

Shade moved down one of the clone tunnels quietly, team in tow. The next intersection they encountered, she called a halt. There was movement coming from the left. She motioned for weapons ready and her troops brought their battalia up, outstretched. Those that came into view were also expecting a fight.

Weapons dropped.

"Donovan." Shade nodded to him, and he to her. Bells jingled as he rotated his wrist, returning his weapon to its sheath. "There's nothing down 114-A3," she explained.

"Nothing the 115 way either. This is beginning to prove a waste of resources."

"Everything looks the same down here," she agreed. "And that's exactly why every inch must be searched…for the small difference. I'll continue ahead," she told him. "You do the same. Return to the Arena when you've cleared the sector. We'll meet up with Balthazar, update the logs, and prepare the next search."

"On your order," Donovan replied and Shade pushed her

hair from her face. In this lighting, Donovan's blond hair looked like dull spikes of dead grass sprouting up toward the shadows and his blue eyes looked gray.

"You're far more menacing in this light, Donovan," she remarked and he chuckled, passing her a drink of water.

"I was going for dashing," he retorted with a smile, walking past. "Forward!" he commanded his unit, motioning to advance. Shade watched him go and took a drink of the water. Her team progressed and she scouted ahead, as usual.

Down the tunnel, she noticed a small sparkle and stopped. Her team was already far behind her at this point and she didn't wait for them to catch up to investigate. She slowly approached and knelt down, examining the source of light. A tiny hole in the bricking had been cut out and a dark cloth draped around it to further conceal it. Shade pulled it away and was utterly shocked to find a globe perched in the darkness, white light shining from inside. She wondered where the sparkle had come from and turned around. When the soft reflection hit the opposite wall, a small shimmer pulled her closer. A tiny metal panel was plugged into the wall.

Shade ran her fingers over it, finding it clear of dust and debris.

"119-A3…" She read the markings on the plate aloud, confused. "There is no 119-A3."

In an instant, she drew her sword and steel met steel.

A pulse of some kind of energy emitted from a device in the Keeper's hand and Jilk was momentarily paralyzed. In the following seconds, the shotgun spray fired back on him, ripping into his gut, and he fell into Slot's arms, dead weight dragging her to her knees.

"Jilk!" She screamed and then fired over the bleeding body at his attackers. Slot and fellow cogwheelers kept up the fray, but Solo soon suffered from wounds of his own as he took several blows and grazes. Slot was raked with claw-blades across her side, and the team was cut down with injuries.

Knick ran into the mess, grabbing a dagger scattered from a corpse and plunged it into the back of the nearest Keeper.

"Fuck you!" he screamed and turned on the balls of his feet, making a break for it. The Keepers quickly followed, leaving the disheveled cogwheelers behind. The .38 in his jacket felt heavy and he jerked it from the inner pocket. He knew as disoriented as he was, attempting to fire while running was a long shot, but he glanced over his shoulder and squeezed the trigger anyway. After nine rounds of hitting nothing, the slide locked back. He grunted and tossed the gun to the side.

Sick and wounded, Knick knew he couldn't keep up the flight for long. He ripped the bracelet of bells from his jacket pocket, unsure of the insanity and credibility of the sort of plan he thought he had.

"What the hell," he decided, stressed, and shook the bracelet hard. The jingles were not loud enough to overtake the sound of his footsteps beating concrete and his gasps for breath.

Shade's angrily looked up into the smiling eyes of Donovan.

"What is this?" she demanded and their swordplay brought her to her feet, crossing down the length of the tunnel. Her head began to feel a little fuzzy and she fought the feeling tooth and nail.

"You're too much Shade! You just can't leave things alone; you have to snoop into everything, kiss Eros' ass at every corner."

"What?"

"We all know you're the favorite," he said over the clanging of blades. "Eros' little prodigy and most beloved!"

"What is this?"

"Tell me, Shade! If you're so good—and, you are good—" he advanced harder on her, pushing her further down the tunnel. "How do you feel now?"

Shade felt her vision begin to slip, head pounding, and knew he'd poisoned the water. Donovan laughed. Several spikes of ice shot up from the ground beneath Shade's feet and she managed to jump out of the way with just a split-second to spare. A Dragon Esper broke out of the walls and Donovan had to move fast to dodge it.

"And Eros' misplaced faith wasn't entirely unwarranted," he muttered. "In spite of the drug, you're still quite an opponent."

They bounced off of the walls in high combat performance, using the Interim powers when needed but to no avail. Donovan kept pushing, refusing to answer Shade's questions of his betrayal.

"He didn't tell you everything, did he? Eros, I mean. Oh, I know he's your shining protector and you are his elite, but do you really think you know anything?"

"Shut up," she hissed, fighting his poison, doing her best to stay focused and conscious but his words were distracting her. She concentrated hard on not stumbling, but her feet were slipping. Her vision started to blur.

Then she heard it. Bells were ringing, her sword was trembling with the call, and she knew Knick was in trouble.

"Ask him about the Battery incident. Ask him about File 13!"

"I know about Battery! A delegate was found dropping information to Mirax! The meeting with the MAAR representative turned out to be a fake; it was a pointless bloodbath!" Shade told him, trying to figure out a way to exit the battle. It would take a long time to get to Knick from where she was and Donovan wouldn't open even a little in the assault.

"Did you know that the traitor delegate was named Sornicus Merëne?—Keep fighting Shade! Keep straining yourself, it'll only make it worse!—Did you know that Sornicus Merëne died half a month before the Battery incident?"

"What?"

"The Regent was the one who made the accusations and ordered the attack. The man who was murdered was an innocent member of the collective promised first look at a relic. This man was named Ross Willem; two months before he was murdered, he stumbled upon discrepancies in the Regent's dictation of a prophecy. This raised the question on whether or not the Regent was supplying truthful information or crossing his agenda with the Oracle's. A lie framed him to his death."

Shade clenched her teeth, trying to get away from the conversation, trying to focus on the combat, trying to find an opening to escape, but his words struck her painfully.

"Eros covered it all up," Donovan all but sang.

"He wouldn't…"

"Oh, he wouldn't? There's no end to the lies, Shade! Ask him about Sector Dawn. Ask him about Daedalus! Ask him about your prophecy!"

An explosion of dark energy sent Donovan flying backward.

When Dr. Bassett's hand touched the stone, he felt a surge of power shoot through his body, slipping up his veins and nerves like electricity with the familiar tingle in his finger-tips. The other scientists inaudibly gasped as the colors within the stone shifted. Bassett was paralyzed by fascination, unable to withdraw his hand. It wasn't until a black blur shot through the inside, moving from one edge to the next, that he lunged back.

The scientists were frozen in wonderment, watching the color show. And then the commotion settled, and one small shape could be made out in the gray. Bassett leaned in for a closer look and everyone else in the room mimicked his response.

Donovan clicked his tongue as he caught his footing and pulled himself from the debris caused by the knockback. Dusty pebbles crunched under his boots as he took a few steps toward her.

"It's that attitude that got you in this predicament in the first place, Shade—this attitude that you're better than everyone else!"

Donovan threw himself into the assault, knowing Shade couldn't have too many more tricks up her sleeve. He had to admit that she was remarkably resilient to the drug—maybe it was arrogance—but she wouldn't be able to put up much more of a fight. It took all of her strength to keep in it.

A whisper in her head caught her off-guard and she let Donovan an inch into her defense from the slip. It took even more power to save herself—power she was quickly running out of. The voice came again, louder, and again—a female's voice—until she could almost make out words.

"Ssvmm... Ssv hm..."

Shade shook her head, blinking; the world drifted in and out of focus and now she was convinced she was hearing things—hearing voices. And then the voice got louder.

"Save hm…save him! Save him! Save Knick Coltin!"

Shade backed through a shadow and a burst of black enveloped her. When Donovan struck again, he hit stone.

An explosion of shadow spilled out onto the street and Shade rolled through. Knick dove to the left, rolling on the ground to avoid hitting her. He was stone for a moment in utter disbelief. He'd been ringing the bells for mere minutes and she had popped out of nowhere.

"Where the hell did you come from?" he exclaimed as she stood to her feet, feeling like a driver assaulted by a razer cutting in front of him. "You just manifested out of thin air! What the hell was that? What kind of shit is this thing?" He waved the bells in front of her. "Hey. What's wrong with you?" he asked, noticing her pale and sweaty face. Shade fell to one knee, breathing deeply, and one eye was barely open.

She saw the Keepers coming in fast and forced herself to her feet, racing away from Knick. In one swift movement, she placed a gash to the side of one of the assassins, and as Knick watched, he could tell something was very, very wrong. Her combat was too clumsy for the woman he knew, like a drunken ballet dancer—an utter mess.

Her sword hit the ground and columns of nethergy rose out of the concrete, catching a few Keepers in their path. Corpses were crowned as they dropped, face first and drained dry. There was a moment's hesitation and the Keepers withdrew, more than aware of who their opponent was.

When they'd gone, Shade collapsed and Knick scooped her into his arms, shaking her more violently than was called for.

"Hey, hey! What's the matter with you? What's wrong?" he asked. One touch of her skin and he felt the clamminess of a fever. "Shit," he muttered, getting to his feet with some serious strain under his condition. She went limp in his arms.

Scholar Marcus Nico rubbed his eyes and yawned as he trudged through the pages in front of him. The collective had been at work for months to discover more information about Maximus Marius Malentos, the Fourth Century Deigno Knight who'd discovered the rumble relic. Tiny snippets had surfaced here and there, but no concrete data had illuminated their eyes in all of the material they'd scrutinized.

It was several hours into the night before Nico came across a peculiar image in his selected book. He referenced another tome to check his source and was shocked.

"My, my..." he muttered and his collective colleagues looked up at him.

"What is it? What have you found?"

Nico peered over his owlish glasses at their faces softened by torch and candlelight and smiled.

"Our dear Maximus is not lord of the rumbling road. This glyph was not his," he replied. There was a communal gasp as Nico flipped the book to show his peers the image he'd stumbled upon and then compared it with the engraving from another tome. "He stole this glyph from some ancient king, Malikiel, who lorded over a much different road."

"...which road?" Antion asked. Nico flipped the book around and began struggling through the text, translating the old languages in his tired mind.

"Aha, it looks like...it says here that...mm. Malikiel was laid on the atla—er, no, that's not right. The...a—al...altar! He was laid on the altar and...mm. Oh." Nico's expression changed as he slogged through the words. "He was gutted and bled dry by his twelve most trusted advisors. Mm, they were trying to appease some ritual deity. It reads that he laid there, alive, for one..." he began mumbling, index twitching to trace invisible math equations. "Subtract the seven...carry the two...ah, yes, yes. For one century! Let's see, with his insides in, erm...jars, it seems, placed carefully around his body, and he was lowered into a pool of blood drained from his very veins."

The collective were disturbed by the dark history and they sat in silence for a long moment.

"The sacrificial road..." Nico whispered, gently tapping the engraving of the poor, dead king.

"What does this mean?" someone asked.

"It means we're all in a lot of trouble," the High Counselor said from the doorway. "This glyph is waking up and it is not as we thought. It is a very dark time we are heading into now...when the bloody king returns. There has never been a sacrificial road since King Malikiel."

"And this man...this man they found, my lady Interim

found," a scholar started, "he is the sacrificial road?"

They all sat in silence, pondering the meaning and the repercussions of such a turn in the tides.

All thought but the High Counselor, who knew too much and said too little.

The Arena was bustling with activity as the Keeper's Kur trainees and elites were fitted for battalia, armor, gadgets, and other things only men with intent to kill should possess. In the far west end, shots popped off at paper targets the trainees had drawn of one another as shouts of "I got you in the neck, ooooh!" and "Right between the eyes, sucka!" stamped the boys as fresh off the block.

The higher-ups chose to do their practice in more dignified silence while targeting a more realistic object— plaster or marble copy statues.

The Arena was like a cellar complete with a paneled wooden floor with yellow straw scattered on top of it. It was the Keeper arsenal, where blades were sharpened, guns loaded, training commenced, and kids became killers colder and more proficient than Mirax with a cause beat into their heads more important than the cogwheelers'. But just like both, check the fine print and read that near-invisible clause that said being a Keeper was for life.

Donovan's team was followed by Shade's as they emerged from the channels, both groups unaware of what had transpired between the Interim. Balthazar's team had just assembled and Donovan quickly joined him, feeling the height complex once again—his 6'1'' versus Balthazar's 7'0''.

"How do you even fit down there?" Donovan asked, but Balthazar was distracted by the return party.

"Where's Shade?" he asked, voice deep and alarmed. It pissed Donovan off that Balthazar cared so much for the prodigal bitch, but he put on a face and played the part.

"I'm not really sure what happened. We split ways down A3 but I doubled back to get some of the water I left with her; she was acting really strange. She just…disappeared in the shadows." He had no problem giving up that much detail, curious to see if Balthazar's concern could fish up information on Shade's mysterious exit.

Balthazar rubbed his dark-skinned, bald head and

recessed into his mind. Protocol told him to immediately tell Eros of the development, but instinct wanted to spread back out in the channels and look for her.

"We can do a lot of neat tricks with these powers," Donovan remarked, "but we can't just vanish into thin air."

He studied Donovan's eyes and decided that following his mind would prove more productive than his gut. After all, no one loved Shade more than Eros.

Knick didn't even weigh the prospects of bringing a Keeper back to the cogwheelers. He just did it, feeling sick and scared. *If the assassins see Shade in this state…we'll both be dead for sure.* At the train, the cogwheelers were getting patched up. He ignored everyone but Slot and Solo, who were sitting on the edge of a train car, door wide open, bandaging themselves. He strained his muscles to carry his gothic bride all the way over to their car.

Solo had large, white patches covering his cuts and his larger wounds were still being sewn up by Slot, who looked like the makings of a mummy with her abdomen, a forearm, and a thigh wrapped up in off-white linen. When she moved her head, acknowledging Knick, he saw her neck was even wrapped.

"What the hell happened to you?" he asked as he rushed to lay Shade in the train car.

"More important, the hell you bring with you?" Slot shot back at him, biting the thread with her teeth when she finished sewing the cut.

"Saved my life. How's Jilk?"

Slot and Solo exchanged glances and Knick feared the worst.

"He ain't dead yet," Solo responded to Knick's expression. "But we don't know if he's gonna make it, either."

Knick felt even gloomier, wishing he could just get the hell out of this town. On the bright side, the bedlam had made him forget how shitty the place smelled; still, it wasn't much of a bright side. The sun never shines on the asshole, and this place was just that.

"I think she's been drugged," Knick said, motioning to Shade and pulling himself into the car when the conductor shouted warnings that he was ready to leave.

"What kind of drug?" Solo asked.

"I don't know."

"Well, what are her symptoms?"

"…Look at her, man! I don't know."

"Aren't you an ex-angel? Shouldn't you know these kinds of things? What are they teaching you up there?"

"Angels use very specific poisons. I doubt they'd be able to poison her; most of their drugs are ingested. They'd never get that close to her."

"Well, it wouldn't hurt to look. Damn, man, put your skills to use," Slot said. Knick pushed his sweat-dampened hair out of his eyes and knelt down, attempting to diagnose the problem. He checked her pulse, checked her fever, pulled back her eyelids to check her eyes.

"Oh shit…" he muttered.

"What is it? What?" Slot asked as she and her brother leaned in to look. Her eyes were rolled back and small black spots dotted along the bottom of her eyeball.

"Ugh…that ain't natural." Solo grimaced.

"That's a…" Knick trailed off, confused. "Gimme the med kit."

Solo crawled over to a stack of crates and pulled the metal box from the corner, dragging it over to Shade's body. Knick prepared a syringe of solistate and ordered one of the siblings to pull her sleeves up. Her veins were dark, purple nearing black, and Knick's heart pulled a triple beat in alarm. He pushed the air out of the syringe and plunged the needle in a vein, injecting the antidote.

"That's powerful stuff. She ain't allergic, is she?" Slot asked, watching the treatment.

"Too late now."

Slot and Solo exchanged glances.

"You musta been a shitty angel. No wonder you got out of the business," Solo muttered. Knick ignored him and settled on the floor, watching the landscape roll by, Shade's hair whipping in the wind, his companions settled in silence.

The train rolled on into night toward Knox and the temperature dropped. Solo and Slot had fallen asleep, her head on his shoulder, backs propped up against the far end of the train. Knick was feeling better with the cool breeze, and the common smells of the steam from the coal mines combined with the passing whiffs of stale, underground water took away the nausea. He was beyond hungry, but the emptiness of his stomach wasn't helping his headache.

He got up and quietly fished through the food crate for some sheet bread and pollot slices. Shade stirred as Knick took his first bite, calling him back to her side. When she saw him there, she was a bit startled.

"What are you doing here?" she asked.

"I could ask you the same thing," he said, a wad of food in his cheek. "You were the one who teleported in front of me, like a bull to the Bark."

"I what...?" she asked, attention divided as she attempted to sit up. Knick fished the bell bracelet from his pocket and showed it to her, swallowing his bite of food and taking another.

"These really work," he said. Shade closed her eyes, trying to remember what happened. Keeper tunnels...119-A3...Donovan. Shit.

"I was fighting," she told him. "Donovan—one of the Order, someone like me—attacked me, but...that doesn't make any sense." She was trying to piece everything together. "It doesn't make any sense," she repeated. "I don't know what he was after. He just kept saying things, these things that don't...make any sense."

"You were drugged," he told her and she knew there was no denying the implications of Donovan's actions; still, she wanted to believe there was a reasonable explanation. "It was an angel drug with a name too long and complicated to repeat, but we—they call it Spotty Death." He paused a moment, stopped chewing and all. "How did you get that inside-a you?"

Shade didn't want to admit it and Knick could read the pain on her face.

"I'm guessing it was some sort of food product, like, uh, moist bread or, uh, or juicy meat or water." The expression on her face gave it all away.

"Donovan gave me some water right before he attacked me," she explained.

"Well whoever this Donovan person is, he isn't a friend to you." He suddenly crawled over to her and forced his sandwich into her hands. "Here, hold this," he said while reaching for her face. "Stay still." He pulled her eyelids back. "Look up." She did and he checked for black spots; Knick felt relieved when there were none. "Alright, lemme see the wrists and elbows."

Shade held out her arms with only a slight amount of agitation. He ran his fingers over the veins in her wrists and then moved upward to the insides of her elbows. All clear, so he took back his sandwich and returned to his perch.

There was a drawn out silence between them as the train rolled on, sounds of wheel on track invading their ears. Occasionally, they passed by tunnels lit well enough to see the scrawling and scribbling of the graffiti gangs in bright colors and twisted, block, or bubble letters.

"Have you changed your mind?" Shade asked him, and Knick frowned. "I mean about becoming a Keeper." He made a face. "You called me," she said.

"You mean it wasn't a get out of jail free card? I told you. Thanks but…I'm not interested."

Shade wrapped her arms around herself, hugging her knees to her chest.

"You want something to eat?" he asked, but she didn't. He stuffed the last bit of his sandwich into this mouth and pulled his jacket off, putting it around her shoulders. "So what now?"

"Where're we headed?"

Knick lit up a cigarette and exhaled on his reply. "Knox. Unloading some russells there, then I guess it's back to Thebes."

"I'll get off at Knox and make my way back to Anshar from there."

"You're going back? After they tried to kill you?"

"As opposed to slumming with a bunch of cogwheelers who want to kill me?" she asked, one slender brow raised. He couldn't argue there. "Besides, only one of them tried to... Whatever he was getting at, I can't easily count him a traitor. It's…complicated. I need to talk to Eros."

"You mention him a lot," Knick said matter-of-factly, puffing on his cigarette. "Boyfriend?"

Shade twitched, recalling Donovan's words, and felt annoyed.

"Why did you call for me, anyway?"

Knick grinned. "Maybe I missed you. Shade. Sovereign of

the Sword of Shadows. That's you, right?"

"Still charming, I see."

"Always." He exhaled gray and offered the cigarette to her. She shook her head so he kept smoking. He flinched when she reached up and brushed his hair from his forehead, checking for the glyph. Nothing. He caught her wrist before she could move it, but he was lost on words so he just stared at her awkwardly and then let her go.

That pivotal moment reminded them that they barely knew each other and that their relationship had been fake in the first place, established in a high stress situation. Whatever connection that had been made half-a-year before was seemingly gone, in spite of the tiny invisible thread that connected them.

"You look tired," he finally remarked.

"You mean aside from the fact that I was drugged?"

"Aside from."

"Things have been busy. Tsh, chaotic, actually."

Knick ground out his cigarette, smoke dribbling from his lips as he spoke. "Wanna tell me what's going on? What's really going on?"

"I should tell you because?" she asked. Shade was under a strict oath she had taken both verbally and mentally that Keeper business remained within the Keeper circle. She'd thrown out glimpses of their affairs to him before, but at present thought she felt like explaining anything to him would be violating the natural order of things. He wasn't an ally in spite of the fact that he wasn't, at the moment, an enemy.

"You tell me. I'm your savior, right?" he asked with a grin but was met with a sharp look. So much for conversation. Silence prevailed again for nearly a half-hour.

"Thank you, by the way," Shade said quietly, watching the blur of small towns pass by through the open car door, "for saving my life." She felt corny and awkward putting it that way, but there was really no other way to say it. Thank you for curing the poison? Thank you for not leaving me there to die? The multiple choice question had answers all bordering too-cheesy-for-reality. Fact was, she'd be dead if he hadn't done what he did; facts were just sometimes hard to put into words.

Knick shrugged off her gratitude to spare the situation anything too sentimental.

"You saved my life, I saved yours. We're square," he told her, lighting up another cigarette. "You've—quite literally—dropped into my life too many times now for me to just walk away."

Shade understood what he was getting at, but noted the way he shifted, focused on the view too hard to be critiquing or appreciating the scenery; he was going to say something else.

Knick clenched his jaw once and took a drag on his cigarette, then met her gaze.

"I wouldn't exactly mind if you keep dropping in," he said and she felt embarrassed by his come-ons for the first time. She had no response and Knick had nothing else to say.

It was on his way home from work that Otto had noticed it—the familiar architecture. It was impossible to escape the small poster on the wall; it stood out to him in a way that it would stand out to no one else. He crept close to it, ignoring the white lettering of vacation advertisement around the central photograph and under the side shots on either side of it.

"That's it," he muttered. The buildings and stone were the same as the ones in his dreams. Some of these places, he realized as he scanned the side shots, had even been in them. Otto's hopeful, baby blues focused on the white letters advertising such a place.

Tonatti Haan, sister city of the capital.

He was amazed to discover the city in his dreams was a place famous in Lotus Maze. It piqued his curiosity even more.

Otto licked his lips and rubbed his sore eyes.

"No," he muttered to himself and kept walking.

By morning, Shade was the first off of the train when it slowed to a stop in Knox; she had no intention of opening up bloodshed when the cogwheelers discovered a Keeper on board. Knick followed her to the door and hopped down onto the ground, leaning in close to her.

"Where will you go now?" Knick asked her, voice hushed.

"If you're right and Donovan tried to kill me, the Order will need to know," she replied, shrugging out of his jacket and passing it back to him.

"So you're going back to Anshar," he surmised. She bit the inside of her lip, staring hard at him.

"I thought about what you said," she said hesitantly, hating to admit he was right. "It might not be the best time to return. I'll wait for word from Eros before acting."

Knick grinned and his face lowered a little closer to hers.

"Was that so hard?" he asked. She spun to go, annoyed, but he stopped her. "What happens after you send your message?"

Shade didn't answer, only glanced back at him.

"Come back," he said. To her wondering expression, he answered, "You told me to call you if I, you know, if I needed you. And, there's something I wanna talk to you about."

Shade nodded after a moment. "Alright," she agreed. "How long will you be here?"

"A couple of hours," he guessed. Shade pulled her silk mask over her mouth.

"I'll see you in a couple of hours, then," she said. Then she was gone, quickly down the length of the train and into the smoke from the stack. Knick watched her go, mind filling up with questions—not for her, but for himself. All of them started with the word "why".

He lifted his leather jacket to his nose and inhaled her scent.

He sauntered down a few cars until he ran into one of his fellows.

"Hey, Cog, you know where they're keeping Jilk?"

"Yeah," the man said. He pointed down the length of the train. "Car 9."

"Thanks," Knick replied. He walked down to it and waited until the cogwheelers occupying it had shuffled out, then he peaked inside to check on Jilk. The bald-headed boss was lying on a bundle of blankets, wrapped neck to toe; his skin was plaster white and the metal rings and studs in his face looked like silver bugs crawling over his porcelain flesh. Knick climbed up into the car and carefully removed each one, then stuffed the piercings into Jilk's front pocket. He debated a moment and then checked for a pulse, afraid he might not find one; but it was there, faint though it was.

"I never meant for this to happen," Knick muttered to his unconscious comrade. "You better pull through so you can kick my ass later."

Knick jumped out of the car and signaled the drop-off to the waiting station workers; they filed out of the hangar, slowly heading for the train.

The woman who stared at Shade was wide-eyed and exotic. She was bald and had intricate, silver henna tattoos on her crown, down her neck, along the length of her arms, covering her hands, and beneath the impressive collection of rings on each slender finger. Piercings and delicate chains dangled from her eyebrows, lips, and connected her nose to her ears. Incense permeated her every pore and clung like smoke to her swab of red and black clothing. The woman's eyes were split like a cat's and colored amaranth cerise with yellow slivers gathered around the almond-shaped iris.

This woman was a member of Bloodsworn, the dark messengers of Lotus Maze. They had stations and outposts from high-society Anshar in Rashrima Haan and Boudarelli to the back-lot dreg towns of the Over There, the Mine, and all of Kishar all the way down to the coal mines below. The Bloodsworn were an absolute neutral party in the world and, for a pretty price, they transported letters, packages, verbal messages, and much more back and forth between the underground mercantile nation and the shining city above. All secrets were safe because, unlike the rest of the world, they didn't care about the profit of politics, just flat profit.

She leaned on the counter, waiting for Shade to finish scribbling the coded letter to Eros warning him of Donovan's actions and possible intent; she left her location tagged in the message with an added notice that it could and most likely would be changing soon. She folded it up, sealed it tight with hot wax and the Bloodsworn seal, and then passed it to the woman, who grinned and took it, tucking it into the leather pouch on the belt around her curvy hips.

"It will be in Anshar in two nights," she said with a thick accent. "I am Hezara, and I will be delivering. How would you like to pay?"

Shade opened her left hand to reveal an earring. Hezara's eyes widened and the corners of her mouth twitched upward, drawn in by the jewelry. It jingled as she picked it up and looked at it.

"The coins were shaped in the Rapenhana River and carved by boneshapers in Darmstadt," Shade explained. "There is only one other like it in the whole world. The bone-shapers say that when the earrings come together, one wearer must kill the other and take the brother earring. Any man or woman wearing a complete set is called an ikret and revered as a warrior of bone."

Hezara plucked one of her more plain earrings from her ear and slipped the Darmstadt one in its place.

"I accept," she said. "Lady of Shadows, it is a pleasure doing business with you."

Knick met Shade back at the train station as the last of the russells were unloaded. He was on his smoke break and ventured away from the crowd to avoid a possible conflict but at the risk of raising suspicion.

"All done?" he asked.

"Done. You?"

He shrugged and threw a glance at the train. "Finishing up now. We're staying a few extra nights. There's rumor of another order coming in headed for Thebes and that's us."

Silence.

"Look," he began. "I need you to help me make this stop. I need you to help me figure it out. When you said assassins, I admit I didn't give the notion much credit. But I've spent the last five months on a serious work-out plan running from and fighting these guys, and I don't even know for what. I quit the angels because I wanted to be done with it all. So I picked up a gig in the Mine as a runner, so what?

"I want to be left alone. That's why I came here. I'm not out to spill secrets to Black Tuesday. I'm not out to save the world. If anything, I'm trying to disappear. I can't spend the rest of my life running from these guys 'til they get me or you guys take care of your shit."

"Is this you volunteering?" she asked. "Or is it a 'you scratch my back, I'll scratch yours' kind of deal?"

"I will do whatever you want to whatever part of your body, baby," he mumbled on gray tendrils. "All I'm saying is that, in the interest of making this nightmare for me go away, I'll help you with the nightmare plaguing you. Deal?" He held out his hand.

"That's very charitable of you..." she muttered, appre-hensive.

"I'm in a charitable mood thanks to your charitable sense of fashion," he said, reinforcing his outstretched hand. Shade took it and firmly shook, once again ignoring the extra commentary.

Hezara had delivered the letter from Shade in two nights just as she promised—normally a week-long trip, at least; the Bloodsworn ways were nearly as unnatural as the Keepers'—and it fell into Eros' hands only a few hours after midnight. He was filled with such rage from the note that it crumbled in his fist. He had immediately ordered the return of the Interim sans Shade and Donovan and, in less than half a day, they all gathered, were debriefed, and now marched to the Arena where Donovan was preparing to lead a team back into the channels.

Eros could read the guilt on Donovan's face when he saw them descending the scaffolding staircase into the Arena.

"Eros," he began on an empty, faux cordial note. "To what do I owe the pleasure?"

"Donovan, Sovereign of the Sword of Frost, resign your blade and bells. You are under arrest with an investigation to follow concerning your potenti—"

"Betrayal," Donovan finished for him, a vampire-like smile spreading across his face as the Interim came off the stairs. "You believe I've betrayed the order but, in reality, I'm upholding it to the utmost degree." He took a few steps backward as he delivered his speech. "You see, the Order is just another power, like Mirax, like Black Tuesday. We even out the score for them, putting us in the supreme position of power. The difference? Our neutrality. And I, Eros, am simply on the winning side of the supreme position."

The flash bomb exploded before the last syllable rolled off his tongue. The chaotic shouts quickly organized as the Kur and Interim scrambled into formation and filtered into the channels.

"Donovan has been learning these paths and routes for months," Eros mumbled to Balthazar and Daelus next to him. "He'll know exactly where to go to get out without leaving any traces behind."

Eros bit back his anger. It wasn't supposed to happen like this. The Keepers of the Balance were the only agency, the only of the three powers who acted in the interest of the majority, not of themselves. The Regent had fled with many delegates and was still somehow taking Keepers over to his side, even in his absence. Now, one of the Interim—the jewels of the Order—had betrayed them. They were falling apart fast, and in the hub of all disorder, there was a new glyph discovered and being researched.

The oldest and most pure organization was rapidly spiraling into dissent.

"Summon Shade back from the Mine, I'm calling an assembly." Eros told his most trusted—the Interim. "I'm invoking Vanguard."

Dr. Bassett was joined by the team of scientists when he dropped the report into Hosef's eager hands. It was the middle of the night according to clocks, but inside the White Tower, all time seemed to have the same bright, sterilized characteristics. Day and night were windowless white walls and the constant hum of air conditioning.

"In a word, it's a mirror," Bassett told him. Hosef seemed disbelieving.

"You're telling me this stone is a mirror, Doctor? I can't see my reflection."

"No, no. It works like a projector—it shows real-time images from another source."

"...a crystal ball?"

"Not at all. Think of it as a portable security camera. One-way, two-way—we're not entirely sure."

Dr. Favre stepped up. "Sir, the data is in your hands. We believe that we retrieved the artifact—our Delta A—in its 'inactive' state. Someone or something 'activated' it during our deliberation. We saw the darkness within the artifact removed, as if a veil covering it was lifted; dark blurs resembling the feet and legs of persons in motion followed the 'unveiling' and the remaining recorded image was of a stone wall with what resembles a metal placard with the words '119-A3' engraved on it. We do not believe it to be an omen or prediction but a location—a real one."

Amil Hosef flipped through the folder of information and

studied the recorded images. He paused over one of the notes.

"What's this about a counterpart?" he asked.

"We believe this artifact has a twin out there, that Delta-A belongs to a set," she explained. "If this 119-A3 is a tangible location, Delta-B must be positioned in front of it—like an eyeball, looking at it."

Bassett took over. "One stone records images and feeds them to the other stone."

Hosef stared at them, thinking, and he grew near edgy at Basset's last explanation.

"And is it safe to assume that the stones work in the reverse? If we're watching this wall, could someone who stands in front of that wall watch us?"

"In theory? Yes." Basset shrugged. "But there's no way to tell for sure unless we find this twin stone."

Hosef closed the folder and nodded.

"Then we will find it," he said, and the meeting finished.

Otto woke up in a cold sweat, sitting straight up and stark white. The clock by his bed read 2:30 AM. Damn, three hours of sleep. He stumbled to the bathroom and splashed his face. Another dream, same girl. He looked in the mirror and noticed how his eyes seemed sunken in; dark circles that looked like the aftermath of a bar fight were a nice backdrop to those baby blues. He felt like he was seeing the dark holes of his sockets and soon his eyes would get sucked in and all he'd be was a skeleton-head.

He tried the back-to-sleep thing, but for six months it hadn't been working. He put on a pot of pitch—the poor man's coffee—and tried for ten-minute cat naps on the kitchen counter. No good. His mind wouldn't shut down.

The girl showed him a wall, and he couldn't get that wall out of his mind. He felt like he needed to find it, get there. In his memory banks, he placed the stone work of the wall and traced it to Tonatti Haan, sister city to the capital. If he took the charger, he could make it there in about a day. He'd have to take a few days off work…

Otto poured himself a cup of pitch and wondered what had gotten into him. He wasn't spontaneous; he wasn't the type to chase after dreams. *Ouch*, he thought. When he put it like that, he sounded really… *Lame.* But something inside told him to get up and go. It was so loud a something that by 6:20 AM, he put in the call to work, poured another cup of pitch, and left for the station.

He had to find this girl in his dreams; he had to find her, find that wall—whatever it was that was slowly killing him every single night. If he didn't, he wouldn't last. His body was wasting away. And the more he thought about this girl, the more he wanted to believe she was real. In spite of the detriment of dreaming about her, something within him wanted to see her most. In spite of her being a figure in his subconscious brain, he felt closer to her than anyone else in the world.

In the middle of the night, Knick dropped out of the cargo train and slipped across the yard to the gate to smoke a cigarette; he had made it his unofficial smoking spot, hoping that he would somehow run into his mysterious Keeper. He knew she was watching him—or he hoped, rather, in case her friends came back to haunt him some more.

He was right, too; Shade was nearby, violet eyes focused on him. She felt compelled to be his guardian and didn't understand why. Since he'd come into her life, her direction she'd once so vastly understood had seemed to disappear.

He stood very still, beckoning to her, and so she answered the silent call.

"I knew you couldn't resist me," he said, but she had no response.

Neither said another word 'til he'd burned through two rettes. It wasn't until he began to light up a third that he found something to say.

"So tell me about me," he said. She cut her gaze to him.

"Excuse me?"

"You know, the prophecy," he said. "When we first met, you said you couldn't let me die because of a prophecy. It's why you wanna recruit me, isn't it?"

She was silent again. He scratched the side of his head.

"And why do you keep touching me?" he continued. "It's not even naughty. I'd be okay with a little chest or across-the-pants action, but it's nothing like that. It's my forehead. You've been way too interested in my forehead, baby. That's a whole level of kink I don't even think exists."

84

Shade hesitated a moment.

"The Regent said you would upset the Balance. You must be killed to protect it," she explained. He noticed her eyes weren't on his; they were higher, trained on his forehead. "That was my job, but," she reached up and brushed his hair away, index stroking the center, "I saw the glyph appear on your forehead," she whispered. He closed his eyes, wondering whether to be annoyed at her obsession with the supposed Keeper in him or content with the caresses.

"Are you sure it was a glyph and not just sweat sheen?"

"It was a beautiful mark. I've never seen anything like it before."

"And do you see it now?"

She shook her head. "No," she confessed. "Just the once, back in the alley."

Before she could lower her arm, he folded his hand into hers, slowly massaging her palm with his thumb. He noticed the muscles in her face twitch ever so slightly; breaking her badass shell was difficult—the ice queen in the flesh. He knew better, though. She'd smiled at him once before.

"I know you're one of us," she said. "A Keeper."

"If that's true, then why hasn't the glyph appeared again?" he asked quietly. She looked from one eye to the other, answerless. Knick felt a breakthrough coming on. "What does it look like?"

Shade yanked her hand away.

"I told you I saw it just the once," she snapped, embarrassed. Truth be told, she remembered every curve and line. He grinned.

"Can I see yours?"

"You could if you were a Keeper."

"Is that you saying no?"

"Yes."

"Well, I've seen it," he confessed, still smirking. She jerked her head in his direction, ready to be angry, but he reached out and began tracing the symbol on her forehead from memory, stopping her voice in her throat. "After the first attack…I was on top of you," Knick explained, "and it was glowing in blue and purple. I, uh, just saw it the once, too but…it's not that easy to forget."

Shade shifted her weight from one foot to the next,

collecting her thoughts. Her gaze remained trained elsewhere, avoiding his eyes even as she spoke.

"He shall be born with wings of heaven's light...and in secret sins will uncover the truth of the pale hands. Marked a beast, the fallen angel will seek the darkness, and be welcomed into their selfish arms," she said, reciting the prophecy Daelus had once told her. "He will hate the blackened palms that feed him for they love him only for his tainted wings, but his knowledge of the white will aid the shadows in the fight." Shade glanced up at Knick. "His blackened wings will spread so far they change the stars of both light and dark."

Knick felt a chill go up his spine; he really hated that people were making assumptions about him and his future.

"That's your prophecy. I know it's none of my business; I'm not a savant—I do not interpret prophecy. Still, I could not allow a potential Keeper to be slaughtered."

"What do you mean it has nothing to do with you?" he asked. "Aren't you the shadows?"

Shade frowned. "What? What do you mean?"

"The shadows," he said. " 'But his knowledge of the white will aid the shadows in the fight.' That's what you said. You're the Sovereign of Shadows, right? Doesn't that mean you?" he asked. Shade just stared at him, mind ringing against her skull with the new possibility. "Doesn't that mean I'm supposed to be with you?"

Shade looked away, flustered with emotion; she had to hide her expression, afraid it would give away the jumbled thoughts in her head. Could the prophecy really be talking about her? She'd always assumed the shadows were the Keepers, who operated undetected throughout Lotus Maze. But the Oracle had named her, and she couldn't fathom how she didn't see it before.

Knick pulled her back to reality, forcing her attention on him as he angled her face toward his, but a vibration that started at Shade's left side traveled through their limbs. Knick threw his hands up and Shade drew her sword. A blue shimmer started at the tip of the pommel of the sword and proceeded up the length of the blade, leaving symbols behind; at the top, a bright light cut out from the metal, engraving the curving letters one by one. When the light had cooled, the power behind the one word was set into the blade, justifying its actions henceforth.

The word was Vanguard.

"What just happened?" Knick whispered as they both gawked at the sword.

"Eros has invoked Vanguard," she replied. "I have to get back to the Order."

She attempted to explain but the hierarchy of it all would have taken more time to go through than she was willing to give. In the end, Knick insisted on going. He stole back into the train yard and gathered a few things in a pack while she waited outside the car. He hopped down and nodded that he was ready to go and they quietly slipped away from the train—a twosome of unreasonable connection moving into a future of unknown potential.

Knick adjusted the pack slung over his shoulder. They were halfway across the train yard when a pair of voices stopped them.

"Sneaking out are ya?" Slot asked.

"With a Keeper?" Solo added. They turned to face the siblings and Shade instinctively went for her sword. He stopped her, noting that neither brother nor sister brandished a weapon.

"You heard?" Knick asked. "Shoulda known. You can't keep your nose outta business not your own."

"Shouldn't talk so loud," Slot told him.

"Why the midnight stealth show?" Solo asked as Slot lit up a cigarette, passed it to her brother, lit another one, passed it to Knick, and finally lit a third for herself.

"Those guys that jumped us a few days back? They're rogue harpers," he explained, briefly running over the situation.

"There're rogue Keepers?" Slot asked, mind-blown with brows pinned back, eyes wide, and jaw slack.

"You leaving because you think we can't protect you?" Solo speculated.

"I'm leaving to put an end to it all. Protect all you want, they'll just keep coming and cogwheelers will just keep dying."

"Mm," Solo grunted. Knick and Shade turned to go, but were stopped one more time.

"You're like...family now, or something, you know?" Slot

said. "If you ever need some backup or anything," she motioned to make a comm call by tapping her ear. "You know where to find us."

Knick rolled over his shock by nodding once, and then he kept going. He hadn't expected a family.

"I don't know how to help you," Shade reminded him as they walked.

"I know," he said, still smoking Slot's cigarette. "I'm coming anyway."

"You said you weren't a hero, right?"

"You said you believe in me." He met her gaze. "Right?"

Shade smiled freely, caught by her own words. She'd almost forgotten.

"Right," she replied. "I do."

Knick mentally notched another victory on his Win Shade Over to Team Knick wall. She'd finally smiled at him again.

Otto felt stiff and achy when he walked off of the charger and onto the Tibble Platform in Tonatti Haan. Not only was the ride uncomfortable but he got even less sleep than usual. The entire trip had taken twenty-three hours and that put his arrival time at dead o'clock.

He checked into his stay room an hour later and struggled for a couple hours of rest before getting up and checking out the city.

The hustle and bustle of the capital's sister city was vastly different than his hometown of Tirmaline. It was almost like being in a whole new country. In spite of that, he felt it was all awkwardly familiar, but not in the I-visited-this-place-one-time-on-vacation kind of way. Instead, he felt intimately familiar with a city he didn't really know.

The explanation was simple enough: Otto had been dreaming about it for nearly an entire year.

His first stop was a tourist vender to pick up a map of the city. He grabbed breakfast and gridded the entire thing out. It would take him days, maybe even a week or so, to cover the entirety. Still, he had to do it, no matter how long it took. He had to find the wall.

He had to find the dream girl.

Part Three

"Unfortunately, the balance of nature decrees that a
super-abundance of dreams is paid for by a growing
potential for nightmares."

Peter Ustinov

The chamber was quiet and dimly lit by floor lamps along the back wall. Ex-Regent Muriel sat in the center of the room and his fellow fugitive delegates created a semicircle on both sides of him. Their heads were bent down, eyes closed, and they were barely breathing through their nose in ritualistic silence and posture.

The high ceiling domed over their heads and the supporting columns around the circular room had almost completely vanished in the far shadows where the former Keeper council knew their guardians watched vigilantly over them.

A loud bang inside the walls vibrated the room and the great doors before their circulet began to grind open with the guttural groaning of ancient cogs grating together. A sliver of light raced from the parting doors to the ex-Regent's chair, canvassing him in mellow lambent. Two figures with the brightness at their backs waltzed into the rooms, front black with the play of light. The ex-Regent lifted his wrinkled eyes and recognized their silhouettes. The former delegates opened their eyes, hearing the clicking of shoes on the soft stone floor. Their awaited company had finally arrived.

The two figures dropped to their left knee and placed their right fist to the ground. They counted out four seconds and stood, waiting in more dusty silence.

The ex-Regent studied them hard with his faded eyes.

"I understand you have been discovered, Donovan?" he said. His voice echoed around the domed room. Donovan lowered his head.

"I have been, your Excellency," he admitted. Muriel turned his pale gaze on the other figure.

"And you?"

He shook his head. "Not yet, your Excellency."

Muriel thought on this a moment and decided it was good.

"Keep it that way for as long as you can. We need them as far from Asgard as possible when the retribution comes down. You shall continue to be our eyes and ears in the Interim."

"Pardon, your Excellency, but would it not be best to have them within the Keeper halls instead of away from it? Inside, they will be slaughtered with the others. Outside, they have a chance to survive and cause problems for you in the future,"

Donovan piped in.

"The Interim have powers not even Eros fully under-stands," Muriel said. "Even without two of their ranks," he lifted his hand barely an inch from the arm of his chair and motioned to the two figures, "they will be so formidable that they may have a chance to succeed in protecting Asgard. This cannot happen. Asgard is the key."

Donovan lowered his head, admitting his fault. He glanced over at his partner, who nodded to him. Private communication filtered between their gazes as the silhouette on Donovan's right promised to get the job done, and done well.

"Asgard *will* fall," Muriel continued, his gruff voice rising in the quiet chamber, "and the Keepers will be destroyed!"

The sleep station ceiling was still the same midnight blue, stippled plastic it was the last time Otto Ferés had opened his eyes; he'd memorized it, having spent more time staring at than sleeping. The shade of the walls, the close quarters compartment, the medical foamotion pad, the temperature regulated Sleep Silks blanket, the tympanic filter—a noise machine designed to lull the brain to sleep—and the breathing regulator were all designed to create the perfect night's rest. Otto was sleeping worse than before. So much for science.

He sighed and pushed onto the door. It whined robotically as it slid out and then up. Otto rolled out and got dressed, bypassing the mirror; he already knew he looked like hell, like one of the walking dead.

He started a pot of pitch at the kitchenette counter, ignored the blinking light on his message machine, and sat down at the two-person table, scribbling notes. His dreams had become more vivid the moment he'd arrived in Tonatti Haan, and his exploration of the city had been fruitful thanks to it. His gridded map of the city was almost entirely blacked out, with the exception of a few inner-city chunks he planned to explore after the sun came up.

The most important detail he'd received was the physical appearance of his dream girl, and he couldn't get her out of his head. The long, blond hair, the crystalline green eyes, and the pale skin made him feel flushed. She wore a simple, white dress. She was delicate, with a round face and a tiny body, but her smile was strong.

The phone rang, startling him from his thoughts. It was probably work again, wondering when he was going to be returning. They'd already left him several messages after he'd stopped calling. He ignored the ringing and eventually it stopped. A single beep let him know another message had been left.

Otto poured a cup of pitch and drank it quickly, finding it and the girl the only things able to keep him going. In two weeks, he'd managed a collective ten hours of sleep. He was crashing hard. He locked up his cubicle, left the hotel, and waited fifteen minutes to catch a street trolley headed for downtown. He ignored the stares from the fellow early-risers; he'd gotten used to the whispers and the gawking.

The drip-dripping of water from the pipes kept the silence of the underground from becoming uncomfortable. Knick Coltin and his Keeper partner Shade had been working their way toward Anshar, and going up was a lot harder than going down. She had been traveling at his pace, since he happened to be incapable of turning into a ball of black smoke and traveling lightspeed everywhere. She liked to remind him of that so he'd learned to tune her out; it was almost like they were married without the perks.

The Mine was far behind them now. They'd gone up into the sewer networks days ago—maybe almost a week—and were hours away from breaking surface. Knick found that the closer they got to Anshar, the more trouble he had calming his nerves.

He finished scouting ahead and walked the short distance back to their pseudo-campsite that included blankets—the end—and saw Shade was still asleep, looking serene with her jet black hair let loose and a blanket snuggled up to her nose. He crouched down beside her and watched, brain brimming with ideas. He mostly repeated the rhetorical questions of why he was with this girl, why him, how did it come to this, and would it really ever stop, but he never came up with any answers.

Knick's gaze drifted down the blanket, eyeing the hint of the curves of her form beneath it. His hand wanted to mold to her shoulder and explore those curves, slip across her side and the valley of her waist to the rise of her hip and then straight down her legs. She had great legs; he wanted his hands all up and down her legs, wrap them around his hips and—but he resisted temptation yet again. Knick put his hand to his jaw and rubbed the scruffiness he'd developed in their journey, biting back his desire to do anything outside of going into mad panic, screaming, and running all the way back to the Mine with arms flailing. He forced himself to wake her.

"Shade," he said, nudging her arm. "C'mon, get up. Time to go."

She opened her eyelids first, violet orbs nearly glowing in the dark. He gave her some room to get up and adjust herself—women always needed to do that in the morning, right? He, like most of his sex, had to take a piss and then rearrange his balls in his boxers, and he was ready to go.

Shade glanced at his back and continued hooking her outfit back into proper alignment.

"Didn't sleep?" she asked.

"No," he confessed. "No offense, but Anshar isn't really my ideal getaway. Down here, I'm safe. Down here, the angels don't come looking for me. Up there? I'm a sittin' target."

"You don't need to worry," she told him. "The Keepers are just as much targets as ex-angels. I know how to get around without their eyes seeing me. I wouldn't let you be so vulnerable to them."

"Ex-angels?" he repeated. "You do realize that I'm the only one. Kind of adjusts that priority list, huh?"

Shade just gave him a look as she passed him. He gathered up the blankets and shoved them in his pack then followed after her.

Dr. Basset and his fellow scientists had been "encouraged" to stay on the project and continue researching the sight stone relic, but it had been, in actuality, a demand. It had been too long since he'd seen his wife and daughters and he was growing restless. The thrill of discovery had waned with worry as the whispers from Mirax officials supervising their progress was causing a creeping feeling in his veins.

The other scientists had started to notice it as well and were becoming unsettled, nearing fear of what was truly at work in their laboratory. But, just like Basset, none of them had the power to leave or ask questions.

Basset had to give himself a mental pep talk to focus on his work; time would fly if he just kept busy at work like it did when he was back in his own lab. If he could just focus, he might make it out of this situation alive.

The narrow streets were crowded by tall buildings made of stacked stone and wooden beams, but there was no one in sight. The two renegades slipped quickly across the cobblestone road, wishing blind eyes upon them.

Shade stopped abruptly at a specific wall and spun to face Knick. He nearly ran into her and had to rock onto his tippy-toes to avoid knocking her over. She stared at him thoughtfully, brow creased, and then jerked a dark mass of cloth from the pack slung over his shoulder. She draped it over his head and let it fall like a cloak down to his feet.

"What am I supposed to be?" he asked. "A mysterious, cloaked stranger?"

Shade ignored him. She leaned forward and bit into the cloth, ripping a strand long enough to tie around his neck to keep the makeshift cloak attached.

"Keep the hood down," she instructed. "No doubt the place will be buzzing about the outsider but I don't want to give them a face to whisper about."

He grinned. "Do you often bring strangers back to the fort?"

"Never." She narrowed a sharp gaze on him. He shrugged, amused. Shade reached out and brushed her hand over the glowing glyph that only Keepers could see. The stones rolled away at her touch, revealing the door to the inside. Knick tried not to gawk. She pushed him in first and then followed; the stones rolled closed behind her. They stood in a small corridor.

"That was fucking cool!" he whispered to her. "Hey, if I become a Keeper, you'll teach me how to do that right?"

She glanced at him.

"I'm just saying, it's worth considering," he mumbled. She yanked the hood further down over his face.

"Follow me closely," she instructed him. "Don't stop unless I stop. Do not let anyone come between us. Say nothing, and keep your head down. Follow my feet."

She spun to go and Knick zeroed in on her ass.

"I'll follow something..." he said and joined her brusque gait. They moved down the corridor and out into the atrium— a golden circle of candlelight and books spiraling up a giant tower. Monks rushed about, sat on railings and in nooks and the shelves of bookcases reading, and muttered to one another over some specific text.

"Welcome to Asgard," she said quietly. "The Keeper Stronghold."

They took the staircase to the right and began the spiral upward. Step by step, the monks stopped to stare and gape. Knick could hear the low muttering begin traveling amongst the collective but he did as Shade directed and kept his head down.

He wasn't sure how far up they'd gone, but she turned quickly onto a new floor and made several turns down a long hallway. He took note of the turns, but the floor and what he could see of the walls looked the same to him. By the time they stopped at a door, he felt as clear on the place as he would any maze—as good as mud.

She opened the door and shut it behind them.

"You can take it off now," she said, so he did. The space was dark.

The room they were in was small—a bedroom. A single bed low to the ground was pushed against one wall with a small nightstand beside it; a wardrobe stood on the opposite wall. A small, round table with two chairs were shoved into a corner next to an old bookcase full to the brim with books that looked like they hadn't been touched in a millennium. All of the furniture pieces had been carved from the same tree, knotted and gnarled and lifeless. A single window was built into the far wall inside a nook and level with the floor.

"How many times?" he asked.

"Hm?"

"Have you brought men up to your room," he muttered. She turned her gaze toward the candles on the table and lit them then crossed to the torches on the walls and set them ablaze.

"Don't be ridiculous," she muttered. "This is the safest place for you. No one will come in here without my permission."

"I see no couch. I guess we'll be sharing the bed," he remarked, tossing the cloak across one of the chair backs. "And it's a pretty cozy bed…"

"Stay here," she snapped, crossing to the door. "Open the door to no one. If you leave, I will know. And best you don't—you won't fare well out there on your own."

He followed after her.

"You're leaving me here alone?" he asked. She nodded. "What for?"

"Eros has called an assembly. I'm late, traveling at your pace in the Mine all this time. Afterward, I will speak with Eros…and he'll know what to do. He may know how to help you."

Knick shoved his hands in his pants pockets.

"You can't leave me alone in here. Just a few months ago, you Keepers were out for my head. Now I'm in the heart of all that shit and the one person I have on my side is you."

"You'll be fine. No one is out for you now. If nothing else, they see you as a science project." She tried to leave again.

"I'm hungry," he said, stopping her midstride. "You can't leave. You need to feed me. I'm your guest. Show some manners."

She glanced over her shoulder. "There's food in the bags. Make due until I return." She opened the door and walked through.

"I'll miss you!"

"Bye," she sang, slamming the door closed behind him. He grinned and glanced around.

The room was pretty empty. He eyed her wardrobe and had to grab fistfuls of pocket to keep himself from searching through her clothes. Knick licked his lips and looked around again, but the pull of the clothes closet was too strong.

"Her fault," he muttered, clearing the space between him and her things. "She was asking for it."

Outside of the door, Shade frowned, trying to push the heat out of her face.

"Stupid," she cursed, and stomped down the hall. A member of the collective came up to her as she walked onto the staircase landing; his eyes flitted over her shoulder, hoping he might glimpse the stranger again. Shade stepped into his line of sight.

"The Baron is aware of your return. All of the Interim are assembling at the Abbey. I thought you should know," he said. Shade nodded once and slipped passed him, slipping down the torch-lit, winding stairs and crossing the main floor to a tunnel at the back of the room.

"Interim," a voice said, reaching out for her. She glanced down at another one of the collective. "I am Marcus Nico, notable scholar of the collective. I need to ask you about the glyph you saw—"

"I'm sorry," she said. "Not now, I'm late." She brushed past him despite his protests and moved throughout the narrow halls and memorized paths until she came to the wooden doors with the old, metal ring handles; the doors were as large as the hallway itself—six and half feet tall and barely two people wide. Balthazar—at 7'—had an incredibly uncomfortable time navigating the corridors.

Agent 44-92-12 turned the corner in the leaky corridor and signaled to his fellow agents behind him. Their infraspec beams cut the darkness, seen only through the goggles fastened across their eyes. The sewers were crowded and quiet, except for the scuttling of rodents and dripping of water.

They took another turn and walked forty paces before coming to a stop. Agent 44-92-12 touched the scrambler in his ear and the high pitched screech came through.

"Dead end," he said, and the screech jumped to every scrambler in the search team. The angels translated the message and immediately turned, heading down toward another unexplored artery of the network. Agent 44-92-12 opened up the panel on his vambracen—a wrist computer— and a 3-D rendering of the network was displayed. He punched a few keys and marked their current tunnel red.

The team moved on.

Shade pulled open one of the doors and slipped inside where the rest of her companions waited. The Abbey was a small octagon with pews and a pulpit on the main floor, a balcony, and a low, domed ceiling.

Balthazar immediately stood for a better view to confirm she was alive and well. Shade scanned the group for Donovan but he wasn't there. Another one was missing.

"Where's Rexis?" she asked, frowning. She felt an arm slide around her shoulders and tug her into a hug.

"You worried?" Rexis asked with a grin, tapping the side of her head with his own. "I was right behind you, but I guess you didn't notice. You walk too fast, Shade. Where are you running off to?"

He moved to stretch out on one of the pews and Shade sighed, relieved.

"Good to see you alive, Shade," the orange-haired Vox said, perched on the balcony railing.

"There was a rumor to the contrary?" she asked.

"We were worried when Donovan returned from the sub-channels without you," Dimitri's water-like voice explained. "We were…baffled to hear you were in the Mine. Eros said nothing but that you were alive."

Shade knew they were looking to her for an explanation but she couldn't give them one. Daelus was watching her with hawk eyes from above. She avoided their questioning eyes by launching into queries of her own.

"Where is Donovan?" she asked, but their grim faces confirmed the truth she feared: he truly had betrayed them. "I see… Dead?"

"Fled," Sonia—the exotic—corrected her. "We're sure he's with the ex-Regent now."

"And the elections?" she continued, pushing out her frustration by distracting herself with other information. Bartimaeus gave a woeful shrug; he was the oldest of them, and often considered the wisest, but even he deferred to Eros's judgment.

"The High Counselor has been the strongest candidate thus far," he admitted. Shade checked the others' faces and could see they approved. She did as well.

Suddenly, Rexis reached out to her.

"C'mere, girl," he called and she came to him and dropped onto the pew next to him. He draped an arm around her shoulders and swatted at her hair a few times. "You okay?" he whispered and, in her quick glance at him, she saw the concern around his eyes.

"I'm fine," she whispered.

"I'll beat it out of you, I find you're lying to me," he warned her. She gave a small, half-smile.

Eros entered the chamber and the room fell silent.

"It's time to brief you, my most trusted, on the situation at hand and deliver to you the new platform from which we will act henceforth," Eros began. "In our time, the act of Vanguard has never been initiated. You, now, are no longer the Interim of the Keeper Order but Champions of Vanguard and possess complete authority over the Order superseded by none save me. The power has been inscribed on each of your blades and will imbue them until the cycle of Vanguard is complete. You will then return to Interim status.

"The ex-Regent Muriel who fled with thirteen of the twenty-six delegates has vanished without a trace. Out of the thirteen remaining delegates, six have committed suicide and the final seven are imprisoned in individual cells, sworn to silence. Donovan, Sovereign of the Sword of Frost, has betrayed us for Muriel and fled; he is still at large and his tracks are cold. He is still in possession of his aegis.

"From this moment on, the Keepers will focus solely on three things: finding and destroying the traitors, uncovering their plans, and deciphering the mystery surrounding the new glyph. The Kur will assist you in these tasks and guard our most precious effects—the Oracle and Enoch. The collective will continue to piece together the truth of the glyph and will double their efforts in uncovering the traitors' plans. It is now our supreme task to find Muriel and his agents...and destroy them.

"A new regent cannot be elected until the Order is set right. Once our enemies from within have been purged, the Order can heal and begin again. Until then, the Balance hangs in the fate of our hands."

Eros bowed his head.

"Show me, Champions, what we are truly capable of in these dark times," he said quietly. After he cleared his throat, he dismissed the group, saying a few things had to be explained and understood before a plan of action could be drawn up and that they were to wait within Asgard for instruction.

After delivering the message to the Keepers, Hezara had made her way to the Bloodsworn headquarters nearby and had spent her time doing local errands. She had just returned from a venture and was preparing a spiritual journey into the beyond when the door creaked open. She sighed and slipped the incense sticks back into the velvet bag and walked to the counter.

"How can I help you?" she asked with her exotic accent. The man that approached her was old and gray with a hunch and feeble limbs.

"Today is the day..." he murmured. "Today is the day when I was to bring in the package."

Hezara raised her slender brows.

"I've brought it," he said. "Deliver it, take it off my hands. I've kept it all this time. They knew, they must've known. They never came for me... I kept it hidden... I kept it safe." He dropped the package onto the counter and, with shaking hands, shoved it in her direction.

"Old Man," Hezara snapped. "No address, no payment... no delivery!" She shoved the package back to him. He tossed a small bag onto the counter and shoved the package back at her. She slipped open the pouch and shook out a tiny gem into her palm. It glistened orange with a hexentriple cut. She lifted her gaze to his terrified eyes. "What has you so spooked, Old Man? You are safe here."

"Safe here," he repeated. "Safe... It's safe. I kept it safe. Deliver it. It's time. It must go to him."

"To who, exactly?"

The Old Man leaned toward her and whispered only two words. "Moscow. Roskolniv."

Hezara leaned away from his foul breath and the Old Man chuckled, wide-eyed and scared shitless. He shuffled a turn and hobbled out of the shop. Hezara looked at the gem one more time and then to the package, unmarked and wrapped with near ancient brown paper.

When Vanguard's Champions had exited the Abbey, Eros and Shade met near the pulpit.

"I am relieved to know you are unharmed. What

happened? he asked softly.

"It is as I described in the letter. I was drugged by the water Donovan handed me and then attacked minutes later by his own sword. Where is he?"

"We went to arrest him," Eros gently explained. "He proclaimed to be upholding the Balance and on the winning side of the 'supreme position'. He's in league with Muriel. He fled into the Keeper Channels; there's no sign of him anywhere."

Shade sighed, disheartened. She hadn't wanted Donovan to be a traitor, but there was no longer any hope to the contrary.

"Shade," he continued. "If Donovan has betrayed us...there's no telling who else might be in league with Muriel. Keep a close eye on your comrades. The Oracle's eyes were blind to this one; we are steering without foresight, so keep these," he tapped the side of her head near her eyes, "sharper than our enemies'."

Shade nodded once, disliking the idea that more of the Order—of the Interim—could betray them. When Eros saw she had nothing to say, he continued.

"What happened down there exactly? he asked. "Balthazar said Donovan told him you...vanished. Into thin air."

Shade nodded. "Knick called it teleportation."

"Knick? Eros repeated, lips curling upward in a smile. "When did you become so familiar with him?"

Shade glared at him and began pacing, ignoring his insinuation.

"I can't explain what happened, Eros. In the channels, I remember a voice telling me to save him, to save Knick Coltin. The next thing I knew, I was near him and...he was being attacked by Muriel's agents. He told me I fought them off then passed out, but I can't remember that at all."

"A voice?"

"Yes. A girl's voice."

"Did she say anything else?"

"No."

Eros put his hands behind his back and adopted the thinking pose.

"Why do you think this voice wanted you to save him?"

102

"He was in trouble," Shade replied, not liking the curious tone Eros had, like he knew something and was trying to trap her into proving some unknown point.

"How could you know he was in trouble?"

Shade frowned. "I doubt the voice would have told me to save him if he'd been having an afternoon tea party."

Eros was surprised by her biting retort. He did not respond, however, only nodded and thought some more. After a while, he spoke.

"I'd like to meet him, your Knick Coltin. I know he's the stranger they're whispering about."

Shade nodded. "I'll bring him in."

"Unnecessary. I'll go to him; no need to drag him through more of our secret city." He raised his brows and Shade realized he knew she'd brought him inside. "Where is he?"

"My room," she replied. He stared at her accusingly. "For safe keeping," she assured. He didn't respond, so they walked back out to the atrium and climbed the stairs with Shade in the lead. When they got to her door, she stopped him. "I'll go in first," she said, "in case…something weird is going on."

Eros looked both baffled and annoyed. "Something weird?"

"You don't know him, he… Never mind. Just wait."

And she slipped inside.

Knick was lying on her bed, hands behind his head, and staring at the ceiling. He sat up when she entered.

"That wasn't too long," he began, but Shade crossed quickly to him and pulled him to his feet. She smoothed out her bed and adjusted Knick's clothes on his body at a poor attempt to tidy him up. "What are you doing?"

"Eros wishes to speak with you," she said. "He's coming in. Don't be a brat; he deserves your respect. If anyone knows how to help you, it's him."

She didn't give him a chance to respond. She immediately crossed the room and yanked open the door. Eros walked in. The two men spent endless minutes sizing one another up as if mere brain power could compare dick size.

"Knick Coltin," Eros began, walking up to him. "The famous Knick Coltin, finally we meet." He pushed Knick's hair from his face to study his forehead but saw no glyph. "Nothing."

Knick backed away, grimacing. "Yeah, she mentions you a lot, too. Feels like I already know you, like long lost brothers."

Shade lowered her head and pinched the top of her nose, counting her breaths to control her anger.

"You are our new Keeper?" Eros asked, but Knick shook his head.

"Don't hold your breath."

"Shade, you may step outside," Eros ordered, but she didn't budge. He sighed and lowered his voice. "You know, before she met you, she was so good at following orders."

"Sorry."

"Don't be. Her actions for you exposed Muriel as a traitor. What I need to know is what happened when Shade came to you in the Mine."

Knick shrugged and rubbed the scruff on his jaw. "She just appeared in front of me, like she'd teleported. She looked...barely conscious. I was being chased by your ex-Keepers so I gave the bells she left with me a good shake. Before I knew it, there she was. She fought them off—barely. It was like watching a bad performance of the Celestial Sky Maiden ballet, or a really good brawl on a Saturday night at Oolongs, depending on how you measure these things."

Eros just listened. So Knick continued, shrugging again.

"She collapsed, so I took her back to the cogwheelers. She had a fever. Did some checkin' into it and found out she'd been poisoned by an angel drug—a drug that Donovan guy of yours gave her. You've got rats, Keeper, and they've targeted her." He lowered his voice. "If it was me, I'd keep better watch over your Princess. You can tell how delicate she is when she's sleeping... How vulnerable..."

Eros twitched, his eyes squinting into momentary slits. Knick grinned, feeling the jealousy rising off of the Keeper, but Eros did not give in to the game.

"Hn. And these bells? Let me see them."

Knick pulled the braided rope bracelet from his pocket to show him. Shade mentally groaned and Eros snatched them up.

"Shade," he began, turning his back to Knick. His voice notched several pitches louder and anger was apparent in the sounds of his consonances and vowels. "You brought a stranger inside Asgard and exposed Keeper secrets. He is not a

Keeper, and we have reason to believe him a traitor. You dropped Keeper technology into this traitor—this outsider's hands! You exposed the lives of everyone here for one man!" he shouted. "Not everyone here can defend themselves, Shade! They depend on us to protect them as much as they depend on us to serve the Balance! You put everyone at risk! You should be ashamed."

Shade bowed her head and nodded meekly.

"As for you," Eros turned to Knick. "I'm sure you're here because you are looking for a solution to Muriel's men coming after you, but I can't help you. All I can tell you is to wait it out while we search for the traitor and deal with him—"

"I can't do that," Knick said sharply.

"You will have to."

"I can't sit around and wait for you people to do your fucking job! I could be dead by then."

"As cruel as it sounds, that's not my problem. Your death was my business in the beginning, but Shade has spared you. The reasons why are still unclear to all of us. Feel free to mount your own investigation, but I will not risk more Keeper secrets on strangers when I cannot even trust my own. And I will not put the lives in this tower in anyone else's hands."

Eros turned to the door, shoving the braided bracelet into his jacket's inner pocket.

"You leave tomorrow morning," Eros said, stopping under the frame. "I will find a room for you. You will have dinner there and are not to leave, is that clear?"

Knick nodded once, glaring at the man's back.

"Good."

And he left. Two men came in seconds later and escorted Knick out.

The swell of the sky made Otto feel nauseous. The dark rain clouds were rumbling and lightning growled angrily just above the tumbling mass. The high concentrate of metrin gas in the air covered the sky in a deep, blue haze. Most people thought it was beautiful, even though it was proof the world had been poisoned.

He crossed off another section of his grid then crumbled the paper back up and slipped it into his front jacket pocket. The headache was kicking his ass, drilling into his brain like a plate-puncher used out in the wastes for terrain remodeling.

He stumbled on the sidewalk and felt his knees giving out; he caught himself on a water feature rim and felt the bile rising fast from the churning pit of his stomach. He puked up black in liquid spurts with chunks here and there—mostly pitch and bites of bark rolls.

Otto wiped the vomit from his mouth and concentrated on breathing, sliding down to the ground. *Great...* he thought. His body was rejecting food. He was falling apart.

He leaned back on the wall and closed his eyes, hearing the sounds of shuffling feet as passers-by dodged his suspicious look. A druggie, that's what they thought; he knew it. He could hear their whispers.

"Mommy, what happened to him?" a small girl asked. The woman with her hushed her.

"Don't look at him," she said. "Stay away from him."

More gasps and whispers.

"You don't usually see this kind of thing here."

"What is the world coming to?"

"Someone should call an enforcer, clean him off the streets and into a cell where he belongs."

Otto didn't have the energy to protest. He wondered why they saw a criminal, not the sick man that he was.

"Help me..." a voice whispered. Her voice. The dream girl's voice. "You can't give up yet. Please don't give up, yet."

"I'll never give up..." he replied. She smiled at him and reached out to stroke his face.

"You're close to me," she said. "I'm right here..."

She pointed to the wall again and he studied it once more.

"I know..." he panted. "I'm coming for you... I'll never stop looking. I'll never give up..."

She could tell by the sound of his voice that he was fading. His breaths were haggard and his lungs were wheezing. She knelt down beside him and wrapped her arms around him.

"Do not be afraid, Otto Ferés."

He groaned. "You feel so warm," he said. "Feels... like...I'm being enveloped in warm light... Tell me, please."

"What would you like to know?"

Otto reached out to touch her angelic face but didn't have the strength to reach her. His arm dropped heavily back into his lap.

"Your name."

"It's Isis," she said. "Now quiet your mind and rest your body. I'm waiting for you."

Otto nodded and waited with her holding him like that. When he opened his eyes, the sky was already dark and rain was pouring around him. His headache had gone and his dream girl had disappeared with his dreams.

"Isis…" he said, feeling tears brimming his eyes. He'd begged her for her name for so long, and finally he knew it.

Slot and Solo were stretched over the same hammock hanging between two stacks of turlosteel crates. Solo's hands were behind his head and Slot was using her brother's stomach for a pillow, feet dangling over the side of the pod-like swing.

Genie's top notch doc had been working around the clock to patch up the injured cogwheelers while the siblings waited in a confused state of relaxation and constant concern. The one patient whose recovery they truly cared about was also the highest on the uncertainty list.

The shipment the cogwheelers picked up in Knox had sent them straight to Genie, a town not too far out from the Cradle, where they were to unload and pull the next cargo headed straight to Thebes. But Jilk hadn't done so good on the road, and Solo didn't want to take him back out until his conditions were improving. They ported in Genie, whether the crew liked it or not.

Solo sighed with a large rise and fall of his chest; his sister fidgeted, deep asleep, and stilled again. Jilk wasn't dead yet, but he sure as hell wasn't alive and well. Solo hated the hang-time, like he was waiting in the fabled purgatory to be sent to paradise or the underworld.

"Hey Solo—" one of the cogwheelers began, storming into the room. Solo hushed him fast and pointed down at his sleeping sister. The cogwheeler nodded and inched toward the hammock. "Sure, sure," he whispered. "Uh, Solo? Don't you think we should, uh…be getting back to Thebes? Boss is wondering what's takin' so long. The shipment is late as it is."

"We go nowhere unless Jilk goes with us," Solo snapped.

"What if he don't make it? What if it's just a body bag you have for a point man, huh?"

"We go nowhere…unless Jilk goes with us," Solo said

again, tone dark. The man nodded and wiped the perspiration off his brow.

"Sure, sure," he said and inched his way out of the room. Solo craned his neck to check on his sister and pulled her jacket a bit higher on her arms to keep her shoulders covered. He rested back and closed his eyes, returning to limbo for a verdict.

There were four guards posted outside of the bedroom Knick was being held in; they called it a bedroom, but it was more like a prison cell. He'd finished dinner ages ago and sat in awkward silence, listening to the rain outside his one window—too small to climb out of and too high to jump from. Besides, when he'd tried to open it, it didn't budge; probably more Keeper voodoo.

Oddly enough, he knew that it was going to go down like that. The angels and cogwheelers both had taught him not to trust the Keepers, and he should've expected the less-than-warm welcome. Something about Shade had given him a small sliver of hope somewhere in the back of his mind, but there was just no tampering with facts—the Keepers couldn't help him and they never would.

He rubbed his jaw but the scruff was gone. They'd allowed him to shave and he had resisted it for as long as possible, but boredom had taken over and he'd been entertained for at least a few minutes. He lazily glanced around the room and his eyes fell on the backpack slumped in a chair by the table. It held something to do, even if it was just the act of changing clothes. He rolled off the bed and crossed the room.

On the other side of the wall, Shade lurked in the shadows, eyeing the four Kur posted by the door. She was burning with anger at Eros for refusing to help and then wasting resources like Kur with simple guard duty. Truth be told, she was mostly angry at herself for acting so childishly. Eros was right to call her out; she'd violated their sanctuary by bringing an outsider in, but she felt tied to him in a way she couldn't explain. Eros was right—he couldn't help Knick. There was nothing they could do but wait.

She remained in the darkness, avoiding the soldiers. No doubt Eros had told them not to let anyone in, especially her. Her hand touched the wall and her fingertips brushed over the rough stones. There had to be some way in.

The darkness pulled on her mind and, in a split second, she found herself stumbling. Instantly, she went to steady her balance so that the soldiers would not expect her of something suspicious, but when she looked up she saw Knick Coltin posed in full glory wearing only what he had on when he entered the world.

"What the hell!" he exclaimed as she spun around with her hand covering her eyes.

"Sorry! I'm sorry!" she hissed, trying not to alert the guards outside.

"Where did you come from!" He shuffled quickly to pull his pants on and buttoned them up.

"Sh—"

"What do you mean sh?"

Shade was by him in an instant with her hand tightly clamped over his mouth. She moved behind him and eyed the door over his shoulder. In seconds, they both heard a key turning in the lock and the door clanked open. Shade yanked her hand back and shrunk behind Knick's form.

"Something wrong here?" one of the Kur asked. Knick shook his head.

"Sometimes I talk to myself," he said hesitantly, trying to decide if saving their skin or preserving his dignity was more important. The guard just looked at him like he was off his tracks and closed the door, locking it again.

"What are you doing here?" Knick asked again, more softly that time. He turned around. "And how did you even get in?"

Shade picked his shirt up and pushed it into his chest, then walked away from him.

"I don't know," she admitted. "I was outside your room— just passing by—and then here I am."

Knick pulled the shirt over his head. "A convenient story."

"The truth," she corrected.

Afraid of the awkward silence coming again, Knick jumped in. He'd wanted to talk to her ever since the meeting with Eros.

"Look, I'm sorry I got you in trouble back there."

"It's not your fault, it's mine. Eros was right. Just because I believe in you does not mean I should risk the lives of everyone here by bringing you inside our walls." She watched him pull up a chair and sit, so she claimed his bed. "One of the reasons we've lasted so long is because we're so secret."

"Why did you even become a Keeper?"

"Being a Keeper is about more than serving yourself. It's about serving the world—"

"Do you think the world appreciates you making these decisions for them?"

"Do you think the world really understands the decisions?" she asked, preparing a practiced speech. Malice dripped into her tone. "If we allowed things to go the way they might, destruction would surely come and they would wail and wonder why it happened to them. Instead, we choose to help maintain a balance to avoid radical ruin and the world whines and cries that we do. There's no pleasing the populous."

"So why not let the tides change?"

"A balance between the powers ensures the longevity of our species. This world may not always be fair, but the tears shed now are nothing compared to the tears that would be shed."

Knick shrugged, still not sold. Shade's tone softened.

"Why did you become an angel?"

"I was born into it," Knick replied.

"Born?"

"Yeah. It's all I remember. I never knew my mother and father—not by those titles, anyway, if they were even around. Well...I donno, this one guy—he was my mentor. He, uh, pretty much raised me. More so than any other angel, he really looked after me, always had his eye on me. Just me, you know? I think *he* might've been my father. I like to think so, anyway."

"I never knew my parents either," she confessed. "And I know nothing about them. Silly, huh? To not know where you came from."

"Not really," he said. He smiled at her. "Peas in a pod, we are. As the saying goes..."

"As it goes."

Knick could tell the awkward silence was trying to return, so he leapt into a new topic.

"So! Since you're such a virtuous woman who believes so wholly in her cause," he reached into his jacket pocket and pulled a wad of cloth out, "tell me what you do with these?" He unfolded the bundle to reveal a rather scandalous pair of panties that had Shade's pale complexion tint several levels red.

"How dare you!" she shrieked as she jumped to her feet. He held one finger to his lips to shush her, unable to pull the smile off his face. He leaned back as she came for him and slipped under her arm to avoid her grasp. She managed to snatch the underwear from him as he went by, settling on the bed. "How did you—Why did you—! You—!"

"If you don't calm down, that guard's gonna come back…"

"Get out!"

"But this is my room!"

"I don't—" She stopped suddenly, staring at him as if she'd seen a ghost. The clothing dropped from her hands and she ran at him, leaning in close. "The glyph," she whispered. "The glyph has reappeared."

It was pulsing in bluish purple light, clear as day, and was not fading. Knick cautiously reached up and took hold of her waist, slowly pulling her into his lap until she straddled him.

"Tell me what it looks like," he whispered. He stared into her eyes, feeling proud in the back of his mind that he was able to steal her gaze away from his forehead. Shade seemed lost somewhere between acceptance of the situation and sheer panic. To his surprise, she relaxed a half-a-second and reached up to brush his hair from his brow.

Her gentle fingertips began tracing the outline of the shape on his forehead; he reached up and mimicked what he felt under her collarbone. She nodded to confirm he'd drawn the right symbol. Then, the glyph disappeared and Shade's hands dropped to her sides. She stared down into Knick's eyes.

"You won't betray us," she said. "I know you won't betray us."

He leaned up toward her face, wondering if he could get away with kissing her, but hesitated in his mind too long so he backed off.

"I have my orders," he told her. "I gotta leave tomorrow."

Shade climbed off of his lap and crossed the room, snatching her underwear off the ground.

"And I have mine. I am to stay within Asgard until Eros

issues commands. With the state of things, our freedoms have been revoked. We have very specific missions now."

"He doesn't want you coming with me," Knick guessed. "Yeah, I get it. So much for coming here, right? That's not so different than everyone else—you only look after your own."

"Knick, th—"

"Don't try to defend them. The only reason you keep following me around in the first place is because you want me to join your Order."

"That's…" Shade trailed off, unready to deny it. "I don't know what's going on, what's happening to us. But you're a part of this, whether you or I or the Keepers like it. Muriel is *afraid* of you—Balance knows why—and that means more than just his assassins coming for you."

"I've thought about it, too. I honestly don't know why. This so-called prophecy doesn't really give any hints, either."

"You're right; I've thought that, too. There has to be more."

"More what?"

"More to the prophecy. Or something else linked to it. I'll talk to Eros—"

"Whoa, whoa, wait," Knick said, getting to his feet. He crossed over to the confused Keeper. "You do realize you say that every other sentence right? 'I need to talk to Eros.' Maybe you should consider he's keeping you out of the loop for a reason."

Shade's expression darkened. "Eros is no traitor—"

"That's not what I'm saying," Knick said quickly to ease her rising temper. "I'm just saying that maybe we should figure this out on our own for a while. The less we discuss with others, the fewer guards posted outside our doors, you know what I'm saying?"

Shade thought a moment and then slowly nodded. "You know…despite what you may think, I'm not enjoying this. Things were much easier before. Things made sense to me, and now nothing does." Shade sighed. "I want this nightmare to end just as much as you do."

"I'm beginning to get that," he said. Shade nodded and let three beats of silence go by before she walked to the window and opened it up. Knick mentally rolled his eyes—Keeper voodoo.

"I should go," she said.

"Shade," Knick's voice reached out to stop her. "If you lay your cards on the table, I'll lay mine. Together, we can create a timeline…and piece this together bit by bit. But we can't help each other if we continue to hold out."

Shade was focused on him, but Knick could tell she was still debating on whether or not it was okay to talk to him about everything.

"I know you don't trust me because I'm not one of your Keepers," Knick continued, "but I'm a part of what's happening here to an extent neither of us understand—you said so yourself. I'm not asking for your club rules and secret handshake… Keep your Keeper cult rituals to yourself. Just tell me what's going on. You trusted me enough to bring me here, you told me you believe in me; let's help each other now."

Shade relaxed away from the window. More points to Team Knick.

"Okay, what do we know so far?" Knick sat down in a chair by the table and touched his fingertips together to form a triangle that he beat against his forehead. "I quit the angels and fled to the Mine. I became a cogwheeler and was trying to remain invisible—relevant? Maybe… I'm not so sure—when you," he pointed at her with his triangle, "came along."

"I was hunting a relic discovered by Krueh-jin traversing the Grey; it was sold to a series of buyers where it was rumored to have wound up in cogwheeler hands, so I was tracking it's shipments across the border territories as it tried to make its way into the Cradle, but the case carrying it was empty.

"I reported back to Eros and learned that Elysium had been broken and a prophecy uttered."

"What's Elysium?" Knick asked.

"A period of silence of the Oracle—"

"Oracle?"

Shade sighed. "I thought you had no interest in Keeper proceedings."

"Well, c'mon, you say Oracle and that tends to perk some interest."

Shade sat in the chair next to him and relaxed into it.

"The Oracle is an ancient and powerful seer. It looks into the tangled web of the future and regurgitates the cryptic words as prophecy. The savants tend to the Oracle, care for it, and record everything it utters to absolute exactness. They then pass this information on to the monks—those men you heard around you when I brought you into Asgard, researching constantly—who pull every bit of information relevant to the Oracle's words from their ancient texts; they attempt to decipher the codes. Again, the information is passed to the Regent and his delegates, who interpret the prophecy and decide what it means and how to act.

"It is believed, however, that fate is like a delicate spider's web, tangled and many. But when that web is interfered with, poked and prodded too much, it begins to crumble. If this were to happen in our world, it would end. Elysium is a period when the fate lines are not to be bothered; it is a time for the Oracle to rest and allow those fate lines to rebuild, the web to strengthen."

Knick was more than surprised to hear about a mystical device that told the future and that it was a key component of Keeper power. Without that Oracle, he guessed, there'd be no Keeper Order to control the Balance. They'd be blind.

Of course, that was just a theory.

"Anyway," Shade went on. She stood and went to the window to feel the gentle breezes on her face. "Elysium was broken. A savant was cleaning the Seer's Cell and the Oracle delivered to us two things: a glyph and a prophecy...about you. My mission was changed. I was to find you and eliminate you. For the Balance."

"And you found me...and discovered that I was an ex-angel and a cogwheeler—"

"And a Keeper—"

"Not yet."

"I saw the glyph appear on your forehead. I knew you must be the new glyph, and the prophecy was either misinterpreted or incomplete...so I came back here and told Eros what had transpired. He went into immediate consultation with the Regent. It was Daelus who came to me with the rest of the prophecy."

"Who's Daelus?"

"Someone like me. An Interim. He told me that we'd learned of angels dispatched to kill you and that if I believed in you...I had to act."

"Those supposed angels weren't angels."

"No, they were Keepers—soldiers turned assassins."

"Then you left to die," he said. They were silent and Knick's muscles pumped with tension. Thinking back on it really pissed him off. "You left to die like it was no big deal."

In the ensuing silence, Shade realized that Knick might have pieced together the revelation that she had gone to die for his sake and it made looking at him extremely difficult. At the time, she didn't think things through; she was guided by pure instinct, acting before her brain told her to move. In the rush, she was lost in a blank chaos, like the eye of a hurricane; when it had subsided, she was bathed in a calm she didn't know. It was euphoric, even.

Dying for his survival made sense. It also made her feelings toward him grow more caring, and more hostile, which she suspected was a product of the former emotion. She couldn't explain why.

Shade moved on with their timeline.

"When we returned, the Regent had fled Asgard with many of the delegates and it had become obvious that he had betrayed us. Our future, it seemed, was plunged into darkness. The relic fell into White Hands and was taken into Heaven. You had no intention of becoming a Keeper or discovering the possibilities of your future. We were blind to the next move except to find the traitor and judge him for his crimes."

"Right," Knick said. "So your Regent wants me dead, but we don't know why. It doesn't seem like it has anything to do with my connection to MAAR or Black Tuesday; if it did, if it *was* for the Balance, he'd have no reason to act secretly outside of Keeper laws, to do your job for you disguised as angels. He'd have no reason to run. So first question: why?

"Secondly, we know nothing about my glyph. No one wants to tell you anything, because if they did…this conversation would be different. Second and third question: what the hell does my glyph mean and why is it such a secret?"

"And why did the Regent betray us? That is something we must answer."

"You find out why he wants me dead, and you find out why he turned his back on you."

"I agree," she replied. "While I'm trapped here, I'll do what I can to pull answers."

"Trapped. That's an interesting word choice."

She narrowed her gaze on him and he shrugged.

"A member of the collective came to me earlier to ask about the glyph. I thought he was just wanting to study you—they're very prying—but maybe he has more information for me."

"Talk to him but...remember...let's be discrete. At least, y'know, for awhile."

"I know," she said. "Try and get some sleep." She paused at the window and then glanced back at him. "People aren't supposed to know their own prophecy, Knick; no one ever has, not until after it had come to pass." After a few beats, she turned away from him. "I'll see you in the morning." And she hopped into the window and leapt out. A black blur shot up into the night. Knick went to the window and leaned on the sill to feel the cool breeze ushered in by the falling rain. His hand went to his pocket where he fingered the other piece of cloth he'd snatched from her room.

The near-silent whirring of the doors as Bassett walked through them was not enough to distract the MAAR associates mumbling down the hall. Their whispers stopped him and he pressed himself against the door's alcove, straining to hear. One of the voices was Hosef but he couldn't recognize the other.

"Another sector closed," one of them said. "The search continues. All of Lotus Maze will be scoured but in using 88% angel output. This is taking too long and stretching our resources thin."

"You must find it," Hosef hissed. "This is too important."

"It's always the last place you look."

"Then look there first."

"Then it wouldn't be the last. If there's an attack...?"

"We'll deal with it as always. Nothing must appear amiss. But the relic must be found."

"What's so important about this relic?"

Hosef scoffed. "Not you or I must know. These are orders, Porter; not mine, *his*."

Porter nodded. "Yes sir, things will progress and quickly."

Bassett slipped out of the alcove and around the corner, avoiding the whispering associates. He'd never heard of the

White Hands being scrambled for anything; not to mention, they were vulnerable somehow.

His brows pulled together as he thought, swiftly traversing the white halls. He needed to know more about the stone—the mysterious stone whose origin was unknown. His fellow scientists and he had run just about every test science had and the object was no more explained than the "why" behind the scramble.

He took the elevator down to the nourishment deck where he could get something to eat. According to the clock, it was lunchtime, but, for all he knew, it was dinner or a midnight snack. When the elevator doors opened on the appropriate floor, he followed the white walls to the double doors and opened one, entered the cafeteria, and was handed a menu. His eyes dropped to item number 32; so far, he'd tried 1 through 31.

"I'll have number 32," he told the attendant. He handed his menu in and took a seat. The place was near empty, as usual. Ten minutes later, an attendant brought his food out and he eyed it with uncertainty. It looked perfect, and he knew it probably would taste that way. That wasn't how things were supposed to be, right? He knew for a fact that perfection did not exist.

This whole affair made him uneasy. In his private thoughts, he said, "Something isn't right here, and someone needs to know." Even in his private thoughts, however, he was afraid he'd said it too loud.

It wasn't quite morning when Eros had the Kur stationed at Knick's door throw a hood over his head and bring him down. Knick could hear the rumbling of stone and feel a cold draft on his arms so when the bag was removed, he wasn't surprised to find himself in the hallway staring at an open door to the outside.

Eros stepped near him.

"These men will take you as far as the nearest Mine entry point and then you are on your own. Do not come back here, ever," Eros muttered. Knick just stared hard at him.

Eros stepped back and Knick noticed Shade lurking in the background. He glanced at Eros and then crossed to Shade and pulled her into a tight hug. Eros narrowed his gaze ever so slightly and his brow twitched once.

"Be careful," Knick whispered, lips pressed to her ear. "There were traitors in your walls. Who knows how many are still there?" Knick glanced up at Eros and noticed the Keeper's agitation. Knick tucked his nose in her hair and closed his eyes. "You become a target because you are the one who believes in me, who fights for me, who was ready to die for me. Don't get comfortable here."

Shade carefully slipped the bells off of her wrist and dropped them into his jacket pocket. It was her turn to whisper in his ear.

"When I discover something, I will find you. If you need me, you know how to contact me." As she pulled out of his hug, she tapped the side of his jacket and he knew she'd left him another bell bracelet. Then, she cleared her throat.

"You'll miss me," Knick said loud enough for everyone to hear.

"I can't miss you if you don't leave, so there's the door," she retorted, annoyed. He grinned in his usual, charming way.

"Oh, you already miss me," he said as she turned and walked away. "That's sweet."

He watched her disappear inside the building and felt anxiousness building up inside his stomach. Eros nodded to the Kur looming nearby. They received his silent orders, threw the bag over Knick's head, and roughly guided him out of Asgard and into the streets of Anshar.

The door to Otto's room flew back and slammed into the wall as he fell into it and then landed with a hard thud on the floor; the sleeping pills he'd purchased rolled out of his hand. He crawled inside and kicked the door closed then tried to use a chair to pull himself up but it tipped over and he hit the ground again, that time with a chair on his head.

He lay there very still for several minutes, trying to calm his heart rate and gather the strength to get back up. His body hurt so much. The tears that welled up in his ducts burned his eyes and the skin around them. He tried slow breathing, but he was too breathless to do it; his body recognized his desperate state, which only made the tears multiply faster. So he allowed himself to cry, and it felt as though his eyes were being burned out of his skull.

After a while, he calmed down. When he was ready, he tried again.

Otto pulled himself up with the table, retrieved the sleeping pills, and stumbled into the bedroom. He collapsed on his bed just as the phone began ringing, but he ignored it. He knew the calls were from work, probably to inform him he'd been fired; somehow, safe-playing Otto didn't care. His only care now was to find and help Isis…the dream girl.

And then he hoped he'd peacefully go into death.

Otto fumbled with the pill bottle until he got the cap off. He tongued his dry mouth to produce saliva, but all he managed was cottonmouth. He felt next to the bed and found a quarter-full glass of warm water. He popped two pills, finished the water, and missed the table when he tried to put the glass back. It shattered when it hit the floor.

Otto rolled over, pills spilled next to him, and waited for them to work. It didn't take long for him to fall asleep.

When the Kur ripped the bag off of Knick's head, he was standing in an industrial ruin; the exposed iron skeletons of old buildings whose concrete flesh had crumbled away were barely standing. The crowded buildings of the surrounding city were off in the distance with plenty of miles of cement wasteland between him and civilization. Not that he was complaining. The city only meant more angels.

He had to admit, though, this felt more like an execution than a drop-off. He could see the manhole down in the ditch they stood next to, but the bleak surroundings, the washed out sky, and the soundless escorts felt shifty and doomsday-like.

When Knick turned to look at his Kur guardians, he was a bit surprised to see them pull their weapons.

"You've gotta be kidding me," he muttered. "I know Eros didn't like me, but—"

The Kur moved passed him, eyes focused down below. He spun around and followed their line of sight. A bald-headed, scarlet-swathed woman had come out of nowhere and was heading for the manhole.

"Find out who she is," one of the Kur told the man next to him. He nodded and he and his partner jumped down into the ditch. They waited in more unnerving silence until the scouts had returned.

"Sir, she's a Bloodsworn returning to Kishar," the Kur explained. The head guard nodded and looked at Knick.

"If you hurry, you won't be traveling alone," he told him. Knick just stared back and then cautiously walked past the four Keeper guards.

He took the rickety metal ladder down into the ditch; two bolts were out, making for a shaky climb down. The bald-headed Bloodsworn woman was waiting for him.

"I am Hezara," she told Knick, "headed for Moscow. I travel quick and light."

Knick shrugged one shoulder.

"Suits me just fine," he replied. He bent down and hoisted the cover off of the hole, let Hezara down first, and then went in himself; he slipped the cover back over their heads and they were plunged in darkness all the way down the tunnel.

When they reached the bottom, Hezara pulled a pair of goggles out of her pack and handed them to Knick, and then she retrieved a pair for herself. They put them on and were thrust into night-vision, the darkness replaced by violet and blue and red light. As they began moving down the leaky tunnel, Hezara began asking questions in her exotic accent.

"What is your name?"

"Knick," he replied.

"What did the Keepers want with you?"

"More like what they don't want with me."

She glanced back at him, her slender brows perked in curiosity.

"They kicked me out of their fortress this morning. Strangers aren't welcome, and they especially didn't like me."

Hezara stopped him. "You mean to say you actually were inside the Keeper stronghold?"

He nodded.

"You do realize that that has never been heard of," she said.

"Yeah, well, one of their warriors has it bad for me." He pushed passed her and kept going down the tunnel, trying not to snap. He was cold and tired and worried. Getting grilled for Keeper info wasn't going to happen. Hezara laughed and followed him.

"So they took you inside their sacred city to kill you?"

"No, 'has it bad'…as in 'a big crush'. You know, sparkles

in the eyes, butterflies in here—" he tapped her exposed stomach with his knuckles, "—warm and tingly and can't keep her hands off me kind of bad."

Hezara only laughed more.

"You're joking," she assumed. He side-glanced at her. "Keepers don't fall in love. Everyone knows that. It is forbidden."

Knick stopped walking; he'd never heard anything like that.

"What do you mean they don't fall in love?"

Hezara's exotic gaze narrowed on him; the lines branching out from her smiling eyes told Knick she found him amusing.

"Keepers have sworn their lives to the protection of the Balance of life. Emotions like love interfere with that oath. If one day a Keeper finds himself between his lover and the Balance, he must sacrifice his lover to protect the Balance."

"That's bullshit," Knick spat.

"Exactly. That is why they do not fall in love. Attachments are forbidden. Only the Balance matters." Hezara turned and kept going down the tunnel. Knick followed hesitantly, frowning.

"How can someone just *not* fall in love? That doesn't seem realistic."

"Have you actually met a Keeper?" Hezara asked, doubtful. "They are entirely consumed by their mission. I doubt they recognize anything else exists in the world."

Knick fell into silence, watching Hezara's back as they progressed through the Grey. *Keepers don't fall in love*, he thought. Shade wasn't like that—wasn't consumed by her mission. True, she was pretty obsessed with upholding the Balance, but she saw more than equilibrium. She had smiled at him.

She had gone to die for *him*, not the Balance.

Knick ran his fingers through his hair, agitated. It was impossible to ignore Hezara's words entirely. Shade resisted him at every angle and had managed to maintain a business-type relationship with him. He was already starting to miss her. Was he really the only one who felt that way?

Slot was sitting on crates next to Jilk's makeshift bed, still waiting for him to wake up. His vitals were slow, but his heart was beating. A coma, the doc had said. But Slot was tired of comas; she needed her boss back.

"You're too pale," she told him. "You were too pale before, so you're really like a ghost now." She stared at his pasty complexion, eyebrows pulled together. "Hate to say it, but you don't look quite human without all your piercings, Jilk." She waited again for him to respond, but he only laid there. She sighed. "Wake up now. It's time to wake up, Jilk. Please."

Solo appeared in the doorway, dropped his pack in a chair, and tossed a tightly wrapped bundle of ham, cheese, and bread across to Slot. She caught it, unwrapped it, and took a messy bite. Crumbs sprinkled onto her shirt and legs.

"We can't wait any longer. Thebes demands its shipment and the doc says Jilk's vitals are stable enough to transport him," Solo explained to his sister. She wiped her mouth.

"Is he sure? I don't wanna put him on that train again 'less we know for sure."

"He's sure."

"Okay..."

They both ate in silence and Slot dropped more of her food on her lap. She couldn't keep her attention on her sandwich; her eyes never left her sleeping friend and comrade.

Marcus Nico clutched the thick tome close to his chest as he walked down the torch lit hallway. He was deep in thought about the meaning behind the latest flux of information: the sacrificial road. He had hoped the Interim would give him a few moments so that he could warn her, question her, attempt to discover some sort of truth not in these ancient texts he scoured. She did not, however, and that was what he'd been expecting.

His eyes flitted to the closed door of the High Study and he lingered outside of it a moment. If only he could go in and look around. That was impossible; the High Counselor was inside, no doubt, with his five priests.

He sighed and moved on, down the hall, up the spiral staircase, and around the circular chamber until he reached a worn, wooden door. He pushed it open and entered the study. Empty. Just the way he wanted it. He quickly fixed a fire and set to work perusing the latest book when the door suddenly closed. He looked up.

Shade of the Interim stood before him.

"Interim," he began, surprised.

"You wanted to ask me about the glyph," she said. "If you were hoping to see the stranger, he's no longer within Asgard walls."

"No. No," Nico stammered. "I wish to speak with you."

Shade crossed the room to the fireplace and took a seat in front of it, soaking in the heat.

"What is it you want to know?"

Nico glanced toward the door, wondering about wandering ears. He moved to the couch and sat next to her. His voice was low.

"Have you seen it appear again?" he asked. She nodded.

"Last night," she told him. Nico's face contorted into concern. Shade frowned. "What? What is it?"

"Last night, the glyph was very active. It was pulsing brightly. It led me to this book," he pointed to the table across the room where the book was laid out, "and then it fell silent. This kind of activity coupled with the sighting of the glyph…makes me wonder…"

"Wonder what?"

"We often regard it as a sign," he explained. "Something is happening with our glyph. Last night, what was happening to him? Any particular activity, or—or emotion!" Nico was gaining momentum, growing excited and waving his hands.

Shade thought back and remembered that he tried to kiss her. She shut her eyes tight to blacken out the image. She thought more and considered again that he had realized she'd gone to die for him. Could he have been emotionally involving himself with her? Her heart thumped hard and a shot of adrenaline traveled up her stomach. What did that mean?

Shade met Nico's gaze and nodded hesitantly. Nico slumped back into the couch, looking more discouraged than before.

"Tell me…what is it? What is it that you know?" Shade asked.

"It is possible that this Knick Coltin is the birth of the sacrificial road."

"Sacrifice?" Shade asked, attempting to mask her sudden alarm. "Sacrifice for what?"

"For...his city—I don't know—"

"How can you not know?" Shade's voice began rising.

"There has never been another sacrificial road before! Not since the first! We cannot know what it means—"

"Who was it?" she demanded.

"King Malikiel, the sacrificial king who, for a thousand years, lay drained of his vitae yet alive to save his city from darkness."

Shade's heart was beating fast. "What darkness?"

Nico stared at her with sympathetic and troubled eyes, glassy with exhaustion and confusion.

"All we know so far is a small transcription from an ancient scrawl that says, 'from within'..."

"Within...himself?"

"No," Nico replied. "It is not 'within' of the...of the self— no. It is a different word, it does not mean the same thing. No, the translation is bad. It means...inside the structure—the city, or something more—the core. Possibly the darkness is a corruption within the ruling body. Perhaps, there was a darkness they feared, like a primordial god, whose temple stood within the city proper and King Malikiel sacrificed himself to appease this god." He motioned to the book across the room. "I was hoping this tome might tell me more."

Shade swallowed hard. "A corruption...like the one within the Keeper Order..."

Nico's expression looked grim, as if he'd already considered such a thing.

"These are dark times we are moving into...as if all the world is about to change." He sighed. "If only I could scour the High Counselor's library."

"Why can't you?"

He seemed surprised she did not know. "No one is allowed to access the High Counselor's library unless he gives them express permission."

"Why don't you ask?"

"I could not ask. It is not my place."

"Whose place is it?"

"It is no one's place, Interim. It is unfortunate; I am sure many answers lie within that library."

Ideas were already forming in Shade's mind.

"If I can get you into his chambers, how much time would

you need to find what you're looking for?"

He turned ghostly white at the mere idea.

"Look," Shade growled. "I need answers. Things are falling apart around us; we're running out of time for rules. If I get you into the library, tell me how much time you'd need!"

"A—a—an hour, an hour, maybe more."

Shade was stiff in thought, brain scrambling for a plan. Nico was studying her, afraid of what he might've gotten himself into. The door opened suddenly, stealing both of their attentions, and they watched a fellow scholar shuffle in.

"Excuse me, my lady Interim. The Baron has summoned the Champions of Vanguard to the Abbey," he said. Shade nodded and he left.

Her eyes met Nico's.

"You suspect much," Shade whispered. "Are there any others?"

"None, save for my apprentice, Antion, who sees my troubled, sad state and worries that something is amiss."

"How much have you discussed with him?"

"Nothing of my premonitions."

Shade got up and crossed to the door. Nico reached after her, over the couch, and called,

"Wait!"

She looked over her shoulder.

"The High Counselor…he knows something. I can see it in his eyes—the look of a burdened man. I see it, too, when I look into the mirror. I see it, too, in Gobol's gray gaze."

Shade considered his words and then left the study.

Otto came awake suddenly, startled and alert. He stared at the sleep station's midnight blue ceiling, trying to recollect the day's events. He remembered vomiting on the street and soaking in the rain. He was still wet when he went to the drugstore and when he came home.

He felt his shirt, wondering if the pills had worked, if he'd finally had a good night's sleep.

Wet.

Otto slid across the foamation pad, pushing pills around as he crawled out of bed. Sharp pains pierced his arch and dug into the bones in his heels and the balls of his feet. Chunks of shattered glass were jammed into his feet and blood was quickly pooling across his bedroom floor.

"Damn it," he cursed, choking on his words as the pain vibrated up through his shins. Otto stumbled into the bathroom, threw the toilet seat down, and sat. One by one, he yanked the shards out, feet over the shower to keep the blood from gushing onto the floor. He caught a glimpse of himself in the mirror and nearly scared himself to death; the face in the mirror looked like that of some scary stranger come to harm him.

His eyes were blood shot and the skin around them was raw red from the tears. His hair had thinned and lost color from malnutrition. His cheeks were sinking in.

"Don't give up yet," he told his body. "We can't give up yet."

He reached into the medicine cabinet under the sink and pulled out a half-empty medkit. There was very little antiseptic but plenty of gauze, so he made do with what he had and cleaned then wrapped his feet.

Though he felt weaker than ever, he knew he couldn't stop. He had to keep searching; he was so close. So he ambled into the kitchen, sat the fallen chair upright, and put on a pot of pitch. There were some bark rolls left on the counter, so he stuffed them with resto paste from the fridge and slowly munched. When it hit his intestines, he felt cramps attack his abdomen in places he never knew could be affected by food.

Otto curled over the kitchen table and did some deep breathing, but his muscles were too tense to calm and his stomach continued to knot in pain. If only he really did know where to get some drugs...he might be able to ease his suffering. Worse than any drug addict, Otto was rapidly deteriorating and deserved a fix.

After a while of lying there, the pain subsided. Fortunately, he didn't lose the few bites of roll he'd taken and, after the excruciating experience, he refused to take anymore. He grabbed a jacket from a hook by the door, walked past the pitch on the counter, and left his room.

Time to get back to work.

The drip-dripping of the tunnels were like a broken record in the Grey. At first, it was jarring, clogging the senses. Then, it faded into the background. Finally, it was the thump-

thumping of annoyance in top form.

Knick wanted to put his fingers in his ears. He hadn't remembered this much noise in ambience when he and Shade had traveled to Anshar. His mind had been on other things then—distracted. Now, he couldn't get the dripping out of his head.

When Hezara called back to him, his ears felt a moment of relief.

"We're here," she said. In the violet darkness, he could see her vigorously pointing down. He came up to her and saw the hatch that led down to another level.

"Finally," he muttered as he bent down and turned the rusted valve. The hatch popped open and swung free. "Ladies first."

Hezara took the ladder down and Knick followed.

The blow to his head was more of a shock than a hard hit. He fell to the ground and stared wide-eyed at the slimy, slick ground. What the fuck just happened?

The scuffling of feet rushed him and he switched into attack mode; Knick swung around as he got to his toes and rammed headfirst into his attacker, yelling on his charge as he took the bulky figure to the ground. They rolled until they hit the wall and Knick fought to be on top. Anger pumped through his fists as he made quick bloody work out of the man's face.

Someone grabbed him from behind, arms around his neck, and lifted him off the faceless man. In this new position, Knick could see Hezara nearby, struggling in the grasp of what he recognized as a Keeper assassin.

Knick flung his head back and connected with his attacker's nose, but the grip did not loosen. He pulled at the man's arms, strained his muscles, but he couldn't loosen the grip. He could feel his face turning red, the pressure on his throat growing.

Hezara was flinging herself wildly until finally she wriggled an arm free. She flung what looked to be a tiny pebble into the darkness down the tunnel before she was restrained again.

A jarring growl emanated from the tunnel and a freakish screech followed. Knick's blood ran cold. What the fuck was down there?

A creature bounded out of the shadows and flew past Knick, racing straight for Hezara. Knick reached out, but there was no way he could have grabbed her. She dodged her head to the side as the feral beast leapt at them.

The maws wrapped tightly around the Keeper's face and pulled him down to the ground. The man screamed and released Hezara. She stumbled away and clutched her throat, gasping for breath. Knick felt the grip loosen around him and he broke away just as the beast turned in his direction. He darted to the side as it bolted by, chasing the last assassin into the darkness. A shriek was heard and then silence.

Knick's chest heaved as he looked to Hezara to make sure she was alright. He was surprised when he saw her yanking a rusted pipe off of the wall.

"What are you doing?" he asked, gasping. "He's dead. That thing tore his face off."

"He is not dead," she hissed, hurrying over to the body. Knick studied the figure again and realized no damage had been done. She jammed the pipe onto the man's throat and there was a sound like a mix between slicing and crushing. "The conjuration is not real; it could never inflict real damage. It tricks the mind, plays on fear," she explained, moving toward him. "These men may die of a heart attack. These men may wake up and realize they were tricked."

Knick didn't have to hear it twice before he sprinted down the tunnel, found the body, and dropped to his knees. He hoisted the frame into his arms and gave the neck a good twist until it snapped. When he returned to Hezara's side, she was retrieving a package from the faceless Keeper's arms.

"What is that?"

"This is what they were after," she replied. Knick was blown away. *Wait a minute,* he thought. *They weren't after me?* This was going to be hell. He had Keepers on him and so did she; what a pair they made.

"Shit," he cursed.

"They grabbed it from me when I first came down. You. Travel with me to Moscow," she said. "I will pay you, but you must protect me."

"Why?" he asked. "You're the Nabari. You have that voodoo whachamacallit. I don't think you need me—"

"How safe do you think I will be once they discover it is

just a hoax? If there was only one of them, even two, I would be safe. But more? Three? Four? Entire groups? I won't survive it."

"Do you know who's after you?"

She shook her head.

"Do you know why they're after you? What's in that thing you're carrying?"

"I don't know," she said. "I'm never to know. That is the promise of the Bloodsworn. I will never open this package."

Knick thought about it awhile and then gave in. He put his hand in his pocket and clutched the cloth he'd taken from Shade's wardrobe.

"Alright. Alright, I'll go with you… To Moscow," he said. Her smile was brief and filled with fear.

"To Moscow…"

They shuffled down the tunnel, alert and afraid.

The train whistled as Slot and Solo finished loading Jilk into the cushiest train car they had. They surrounded him with blankets and squished pillows under his comatose frame. Slot patted his clammy head and followed her brother back out into the train yard where they helped the cogwheelers load up the last of the shipment.

When everything was packed up, locked down, and ready to go, they all hopped a car and Solo whistled at the conductor. The train hissed again and, in just a few short moments, the wheels slowly began to turn, rods pumping, steam curling up toward the cavern's ceiling, and they were off.

Solo watched his sister take up a position where she could keep an eye on their sleeping boss. He turned his gaze to the scenery passing by—to Genie rolling past until there was nothing left but the subtunnels, the graffiti, and the sound of the train on the tracks.

It would take a few days to get to Thebes.

Solo glanced back at his sister. She smiled at him and signaled thumbs up. He smiled too and did a thumbs-up back at her.

The Champions of Vanguard stood in a line before the Baron and hundreds of Kur stood at their back. The assembly was organized in the Arena beneath the Keeper stronghold. The collective were crowded on the wooden catwalks above, overlooking this historical event. The High Counselor and the Cleric stood behind Eros as he spoke, faces set in solemn geometry. Eros was giving a speech, delegating orders, informing the Order what being a Keeper would mean in the coming days.

This transformation was a change that terrified all in the room. What would this mean? The Keeper Order had never failed, and now it was entering a militaristic regime for pure self-preservation.

Betrayal was the greatest of all evils.

Shade felt as though she inhabited someone else's skin, as though she were looking into a time and place she did not belong to. Her gaze dropped from Eros on the platform and sank to the floor where she escaped into private plans of breaking into the High Study. She'd appeared in Knick's room simply by willing herself there; perhaps she could do the same thing to enter the study.

A brush against her right wrist pulled her out of her mind and she glanced at her side. The long-haired honey-brunette beside her had a sudden frown on her face. The woman felt Shade's bare wrist and knew her bells were gone.

"What happened?" she whispered.

"Sh, keep it a secret, Sonia. Please."

"Where are they?" Sonia asked. Shade hesitated.

"Halfway to Kishar by now," she replied. Sonia understood what that meant.

"You gave them to that outsider."

Shade did not respond.

"What will you do?" Sonia asked. "Without the bells, your sword is just a sword… You have no power."

Shade balled her hands into fists and kept her gaze straight ahead.

"I don't need those bells to effectively use this sword," Shade muttered, and there was something dangerous in her voice.

Sonia shifted her gaze back to Eros. The future, it seemed, was tangled by the unknown. She couldn't help but wonder if the fate lines were, indeed, collapsing around them.

The door to Dr. Bassett's private room flung open and he leapt up off of his bed at the intrusion.

"What in the—" but he didn't get to finish his sentence. The men that had entered were angels, two of them, and they silently reached out for him and each took an arm. "What's going on?" Dr. Bassett asked. "Where are you taking me?"

But the angels did not answer. They dragged him out of his room and into the hall, down to an unmarked elevator, and the doors closed tightly. He couldn't tell if they were going up or down, but he guessed it was down. He stood between them and felt as though crammed into a tiny space; panic welled in his chest and he thought he might cry. He felt squeezed between his captors; their starch-pressed white suits and silver-lens sunglasses stripped them of any humanity they might have once had. The wire that coiled from their jackets into their ears looked like an exposed part of the machinery he sometimes believed lay beneath the surface of their skin.

Dr. Bassett hung his head resignedly. Could they have known he doubted the project? Could they have known he overheard Hosef? But how? He tried to put his mind to better thoughts: to his charming daughters and his beautiful wife. He longed to see them again. Would they still be safe even after his death?

That's what this had to be: an execution.

The elevator stopped moving and the doors slid open. He was once again roughly yanked down a dimly lit hallway, still with white walls, toward a door. His heart pounded and his stomach churned. He wanted to kick and scream and fight back, but he was rigid with fear.

The door was pushed open and he was thrown out into a concrete yard. Bassett waited for the plunge and tried not to look as terrified as he felt.

"You have been released from your contract," one of them said.

"You are free to go," the other explained. "Say nothing of what has transpired within these walls and your obligation to Mirax Augmentation and Aero-cognition Research is concluded."

The doors banged closed and Dr. Bassett stood speechless before the impenetrable tower. He stood outside of Heaven, stranded and alone, and felt such relief that tears fell down his cheeks.

He was free.

Part Four

"We have sworn, and not lightly. This oath we will keep. We are threatened with many evils, and treason not the least; but one thing is not said: that we shall suffer from cowardice, from cravens or the fear of cravens. Therefore I say that we will go on, and this doom I add: the deeds that we shall do shall be the matter of song until the last days of Arda."

J.R.R. Tolkien

The echo of soft voices under the domed ceiling far underground sounded ominous even to those in the shadows that served the voices. The reverberations bounced off of the columns and walls all around with the illusion they spoke from all angles. Sometimes deep, sometimes biting—the voices were like haunting ghosts, and they belonged to ex-Regent Muriel and his fugitive delegates, all deep in conference concerning the latest Keeper activity.

"The Bloodsworn woman and Coltin have nearly breached the Grey into the Mine," one of the delegates informed the group.

"Our assassins continue to fail," another observed.

"And what of the angels? What do we know of their progress?" a third questioned.

"They are close," Muriel answered.

"We cannot wait forever. Time is of the essence," a fourth murmured.

"Patience, Greelo," Muriel said soothingly. The door to the chamber thundered open. "All is moving according to plan."

Donovan swept across the room and dropped to a knee before the circulet.

"You're Excellency," he said firmly. "Most honored delegates."

"What news bring you from our spy?" Muriel asked, anxious to hear the developments.

"The final elections for a new regent are being held," he replied. "Shade's insolence has cost the others. They are all confined to Asgard until a decision has been made and a new regent sits in your place."

Muriel frowned for a moment, agitated at the circumstance. And then his brows lifted from their scowl and a smile crept into his lips.

"My lord?" Donovan queried, confused by his master's sudden joy.

"Fear not, lord of frost," Muriel said. "From what we've seen of Shade, she will, no doubt, do as she wills and leave Asgard. Curious, isn't it? She used to obey every order without question."

"Coltin has corrupted her," Greelo interjected and Muriel nodded.

"Yes," he agreed in a low and growly voice, eyes distant

in thought. "A new regent will soon be elected," he continued, "and we all know who that will be." A sudden scowl came over his face and he gripped the arms of his chair. His rotting teeth were revealed as he barked out the name. "EROS!"

The private lounge of the Interim was warm with two hearths popping and cracking at both ends of the room. There were two old, wooden tables with four chairs each—one in the center and one against the inner wall between the bookcases that lined the space. Couches were squared around the hearths. A malanga table stood in one corner.

Shade surveyed the room and was comforted by the sight of the Interim gathered together. Vox was lounging near the far fire, soaking up the heat with her sheer layers draping over her slim figure and her orange hair looking like part of the flames. Dimitri sat near her, head-to-toe in dark blue with a fashion similar to Eros's. The small window in the center of the long wall was open and Balthazar was standing next to it, his strong arms crossed over his chest and a deep crease in his brow. Bartimaeus was playing himself in malanga, and Sonia was sitting at a table with Daelus; she was carving at a block of marble and he was nose-deep in a book.

Of course, Eros was not present, too busy with Order affairs to lounge, and Donovan was a traitor. She sighed.

"Ey. Cheer up, girl," Rexis commanded playfully, swatting at her hair as he walked past and dropped into a chair beside Daelus. He pulled the one across from him out and threw his feet up into it, provoking an annoyed glance from Vox.

Shade gave a short nod.

"Why?" Sonia asked. "It's your fault we're grounded. You know that, right?"

Shade cut her eyes to the golden-skinned woman and met her emerald gaze. Sonia was staring sharply at her and the others lifted their heads in curiosity, wondering where this unspoken challenge would lead.

"My fault?" Shade echoed quietly, darkly.

"You defied Eros long enough," Sonia insisted. "First the Regent, now the Baron—when will it end?"

"Her defiance proved the Regent the traitor he is," Rexis snapped and all eyes turned to him.

"And we are grateful that insolence served the greater good," she retorted, "but how many more times must she rebel? Eros is no traitor! We all believe that. Defying his every word?" Sonia turned her attention back to Shade. "What are you digging at? Honestly, you were once the best of us—"

"And she still is!" Rexis shouted, doubling his effect with the loud scraping of the chair as he shot onto his feet. "Shade showed the Regent's true colors. We should look at her actions and trust her judgments. No one believed the Regent would betray us. No one believed Donovan would betray us! Who else can we really trust?"

Shade flicked her eyes to Rexis. Sonia suddenly stood, throwing her chair back as well.

"What are you saying? That Eros is a traitor?"

"I'm saying we should be cautious," he corrected her, "and we shouldn't trust any convention we once thought was infallible. We live in a sand castle now...one wrong tide is gonna sweep us all away." The room was silent. "If any-thing...you should thank Shade for showing us how fragile our fortress is, ey?"

Rexis turned and hooped his arm across her chest and took hold of her shoulder. He put his forehead to her temple. Sonia stared at his defiant gaze cast over his shoulder and took a look around the room. Their faces were unreadable.

"Thank her for showing..." she mumbled and trailed off. "Did we really want to know?"

"Ey?" Rexis hollered.

"Did we really want to know?" she snapped. "I'm only saying what we're all thinking. If Shade had done as she was ordered and killed Knick Coltin, things might not be falling apart around us!"

Shade started toward her but Rexis maintained a firm grip on her shoulder. She captured her anger in clenched fists and gritted teeth until she managed to control the swell of fury. Sonia was afraid; they all were. Blaming Shade for that would not justify Sonia's frustration. The truth was, in spite of Sonia's argument, she had not betrayed Shade's secret: that she had given her personal bracelet to Knick and now was incapable of using the nethergy of the Shadow Sword.

"Tell us why," Vox chirped gently. "Why did you spare him, Shade?"

All eyes turned to her and Rexis lowered his arm. She met each of their eyes and wondered what she would say to them. She didn't truly know the answers herself.

"I was going to…" she began hesitantly, "but…then I saw the glyph. It was like nothing I'd ever seen before." She remembered the glowing symbol on his forehead. "It was beautiful," she told them. Her memory shifted from his forehead to his eyes, half-closed and impossibly close, and then to his parted lips and the hot breath on her mouth. Her cheeks blushed slightly and she stumbled on with her explanation. "I could feel it. There was something important in him. I couldn't kill him—it felt wrong, felt forbidden."

"But to die for him?" Sonia asked and Shade recalled the event in her mind. "Why?"

"He is…the One," she said matter-of-factly. A sudden inhale shuddered over the room.

"How can you be sure?" Dimitri's gentle voice disturbed the silence.

"I sa—" but she stopped when her eyes settled on Daelus and his perceptive lavender eyes. He was far too close to Eros and she couldn't trust him not to relay her words to the Baron. "I just know. It was a feeling."

The room was quiet save for the popping of the fire and the light rain that had just started to fall. Finally, Balthazar pushed off of the wall and nodded his head in her direction.

"I believe in Shade." His deep voice resonated around the room.

Rexis put his arm around her again. "So do I." He turned her around. "Let's go." And he led her out of the room. "Ey, I'm sorry, I didn't think they'd go so far."

Shade shook her head.

"They have every right to question me. So do you, Rex."

"Oh, Shade, you know me too well to pull that bullshit on me." He flipped her hair once. "Best friends trust each other. You don't want to tell me everything, fine. But I'm here for you. You know that." Rexis stopped her and lifted her chin. "Ey?"

She nodded. "Yes."

He flashed one of his famous, roguishly charming smiles and his burnt orange eyes glittered mischievously. He pushed his dark red hair out of his eyes and left. Shade exhaled a deep breath.

"I'm sorry, Rexis," she whispered. She couldn't tell him that Sonia was right—she was defying Keeper Law. That night, she was going to break herself and Nico into the High Study.

Otto limped down the sunny sidewalk until he was able to scribble over another grid on his crinkled map. He wiped his brow, taking haggard breaths, and shuffled toward the closest bench; he had to latch onto a railing for support in order to make it. These days, walking across a room put him out of breath; exploring the city had become nearly impossible and the amount of ground he was able to cover each day diminished significantly. He was averaging a few blocks at his snail's pace, but his body was too weak to go any faster.

Otto laid his head back and closed his sunken eyes to claw at even a moment's rest. The sun beating down on him would've normally felt nice, but he lived with fever and the sun just boiled his brain twice as fast. He threw his bony arm over his eyes and it took all his energy to get it there; he was too weak. He wondered if his legs wouldn't snap out from under him for just taking too heavy a step.

A sudden shadow fell over his face and he peaked from under his arm. Another enforcer was staring at him disapprovingly. He'd been hassled by several of them lately, all figuring he was a drug addict in the wrong part of town. He was disturbing the peace—that's what they said.

"Son," he began, and Otto registered the shock on the enforcer's face when he lowered his arm and revealed his gaunt face.

"I'm sorry... Sorry," Otto grumbled, shifting into a standing position. Used to be he could just hop up; now, he had to help himself onto his feet like an old man. "I'm moving along. I don't mean trouble."

The enforcer reached out and caught Otto by the shoulder. When he glanced back at the man, there was a seriously concerned look on his face.

"You need help, son," he said matter-of-factly. The

kindness touched Otto deeply and he tried not to cry—it hurt like hell to cry—but this man was the first to stop to help him.

"Yes, sir," Otto confirmed, already feeling the burn at the back of his eyeballs.

"Tell me what drug it is. I know all the best clinics in town—"

"No, sir, I'm not on drugs," he told him. "I swear," he added in response to the enforcer's skeptical expression. "I can't sleep. I can't eat…"

"How long?"

"Over a year now. It's gotten worse the past couple months…"

The enforcer nodded and awkwardly patted Otto's shoulder. "Well, you come with me. I know a place that can fix you up."

Otto was about to refuse when he suddenly heard her voice in his head. *Go*, Isis said. *Go with him, Otto.* Otto no longer had a mind to question his lady, so he put on his best smile.

"Okay," Otto agreed.

"The name's Fischer." He offered his hand and Otto shook it.

"Otto," he replied.

"Otto," Fischer echoed. "Wait right here."

He left him on the bench and nearly disappeared down the street. Just before he was totally out of site, he stopped at an electronic reader and flashed his badge. Otto was surprised when the gated rectangle next to the reader suddenly had an enforcer vehicle inside it. The enforcer climbed in and hovered back down the street to the bench where he was sitting. Fischer got out as Otto got to his feet, put a fatherly hand around his shoulders and helped him into the hovec.

When they were sailing down the street, Otto referenced his map and realized they were moving into already explored territory. *Damn*, he thought; he had hoped that, at the very least, he would be going to a part of the city he hadn't seen. He wondered why Isis had sent him with the enforcer.

"Sightseeing?" Fischer asked when he noticed Otto's map.

"Yes, sir."

"First time in Tonatti Haan?"

"Yes, sir."

"Where are you from, son?"

"Tirmaline."

"Ah, Tirmaline." He seemed pleasantly surprised. "I met my wife in Tirmaline, God rest her soul. Beautiful city."

"I'm sorry," Otto offered, but Fischer shook his head and rubbed his left wrist. He noticed a watch on the man's wrist and wondered if it was a manly tick or a habit developed in grief.

"It was a long time ago," Fischer assured him. "How about you, Otto, are you married? I'll be honest, you don't look married. You look a little young for marriage."

"No, sir, not married," he replied with a small smile.

"Girlfriend?" he asked, using the holo controls to steer the hovec into a right turn and then an almost immediate left. He saw in his peripherals Otto shake his head and heard the hard and heavy breaths.

The car hovered with a high-pitched purr and a strange whirring sound that occasionally chimed like a tuneless cricket. Most fascinating to Otto was the advanced holo-steering. He'd never driven one of the garbage trucks he used to ride in back of, but his old buddy Mick had shown him the inside before. It seemed complicated.

Fischer must've noticed him admiring the console. "Fancy, huh?" he asked and Otto gave a short nod. "It's the noises I like. Comforting, in a strange way. What is it that you do, Otto?"

"I am...er, was a waste collector back in Tirmaline."

"Was?"

"Yes, sir. When I came here, I... Well, it's been a long time now. I'm pretty sure that job is long gone."

Fischer eyeballed his passenger, and Otto guessed he was thinking that was a classic sign of a drug addict. The enforcer said nothing, however, and he was temporarily relieved. The company was welcomed; he had not only been alone for what felt like months, he had been shunned by every person passing by.

The enforcer finally pulled the hovec onto the side of the road in front of a shop Otto actually recognized. It was a small shop crammed between two other more impressive looking structures. The store sign was scrawled in black characters on brown canvas that read *The Dark Mermaid*.

"Here we are," Fischer announced. "Masha has the best metabo-menu in Tonatti Haan. Don't let the humble appearance fool you. She draws in quite a crowd." He nodded to the black iron relief of an exotic and striking mermaid just above the canvas door.

Fischer helped Otto out of the hovec and into the establishment. It was small but empty—clutter free. A simple counter and a layer of cerulean beads blocked the back door. A table and two chairs were cramped in the left corner; on the right, a bar in front of a tiny kitchen was lined with four barstools. The shop was empty and quiet.

"Masha?" Fischer called and a dark-skinned woman appeared through the wall of beads. Her hair was twisted into long ropes, decorated with shells and beads.

"Fischer." She smiled when she saw him. "What can I do for you?" She suddenly noticed Otto standing next to him and frowned. "You know I can't treat him, Fischer. He needs to be taken to the clinics, first."

"Go ahead and tell her what you told me," the enforcer told Otto. He rubbed his brow as Masha came around the counter and leaned on it.

"Ma'am. Just over a year ago, I started having strange dreams," he explained. "And then I couldn't sleep. At first, I'd toss and turn or just wake up too early. Now, I'm lucky if I get to sleep at all. But every time I do, I see those strange dreams."

Masha frowned. "How much you sleep this week?"

"Maybe…four hours, ma'am," he replied. Masha and Fischer exchanged worried glances and Otto continued. "My body's rejecting food…I can barely keep anything down. I know I look like an adrenaline junkie—believe me, if I were you I'd think it, too—but I'm not. I swear I'm not. I've never touched a drug—not ever, except when I split my arm open on a job and the surgeon had to put me under."

Masha smiled and gently patted his shoulder. Her electric-blue eyes flitted beyond him to the door.

"Fischer," she began, "how many times have I told you not to park in front of my shop?"

"He can barely walk, Masha—"

"I can't bring in customers with an enforcer blocking my way. Move it, please."

He nodded, but hesitated. "You can help him?" he asked.

Masha nodded. "You'll help him."

"Yes," she nodded again. "Now move that hovec."

Fischer did as she asked and Masha ushered Otto to the bar and helped him onto a stool. He buried his face in his hands and took deep, slow breaths. His body ached so badly. His eyes burned in his skull. His head felt fuzzy between the spikes of pain that resembled nails being hammered into his brain.

A clunk before him opened his eyes and he eyed the bowl of chaka soup Masha had laid out. He turned a sympathetic gaze on her.

"I can't pay you," he mumbled, but she shook her head. There was a stern expression in the lines of her aging face. "I don't think I can eat it…"

"Try."

So Otto reached for the spoon, but the older woman suddenly snatched his wrist. He winced at the pain, afraid she might snap the bone in half. He clawed at her with his other hand but his fingers were too weak and her grasp too tight. He looked at her face in alarm, trying not to scream, and silently pleaded with her to let him go, but her gaze was hard.

Finally, she released him. He gasped in relief and cradled his wrist into his chest.

"She told us to look for you," Masha whispered. "We were to look for you. She said that a time would come when we must help her by helping you."

"Who?" Otto asked, terrified by the woman's intensity.

"*Her*. The girl in the white dress," she replied in a hushed voice. Otto's already gaunt complexion paled in shock. "She told me to tell you that when the shadow is in trouble, you must come here. She said that she will be with you. She said that I must guide you. The number is eight."

Masha's eyes flicked up to the door but Otto was still frozen in stunned silence. *Someone else has seen her…? Someone else…has seen her…* He felt a sudden swell of hope and surge of energy. He wasn't crazy. He absolutely wasn't crazy. He dropped his head onto the bar with a thunk and closed his eyes, trying hard not to cry.

"I'm not crazy," he groaned so quietly that even Masha couldn't have heard.

"Come on, eat the soup. This one is stubborn," she

announced suddenly. "Come on, come on. Try it. You'll like it, I promise."

Otto picked up his head and noticed Fischer had returned. Masha was smiling and he understood at once that her words were a secret meant only for him. He gently took the utensil and spooned a humble amount of soup into his mouth.

"Tastes good…better than how my mother used to make it." He waited to see if his stomach lurched; so far so good. He tried a bigger bite and then another. *Magic soup?* He was amazed he was able to keep it down. But when he took another bite, his insides suddenly churned.

The spoon clattered against the bowl and table, and then fell to the floor. He slid away from the bar, covering his mouth, and then sprinted out of the establishment. Fischer started to go after him, but Masha stopped him with a hand on his arm.

"Give him room," she said quietly. When she pulled her hand back, she tucked her fingers into her palms, still feeling the burning of Otto's pulse on the tips. The girl had said his pulse would be seven weak beats and an incredibly strong eighth, and Masha would know that boy was the one she waited for.

Outside, Otto heaved onto the sidewalk, both arms wrapped around his stomach. People scattered onto the street to avoid the spatter of vomit, mumbling and shrieking and cursing to themselves. The soup collected on the path looking just like it had in the bowl, almost as if he hadn't eaten it.

Otto wiped his mouth and slumped against the closest lamppost, gasping for air. It truly had been too good to be true. His vision came into focus across the street and suddenly he felt his stomach knot in anticipation. There was an alley directly across from *The Dark Mermaid* that he'd never seen before.

"I could've sworn," he mumbled, "could've sworn I went past here a dozen times…"

Something in his bones told Otto to run. He crossed the street and moved into the alley. When he glanced back, no one had followed, no one had looked; it was as if no one had even seen him go in. He shuffled down the long, narrow space, arms stretched out to grab at the walls, at objects—anything to hold him up, help him propel himself down the alley faster. He limped on as fast as he could, heart pounding through the twists and turns.

The stone. It was the same stone from his dream. He'd been through this alley before in his dreams—he'd been through before, chasing her.

The alley opened up into a small section; there was another alley on his left and an alcove on his right. Otto dropped to his knees but barely felt the pain rocketing up through his femurs. His hands shakily caressed the bricks before him. Tears dripped from his eyes.

He'd found it. He'd finally found it. He was finally at the wall.

The drip-drip had almost completely faded into the background. Knick Coltin barely heard it anymore, not even the subtle breathing of Hezara lying five feet from him. The ambient silence pushed into his ears like cotton stuffed too tight and his eyes were glazed trance-like. He gripped the blue bandana between his dust-blackened fingers and held it two inches above his face. He could barely smell her on it; her scent had faded quickly in the Grey. Still, whether it was a fragrance or just a memory, he could still feel Shade in the strip of cloth—the bandana she wore the day they'd first met. It felt years in the past.

Knick dropped his arms to his chest and closed his eyes. He couldn't push out the anxious swirl in his gut—some mysterious venom that churned his stomach and caused his heart to suddenly palpitate. He couldn't remember when it started, but whenever he traced the roots of his uneasiness, it always ended with the same cause: Shade.

He was positive she was alright. She knew how to take care of herself. Still...the nagging feeling, the disquiet prick...it just wouldn't go away.

"Fuck..." he muttered under his breath.

"She must be very important," the exotic woman interrupted his solace, thick accent curling over every syllable. Startled, Knick jerked in the direction of his Bloodsworn companion. "To trade your heart for a piece of cloth, I mean."

"What?"

"You coddle that rag like it's a person. You cling and stare and grasp it like it might run away from you. So who is it supposed to be, hm?"

"Just someone I know," he mumbled irritated and turned over. "Shouldn't you be asleep? It's too early to start working my nerves, Zara."

She lifted her pierced eyebrows and smiled under the tattoos. Her cat-like eyes cut the darkness of the tunnel they'd camped out in and tracked him like a spotlight in a prison yard.

"Someone you know?" she balked. "Should I cut off a scrap of my attire so you can stroke it in the dark when we part ways?"

"Okay, there's no stroking," he snapped, sitting up. "I like holding it, okay? It makes me feel closer, connected. It reassures this internal alarm that she's all right. I feel like...I don't know—like I'm not moving further away from her. Not for no reason."

Hezara planted her chin in her palm and clicked her canines together—a thoughtful tick Knick had become extremely familiar with during their time together.

"The Keeper again?" she guessed. Knick shot a glare at her but her expression seemed unusually neutral. He conceded and confirmed with a nod. "You aren't a Keeper. I don't understand why you feel such concern."

"I fucking wish I knew," he groaned, dropping his face into his hands. He rubbed down his forehead and cheeks to his jaw and then slumped limply. "She has done nothing but fuck with my life since she came into it all because she believes. She believes hard."

"In what?"

"Me?" To Hezara's skeptical brow, he added, "Seriously. I had a hard time swallowing it myself. I don't believe in anything anymore. But fate keeps throwing us together."

"You don't seem like a man who believes in fate," she mused.

"I'm not," he confirmed. "I'm not a lot of things she's proving me to be."

"It bothers you."

"No," he admitted. "But something is. I can't explain it, but I'm worried about her. Something feels like it's coming— something bad. And she...she's too trusting." He shook his head and rubbed his jaw; the rough stubble of a beard was getting longer. "I should be more worried about my own ass,

145

right?"

Hezara shrugged like she couldn't disagree.

"So, if you feel this way…why leave?"

He narrowed his eyes. "Forget it. I don't want to talk about it anymore. If you're up, let's go." And he stood up. Hezara rolled onto her ass and threw her weight forward onto her knees. A bang far down the tunnel resonated and froze them both mid-motion. They listened for another noise and their blood turned to ice when a second clang echoed.

Hezara's wide eyes shakily turned to Knick and he motioned for her to get up. She quietly got to her feet.

"They heard us?" she guessed in little more than a whisper. He slowly inched toward his Bloodsworn companion.

"We make a break for it. Drop an illusion; it'll buy us time. The next drop-entry is no more than forty yards," he hissed.

Hezara pulled three beads out of a pouch on her belt and dropped them to the ground. The explosion of gray smoke whipped around them as the three monstrous hound illusions darted off in the direction of their master's pursuers.

Knick and Hezara broke into a sprint down the passageway, dipping in and out of low heiron guide-lights. The clamor of feet followed by the sudden horror-filled screams caused their hearts to pound. It wouldn't be long before their hunters realized the beasts were just illusions and they were closer than Knick had thought.

They skidded out of full speed so fast that Hezara's fingers skimmed the ground like brakes. Knick twisted the valve on the hatch and waved her into it.

"C'mon, c'mon," he rushed as she scrambled down the ladder. Knick took the rungs only to seal the hatch and then dropped down to the ground.

The pair raced down the tunnel as fast as possible, surrounded by the echoes of vibrations from stomping feet above them. A strange crack behind them sent shivers up their spines and startling screeches like caws of exotic birds filled the passage in front of them. Knick pulled Hezara back as he slowed, frantically searching the darkness ahead and behind.

"What is it?" she asked, voice betraying her near panic. He shook his head. "Vatan da na," she muttered. "Vatan le cordnara ses shei. Vatan d—"

"Sh!" he hissed, interrupting her unnerved prayers. More

eerie cawing, followed by throaty pigeon coos coming from behind them. "Go!" he exclaimed and they continued down the tunnel.

The heiron lights suddenly blinked off and the darkness chased them until they were plunged into total black. They immediately brought their infrared goggles up to their eyes, but there was nothing they could see. The darkness was unnatural.

Suddenly they tripped and fell flat onto the hard surface with loud smacks. The terrifying noises growing louder stopped. Then, all at once, a bright light flashed above their heads and eerie faces surrounded them. Some wore shiny black gas masks and had large, empty goggles bolted onto their heads. Others had ghostly skin and long, thin hair with moon eyes squinted in their direction. Fuzzy, monkey-like shapes were humps on shoulders and backs with reflective eyeballs like giant, round coins.

A mocha-colored arm extended from the shadowy ring of confusion and caught Knick by the collar. He hoisted him up and Knick came face-to-face with a blue-eyed man.

"The Keepers are smarter than that," he said quietly. "You make it too easy to track you." To his fellows, he said, "Ita. Kowa e yo. Itai."

The light blinked out and those empty goggles blinked on to be orange orbs floating in the dark. The reflective eyeballs glowed yellow and red; only one pair shimmered blue, just like the mocha-skinned man's eyes.

Knick and Hezara were set onto their feet and herded into the black blindly. Strong hands guided them roughly, bodies surrounded them—for their protection or security against them, Knick wasn't sure which. They took countless turns and slopes until neither the ex-angel nor Bloodsworn nabari could remember which direction they'd ever come from. Then, at the turning of a valve and the creaking of a heavy door, they were shoved into a large cave alight with cool spectrum. Torches, fire pits, lanterns—all burning with blue and purple flames. There was strange phosphorescent fungus—moss and mushrooms—growing on the cavern walls and through cracks in the tunnel floor.

The place was a camp complete with pitched tents, work tables, wagons, cantina, and watchmen. It was the traveling home of the Krueh-jin—the nomadic gypsies of the Grey that scavenged for relics, artifacts, and scrap. The people were deep-dwellers and walked with a bit of a hunch. Their figures were slim but strong; their hair lacked luster and skin lacked pigment from dwelling in darkness. Many wore infrared goggles to navigate, but most worked well in the lowlight. Then there were the legendary moon-eyed—their eyes shined to see in the darkness; they were hypersensitive to light but could hunt in pitch black without pause. Their eyes looked like white moons.

More monkey-like animals skittered freely in the camp and their coin-like eyes followed their movements.

The scavenging band pushed Knick and Hezara to the center of the camp where an old woman emerged from a tent. The mocha-skinned man went ahead of them and whispered something to her. She met Knick's gaze, crossed her arms, and smiled. When they were stopped in front of her, she tilted her head to the side and wavy, gray strings drifted across her wrinkled forehead.

"Lethan, here, tells me Kada-Ma pulled you from the ex-Keepers' grasp…but it's too early for you to come," she said mysteriously. "Where are you and the 'Sworn headed?"

"Moscow," he replied. The crone clicked her tongue and made a wet echo in her throat.

"Too far. You will stay the night with us, and then you must leave. We have only one rule: information freely given, information freely received. Otherwise, it's a trade." She grinned again and her teeth looked sharp in the lowlight shadows. "And none can afford such a trade. After all, you have nothing to give. Perhaps…a mysterious package."

Hezara tightened her grip on the box and a low hum of laughter rippled through the cavern. They were suddenly aware of the audience that had silently gathered to watch.

"You must not fear that here, 'Sworn. Not if you keep your tongue tight from curiosity's gallivanting. The tongue is the reigns of curiosity, in fact."

Another ripple of laughter.

"You know I'm Bloodsworn," Hezara warned. "You know my mission. Do not interfere."

"Your mission means nothing to us, 'Sworn. We only know the holy rite of trade, celebrate the divine bargain between two men."

"Let's just go now," Hezara whispered to Knick.

"The Keepers still hunt," the crone interjected. "We will mask the trail and safeguard your sleep—"

"Why?" Knick asked firmly.

"Knick!" Hezara hissed, tightening her hold on her package.

"She asked us a question. It's fair we ask one in return."

More laugher and the crone grinned. She brushed her gray waves from her wrinkly face and tilted her head back.

"They learn so quickly, Kada," she announced with mirth in her throat. "I accept your question, though if I were you, I'd not be so eager to find wormholes to wiggle through. Still. You ask why. Why. You are not yet meant to be here, but not ever meant to be there with them. Therefore, we will save you from them and set you back on the road back to us. There. Your question has been answered."

"Wha—"

"*Knick!*" Hezara cried. The cavern filled with another brief hum of amused men and women. The old woman was chuckling, too, with her eerie eyes narrowed on them.

"Lethan," the crone called and the mocha-skinned man came to her side. "He ta ta, mori mo yuubi. San." To Knick and Hezara, she said, "Lethan will take you to your place." And she turned her back on them in such a finite way, they felt momentarily shut out, as if great doors had boomed closed in their faces.

Lethan motioned for them to follow him and the blue-eyed creature on his shoulder mimicked the motion. They trailed behind him through the camp, which extended deceivingly far into the cavern. He stopped at an alcove full of empty tents and a cold fire pit and waved his arm.

"Whichever place pleases you," he murmured, "it shall be your place for the night."

Then he left them to their preparations. When Knick and Hezara had each selected a tent and laid out their blankets, the crone came by with a satchel of food that she tossed at their feet. Then, she bent to light their fire with blue flame. She used a long stem that smoked like incense and a spark block.

"The wood is special," the crone explained to their curious eyes as she worked to ignite the stem. "It is brought in from the Kinkelaar—the forests of the lehn." After a few moments, a spark set the stem on fire and she gently placed it in the pit. It took only a second for the logs to catch fire. "They burn easily," she informed, "but they burn long."

Knick opened up the sack and withdrew bread, cheese, dried razer, and speir fruit.

"I didn't see any trees or a farm when we came in," he remarked and held up the round, green fruit.

"Our existence depends on trade," the crone explained. "The Kada-Si you see—the men with goggles—they make frequent trips to the top and down below to bring us what we need to survive. That is why they have not been shined or walk in lowlight, so that they can withstand the light."

Knick tossed a spear fruit to Hezara and broke a piece of bread in half.

"You have weird animals around your camp," he observed.

"Knick," Hezara snapped. "Stop it."

"I'm not asking questions," he assured her. "I'm observing. Information freely given, freely received, right?" He eyed the crone. "You don't have to elaborate."

She grinned and stood up.

"The lunalehn are descendants of the Lemuroidea family. They come from Kinkelaar and live in the trees that we burn. The lehn hunt with us, scour with us. They are not pets, but treated just as any people of the tribe. We respect them as we do our own."

The ex-angel and Bloodsworn nabari glanced around at the lehn dipping in and out of lowlight. Their long, thick tails curled around their feet—some with rings, others with long stripes, and some merely solid. Some lehn had small, mousy ears and others giant, fuzzy ones. Some had manes, some did not. But all had those giant, round eyes—yellow or red only.

Except for one.

Two pairs of blue eyes stuck out in the dark.

"Lethan's lehn is different," Knick remarked as the crone turned to go. She glanced back at her guests.

"Lethan and Whiskey are very special," she whispered quietly, the feeling of an inescapable regret blended thoroughly in her words. And then she walked away.

"You've been clinging to that box since we got here," he

mumbled after observing Hezara. "You can put it down to eat."

"It is my duty to protect this parcel with my life—to see it safely from the patron to the receiver. That is my oath. What is inside is not for me, not for anyone but who it was intended for. Once in his hands, I care not what is done with it. But I can never open it and I can never let anyone else do so."

"Don't you want to know why they're trying to kill you?" he asked her. Her amaranth cerise eyes dropped to the blue fire and she ate the tender fruit in silence.

Shade found Marcus Nico changing one book for another on a dusty shelf under the golden lighting of the apex of the library tower. With his back to her, he didn't notice her silent entrance to the stair landing.

"You've gone high up to get away from me, Nico," she mumbled. Startled, he spun around and threw his back against the tall case, his thin hands clutching the book tightly to his chest.

"Interim," he breathed, relaxing a little. "No, I… No. Get away from you, I would never. What you are proposing, I…it is too much. I cannot. The risk is—I cannot. It is too great."

"You can't be afraid," she said simply. "If you do not help me—if you ignore your own gut—you could put us all in danger."

"We don't know for sure!"

"Exactly. We don't know for sure." She took a step toward him. "Nico, I'm not asking. If Knick is in danger, I must know. I will not be kind to those who do him harm—cowardice included. Tonight is the night."

"No!" he exclaimed and his already eccentric spasms were enhanced by his twitchy nerves. He swallowed his voice and gathered his courage, lips rolling together in anxious preparation. "Please," he finally said as calmly as he could manage.

"I'm sorry. I cannot sit behind these walls and wait for something to happen."

Nico hung his head; his eyes were gently closed, brow pinched in the right corner with resignation. Of all the taboos to break, this was the worst his sheltered mind could consider, and yet he could not stand silent in the silence when the gnawing feeling of deception chewed away at his conscience.

"Who are you serving?" she hissed. "The Collective answer to the High Counselor, the Interim to the Baron—we all to the Regent, yes. But every Keeper's true master is the Balance, and that is the highest authority we serve."

He remained quiet. Her words penetrated him like hot lead and left a brand on his momentary cowardice. Every scholar had been taught from the moment they took the oath to seek the truth; every Keeper had vowed to serve no master but the Balance. He should not have to fear the High Counselor's retribution for refusing to break his vows.

"Of course, you are right, Interim. Tonight," he said solemnly. "Tonight we will go."

The sudden sound of footsteps on the stairs set them both alert. A scholar spilled into the room, huffing and panting from what appeared to be an exhausting run.

"Lady Interim," he wheezed, "Champion, I mean. Scholar Nico. The elections...they've finished! All are gathering in the Arena—"

He barely got the words out before Shade and Nico bolted past him. He shuffled after them with a last deep inhale to keep him going. Down twenty-three flights of stairs, the scholars followed the charging lead of the black-haired woman, through the tunnels past the Abbey and down three more flights of stairs until they descended into the cavern already humming with the buzz and shuffle of excited Keepers.

Eros had already started his speech.

"—and it is during such a grave time that we have found our strength and reason. With all energy thrown into the troubles controlling our faculties, it is a wonder we have been able to pick ourselves up out of this sedentary struggle. Never before has a Regent of the Order betrayed his charges. Never before have the collective, the guard, the naga been called upon to fill the void left by a thoughtless traitor. With our duties temporarily abandoned to search for a new leader to guide us in these unpredictable times, tensions have risen and questions have multiplied. I apologize for the silence that met you...the silence of the Regent's empty chair.

"And now, people of the Balance, I am pleased to announce that a new Regent has been elected to carry the great torch of the Order through this darkness, back to the light. Taylor, if you will." Eros motioned to a scholar who shuffled forward and handed him a slip of paper. Eros held it gingerly in his fingertips as his deep, blue eyes looked out over the crowd. "People of the Balance, our new Regent of the Order is—" He opened the slip of paper and stared longer than necessary at the word scrawled there. Finally, he looked up. "Our new Regent...is me."

A shockwave of momentary surprise followed by a tremor of joy swept across the Arena, down on the main floor, up on the rafters, on the scaffolding and catwalks, and on the balconies and in lighting nooks. Shade frowned.

"What?" she whispered, still lagging behind in the shock. *This isn't really happening...is it?* She looked over to Nico, whose eyes were round and brows drooped, and the fear she read on his face reverberated in her bones.

She looked back down at the stage where Eros was being received. The High Counselor had the smallest hint of a scowl on his tired, old face. Her gaze moved beyond to the celebratory motions around the cavern. The elation boomed around her and caused her skin to crawl like thunderous warning.

Otto was walking, but not in the real world; he was walking in his dream. Isis—in her white dress with a bouncing fall of blond hair and porcelain pale skin—led him through the city and straight to the wall he'd searched for and finally found. He felt lighter than a feather in her soft presence, chasing after her tiny frame, eyes on her slim back, in blissful slow motion.

Isis stopped at the wall and her delicate hand gently hovered near it. She twirled on her toes with the grace of a dancer and her crystalline green eyes were stark against her white skin and light hair.

"Otto, listen to me now. You must do exactly as I say." Her voice was gentle and angelic. "Do you understand?"

"Yes," he whispered.

"Follow my footsteps exactly as I step them—take pauses where I pause and do not delay a second longer or rush a second too soon. Do you understand?"

"Yes."

She smiled with pale pink lips and motioned him closer. He stepped slowly, enraptured by her light—like some divine brightness illuminating everything, softening all shapes, drowning out the harshness of the world with its intensity. Isis took his hand with one and lifted her other hand to the wall. She touched the stone and suddenly there was a door.

Into the belly they went, darting across a round vestibule and into another door. She led him down a long and twisting tunnel in surreal motion, pausing and sprinting, ducking and darting. He noticed the stone was a dark gray but cut into a smooth, refined surface. The pace continued until they came to a flight of stairs. They took two flights down to a new level where he followed her into another series of lefts and rights. He noticed these walls were even darker, impure with black patches and white spots, and infested with mold. The rough and uneven surfaces would've tugged at his clothes had this not been a dream he seemed to glide through.

Finally, Isis knelt into an almost invisible nook, pushed into the side, and disappeared into a hidden passage. Otto followed her inside and quickly closed the door behind them. They would've been in utter darkness if not for her light.

"Otto," she said softly. "You will wait here for three days. You must bring enough sustenance to last you. On the third day, you will hear terrible things."

"What will I hear?"

"Screaming. Thunderclaps. Scuffling feet. Do not be afraid. So long as you do what I say, you will never be in danger. Do you understand?"

"Yes."

"When you hear these sounds, you must crawl down this passageway. Follow me now."

Isis crawled down the tunnel until it lifted to allow her to stand. Otto still had to crouch in the narrow space. He noticed her white dress was unblemished. She led him further into the walls and around a corner until they came to a particular spot where a stone jutted out further than the rest. Isis removed it to reveal a tiny grate. Of what he could see in the room roughly twenty-five feet below, it seemed to be some type of cell.

"You will watch here until the room empties." They watched shades of people shuffle about and then depart. "When it does, you must quickly follow this passageway down." She began moving again and he was quick to follow. The slope spiraled downward for twenty-five feet and stopped at a small hatch. "Do not hesitate," she warned as she pushed against the door. It swung outward with a heavy scrape.

Isis darted into the room and Otto shuffled in after her. The room was entirely empty. Not even a stool or blanket filled the cell. When Otto's wandering gaze returned to Isis's crystalline green eyes, he was captured by the seriousness in her expression.

"You will not have long, Otto. Not long, but long enough—and you must work as quickly as possible if you are going to succeed."

"Succeed?" he asked. "In what?"

"In saving me," she replied.

"Saving you?" he echoed. "There's nothing here."

"I'm not allowed to see this room. I was never meant to see it. I was never meant to see myself. I do not know what will be in here—what you will face. But Otto, I beg you…please, hurry."

Though he did not understand what she was saying, Otto nodded earnestly.

"Anything," he rasped, "to help you."

She smiled gently and his pain was momentarily lost in her grace.

"When you have me safely secured, return to the secret passage and seal the hatch tightly. Climb the spiral ramp and replace the stone on the grate. Return to the alcove and wait there."

"For how long?"

She did not reply, so he only nodded. Isis crossed the room to stand before him. She reached up and gently touched his cheek.

"Otto…the whole world needs you now."

"The whole world?" he choked, somewhere between smiling and crying, and bashfully stared at his hands. "All I need to know is that you need me…and not a thing in the world will keep me from you."

Her hand dropped back to her side and he instantly missed her touch.

"I regret your part in this will not end," she said softly, prompting him to look up at her. She began to fade away.

"Please don't go," he whispered, but it was too late. She was gone. The dream was gone...

And he was staring up at the stippled, midnight blue ceiling of his sleep station. Otto pressed his hands to his forehead and shut his eyes tight, holding on to every last fast-fading image of his dream girl until all he could see was darkness and memory.

He rolled over into more pain and tucked his bony arms under his head. Soon he could die in peace.

Shade was naturally at home in the shadows, Nico observed, and looked every bit a shadow herself. Unlike him. He felt so utterly obvious; standing there waiting for Asgard to fall quiet felt less of a camouflage than pacing under torchlight with a book in his fists.

They must've waited for hours. Nico's shins were already starting to ache from the stagnant pressure. He wasn't used to getting older. There was once a day when he stood for hours and hours reading passage after passage in the great spiral library of the Keepers. He was no longer that young man and wished his Interim friend understood his aging body required frequent rest.

Finally, the door to the High Study clicked open and the High Counselor's five priests shuffled out. The Counselor did not come with them and the door softly closed. The priests passed right under Shade and Nico's noses but were not even suspicious of their presence. Nico glanced up at his mysterious companion and wondered if she had somehow cloaked them with her dark friends.

The two Keepers had to wait three hours more, until the candles had burned low and Asgard was shushed. Though the stronghold never truly slept, the hallway traffic was almost entirely eliminated and those that did haunt the night typically remained glued to the bookshelves of the library tiers. Nico was usually one of them. The High Counselor finally emerged from his chamber and locked the door tight with a heavy, iron key that he dropped into his pocket as he left. Nico noticed a book tucked under the old man's arm. *Late reading even now, Counselor?* he wondered.

When all was quiet, Nico peered up at Shade.

"How are we to get in?" he whispered.

She did not answer, her face set in solemn focus. She pulled Nico close and closed her eyes. He waited with a slight blush to his cheeks for something to happen, but nothing seemed to change around them. Her free hand pressed to the wall, slowly rubbed the dull stones.

Nico sighed and glanced around, unsure how long they'd be standing there like fools. His eyes fell on a cluttered pile of books and papers and he frowned. *Who left that there?* he thought. *Better yet, when? We were standing here all this time—* The room suddenly whirled around him as he realized the pile of books and papers were not shoved in a corner of a dark hallway, but rather set against a bookshelf.

Nico spun out of Shade's grasp and realized they were standing in the middle of the High Study. His wide eyes and gaping jaw effectively conveyed his shock but his perplexed expression was ignored by a pokerfaced Shade.

"H-how?" he stammered, but she brushed by him to light the table lamps.

"We don't have much time and we won't waste it with pointless questions. Find what you need and let's go."

With light—as little as it was—penetrating the dark chamber, Nico was able to see more clearly. The High Study was in two tiers with just a few steps separating them. There were no walls, only bookshelves packed tight with large, thick, and crinkled volumes. The floor was covered in stacks of books and papers and a narrow path between the door and the High Counselor's desk had been formed. Veins of walking space spidered out so that some of the shelves were reachable, but the clutter of knowledge felt endless.

"Back there," he motioned and carefully led her up to the second tier. As he worked his way from one side of the room to the other, he muttered with bubbling mirth. "I've always dreamed of this!" he told her. "Can you imagine the knowledge between these leaves? The secrets that lie within? So much of our world—our history—hidden from us in this tiny room."

"You aren't here for that. Find the information on Knick."

"Well to know about Knick, we must find information on the sacrificial road…and to do that, we must read of King Malikiel." He came to one of the far shelves and his fingers wiggled in anticipation. "This is it!" He reached out with his right index and began running past the titles. Suddenly, he stopped.

"What?" Shade pressed, eyeing the shelf. Between two wrinkly volumes was a gaping, black, empty space. Her blood cooled.

"It's gone," Nico whispered, and suddenly remembered the book tucked under the High Counselor's arm. "He took it."

"Who?"

"The High Counselor," he replied. "I saw him carry a book with him. Unusual, no? Why would he bring anything with him, out of the library? We live in this tower—we stay put to study and retreat when we sleep—it makes no sense unless—!"

Shade waited a moment for him to finish, but he only stared at her with a wide expression of revelation.

"Unless?" she prompted.

"He would go so far to protect some vital information as to sleep with such a precious book even after he locks the High Study up tight."

"Protect?" Shade echoed, "or hide?"

Nico's grim face let her know he was thinking the same thing. He swallowed and motioned her to follow him to the High Counselor's desk.

"I only saw the book with him. Perhaps he left notes behind..."

As Nico set to riffling through the layers of pages, Shade watched over his shoulder, scanning the passing leafs for things she did not recognize. A drawing of a glyph fluttered in her peripherals and she stuck it to the table with the swift jab of her index and middle fingers.

"Wait," she commanded, and her scholar friend froze. "What is this?"

"What are you saying? It is the new glyph. How can you ask such a thing? You brought us the si—" Nico stopped midsentence as the revelation sunk in. He didn't even notice Shade's hand slip away from the page or her body step away from him.

He slowly turned around and was, for a moment, struck with fear from her dark expression. The shadows from the far end of the room had unnaturally gathered around her. Those unusual violet eyes of hers shimmered under a terrifyingly beautiful scowl.

He realized she was waiting for him to explain—waiting on the brink of some terrible vengeance. He was afraid, but not for himself. What were the Keepers hiding from their own people? For their sake, he hoped Shade did not find the secrets too vital.

"Th-the glyph," he stammered, voice seemingly caught in his throat. "The one the p-prophecy spoke of…this is the s-s-symbol—" he blinked furiously and twitched as he forced the words out "—of the sacrificial road—w-which I'm guess-s-sing isn't the glyph you saw on Knick."

"No," she replied curtly.

Nico faced the desk again, gaping open-mouthed at the drawing before him.

"Why?" he whispered at the pages. He had always thought the Keepers did not have secrets among the clan; he had always believed in the truth of the Balance. What was the purpose of such a deception and how long had this sort of situation been going on? Years? Decades? Millennia? But all he could say, and with barely a voice, was, "Why…?"

There was a scraping sound at the door like a key forced into the lock and his blood froze. He spun to Shade for help. Then he heard the click of the bolt sliding free. The door flew open and a dozen Kur flew into the room, knocking towers of books to the floor and scattering papers into a fluttering pile of academic snow. He felt in the chaos hands tightly gripping his arms, but the blood rushing in his ears drowned out every sound but that of the falling paper.

Between the swaying leaves, he saw the dark blue eyes of Eros staring up at him with a terrifying scowl on his face, and he thought that, in that moment, he saw Shade in the Baron's place. As the Kur dragged him through trampled books, he twisted around to see Shade. The Sovereign stood gathered in the darkness with one hand on the Sword of Shadows. He realized the Kur had not seen her and knew that the shadows had protected her—probably without her command.

Before he disappeared through the door, the storm of leaves shifted so that he could clearly see her pale hand tightly gripping the hilt of her blade. He understood her hesitation…but understood she had been ready to fight for him. It was a momentary sliver of happiness in his overwhelming swell of terror.

And then he was gone.

When the paper settled and the room cleared of most of the soldiers, Eros stood mumbling to Daelus while two sentinels guarded them. Shade stepped out of the darkness. Daelus was the first to notice, with a shocked and concerned expression. Eros turned expectantly.

"I should have known," he said, clearly agitated.

"Are you going to arrest me, too?" she snapped as she stepped down from the top tier.

"As if that would help."

She crossed to them and stopped once she threateningly entered Eros's space.

"We need to talk," she said darkly.

"My thoughts exactly."

A loud shriek shuddered sharply in the cavern walls, startling everyone from their quiet. Hezara flew out of her tent and darted further into the camp.

"It's gone!" she screeched. "It's gone!"

Knick stumbled over to her just as the gray-haired woman—pulling a heavy, furred skin tight across her shoulders—and several Krueh-jin guards approached.

"It's gone!" Hezara shrieked again, grabbing the old woman tight by the shoulders; the guards closed in but a wrinkled hand bid them stay back. A deathly glare in Hezara's cat-like eyes focused on the crone. "*You!*" she hissed. "You've taken it, and I demand it returned!"

"I've taken nothing!" the crone bellowed. "Do not accuse me—it will be the last you ever do!"

"Give it back!" she screamed and her biceps flexed and churned, tossing the woman back and forth. Knick pulled Hezara back and pinned her arms behind her.

"Snap out of it!" he begged, but she twisted and bucked in his tight grasp, grunting and shrieking in rage and panic.

The crone fixed her fur on her shoulders and muttered something to one of the men next to her. He and his fellows spread out into the camp and shouts began echoing in the cavern.

"Hava da! Ketoshi! Hava da!"

Several lowlights were snuffed and the camp dimmed

around them. The scurry of lehn and human feet filled the space like the flutter of a hundred wings all together. The crone smiled and motioned for Knick to bring Hezara. He followed her back to the central ring where they'd first been brought—dragging his Bloodsworn friend—and believed this particular site held authoritative significance in their hierarchy.

"What's going on?" Knick asked, still fighting Hezara's squirming in his arms. "Cut it out," he told her. "You'll rip a ring out of your face!"

"I told you we do not tolerate theft here," the crone replied. "The Kada are looking for your package now, 'Sworn. Rest assured, it will be returned."

Hezara calmed down and jerked out of Knick's grasp, but the violent look of rage was still in her eyes. Her muscles were tensed and nostrils flaring; she didn't notice the crowd creeping up on them.

"You put it on the table when you brought it up!"

"*You* put it on the table when you brought it here!" the crone rebutted. "Don't you think everyone saw your precious cargo the moment you entered Krueh-jin camp? We have laws! If someone disobeys these laws, they do it on their own!"

The two women huffed at each other in a standstill and Knick was relieved when a new shout interrupted their glaring contest.

"Negola! Negola! Negi ii gandu reta! Negola!"

"What are they saying?" Hezara demanded.

"They have found it," the crone replied, "and the culprit."

Knick sensed some regret in the old woman's voice and spotted apprehension in her furrowed brow. The three waited on edge as the retrievers pushed through the crowds and Knick's stomach churned a little more each time he heard the whispers and gasps grow louder.

The crowd broke and a mocha-skinned man was tossed before the crone. A blue-eyed lehn, restrained, was thrown next to him.

"Lethan…" the crone whispered, sorrow in her eyes. Knick frowned. Hezara's package was presented to the old woman, who turned and extended it to Hezara. "Your package, 'Sworn."

Hezara snatched it up and hugged it tightly to her chest. After a moment, she held it out and checked it over until she was satisfied it had not been damaged, much less been opened.

"We've stayed long enough," she muttered. "Knick, let's just go."

"Hold," the crone commanded, and her hard gaze was focused on Lethan, who remained slumped on his knees, head hung low to the ground. Whiskey, his lehn, had curled up beside him, head to the ground. "I am Sabal, chief of this tribe, and our laws have been broken. It is my duty to enact the will of the Krueh-jin. Justice come to this thief!"

She held out her hand and a jeweled scabbard was placed in her palm. She held the sheathed weapon out to Hezara and the gems glittered darkly in the lowlight. Hezara looked baffled by the gesture.

"You were wronged," the crone explained ritualistically, "and now you punish the devil who wronged you."

Hezara's cat-like eyes darted around the crowd, inspecting the solemn faces observing this trial. She looked at Lethan, curled over and silent, and then at the hard gleam of the crone's eyes.

"I just want to leave," she announced. "Keep your revenge."

Sabal thrust the scabbard at her again.

"This is our law. Justice is not a choice. Your thief is a thief because he did act, and now you must act. It is not a question of 'you may' or 'you should', but you *must*, because he did. Do you understand?"

Hezara hesitated and the crone offered the weapon again. Finally, she took hold of the hilt and yanked a sinister dagger out of the scabbard; it startled her for a single heartbeat—like pulling the wolf out of the sheep's skin.

Knick watched Lethan. He was perfectly still; not a single flinch, much less the trembles of fear, passed through his skin. And he was utterly silent, refusing to defy the accusations or accept them. Something was off. As an angel, he'd interrogated plenty and killed even more. No one went silently. This was wrong.

"What are you doing?" Knick asked Hezara as Sabal stepped aside and let her pass.

"I want to be gone from this place," she replied. "So let this be done."

"What? No. Are you crazy?" He turned to Sabal. "Can you

seriously do this? Didn't you say they were special?"

"This is our law!" Sabal cried. "Justice be done!"

Hezara reached around Lethan to cut his throat but Knick leapt to her side and grabbed her elbow so tight that she winced. She tried to jerk free, but she couldn't move. He twisted her arm away from Lethan's neck.

"What are you doing?" she hissed.

"You can't kill him because he took your box! There's nothing wrong with it. No damage done. Let's drop it and go."

"You heard the crone!"

"Bullshit. You still have a choice! No one's forcing you."

The dagger clattered to the ground at Lethan's knees.

"Fine," she snapped. "It's done. Let's go."

Knick looked over his shoulder at Sabal's stern face. "We're leaving," he told her. "We're done here."

"You have spared him, boy. His debt belongs to you, so now does his life." She motioned to someone nearby who cut the binds on Whiskey and pulled Lethan to his feet.

"Not necessary," Knick told her. She glared at him.

"You've interfered with our laws once. Do not try it again," she hissed. "Lethan and Whiskey are yours now. They will take you to Moscow. Now you must leave."

Several burly figures approached.

"We will see you again…boy…" Sabal muttered and Knick felt his skin crawl. She glared at Lethan. "Go, outcast, and fulfill your master's will."

They were aggressively escorted out of the camp and to a black tunnel off the side. Backs were turned, shutting them out, and the silent dust of the darkness ahead greeted them with a musty smell.

"I didn't see that coming," Knick muttered. "And Zara? You pull that shit again, *I'll* kill you."

"Shut up," she hissed and eyed Lethan. "It's not like I wanted to do it."

"I'm sorry," Lethan said quietly as Whiskey crawled up his leg and hung onto his arm. The lehn gently touched his chin, trying to comfort him.

"No harm done," she replied warily, "as long as it does not happen again."

"I promise you, it won't," he replied.

The awkwardness in the air set them all in motion down

the dark tunnel in tense quiet. Soon, phosphorescent mold began appearing—first as tiny dots near crevices and then in large patches on the walls and floor. And with the mold came the pungent smell they'd only faintly whiffed back at the beginning.

"What is that?" Hezara asked, hand to her nose.

"Mold," Lethan replied softly. "Moscow is surrounded on two sides by water."

"It's goes all the way?"

He nodded. "It's poisonous if ingested, so be careful."

Hezara pulled her goggles up to her eyes and then wrapped a swathe of cloth around the lower half of her face; she pressed on ahead without them. Knick glanced over at his mocha-skinned companion and, in the phosphorescent glow, noticed the tender bruising on his face.

"Are you all right?"

"I'm fine," he replied. "And thank you."

"Don't thank me. Thievery shouldn't earn you a death sentence." Knick began moving after Hezara and Lethan followed. Whiskey hopped up onto his shoulder and his thick tailed curled around Lethan's neck.

"It is the only crime our laws punish with death," he explained. "Murder, adultery, rape, slander, greed—they are measured as equal sins. The offender is beaten and left to rot, forever an outcast."

"You beat rapists but kill thieves?"

"Our survival is in trade—information, objects, people. Thievery is an affront to the Krueh-jin livelihood. It is the one sin that affects the survival of the whole clan and death is the only response."

"So why'd you do it?"

Lethan was silent, head hung low. They traveled the rest of the way in silence.

"What were you thinking?" Eros snapped as he and Shade walked brusquely down a corridor and turned into the next one. Daelus quietly trailed behind them.

"I'm tired of not having answers. Everyone is content to sit on their asses while nothing gets done. I'm through with that. I want to know what's going on."

"You think nothing is being done?" he balked. "You think

that the collective scour books day and night for nothing? That your fellow Champions are fighting for nothing? Have you changed so much that you think you are the only one capable of doing something?" He shook his head. "You're letting this go to your head, Shade."

She flushed in embarrassment for only a second and then the anger took over again.

"Aren't you just the same? Hasn't this gone to *your* head?"

"What are you saying?"

"Eros, why are you regent?" she asked. He stopped and faced her.

"Because I was elected, and I promise you that I was just as shocked as you were."

"I doubt that."

He narrowed his gaze on her and she could tell he was fighting her getting under his skin. He closed his eyes, sighed, and then kept walking. His voice had calmed when he started talking again.

"You've been disobeying one order after the next—"

"Order?"

"Not mine. The Keepers'. We have customs, Shade— customs you once observed. Not bringing outsiders into Asgard walls, not trespassing into the High Study."

"I did what I had to do."

"Why did you have to do anything? We are your people, Shade. You can come to us with these concerns and requests! You can trust us—"

"Like hell I can!" She grabbed a fistful of his collar and slammed him into the wall. "You lied to me!"

Eros was wide-eyed in shock at her outburst and only gaped at her. Their glyphs flared in sync and Daelus, stunned, was the only one to notice.

"What…do you mean? Lied?" Daelus stammered.

Shade slammed the scribble of the sacrificial glyph against the wall and the shadows traced the lines, burning through the paper and scribing it into the stone. She backed off, gaze locked on Eros. The men gaped at the scar on the wall and Eros ran his fingertips over it.

"Shade…" he began.

"You lied to everyone—"

"Shade—"

"Since the very beginning! How could you?"

"Shade!" he exclaimed. "I didn't lie to you."

"You just left out parts of the truth. It's the same thing—it means the *same thing*! You want to talk about trust, Eros? You have no right!"

"Shade, listen to me," he pleaded. "I would never betray you. Never. I trust you more than anyone." He straightened his clothes. "The more time you spend with Coltin, the more you lose your trust in the Keepers. I understand the Regent's betrayal has upset you—as it has us all—but now you're seeing treachery everywhere."

"That's not true—"

"Shade, you are the best of the best but, right now, you aren't thinking clearly. And Coltin is poisoning you against your family. You can't see it now, but think about why the Keepers of the Order—a system that has stood the test of time—would be lying to you now?"

Shade flinched and opened her mouth to say something but the approaching footsteps closed it again. Bartimaeus appeared.

"Baron," he began. "The spies have returned. The Champions are gathered."

Eros and the three Champions made their way to the Abbey and Eros immediately went into private consultation with the cloaked scouts. Shade, Daelus, and Bartimaeus joined their companions in the wooden pews. Rexis put a hand on the top of Shade's head.

"Something's up," he whispered. "Looks like a development."

They waited quietly and soon Eros turned to address them.

"Our spies report that one Doctor Robert Basset has just been released from a MAAR contract. He was brought on shortly after the last relic was taken into their custody and we believe he may have information on the situation.

"One of you will retrieve him and find out what he knows. Basset also has family that will be put at risk once MAAR discovers we have the doctor; they must be relocated. Which of you will volunteer for this?"

"I will go," Shade said.

"No," Eros replied immediately. "Though the grounding

is officially lifted, you are forbidden from leaving Asgard until—"

"Why?"

"Because you have proven yourself to be acting outside of Keeper influence and I will not trust Basset's information or his family's lives to your whims."

Rexis noticed her fists clench. It was unusual to see them at odds and everyone in the room was more than a little taken aback.

"I'll find Basset," Vox volunteered. Dimitri stood up.

"And I will retrieve his family," he said. Eros bowed his head to both of them.

"So be it."

And the meeting was over. The Interim filtered out and the spies had disappeared without being noticed.

"Eros," Shade began before he could leave.

"It's not up for debate," he interrupted her. "The others can handle this—and everything else thrown our way. Muriel is in the wind, the delegates are still not talking, a new council must be elected, and I have enough to deal with without having to track your every move. It's enough I have to keep my eye on you in Asgard; I cannot afford to watch you beyond these walls. Is that understood?"

Shade swallowed back her anger.

"Yes," she replied and walked out, passing Daelus in the hall.

"Are you sure about this?" Daelus asked Eros as he exited the Abbey.

"She's like a whole new woman, Daelus," the Baron sighed.

"I don't agree," he said. "She's always been this way... only her sights were never set so close to home." He intercepted Eros's raised brow. "Well, she used to be a lot better at following orders...and at not thinking too much."

"I'm scared, Daelus," Eros admitted.

"Of what, sir?"

"That I'm losing her...that she's slipping away from me..."

Daelus lowered his head. He wasn't sure how to respond. Eros only stared at his empty hand—at the fingers that used to stroke her soft, black hair.

The sound of water reached their ears long before the group reached the exit into Moscow. The mold had grown brighter and covered the tunnels almost completely. It had grown over every potential marker they might pass and it was easy to miss turns in the glow with everything blended together. Lethan had been invaluable in guiding them down the right path.

Plus, there had been no sign of the ex-Keepers.

Conversation had been kept to a minimum due to the harsh smell and lack of anything to relate to. Hezara was still sore about her package and Lethan was probably still depressed over being kicked out of his clan. Knick found small things to talk about here and there, but mostly it was over in a couple of minutes.

Finally, they were descending a ladder and crouching next to a rough opening down into a rocky decline on the edge of the city. Hezara was the first to go down. Lethan picked her up at the waist and eased her onto the surface, grasping her arm then hand so that she easily slid down the way.

Knick climbed into the gap next and Lethan reached out to help him. Knick grasped his hand tightly.

"We can take it from here," he said.

"But—"

"Go back to your tribe. Tell them you fulfilled my will and I released you. You shouldn't have to live like an outcast over something this minor."

"Knick, I—"

"Hey. I don't need a servant. And you don't deserve to be one." He gave Lethan a firm nod. "Take care, man. Maybe we'll see each other again."

Lethan eased Knick down the slide and watched his two companions collect at the bottom. After Knick had explained to Hezara why Lethan wasn't coming, she looked up and gave a simple wave. Knick just glanced back. Then they were off and Lethan disappeared in the dark.

The walk into the city took less than an hour.

"So where are you taking this thing?" Knick asked once they started passing civilized structures.

"A man called Roskolniv."

"And who is he?"

She shrugged.

"Right," he muttered.

Once they had gone further into the city, Hezara stopped to ask around. It only took one person to set them in a direction.

"Kirill Roskolniv? The old lawyer? He lives in a beach house about five miles west of here. Take Jimps Road out to Lyrin and follow it uphill. It's the first place you come to—can't miss it."

Hezara thanked the informant then she and Knick were on their way down Jimps. They hopped a tram to the city limits, got off when they reached the sea, and followed Lyrin Road left—since the dead end only went uphill one way. They followed the rocks lining the road, separating the sand from the street. Just as Hezara's information had said, they found the rutty old beach house isolated at the water's edge.

The hollow thunk-thunk of their feet on the boardwalk was met with a plip-blup of water lapping at the support beams underneath. The door was swung wide with a screen in its place, showing them right into the hallway with a glimpse of the living room in the back. Knick knocked on the side of the house twice but there was no movement within.

"Roskolniv!" Hezara shouted. The word vibrated out to the water and was swallowed up. Then there was the empty smack of a screen door in the back and footsteps shuffled toward them.

The man that appeared looked hollow. His brown hair was muted with gray and his skin was pale. His eyes looked up at them with the utter disregard of a man who had lost all meaning to live.

"What?" he grumbled with a deep and scratchy voice stripped by alcohol and tobacco.

"Roskolniv?" Hezara asked.

"Yeah?"

Hezara held out the package.

"Moscow. Roskolniv. Those were my instructions," she said. "I am Hezara of the Bloodsworn. This package belongs to you."

The man hesitated a moment before opening the door and stepping out onto the porch. He took the box in one hand, carefully turning it over until he was satisfied it was entirely unmarked. Knick and Hezara had already started back down the boardwalk.

"Who sent this?" he called after them.

"A ghost," she replied over her shoulder, remembering how close to death the old man had been.

Roskolniv grunted and ripped back the brown paper. The marking in the marble underneath caused his heart to thump wildly. The curving lines and accompanying dots was the symbolic signature of only one person...and that person was dead.

The box clattered to the floor and Roskolniv stumbled back into his door, ripping out the screen as he fell through. He tried to scream but couldn't breathe. His hand clawed at his chest as if he could open up the airway if he scratched hard enough, but the pain squeezing his heart and bearing down on his lungs was too great.

Knick and Hezara whirled around and ran back to him.

"What the fuck!" Knick yelled, kneeling at the man's side. He hoisted him up just in time for Roskolniv to lurch and vomit. "Help me get him up!"

Hezara scooped up the package in one arm and used the other to help Knick drag him into the house. They set him on the couch and she ran into the kitchen, yanked a glass off a drying cloth on the counter, filled it with sink water, and brought it to Knick.

"Here, drink this," Knick instructed the man, but he wasn't listening.

Roskolniv's eyes were wide with fear and his face was near purple from lack of oxygen. His trembling hand gripping his chest was so tense that the skin looked ready to rip to allow the muscles and veins more room.

Knick grabbed his hand and gripped it tightly. He forced Roskolniv to sit, still holding his hand tightly, and gripped his jaw.

"Look at me, Rosk! Breathe!" he commanded. "Breathe!"

Some strange glint of familiarity in the man's eyes as he stared wildly at Knick put him on edge. He clamped onto Knick's arm and the two were locked together. Roskolniv tried to suck in some air but he couldn't feel any filling his lungs, like his throat was closed up tight. He was panicking even more.

"Zara!" Knick exclaimed. She offered him the water. "Forget that, just hit him with it!"

She tossed the water onto Roskolniv and he sucked in a breath out of shock.

"Good," Knick coached. "Just like that, keep breathing!"

Now that Roskolniv had started, he kept going. At first, he was inhaling and exhaling ninety-miles-a-minute, but eventually he was able to slow it down. Once his heart was calmer and his flesh had flushed to a lighter shade of red, Knick let him go and backed off.

Roskolniv's head dropped into his hands and his shoulders slumped, shaking as he sobbed.

Dr. Basset exhaled hot air, finished wiping his lenses, and put his sunglasses on. The line he stood in moved up one and he stepped the two paces forward. The Kahli district was always packed at lunch time and the hum of conversation sounded more like a roar when thousands of people were all doing it at once. It was the hub for business men and women at lunch, a hangout for everyone calling themselves a serious artist, a jog spot and day-off stop for housewives with girlfriends and young children. The square was packed with eateries and hydration stations mingling with hundreds of shops, all housed ground level of sparkling office buildings. The square was surrounded by golden arches and tall, wide steps that descended into beautifully manicured gardens with cool, relaxing fountains and ponds.

Kahli was one of the most beautiful districts in all of Lotus Maze.

It was pleasantly warm and unusually bright, easing the shakes out of his body. It had only been a few days since he'd been released from his MAAR contract, but he was still worried that, at any moment, they would break down his door and hurt his family, hurt him.

As the hours ticked by and one day turned into two, he slowly felt the anxiety wallowing in his stomach start to fade. His guilt, however, only grew—his guilt at his silence.

He moved up in line again and, after ten minutes, finally stood at the window.

"Somen noodles," Basset told the attendant. As he waited, he checked his holocard and skimmed through the morning-to-afternoon transition's information flux of business. Between his attempt at concentration on work and his side-tracked mind worrying about the angels, he didn't even notice the orange-headed girl with the sheer and draping layers approach him.

"Dr. Basset?" she asked, pulling her pale-pink lips into a bright smile. The moment he made eye contact, he instantly knew something was wrong. "Please act normal. I'm merely a curious girl wondering about the food here."

He frowned, deadlocked with her gaze. The attendant brought his noodles but he didn't notice.

"MAAR's eyes are always on you," she said, and his blood instantly froze. "Please, Doctor. Your cold noodles are going to get hot if you don't take them."

Dr. Basset attempted to steady his shaking hand as he grabbed the bowl and paid the woman. He followed the woman to a table and found his legs felt as though they had the consistency of gelatin. They took a seat under the umbrella, but Basset couldn't even touch his bowl. He'd suspected they'd keep an eye on him, but he was hoping it wasn't like that. He was pretending it was different for his sanity's sake. Ignorance is bliss, and what-not.

But hearing it said aloud like that shattered his already fragile illusion.

"Who...are you?" he asked. His words sounded forced, and they had been. His heart was thumping wildly.

"My name is Vox, Sovereign of the Sword of Flame, Interim of the Order, and Keeper of the Balance." Her amber eyes flickered like fire momentarily. Upon hearing her association, Dr. Basset nearly knocked his bowl off the table.

"K-Keeper?" he stammered. *This is trouble...this is serious. My girls,* he thought, *my wife... Shit!* "How do I know you aren't MAAR?"

"MAAR's street agents are the business men in line behind you, the woman by the hydration station, the clerk serving your noodles, the teg-head with the newspaper a few tables down bobbing his head to dream-trance. A MAAR street agent would spill somen on your jacket, apologize, and attempt to buy the cleaning bill—never approach you and claim to be a Keeper."

He felt a lump form in his throat at the idea and wondered

how many agents he'd met in his lifetime. Had everyone been a fictional creation of the White Tower? Between panicking over their safety and fearing this woman in front of him, Dr. Basset's instinct to protect what he loved with all of his might rose out of his gut and into his voice. He narrowed his gaze on the woman called Vox.

"What do you want with me?" he asked.

She smiled.

"Good, you've found your resolve. You'll need it. Please, understand I have no intention of hurting you, Doctor. Unfortunately, I cannot leave you alone. For your sake, please do as I say: laugh, point at the soup, relax. Let's pretend you were on edge because I told you some scary little fact about noodles."

Dr. Basset swallowed the lump in his throat, forced the tension out of his back, and tossed his head back when he laughed. He pointed to the soup and then made friendly gestures with his hand as though he were talking about it. He found himself mumbling under his breath what the conversation might've been like had he not been in this mess. Then, he opened his canisters of dipping sauces, pulled the vacuum seal off his chopsticks, took up a huge clump of noodles, and offered it over to her. She shook her head and so he began to eat.

"Thank you," Vox said, and she smiled warmly. "It has come to the attention of the Order that you were recently contracted and released by MAAR. We want to know why."

Dr. Basset took the opportunity of noodles in his mouth to hesitate. He did not want to cross MAAR. However, he had heard the stories of the Keepers and every ounce of propaganda that Mirax pumped out. He was just as afraid of them as he was of MAAR—maybe even more.

"Whatever you know of the Order, sir, please allow me to ease your mind. Our only interest is the security and longevity of everyone in this world. If some have to die for that, it is regrettable. It is a heavy burden to take an innocent's life and we avoid it at all costs. We willingly and guiltlessly eliminate those that easily put others in harm's way.

"You need not fear us at all. All we ask is information that may or may not be vital to the security we aspire to maintain," she explained. Dr. Basset noticed her eyes casually flick around the lunch square, constantly keeping watch. "I am ready to fight for your safety at any moment, Dr. Basset. If things go unfortunately, I promise you that I will give my life to see you to safety."

"I have a family," he told her quietly, "two girls..."

"We know. Someone is already with them now. He is prepared to protect your family just as I am prepared to protect you."

He dropped the chopsticks in his bowl.

"It was a stone," he said bluntly, "a perfectly round and polished stone with strange psychic properties."

She frowned and stood up.

"Please come with me."

He stared at her, a little surprised by the sudden movement.

"Now."

He got to his feet and began walking with her. Although they weren't even walking fast, he could sense in her steps that she was aiming to get out of the square as quickly as possible. His heartbeats quickened.

"What's wrong?" he asked.

"MAAR is making its move. We need to get away from these people to minimize casualties. I cannot fight their numbers effectively with the battlefield crowded by the panicking guiltless. Once we get clear, I'll stand ground and you must do exactly as I say. Is that clear?"

"My family—"

"Is being collected and brought to a safe place—the same place I will be taking you. You'll be united with them soon. You will explain everything you know about this stone and what you saw or heard while under MAAR's contract to someone in the Order."

It was when they reached the golden arches surrounding the square that the crowd began to thin and Dr. Basset became aware of the gentlemen casually following them. Out of the corner of his eye, he saw one of them lift his hand to his ear. He faced him head on and read his lips: they've entered the gardens.

"Keeper," he mumbled, but she was already well aware of the situation.

"Run," she said coolly, and they both took off in a sprint.

They barely ran ten yards when the angels stepped out of the surrounding scenery as though they'd come out of the walls themselves. The Nightwalkers were brought up threateningly and the silver lenses reflecting light made their eyes appear to glow.

Vox put her hand to the hilt of her sword that suddenly appeared out of her layered clothes.

"Basset, listen to me. Get on those stairs," she ordered him. It took him a moment but he did as he was told. "You have to stop hesitating! It could be the difference on whether or not you make it through this!"

She yanked out her scimitar and struck the ground then made a sweeping motion as though she were drawing a circle. The bells on her wrist jingled. A wall of fire shot out of the ground and traced a protective path around Dr. Basset. He fell back onto the stairs in shock.

The scattered throng fled in sheer panic, widening the stage for the inevitable battle.

"Leave him!" Vox exclaimed to the angels. "Do not engage!"

The angels drew their preferred weapons from the polyspace of the Nightwalkers—maces, swords, spiked clubs, morning stars, and all manner of vicious killing instruments.

The fang of her blade glowed with the scar of Vanguard down the curving and vicious steel. Her amber eyes shimmered like burning hot embers and her short, wild spikes of orange hair looked more and more like the chaotic flames she mastered.

The angels were the first to attack. Vox dropped to one knee and stabbed the ground again. Columns of fire twisted out of the ground and instantly burned several of them to charred bone. The others that escaped the blazing fury were met with the ring of her blade. The longer their weapons were in contact with Vox's, the hotter they became, until the metal glowed bright red with heat and they were forced to abandon them. The scorching cuts she left on them singed their suits and seared their flesh.

Still, angels came. And one by one, the mistress of fire cut them down, the bells on her wrist chiming and jingling all the while. Dr. Basset knew she couldn't keep going. She was one woman—the angels were thousands. They'd never stop.

A blur stole his attention from the fight and he saw more angels descending the stairs, coming at him from him both sides. He clenched his fists, sweat dripping down the sides of his face. Could they get through the flames? Would they even try? Perhaps they didn't need to in order to kill him.

"Vox!" he shouted and she turned a sharp eye in his direction.

In a graceful blur of turns, Vox's sweeping blade raised another wall of fire directly under the angels she was fighting, throwing them into screaming fits. The lightweight sheers she wore danced with the fire, never once catching flame or even singeing. Her second spin sliced a scar of fire in the air above her head. Her palm stretched up toward the burning streak and closed her into a fist as though grasping the fire.

"Get down!" she demanded and he dropped instantly.

A ball of fire exploded at his side, engulfing several angels. He glanced up and saw her pull more fire out of the sky and it, too, exploded near him, taking out the rest of the advancing agents of MAAR. With everything around him burning, Dr. Basset slowly stood to observe the destruction. Among the blackened bodies, he noticed markers of the angels — a hand with the silver tattoo, a pair of half-razed silver lenses, patches of white suit, bald heads.

Through the heat's quivering blur, Vox stomped toward him. With one jerking motion of her scimitar like the parry of a blade, a section of the ring of fire around him instantly died and created a path. She motioned for him to follow and he immediately obeyed, positive there were more angels on their way.

The door to the High Study was thrown open and Shade's dark silhouette appeared in the frame. The High Counselor peered over his half-moon glasses with tiny and tired eyes, poised mid-reach to place some books back on his shelves.

"Shade," he said with a smile. "The collective helped me order my study back together. Perhaps the mess was needed — it helped me get to organizing decades of old clutter." He noticed her glare when she folded her arms over her chest and leaned against the doorframe. "You know, Shade, if you really wanted a look at my library, all you had to do was knock — "

"I am *not* here for games, High Counselor," she interrupted him. He slipped the book on the shelf and nodded.

"Yes, I know." He waved her over. "Come in."

She took one step inside and kicked the door closed. The High Counselor managed to put one more book away before he sighed in exhaustion and shuffled over to his desk.

"I want to know about the sacrificial king," she said bluntly.

"Yes, King Malikiel," he began, slumping into his chair, "was the lord of ancient and powerful Mesopotamia."

Shade leaned back on the door, arms still folded across her chest, and narrowed her gaze on the old man.

"The legends say he was sacrificed to save the city from darkness—a darkness within," she said.

"Yes," he agreed. "That is what they say. I know, having rewritten many of the texts myself."

"You?"

"The bloody king—that is what he is called. A dangerous and dark symbol of our weakness. It wouldn't do to have the truth, now would it? History should inspire righteousness, not burden us with the veracity of our preordained failure."

"What are you saying?"

"Malikiel did not willingly go to the altar," he replied, "nor did he ever intend to sacrifice himself. Truthfully, he was murdered by his very own flesh and blood. The ritual was staged—that has been the consensus for many millennia— though some of us believe it never happened at all. Still, his brother, Mahmud, killed him for his power and he became the sacrifice to save the city from Mahmud's wickedness fueled by his jealousy."

"Tch, romantic bullshit."

"Possibly. And now the bloody king returns."

"Why?"

"The Sages predicted he would return to reclaim."

"What do you think?"

He smiled. "Romantic bullshit, as you put it." He pushed his glasses up his nose. "But after his brother's betrayal, King Malikiel refused to leave us without warning for the future. He left us the Enoch, born from Malikiel's line."

"Born?" she breathed, shocked, but he did not elaborate.

"Apparently, poison still clouds the Sight. Neither the

Enoch nor the Oracle ever saw Muriel's betrayal coming. Still, he cannot conceal his treachery." The High Counselor linked his long, knobby fingers. "The Sages of the First Days saw all that was to come and wrote it down. That is why Mahmud was never able to hide his sins, or so we believe. Though most of the scrolls of aeternus are lost, we collect as many records as we can—we have been for lifetimes."

Shade pushed off of the door and slowly approached his desk as he continued his train of thought.

"They give us clues to the roads, you know. They are how we learned to craft the weapons"—he motioned to her aegis—"to interpret the prophecies, to understand the glyphs," he explained. One of Shade's brows dipped in confusion. "Each glyph has a particular marker that reveals the fate of the bearer—a mark that separates the monks from the kur, the savants from the naga, the Interim from the Primordials."

He motioned her closer and pointed to the glyph on his forehead.

"Do you see these three dots among my sigil? They have a hard focus but a reserved disposition associated with scholarship. They are arranged in a triangle, representing wisdom. Mine points upward, meaning I sit at the head of the hierarchy and shepherd the collective; the collective's triangle points downward, showing that they are being shepherded. The solid bottom line of the triangle is the firm base on which academia rests, as well as what I rest upon, but when turned upside down, it becomes an umbrella of knowledge. Do you understand?"

Shade, fascinated, did not reveal her intrigue. He was trying to bait her with a new topic but she had come for answers, not chit-chat. She cocked her head to the side.

"Before, you said you rewrote many of the texts."

"I did. I imagine you're wondering why the tales are so different. I...*chose*...to leave certain details out. Well, perhaps that isn't the correct word. I was *encouraged* to."

"By whom?"

He smiled. "Don't you know?"

"The Regent."

Shade frowned and reflected on what she already knew to be true, even without the High Counselor's confirmation. The corruption went much further back in time than the day of the betrayal.

"High Counselor, I need to ask you something."

"Go ahead."

"Tell me, why is Eros the new regent and not you?"

"In the past months, the Keepers have come to trust Eros implicitly. Before now, the collective never had cause to fear, but Muriel's betrayal left them all frightened. Eros inspired confidence, offered them security through military action. The Kur and Interim already followed him without question. It is no surprise that he was elected."

"I don't like it."

He sighed. "Perhaps even more than the Regent himself, the Primordials bear the burden of the Order. Eros is no different than Camilla—the Cleric—or myself as High Counselor. We all bear the responsibility of where we are today as an institution and a force at work in the world."

"What does all of this have to do with Knick?"

"He is…a force in this world, too, Shade. A force on his own…and a force through you."

"If he isn't the sacrificial road, then who is? And what is he?"

He intercepted her agitation but ignored her question, desperate for her to understand at least one thing.

"You are like a great Phoenix, Shade, burning brighter and brighter—brighter than any bird in this aviary could hope to be in a millennium! You must pace yourself, for his sake, before you burn up in your own power."

She turned to go.

"It's too late for that, High Counselor. The ripples have already started spreading."

The High Counselor gripped a book with white knuckles under his desk. He hesitated, but couldn't bring himself to show it.

"Shade," he called as she opened the door. "I'm sorry. I can't help you."

"No shit." And she walked out.

The housing district in Molatta was constructed in the walls of the Mora Crater just less than a mile into the earth. 520 stories with 400 apartments per level set the minimum resident count at 208,000, though the census counted three-quarters of a million living in the hole. It was a top-notch complex with state-of-the-art filtration systems and security press. The elevator ride straight from floor 1 to floor 520 took roughly four minutes thanks to turbulence buffers and acute gravity modules.

The Mora Complex was also the home of Dr. Basset and his family. Floor 334, apartment 97. It had taken Dimitri two minutes to get there after one stop at 287 to let an old woman off. The belt rotated him around to the 90's where he walked the rest of the way to his destination. He stopped in front of the blank, white door and a holopad appeared. He touched his fingers to it and an automated voice announced,

"This is the home of Dr. and Mrs. Robert Basset. Would you like to page them, leave a parcel, or record a calling card?"

"Page, please," he replied.

"One moment." On the other side of the door, the automated voice announced, "Mrs. Basset, someone is at the door for you."

"Thank you, Mora," she replied, got up from the couch, and strolled to the door. With one flick of the holopad, the door phased out like a two-way mirror; she could see the man on the other side, only he could not see her. "Yes?" she asked, skeptical of the stranger calling.

"Mrs. Basset," he began, "my name is Dimitri, Sovereign of the Sword of Seas, Interim of the Order, and Keeper of the Balance. I am here on behalf of your husband."

"Keepers?" Her voice was suddenly unsteady.

"Yes, ma'am. This matter is concerning the contract for MAAR your husband was recently released from. It would be in your best interest to gather your girls and come with me."

"I don't think that's such a good id —"

"I know you're frightened, ma'am, but I assure you...we have little time to waste. I am here to protect you."

Suddenly the two-way mirror opened up and he could now see the scared woman on the other side of the door. A normal housewife, dressed for a day in with a fold-neck sweater and roll waist wide-leg pants. She was holding a cup of tea with trembling fingers.

"Please leave or I'll call security!"

"I'm sorry, I can't do that. To minimize the risk to you and your daughters, it would be best to come wi —"

But the trap had been sprung. The door suddenly disappeared without Mrs. Basset's order and the sniper laser appeared on her forehead. Her cup slipped from her hands. Dimitri whipped his katana from its scabbard on his back and spun it over his knuckles. The crack of the rifle was so far away.

As the glass shattered on the ground, the tea gathered and rose, shifting form, particles multiplying, and the green substance created a wall of liquid just in time to stop a sniper bullet in its tracks. It captured the hot metal and crashed to the floor.

"Get inside!" he yelled, pushing her into her apartment and as far away from the door as possible. She screamed and stumbled, jelly-like in terror. Her girls rushed down the hall to the living room, crying out.

"Mom, what's wrong!" the eldest exclaimed.

"Momma!" the youngest cried.

She gathered them up in her arms and hugged them, wide-eyed and shaking in a ball behind the couch.

"Who are they? What do they want?" she exclaimed.

"They want to kill your family," he said bluntly. "Another team was dispatched to take your husband. My comrade is with him now."

"Oh god, Robert," she cried. "Why?"

"This isn't the time. I will get you all out of here safely, but you must do exactly as I say. Now, quickly, get up." Dimitri glanced around at the door and could see from far off the kill units moving into position. "Is there an open water source anywhere nearby?"

"W-water?" she stammered. "Th-there's water at the bottom of the abyss—the great lake we draw our water through."

"Good. I will go out and create a barrier, but you must run immediately when it rises. Do not be afraid. Follow me, is that clear?"

The mother nodded, holding her girls tightly. Dimitri sprinted back out into the breezeway and dropped to one knee. His katana came down hard on the concrete and a great rumbling shook the whole crater. The sniper-shots plinked off of the barrier his weapon had created, the hot glow of Vanguard visible in the scope. The bells chimed musically with the sounds of the gunfire.

The churning in the pit caused many to try to exit their homes and a mass of internal panic swept over the complex as the doors refused to obey their owners' commands; the network had been entirely hijacked by MAAR, the very company that had produced the security system.

A loud screech filled the pit and the water took the form of a gigantic hydra rising out of the lake. It's seven, watery heads roared and shrieked and whipped back and forth as the beast made from the sea climbed higher and higher. Its necks stretched and whirled, chomping viciously at the kill units and snipers who all turned their fire to the mythical beast.

The women behind Dimitri were huddled together, cowering in fear, and the youngest wet herself.

"Run!" he exclaimed, and the mother pulled her daughters to their feet and yanked them into the breezeway. Dimitri took the lead, katana ready for when they met the kill teams that had survived the hydra's assault.

The hydra's many heads let out more shrieks flooding the levels with their swinging heads and twisting necks. Their vicious maws chomped at their assailants with ease as the water they were created from easily molded around the building.

As Dimitri and his charges dodged the surges of water that randomly shot into the hall and trudged through the pools collecting, the youngest girl sobbed and cried. Her big sister picked her up and carried her, drenched from head to toe. They reached the elevator and piled in; water piled and filtered into the car as the doors closed, leaving them standing in a puddle up to their knees. Though the lights flickered and the machinery whirred, the elevator began rising and the numbers counted down faster and faster as the seconds ticked by.

"Where are you taking us?" the mother asked.

"To your husband and someplace safe," he replied. "I promise you, I won't let anything happen to you. Do as I say and everything will be all right. When these doors open, I want you all to be crouched in that water."

The eldest lowered her sister into the water and she and her mother crouched down. Dimitri stirred the water with his weapon and it trembled under the influence of the aegis. The numbers on the door flashed: 5, 4, 3, 2, 1.

Bing!

The water shot up as the doors opened and a spray of bullets instantly lodged in the liquid. Dimitri brought his blade back in a mid-position thrust, his palm against the pommel. His bells jingled as he propelled the blade forward and the water with its thousands of bullets flew forward with deadly speed.

Even with the Sovereign of the Sword of Seas bearing his almighty power, the horde of angels collected on the rooftop did not stop coming for the trembling family trapped inside an elevator.

The dark living room of the beach house was lit by dull light filtering in through the windows as the afternoon turned late. It bounced off of the haze of cigarette smoke and caused the wispy tendrils to glow. The clock on the wall tick-ticked over and over again, melding sounds with the crisp of tobacco and the haaa of exhaled smoke. Hezara lounged lazily on the window seat, staring out at the dark water of the Thysees Lake in the cavern bay. Knick smoked, leaning into his perch on the fireplace mantle. Roskolniv was still sunk into the couch, head down, eyes glassy, and a rette between his gnarled fingers. There was a glass of amber whiskey and a full bottle on the table.

The story felt coming in the air like a storm of torment raging twenty-five years.

"Her name was Red," he said, "and she had the reddest hair I'd ever seen—like crimson on fire. And she had these stone gray eyes peppered with more red. She was fucking beautiful—the most beautiful fucking woman I've ever seen. I don't know how I went so long without her.

"It's karma, you know? For hopping in bed, one girl after the next. Never taking relationships seriously. Get bored, move on." He inhaled his cigarette, worked around the words, and then exhaled the smoke. "But her I wanted more than anything. And I got her—I *had* her. But it wasn't enough. Red was what I never was—not in a million years, no matter how much I pretended to be. She was free. And she had another lover…

"The job. She was always working. Working, doing what? She wouldn't tell me, but she was always sailing off with that freaky crew of hers, always crawling into the Grey, always going off on some crazy adventure. Top secret. Bullshit, man. Fuck." Another inhale and exhale. "I even begged her to stay, to move in with me, to just be mine.

"She said, 'sorry Rosk but this is more important than you.' More important..." His face contorted in pain at the memory. "I didn't care. I still loved her. I needed her. Even when I broke down, she kept her cool. She smiled and told me she'd be back. She kissed me, fucked me, and always said, 'Seein' ya'. Except the last time. The last time, she said, 'Bye, Rosk.' Bye like she knew."

Hezara's cat-like eyes were focused out the window, but her ears were soaking up the story, attention undivided. Knick lit up another cigarette and burned, feeling a dangerous connection between Roskolniv's story and his. And this man's pain was ugly and twisted. Clearly, Time—the great healer—had done nothing but fuck him over.

"I heard the fight and went to the window. Saw her ship in port. Sprinted down to meet her, scared the shots were at her and prepared to play it cool when I saw they weren't. The crowd was thick, tight. And she was laying there with half her crew. The men in hoods withdrew, went after the ones that escaped. I didn't even get to say goodbye—her eyes were dull and pulse dead. Pulse was..."

Hezara and Knick said nothing when he started crying. If there was any reason for a grown man to cry, this was it. Maybe it was karma...but the punishment didn't really fit the crime. That's what they thought. Roskolniv dropped his cigarette and it smoldered on the floor, burning a black spot in the stained rug. It smelled like a mix of fire, smoke, and old piss.

Another hour rolled by and the tick-ticker chimed pathetically. The house was falling apart at the same rate as Roskolniv. The old man reached out and pushed his hand inside the torn paper, shoved it aside, and ran his fingers over the marble box and the rough scar across the top.

"This was her signature," he said. Then he opened it up. The musty smell of twenty-five years was released. A wrinkled and old piece of paper sat on top. He took it gingerly in his rough paw and carefully opened it up.

Rosk

You're getting this 'cause I'm dead. Gru's been holding it all this time, waiting to send it out. To you. Waiting til it was safe. I know you'll hate me, but I couldn't put you at risk, kid. This is important, so buck up and bear it. I hope the trail is dead by now. I don't want to bring you trouble. I'm afraid it can't be helped. If a man named Hermes comes knocking, don't ask questions. Send this box to the bottom of Thysees. He'll destroy it. I know Hermes works for Muriel, but I don't think he's one of his lackeys. Gone rogue under the old fool's nose. They're both after me, but if I'm dead, he's the one that killed me.

It's been 25 yrs. I hope you settled down with some nice girl. Yeah right, you need a bitch like me to keep you in line. So I hope she's a bitch. Remember when you asked me to move in? Well I'm coming home to you. Well, was. Since I'll be dead when you read this. You asked me if I loved you. I left. So in case you never get to hear me say it, I'll just write it now. I love you, Rosk. There. We belong together, didn't you always say that? I believe it, too. Now that my work is done, I'll give you this one wish.

See you tomorrow, or I'll see you in hell.
Red

He rubbed his face, caught between despair and rage. After all this time, he had his questions answered: who killed her, why, would she ever stay, did she love him? She did. She did love him. She was coming home to him.

Roskolniv peered at the object inside the box, packed tightly around black squish. He lifted the black marble statue and rolled it into his palm. There were hardly any veins in the polished stone, only faint gray flecks. It was in the shape of a tall tree with five large and gnarly roots. Near the top of the tree, a wide plain holding a grand city was carved.

"So this is what Muriel wanted and Hermes sought destroy?" he mumbled. Knick suddenly looked up.

"What did you say?" he asked. Hezara twisted around and Roskolniv showed him the statue.

"This is what Muriel—"

"The ex-Regent Muriel?"

"Regent of what?"

"The Keepers."

There was an awkward silence.

"You mean the Keepers killed my Red?" he growled. Roskolniv raised the statue high and tossed it angrily, but Knick lunged and managed to catch it before it hit the ground. He twirled it around in his hands, scouring every centimeter. On the belly of the plane, the Keeper symbol had been carved.

"You don't know what this means?" Knick asked, pointing to the statue. Roskolniv shook his head. "Tell me what the letter says."

Roskolniv handed it to him and Knick read through it twice as the old man finally took his shot of whiskey and poured another. Muriel was definitely the ex-Regent. He'd never heard the name Hermes before, but perhaps Shade knew.

"This is Keeper, all right," Knick informed them.

"Do whatever you want with it, but leave the letter with me," he replied. Hezara turned more on the window seat as Knick passed the letter back.

"You're giving it up? Red died to protect it," she reminded him. He gingerly held the old paper in his fingertips, gaze locked on Red's scribbling.

"She died coming back to me... Besides, it's been twenty-five years. It's over now. I just want peace...and then to find her in hell." He slipped a cigarette out of his pack and Knick bent to light it for him.

"Take care," Knick muttered and the old man smirked and took his second shot.

"You look just like someone I used to know," he muttered. Knick poured him a third.

"Maybe you'll see him, too," he said, "in hell." And then he headed for the door. Hezara jumped to her feet, torn between the departing Knick and the despondent man on the couch.

"Roskolniv—" she began, but he held up two fingers to shush her. He lifted the shot glass to his lips, the letter still curled into his palm.

"Don't try and save me," he said. "Just let me drown."

She stayed only for another half-a-minute and then followed Knick outside and found him halfway down the boardwalk.

"Knick, what the hell is going on?" she asked. He tossed the statue to her. "Going to find your Keeper friend?"

"Doubt I'd be able to see her if I did."

"Then what? Tell me what's going on—what is your connection to the Keepers?"

"About a year ago, I was attacked by her—by Shade. She said the prophecy wanted me dead. Then she claimed she saw a glyph on my head and wound up saving me. Muriel—the man in that letter to Rosk?—he was their Regent, their fucking boss. He betrayed them and abandoned the Order. Something to do with me dying, but no one knows why. I've spent the last six months running from his lackeys."

Hezara's ringed brows were pulled together.

"There's trouble…in the Keeper Order?" she asked.

"Big time."

"We have to find out what this means."

"Pff, fuck that. Too much trouble."

"What do you mean trouble? Weren't you so gung-ho before? You followed your Keeper girlfriend around, pine over her clothes, and now you suddenly don't care? We've found something important. We need to figure out what it is, help them if we can. The Keepers have their own set of laws, but they've only ever hurt the oppressors."

"Not sure it's related at all. It's two and a half decades in the past! Besides, this sounds a bit noble," Knick muttered, "and I'm not really the hero type." He scratched at his fuzzy chin and rubbed the beard thickening on his jaw.

"Suddenly you think this makes you a hero? Because you care? Even *dogs* care, so we'll say you're a dog," Hezara snapped. "Go back to your life if it really doesn't matter. No one will miss you. But this statue surfaces after twenty-five years and he's after it all this time? There's a connection between you and it, bet your ass on it."

Knick stomped out his cigarette.

"Well," he said around tendrils of smoke, "when you put it like that…"

She tucked the statue into her satchel and they made their way back to the road.

"I have a friend who deals in artifacts and he owes me a favor. I'll go to K-City and find out what he knows. What about you?"

"Back to Thebes. I need to check on a friend."

"Then I'll meet you in Thebes when I find something. If

you leave for any reason, send word through the Bloodsworn. Tell them you are Hezara's kadan and they will go for free. Do not abuse this power."

"Be careful," he muttered.

"Tch. You, too."

Otto stood in the alleyway staring across the turnabout to the wall where Isis had stood in his dream. It was a solid wall—not a hint of where a door once was or could even be placed. A solid wall. But he was going to have to go through it.

This is what it comes down to, Otto, he thought. *Whether this is a sick dream you'll wake up from or reality...either way, you're going through that wall.* He wrapped his thin arms around himself and stepped out of the alley. At the stones, he stopped and looked up. It went on for forever, speared straight up into the sky. What was this place anyway? Who did it belong to?

He sucked in a deep breath and lifted his hand. He remembered all the moves, the timing, the way. He was ready.

"I'm coming," he whispered. "Isis, I'm coming."

He touched the stone and an ancient symbol glowed brightly. The bricks shifted and suddenly there was a door. His jaw felt slack but he had no time to gawk. He sprinted across the entryway and pushed through another door. He counted a few seconds to make sure there were no footsteps on the stairs he'd glimpsed in his sprint and he was off again.

The tunnel looked exactly as it had in his dream and every turn he came upon opened up into another tunnel he recognized. He paused at the doors and corners to listen for footsteps, never tarrying more than a few seconds, until he came to a large intersection. He rolled across the way and threw his back against the smooth, dark gray stones.

Boots echoed on the cobbles and he nearly stopped breathing, already winded from his degenerated state. His bones were aching at all of his sudden movements, but he had to put it out of mind. He peered up out of the shadows and hoped the stranger wouldn't hear the pounding of his heart as the figure swept around to the right and took the tunnel he'd just come from.

Time to move again.

Otto shimmied down the pathway and turned, following

it to a flight of stairs. The sound of gunfire and swordplay somewhere far below him forced him lower to the ground. He cowered against the wooden rails and peered through the crossbeams into the cavern below. It was like a great arena beneath him where fighters gathered and trained.

As quietly as he could, Otto descended two flights and crouch-walked off the landing and into a dark corner. The rough stones scratched at his shirt and the pack on his back. He ran his fingers across the dark rock and saw black patches and white spots with clusters of mold all throughout. It was exactly the same as in his dream.

The person who passed by him descended the stairs even further and he wished he could explore the place more. It was impossible, and he had to keep moving. So, on he went into the series of lefts and rights that Isis had taken him through.

He knelt down at the alcove and pushed, but he was so weak it barely budged. The pat-pat of boots in the distance was drawing closer. He pushed harder, straining his muscles until he heard both a pop and a grind. The door swung open and his arm hung limp. He scurried inside, knowing the boots were almost upon him, and gently closed the door.

The footsteps traveled past him and faded down the hall. Otto sighed and held his right arm against his body, cursing that it had to break at such a vital time. There was also the darkness. It was so dark inside the wall. When Isis had been with him, her light had brightened every space. But this time, he was alone and in total black. He waited for his eyes to adjust, but they never did.

He slumped back against the wall and closed his eyes. Now that he was in such thorough darkness, would he be able to sleep?

The gallows looked as though they swayed in the torchlight; with the hanging chains swinging back and forth, the whole sector seems to be rocking from one side to the next. The old, wooden door that separated the rest of Asgard from the gallows swung open and Shade appeared in the doorway.

Rank stood up from behind his desk, 6'4" with black skin and dark eyes. He was intimidating as hell to the Kur and collective, but Shade wasn't the slightest bit unsettled.

"Rank," she began. "I want to see Nico."

"I'm sorry, Shade," he replied. "I can't let you do that."

"Why not?" She frowned.

"Eros's orders. You aren't to have any contact with the scholar." He genuinely seemed sympathetic, face contorted apologetically and his shoulders curving into a limp shrug. "Sorry," he said again.

She spun out of the room and stomped back up the staircase, the sounds of training drifting up from the arena, and made her way through the maze-like turns of the belly of Asgard. She passed the Abbey and went out into the main spiral, working her way up the stairs until she turned off onto a new floor.

The Office of the Baron was a few doors down and cracked. She heard voices inside. Eros, Daelas, Vox, a male stranger. She pushed open the door and stepped inside.

"Shade," Eros began, a bit surprised to see her. She opened her mouth, intending to confront him on his forbidding her to see Nico, when the stranger suddenly exclaimed,

"It's you!"

She frowned at him. She didn't know him; she'd never seen him before in her life. Because he was with Vox, she assumed he must be the delivered Dr. Basset, but had no idea why he was gaping at her.

"It's you," he continued, "the one I saw in the orb. You were fighting a man with spiky, blond hair."

"How did you—"

"Shade," Vox interrupted, voice slightly trembling with worry. "Has Dimitri returned?"

"No," she replied and shook her head. Vox frowned, eyes glossy with distress, and she looked to Eros for guidance. He lowered his head. "What's going on? Is Dimitri in trouble?" No answers. She turned to Basset. "How did you know about my fight with Donovan?" Nothing.

She whirled around and stormed out of the office.

"Wait!" Daelus called, running after her. "Shade, please, wait." He caught her by the shoulder, took hold of her arms, steadied her and forced his gaze into hers. "What are you about to do?"

"I'm going to get some answers. Clearly there are none here."

"Shade," he warned, concerned, but she wouldn't hear it.

"Don't," she said. "Run and tell Eros if you must, but I can't wait to be brought into the circle."

"Run and tell?" he echoed. "Shade, I'm on your side!" He lifted his hands and held her cheeks in his palms. "I just don't want to see you in danger. I'm worried about you. You're deep in this and Muriel is targeting you, too. Please, believe that."

"I don't trust you," she said bluntly and Daelus's hands fell limp at his sides. His crushed expression was more hurtful than Shade thought it would be. "You're too close to Eros. I can't trust you."

"Shade… Once, you were that close to him. Can't you believe in me now? Don't you know how I feel?" But she didn't; he knew she didn't.

"Sorry," she muttered and pushed past him. She paused midstride, the battle with Donovan fresh in her mind after Basset's declaration and, now that they were alone, a question she'd been itching to ask Daelus about entered her thought train. *Ask him about Daedalus*, is what Donovan had said. "Who was Daedalus?"

"What?" he gasped.

"Someone once mentioned a man called Daedalus…a name similar to yours." She glanced back at him. "Do you know who he was?"

His face was contorted in pain.

"Yes," he replied. "He was a man who died to protect an innocent girl from a prophecy the Regent greatly feared. He wanted her to live, and so he took her place; he brought the prophecy onto himself." He swallowed hard. "He was deeply in love with her."

Shade stared at him a moment longer and then walked away.

"And I still am," he whispered to himself, but she was too far to hear.

Shade stopped the first monk she saw.

"Where can I find Ralph Gobol?" she asked.

"Gobol? He's not here. He left Asgard yesterday, headed for Isahli in Ca'aramiriel. Something about information on a relic."

Shade's blood froze. She remembered Donovan's story of Ross Willem and how he was butchered for questioning the Regent. Somehow, the circumstances seemed the same. She moved to the nearest window and threw it open.

Sorry Eros, she thought. *Looks like you can't depend on me after all.* She wasn't going to let the only person left with answers take them to his grave. And with that, she leapt out of the window, exploding into the mysterious ball of black, and shot off into the dark sky.

The tunnels were dripping with water in every direction, echoing in the silence as thirty angels quietly shuffled through the dank corridors. Their lights bounced across the stones as they explored. Finally, the squad leader held up his fist and the group stopped. He knelt down and carefully swept the black film away from the wall. There, in a tiny alcove, a globe was perched in the shadows.

A tiny glint reflected off the face and he moved to the other side of the tunnel. He rubbed at the wall and the metal plate shimmered.

119-A3.

He lifted his hand to his ear and touched the scrambler. There was a loud screech his brain translated as a request for status. He grinned.

"We've found it, sir."

Part Five

"Destruction cometh; and they shall seek peace,
and there shall be none."

Ezekiel 7:25

The voice that cried out in the dark held the sound of a thousand souls weeping. Deep underground, her voice resonated up through the earth and the knights that knelt around the lake did so in reverence to her sorrowful song. And though she never sang again, the knights still bent their heads in reverence at the memory, truly believing her song had been for them, their song from this lady of the lake.

The last bells rang with his death, one chime for
one heartbeat, and the good king fell.
Take up the sword, he had, and cast away the ugly bane
of war for a bride to walk beside him.
She could not save her king or serve his undoer.
Curse the Oracle! Curse the powers! Curse the god!
And though lamenting sobs did cry out
in hideous anger and mourning,
not a clarity cooled their aching minds.
The Sight is poisoned by treachery and
there are no ears to hear a coward's words. Eternal.
The city waned and the veins ran dry.
That primordial power was locked away, hidden from the world,
waiting, waiting, waiting. The Bride, she wept, and remains,
waiting, waiting, waiting.
The weapon of the ages sleeping inside
the breast of a woman in love.
Madness take this homunculus when the time comes.
The curse first set in ancient blood covers a kingdom,
and no child born of scales will escape the final coming.
When the one appears bearing the marking of Tiamat,
all shadowy curtains shall fall from their perch to become
the One's dark cloak, dark sword, dark heart.
The coward flees!
Beware the scar on the wall, the bloody king,
for the walls of the body will crumble, the scales scattered.
The bloody brand marks the living,
beating heart of Ásgarðr, rupture.
Dissention! Distrust! Damnation! Beware the scar!
The end is near!
All the soft voices crying as one until their blood
becomes the tower's blood,
until the hearts of the beast and all the bodies within

stop as one.
A thousand souls.
Lament them, their innocence, snuffed in a single night.
Lament them...for they perish to once again open
the dusty doors of the dry city,
to waken the Bride. Together, spirit and mortal, at last.
The Bloody King, the Father, the Coward,
the Shadow, and the One
bear the Sight unto the Bride, and she will again
open her eyes.
All the scales to be hidden away.
The precipice of unknowing lies beyond, for even
the Sages could not see beyond procession's veil.
Lament, for the time is near...

The Office of the Baron was filled with silent tension as Vox threw a black bag over Dr. Basset's head and escorted him out. Eros shuffled his papers on his desk while Daelus stood quietly by, remembering Shade's words.

I don't trust you. It stung much worse than he was prepared for; his heart was being squeezed inside his chest and his lungs felt tighter, smaller, like less air was filling his body every time he took a breath. *Who is Daedalus?* It caused his heart to pound even harder against the constriction. He told her—he'd always wanted to tell her. Did she understand? Probably not. Still, he never wanted to keep anything from her. He hoped she would understand someday. He could wait. After all, he'd been waiting for over twenty-three years.

"Something wrong, Daelus?" Eros broke the silence, noticing the pained look on his friend's face. Daelus looked up and immediately forced his expression back to neutral.

"I'm fine," he replied.

"How long have you stood by my side?" he asked with a small smile. "You can't hide your pain from me. Tell me." He motioned for Daelus to sit; the Interim crossed to the chair but did not sit, only held the back of it.

"I'm worried, that's all. Things are getting worse."

"You're thinking of Shade," Eros assumed and Daelus hoped the heat in his cheeks didn't show up as red in his skin.

"She's part of it…"

"Daelus… Don't think I've forgotten what you did for her. Am I a fool now? You think I don't see your eyes when you look at her, hear your voice when you speak to her? It was you who suggested she run from the Keepers to save herself from the Regent's retribution. You spoke for her, defended her. I'm positive you told her Coltin's prophecy."

"Eros—"

"Do you think that I'm a fool, Daelus?" His voice was still gentle and he gave another small smile to ease his companion, but the Interim did not feel relieved.

"Love is forbidden—"

"Many things are forbidden, but it does not stop them from happening. As sure as the Regent betrayed us, the Keepers have been dabbling in the forbidden since the dawn of the Order. We're human, Daelus. We cannot help it." His eyes momentarily glazed over with the pain of a deep memory. "Shade was born from the forbidden."

"Sir?"

"It's nothing." He cleared his throat. "Times are dark, Daelus. Will we recover from this and return to the Order we always were? I'm not positive we will. You best make sure you have no regrets."

"Are you telling me…that I should—"

"I'm telling you not to have any regrets," Eros said simply. "Take that however you wish. So long as you don't forget your purpose and you don't forget your duty." Eros motioned a member of the Kur to him. "Summon Shade."

Daelus watched the guard leave and glanced at Eros.

"Shade?" he asked warily.

"The relic taken into MAAR custody was a sight stone and Dr. Basset saw Donovan's attack on Shade through the stone. That means the brother is somewhere in our tunnels. I don't see how MAAR could know the tunnels link with Asgard, but it wouldn't do to have them come any closer to us than that. Shade will need to take us to 119-A3 so we can take appropriate measures."

Daelus shrunk back to the side of the room, wondering how Eros would respond when he discovered Shade was gone.

He wouldn't be the one to tell him—he'd quietly promised Shade that much. He had hoped her secret would be kept longer.

However, Eros's other words had excited him. The potential caused his stomach to knot and flutter even though he was positive there was no room in her heart for him. Hope. Hope affected him with feelings he'd only experienced when looking at her, thinking of her.

Rexis suddenly poked his head in. Another one Daelus was jealous of. Rexis was her best friend; he could speak to her freely, touch her as he pleased, and simply be in her presence for no rhyme or reason. Daelus closed his eyes and lowered his head. It felt defeating.

"Come with Shade?" Eros asked.

"No. Come to ask if you've seen her." Rexis said and Eros frowned. "Why? Were you looking for her, too?"

"What do you mean?"

"I haven't seen her anywhere. She's not in Asgard. I was wondering if you sent her out—" But Rexis stopped short with the sudden scowl that crossed the Baron's face. His glare caused him to flinch backward.

"What do you mean she's not in Asgard? I forbade her from leaving these walls!"

"I…don't…" he mumbled, at a loss for words.

"Find someone who may know where she's gone! I want everyone who saw her last in my office in twenty minutes!" he boomed. Rexis quietly slipped out and shut the door behind him. Eros caught a glimpse of Daelus's guilty face. "Do you know anything about this?"

"No, sir," he replied, but Eros was positive that his most trusted man had lied to him; he was positive, because Daelus had never lied to him before, and this time the words were heavy with shame.

He couldn't fault the man. He'd been in his place many times before. At least he could tell that Daelus felt guilty; Eros' lies had come as easy and remorseless as the truth.

A deep cry from down the hallway caused Eros and Daelus to frown and step out of the office. Several monks and Kur were gathered to the High Counselor, who was gaping at the wall and shaking terribly.

"High Counselor," the Baron exclaimed. "What's wrong?"

The old man was pointing now, trembling violently, with his vocal chords locked in a gaping loop.

"The wall," he cried. "The wall!"

Everyone examined the spot. The sacrificial glyph had been burned into the wall by Shade's shadows when she'd accused Eros of lying to her. The Baron ran his fingers over it, painfully remembering the moment.

"Shade did it in a moment of anger," he explained, turning to face the High Counselor. The news only upset him all the more.

"No," he muttered, knees buckling under him. "I knew it. I knew it! I didn't want it to be..."

"High Counselor!" Daelus exclaimed as the elder collapsed into the arms supporting him.

"I have made a terrible mistake," he groaned.

The Baron looked up at the supporters. "Take him to rest."

They nodded and carefully eased the old man to his feet. Daelus and Eros returned to the office, and the haunting whisper of the High Counselor's repeated mutterings of, "A mistake...terrible mistake...it's too late..." set Daelus on edge.

The barge docked in Thebes early that morning. A single day was all the trip from Moscow to the capitol took. Knick Coltin stretched, nodded to the deckhands as he moved to the ramp, and sauntered onto the dock. Luckily, the port was on the edge of the heart of the city and Black Tuesday's guild hall was less than a mile from the docks.

He walked the way there, filled with the sights, sounds, and smells of the familiar city. It had been—what?—nearly a year since he'd been in Thebes. He wondered if Solo and Slot were still here; he remembered them saying they were heading back. He wondered if Jilk had recovered or... Well, he wondered.

When the creep of grime and the sickly sweet vapor of sugar beets encroached on his nostrils, he knew he was close. Though the air smelled funny and gave his stomach a less-than-thrilling whirl, he knew there was a stand on the corner selling delicious meat buns that would cure his ripe belly. Jilk loved those meat buns.

"Damn it," Knick cursed. He didn't want to admit he was scared, or that his churning stomach wasn't entirely due to a bad smell. He rubbed his jaw and the untamed mess of fur on his face scratched his palm. "I need to shave."

He rounded the corner and pushed his fingers back into his greasy hair, anticipating meat buns and a shower. The steps to the guild hall came into view and he paused a moment, waiting, expecting to see a metal-head scowling but afraid there'd be a wooden box instead.

His heart lightened a little bit.

From far off, Slot eyed him and her jaw dropped. She swatted her brother with the back of her hand, a smile creeping into her lips. Solo turned a frown on her and then followed her outstretched arm and pointing finger to where Knick was standing, frozen to the spot, hands in pockets. Solo grinned and waved with his whole upper body—a long sway from side to side with his tall torso and lanky arms. Slot messily transferred her lunch to Solo's lap as she jumped up and began sprinting in his direction.

Knick tried to hide his grin and not give away how happy he was; he had to keep his cool reputation alive, so he just sauntered toward her. She jumped into him and threw her arms around his neck. He kept his hands in his pockets but affectionately pressed the side of his head to hers.

"Knick!" she screamed. "Shit, shit, shit! You're in one piece! I expected you to be missing an arm, at least." She dropped down to her feet and he took in the different assortment of band aids on her nose and cheeks.

"You're talking to me?" he asked. "What about you? What's with all this all the time?" He motioned to her face. "How is it you aren't missing any body parts?"

"Jilk says I am," she replied. "He says I'm missin' two parts: female and brain. I told him he could shove it."

"Jilk? Is he…?" But Knick couldn't ask the question, feeling the lump in his throat preventing him. Her suddenly sad expression dashed his hope.

"Not yet," she replied quietly. "But I haven't lost faith yet, so you don't either, kay?"

He nodded once and studied the Street Gun in front of him. She talked like a boy, dressed in layers and rags, was covered head-to-toe in dirt, always had some type of wound on her that she treated like a paper cut—big or small, and her chin-length hair was a permanent mess. Still, Knick had to disagree with Jilk. Slot's warm heart was definitely female. Plus, she had the longest eyelashes he'd ever seen, making her irresistibly cute in the urchin kind of way. Diamond in the rough, so to speak. Solo knew it, too, and Knick figured that was why he'd kept his sister dressed up in muck: to keep the boys away. It worked.

Slot tugged on his leather jacket, at the red racing stripe.

"C'mon, Bix just put out a fresh batch of meat buns so they're nice and hot—just like you like 'em," she said, yanking him along. They met her brother near the stand. Knick, Solo, and Bix all exchanged manly nods as greetings and Knick ordered up half-a-dozen buns.

"Where is he?" Knick asked.

"Cogclock," Solo replied. Knick recalled the strangely assembled building—giant cogs, wheels, and bolts hollowed out and welded together to form a brass sanatorium. "What?" he asked in response to Knick's cringe. "It's sanitary, they swear by it."

The walk over to Cogclock Hospital was a short one and Knick wasn't entirely sure he wanted to go in. They stood outside the back door, chomping quietly on their food. These moments were what Knick remembered most about being a cogwheeler; standing around with the siblings and Jilk, silent, with the sounds of the city in the background. He ate all but two buns, saving them for his metal-faced friend. The reverse blast on the punk was stuck in his memory banks.

"Shit," he muttered. Slot slumped over and rested her head on his bicep, a Heavy's way of comforting a tormented soul.

The sound of footsteps didn't mean much, in spite of the low traffic around the back of Cogclock, until they stopped nearby. The cogwheelers looked up and Knick's jaw tightened. He counted no less than ten ex-Keeper agents spread out in front of him, blocking the exits and trapping them against the brick. They were wearing white layers as though they might still manage to pin the murder on the angels.

"Knick Coltin?" one of them said.

Slot gritted her teeth, staring straight ahead. Knick felt her muscles tense and knew she was prepping herself for a fight. He wanted to warn her, but he was afraid any sudden movements would cause the agents to react. Even a Heavy didn't stand much chance against ten Keepers, right?

"You followed me all the way here? Persistent. Mind if I smoke?" Knick reached into his jacket pocket after the man nodded his approval and lit up a smoke. He passed it to Solo and then lit one for himself. Slot didn't smoke when she fought, her brother didn't allow it; something about burning her own eyes out on accident.

"You're a hard man to find," the ex-Keeper admitted.

"Harder to kill, apparently," he replied around the butt of his rette.

"Apparently," the ex-Keeper agreed. "We intend to rectify that today. You've kept this game up long enough and we're tired of playing. It's time for the Priori to end this."

"Priori? Is that what Muriel calls his traitors?"

"His elite." The ex-Keeper grinned.

"Well," Knick puffed his rette, "what are you waiting for?"

"Muriel sends his regards," the Prior said, drawing his weapon.

A loud bang cut the silence and the Prior stumbled backward, gaping. His stomach and chest were stippled with shrapnel, blood seeping through twisted meat and white cloth. The ex-Keeper stared at his mangled torso and then looked up. There was the cranking of a shotgun being cocked then BANG. A second blast knocked him to the ground and he pooled blood, eyes empty.

Jilk was standing up on the emergency dock, skin pale and sweaty, body in a crouch to support his still-healing gut, and a thin drape the color of washed out cobalt clung to his skinny form. The black shotgun was cradled in his arms, cocked and ready for another round.

Knick felt the corner of his mouth twitch up in a grin. *Damn, you look cool right now, you son of a bitch,* he thought.

"Slot," Jilk said, voice raspy but strong. "Show these fucks how *you* play."

She stepped forward and pushed up her sleeves then cracked her knuckles. The ex-Keepers started to reach for their weapons, but Jilk angled the shotgun up.

"Uh uhn," he growled. The ex-Keepers froze, their meaty companion in a heap on the ground in their peripherals. They backed off, stuck in the crouched shuffle, prepared to be attacked.

The brass knuckles that Slot lifted out of her coat pocket and slipped on her fingers were studded with sharp spikes.

"That's right," she mused quietly. "Last time, you didn't get properly introduced." She flicked the messy hair from her eyes and clenched her hands into fists.

"Hey!" Knick hollered and the ex-Keepers glanced at him nervously. "Incredibly brave...or enormously stupid? You be the judge." He grinned and the agents looked back at Slot. The expression that passed over their faces all said the same thing: wait, she's taking on all of us...alone?

Slot dashed forward so quickly, the agents barely knew what had hit them until her right fist connected with one of their jaws and a loud crack sounded. She ducked and spun under the falling body, using it as a dividing shield between two halves of her assailants. Her left fist buried into another's gut then hooked his jaw. She reared back her arm and shattered his breastplate when she made contact, throwing him into two of his buddies.

Knick and Jilk exchanged smirks. Solo just watched his sister in action—always worried and always amazed. He and Knick were Gunnies; they stayed back, they remained tactical, and they knew when to pick a damn fight and when to avoid one. Jilk was a Cogger—the brains of the unit, versatile, strategic. Somehow, the girl of their group—and the tiniest of them all—was brute force at its finest.

As the ex-Keepers shuffled and bobbed to dodge her deadly fists, they lost their edge focusing on her spiked knuckles. Having taken out two men in less than a minute, they were a little nervous to move within arm's reach. Plus, Jilk's shotgun was forever trained on them should they make any sudden and unfair movements.

They attempted to position her back to Jilk so that they could strike out without fear of getting blasted, but that only made her laugh.

"Jilk!" she exclaimed. "D'you see?"

"I saw," he replied. "Hey, you think I'm here to protect her, huh?" He shook his head. "No, it's the other way around."

The skirmish that followed included kicks, punches, cracked, snapped, and shattered bones, and a few flying chairs from the waiting patio. With bloody knuckles and a heap of bodies under her boot, Slot glanced over her shoulder at her brother and smiled. She gave him thumbs up.

Solo grinned and thumbs-up'd right back at her.

Angel agent 22-76-43 stood at the front of his attack force, all scattered into expert hiding behind him. The mechanical vambrace clamped to his wrist forearm was beaming light out of the projector eye. The schematic shown was of the tower not one-hundred feet in front of them, sealed protectively from head to toe with magic or scientific intelligence—he wasn't sure which—so that they couldn't get an appropriate read inside.

"Captain," 67-12-34 said, approaching from enemy objective. He handed over another chip. "Here's the last scan of the tower."

22-76-43 yanked the old chip out and dropped it on the ground with the rest of the discards, and then plugged the new one in. The light beam flickered and then brought up the latest schematic.

"Useless," he cursed quietly. "Let's go in and drop a flash. We'll get that scan. Go ahead and drop the slugs in with the flash; they won't interfere."

"Sir," 67-12-34 said, nodding once before moving off to the rest of his unit.

The captain glanced down at the silver wing tattoo on the back of his right hand before lowering his arm back to his side. The silver lenses covered his eyes and his bald head was smooth when he ran his hand over it.

"It's over for you," he growled. "Never again will you interfere in Heaven's holy business."

The tact teams moved into position under his orders and lined up in the alleys outside of the tower. Four men brought cases up and placed sonic charges two feet apart in a large square on the wall. They backed up and hit the detonation; the whining whir as the charges connected and built momentum grew louder with every second.

The whole street trembled with the explosion. The base of the tower burst forth, wall chunks crushing two angels in the blast, and a cloud of dust was thrown up into the air. A large opening was visible through the cloud and two angels used it to usher the flasher into what they thought looked like the entry to a giant library.

The flasher was merely a metal rod on a tripod. After thirty seconds, red lasers flashed out of it, recording the measurements of the internal structure; it mapped blueprints nearly instantly and downloaded them into nearby comm-units.

Captain 22-76-43 grinned when the schematics finally showed up in his projector beam. He sealed the mechanism and touched the scrambler in his ear.

"Go."

When Asgard rocked as though there had been an earthquake directly under their feet, Eros jumped up from his chair and braced himself with his desk. Daelus stumbled over to join him, both men eyeing each other with a sudden feeling of dread.

"What the hell was that?" Eros asked, taking the words right out of his friend's mouth.

Below them, monks and scholars were coughing and hacking from the inhalation of dust, slowly meandering to its source. Had the wall really just exploded? But why? It wasn't in the collective's nature to be afraid of the outside world. The Keeper Order had stood proudly throughout history and had never been in danger from the creatures outside their walls.

A tiny disc suddenly cut through the debris cloud and landed on the floor near the metal rod on a tripod. Murmurs of wonder and confusion made its rounds among those gathered. Suddenly, it glowed with the shimmer of polyspace and large, black shapes began pouring out. Like thick noodles, these shapes bounced out, flying toward the collected men.

The slugs latched onto their legs, their arms, torsos, necks, faces and clamped tight with tiny claws. A burning sensation sizzled the skin under the black leach and sent the murmurs of curiosity into terrified screams of panic and pain.

The chaos that erupted spilled onto the upper levels, the marked collective swaggering and shrieking in terror and confusion. Their brethren ran to them to help, stricken with horror when they saw the black slugs viciously attached to their friends. They tried to help pry them off, but more slugs were squiggling up the stairs and lashing out at the unmarked monks.

A flood of angels poured into the building, armed with rifles loaded with assassination. Flashes from muzzles lit up the debris cloud as one scream after another was snuffed out, spreading the chaos further and further up the tower.

Captain 22-76-43 stepped into the Keeper tower, silver lenses focused on the holo-display of his vambrace. The bodies with slugs attached showed up on the readout, and disappeared when his men took them out.

Ralph Gobol realized his grave mistake about thirty seconds after he'd arrived at the promised meeting point. Isahli was quiet—a vast and empty necropolis of aviation. Mammoth metal wings spanned out across the five-mile stretch, bound and melded together to form a sort of unlevel plain. Abandoned cabins once doubled as houses and businesses were scattered among the wings and tails, some level with and some half-sunk into the metallic mesh.

Gobol pushed his hand through his short, course hair. The excitement he'd felt began to wane as his stomach began to twist into an anxious knot. His mouth dipped in apprehension and his brown eyes drooped with his fear. The bleak sky was blank and gray.

The particular spot chosen had taken Gobol nearly an hour to reach, and the vacant whistle of wind on the gray steel felt forlorn. He took a moment to scan the aviation graveyard and took in the sights of the recycled planes—some wings twelve meters thick, some rusted, some with faded paint in red, white, green, blue, or purple. The degenerated state of the abandoned sky-city—for that was what it was called, being constructed from sky machines—was the warning bell that told him he had made a grave mistake.

While he took a second to decide whether he wanted to fight for his life or was resigned to die, the Priori sprung their trap. A number of Muriel's elite that Gobol did not have the calm to count sprang up from the cracks in the aeroscape and moved toward him. It was about that time that he decided he wanted to live.

"Don't run, Gobol! Don't make this harder on yourself," one of them shouted at his back as he turned and furiously ran. He didn't recognize the voice and it made him realize just how sheltered the collective were—buried in their books and scrolls, researching day and night, happy by any scholar's standards, and yet he had no idea who this former member of his organization was.

Gobol hoisted himself over the top of a wing and slid down the slope of another. He scrambled to his feet and ran, clanking every step of the way as the metal echoed his heavy and frantic steps. He couldn't hear the Priori behind him but he could feel them closing in.

"Don't stop," he urged his body. The rising sensation of the subconscious need for survival was blurring his vision, gripping his heart, pumping his blood. It was true, then, that even the gentlest of creatures would fight from the crowded corner.

A Prior cut in front of him and Gobol lashed out, but his fist was dodged and the momentum sent Gobol tripping flat on his face. He was kicked into a roll and tumbled down another slope. He stopped near a crevice between wings and got to his feet as the Priori surrounded him.

"Why?" he begged to know, always needing to know.

"You're one of the last, Gobol," one of them responded. "Soon, there will be none left—none who know what the Regent knows."

"You can't mean...but the Keepers—"

"Won't be a problem anymore," the Prior finished, and then they closed in. Gobol winced, fists clenched and muscles strained. This couldn't be the end, could it?

"Gobol, get down!" a woman screamed from above. This voice. He knew this voice. Shade! he thought. All the collective knew the voices of the Interim—their saviors, protectors, heroes! He dropped to the ground and covered his head as she landed in a black and smoky blur, rocking the plane's wing with a creak and groan.

Gobol lifted his head to see the smoke clear around her form. Shade was knelt over a Prior, sword buried deep in his skull, and a terrifyingly beautiful scowl was set in her face. He felt the tremor of hope vibrate through his body when the Priori took a cautious step back.

"You can't stop this, Shade. Now we'll kill you and the monk!"

"Tsh," she muttered, yanking her bloody sword free from the skull at her feet as she stood. "I've killed enough of you to know I can."

Another Prior gritted his teeth and Gobol sensed the same fear in him at the sight of Shade that he had felt at the sight of his assassins.

"Stop us or stop the Priori sent after your beloved Coltin?" he asked. "As we speak, his life is at stake."

She grinned darkly. "Then, many of your people will die today, Grul. Gobol," she glanced back at him, "get *down*."

Her movements came in flashes, black hair flowing around her movements like silky shadows. The Priori scattered out of her reach and Gobol crawled across the wing to the crevice. He lowered himself into the darkness, feet kicking for a foothold, but lost his grip and fell. He landed hard on the ground, twisting his ankle when he did, but was able to stand well enough.

The network beneath the plain above was a twisted and dark labyrinth of sharp metal and trick mirrors. A thick web of beams twisted between the sunken cabins and wrecked winglets, stabilizers, rudders, and engines. The light that filtered in from above barely illuminated the belly of the aeronautic necropolis. Gobol hoped to remain in that single spot until the fighting was over, but two Priori dropped down into the crevice after him.

Gobol nearly tripped when he ran forward and hopped up onto a winglet. He didn't even feel his ankle screaming at him as he navigated the dark jungle gym. This time, he could hear the Priori coming after him, lending a warped sense of comfort to his palpitating heart.

Gobol lost his footing against a rough tear on his path and tumbled down a dislodged rudder like he was riding a slide. He hit the bottom hard, smashing his back against the blades of an engine. He cried out and then clamped his hand over his mouth, biting back the pain. He could hear them coming, trying to find the best way down the rudder.

He scrambled through the inlet and squeezed through two fan blades where one was missing. The wire mesh was bent and warped from the wreck and it took only a few kicks to knock it loose. He crawled around it, ignoring the tears to his clothes and scrapes to his skin where the broken metal caught him. He had to crawl under the compressor, barely fitting; his fingers clawed at the base, dragging his bunchy robes through.

Once on his knees, he took off the thick over-layer and pushed forward.

The fuel nozzle was dripping—who knew how long it had been—and a puddle of something shiny and black had pooled there. He used his discarded robe to cover it and pass under the combustion chamber to another crawlspace. The back of the engine had blown out and he was able to drop down to safety without too much of a struggle.

Without stopping to see if he was being followed, Gobol scrambled through the labyrinth in search of another way up. Metal beams mashed together made a decent ladder and he felt his way up, plunged into a column of blackness. His sweaty fingers curled around the edge of a beam and he hoisted himself up, cutting his knees on the sharp edge. He shuffled down the curve of the beam to a support column, climbed the slot holes, and stretched onto his tippy-toes to reach the next self-declared rung on his makeshift ladder.

As Gobol pulled himself up, he came face to face with one of the Priori.

"Ah!" he screamed, falling backward into the darkness. His spine hit a jutted wingtip and he was able to reach out and grab it before falling further. He climbed up as the Prior jumped after him and ran along the span.

The wing groaned under their banging. By the time Gobol neared the other side of the wing, it began tilting down. He slid and jumped, grabbing onto a horizontal stabilizer. The elevator drooped under his weight. The Prior leapt out at him but Gobol's frantic kicking swung the stabilizer free, swinging him away from his assailant.

The Prior hit the other side of the newly created abyss, banging against the side of a sunken cabin. He dropped five feet and was speared through the chest by a rusted spike of broken metal. Gobol felt the bile rising in his stomach at the juicy squish the body made when it connected with the aeronautic dagger. He forced it down, still kicking in the air, and managed to swing the elevator over the side of the over-turned cabin. He rolled, barely managing to catch himself on a shattered window before he went over the edge.

Gobol pulled himself up and ran along the side of the fuselage toward the cockpit where light was filtering in from another crevice in the sea above. The tut and clip of footsteps climbing after him caused his feet to move faster toward his escape. He reached up and hoisted himself onto the next level but the Prior was right behind him. He stumbled onto a wing but was tripped by his pursuer, falling hard onto the aileron. It whined under his weight and pushed down like it would fall but another wing was crunched beneath it, preventing him from rolling off. He kicked away from the Prior, still on his back, but couldn't escape the knife that plunged into his gut.

He cried out and kicked again. The aileron released when he pushed himself off and the Prior was thrown back. Gobol got to his feet and ran for the crevice. He glanced back and noticed his assassin race across the wing. He sunk into the flap but managed to jump out before the flap rusted loose and crashed through a gap in the support wreckage.

Gobol hopped onto a rung and climbed. Shade's blade slipped into the crevice next to him and plunged into the shoulder of the Prior directly behind him. She pulled out and struck again, cutting his throat open. Gobol looked away as the blood splattered out and the body fell away. Her pale hand reached out and helped him up and into the light.

That's when he felt the pain in his stomach and saw his own blood on his hands.

When the wall had exploded, Eros immediately knew something was wrong.

"Tanahk, get the Kur downstairs immediately!" the Baron exclaimed to his Captain. "Form a barrier between the intruders and the tower! Have Delia and Kallo assemble a team to get the Enoch out immediately! Send Bashyl for the Oracle!"

"Sir!" Tanahk shouted with a salute, swishing quickly from the office.

The rumble that followed the explosion could only mean one thing: invasion.

"It looks as though we're too late," he said quietly. "This was the intention all along, don't you think so?"

"Sir," Daelus agreed somberly.

"Daelus, gather the Champions," he muttered. "Tell Vox to get Dr. Basset out of here. We need to get the collective to safety." Eros reached for his hilt and lightly touched the pommel. It had been a long time since he'd had to draw the

Sword of Scars.

"Yes, sir," he replied, crossing to the door.

"Daelus—"

"Sir?"

"If Shade comes back…"

"I will," he promised, then sprinted down the hall.

He took the turns at top speed, swiftly dodging monks and scholars coming out of their rooms in confusion. Kur swept around him with orders from their leaders passed down from Tanahk. When he reached the spiral—the great staircase—the swell of screams practically hit him in the face.

"Daelus!" Sonia cried from above him. He looked up and saw many Champions gathered. Vox came up from another hallway, Basset in her grip.

"Sonia, take Bartimaeus and Rexis below. Eros is headed down with the Kur. We're under attack. Angels—they're inside. Balthazar, hold this floor. Get the collective off the spiral and out of the halls."

They nodded so he knew they understood. Sonia and Rexis leapt over the railing, bursting into a ball of black as they dropped. Bartimaeus gave Daelus a concerned glance and then followed their lead. Balthazar's fists clenched and he turned, barking orders to the collective gathering around him.

"Get back to your rooms!" he boomed. "Until you are told otherwise, Asgard is not safe. Get back!"

Daelus turned to Vox.

"Get him out of here," he told her. She gave a curt nod and pulled Basset down the stairs after Eros. She got off at a different floor than he did, tugging the confused doctor behind her.

"What's going on?" he cried, frantic and unnerved. "What are those screams? Why are they screaming?"

"Shut up!"

"Where are my girls?" he screamed. "You said they were brought here! Where is my family! Where the *fuck* are my daughters!" He stumbled. "What's going on?"

Vox slammed him into the wall and ripped the mask off of his face.

"We're under attack," she hissed, eyes flaring. "Please, calm down. You're family never arrived. Now it's up to us. We have to go *now. Quietly.*"

He nodded, brow pulled tight in a frown. Vox was moving again and he was stumbling after her, down halls like a maze; he was lost in the chaos, in the static scenery, and couldn't get the screams out of his head. He saw her hand on her sword and wondered if there were really enemies ahead of them.

He glanced back. Could they be behind them as well? The hallway was empty. His eyes went back to Vox, to her hand. It was then that he noticed her fingers were trembling, knuckles were white.

Basset swallowed hard and wondered where his family was and if he would ever see them again. *What is this nightmare?* he thought. *What have I gotten into? Where is my family?*

"Do you want to stay behind and fight?" he blurted. "You can, just find my family! Help me find them! Don't run away!"

She whirled around and every bit of her seemed to flare like a fire stoked with a sudden wind.

"Don't you think I want to?" she exclaimed. "But I was told to get you out of here, and so I will! Now *move!*"

Basset reluctantly nodded that he understood and they were on the move again.

In the lower levels, Kur were filtering around panicked scholars, but the angels did not give them the opportunity to form a barricade. The slugs lashed out at every life form and the soldiers' ranks were dissolving before they could form.

The Baron's plan to blockade the fourth floor was pushed back all the way to the sixth. Bartimaeus had stepped forward with his sword held vertical and the free hand braced against the flat of the blade. The bells on his wrist jingled and a bright glow emanated from the fuller, spreading out in smoky ringlets of yellow light.

The sun-like shield that exploded forth blocked the stair well and repelled the angels back onto the spiral and down into the lower levels. The Sword of Suns pulsed and vibrated with the energy and even the Kur behind the Sovereign had to back away and lower their heads.

Eros came up and put a comforting and confirming hand on Bartimaeus's shoulder. He then turned to face his men while the Champion concentrated on holding the shield. Rexis and Sonia stood nearby, swords drawn.

"We hold this position," Eros commanded, and his mere presence inspired courage. When he drew his sword, the crowd shuddered backward. "Let me through," he said quietly to Bartimaeus.

The older man nodded and released the bright shield. The angels that came close were cautious, guns raised. Eros made a sweeping motion in front of him, and the angels were hit with an invisible blast. Long wounds opened up all over their bodies and blood sprayed the walls. They collapsed in heaps and more angels took their place. They, too, spurted blood and fell.

What no one else knew was that beneath the Baron's clothes, tiny wounds also opened and blood trickled out, leaving temporary but no less painful scars in his own flesh.

Basset followed Vox down a multitude of corridors and into a smaller stairwell. It was tight and packed with webs, as though never used. They only descended a few flights when another explosion rocked the tower. A debris cloud rocketed up through the narrow space and his eyes, nose, and mouth were filled with the chalky and dusty taste of stone. Through the haze, he saw a bright streak of fire and then felt the heat when it blasted down into the well.

The flames sucked up the cloud like a vacuum and more screaming filled his ears.

"Try me!" Vox screamed and her challenge echoed off the walls. She looked as vicious as some eternally blazing fire from the deepest circle of the underworld.

Across the way, another explosion rocked the tower. The angels were finding new ways to ascend past the Baron's blockade.

Vox cursed under her breath, pausing only a second in her desire to return and help her friends—her family. She cursed again and yanked Basset after her, quickly descending the spiral staircase still partially in flames. They ducked between columns of heat and patches of material they couldn't make out still on fire.

Eventually, they went so deep, Basset was sure they'd gone underground. The narrow tunnels were overrun with webs and he didn't want to think about what would be crawling on him after they'd gone through. Vox, apparently, had thought it through; the entire corridor was flushed with a rush of fire and then they were sprinting down the passageway.

"Almost there," she promised. "Almost there."

A small manhole cover came into view. Vox slid to a stop, hoisted it off as though it were weightless, and pointed down.

"In," she commanded. Basset looked once at the black hole and once at Vox. Her blazing eyes were not to be crossed. He jumped into the darkness and the Sovereign of the Sword of Flames went in after him.

After her physical display, Jilk had patted Slot on the head and eyed the band-aids on her nose and cheeks.

"What happened to you, anyway?" he had muttered. "All the fights you get into, and you're the one who hurts you the most. That's some backwards shit, Slot."

The Heavy then latched onto Jilk in hug format and had not let go since, through checking him out of the hospital, walking across Thebes, and getting their boss some food. Now, they were sitting on the grand steps leading into the guildhall under some shade far away from the crowd.

Jilk was leaning back against a column, dressed in hospital pants with a long overcoat. He was shirtless with white gauze wrapped thick and tight over his abdomen. The first thing he'd done after checking out was put some of his piercings back in. A couple earrings, an eyebrow ring; it was surprising he rejected the full entourage.

He was still pale and sweaty, aside from the blush in his cheeks caused by the Heavy clinging onto him. His face was turned away from hers, mouth hardened as he pretended the affection didn't faze him, but he couldn't stop his cheeks from flushing. Her arms were wrapped around him and her head was nuzzled into his chest. His arm slumped over her back.

Knick glanced over at Solo, stretched back on his palms between the two columns they'd claimed. He was eyeing Jilk and his sister with a bit of a glare. Knick grinned and tilted his head back, resting it on the stonework.

They were all smoking, with the exception of Slot, who was forbidden to smoke as long as she was clinging to her boss.

"What did I miss?" Jilk wanted to know. "I remember what put me down. Still don't know what the fuck it was all about."

"Rogue harpers," Knick replied, exhaling smoke.

"No shit?"

"We didn't believe it either, at first," Solo announced. Eyes went back to Knick for his explanation.

"Remember that job back in Britz?" he asked. Jilk frowned a moment, thinking back. "With Reemer—out by the Ox. We were dropping off sydolis b. waiting for Reinhardt to interfere?"

"Right, right!" he exclaimed. "Shitty ass job."

"Right. Well, that's when I met her."

"Who?"

"5'8'', pale skin with long, black hair and violet eyes."

"Gothic—right, I remember."

"Right. She's a Keeper, Jilk. She was trying to kill me and found out that I was ex-angel and cogwheeler. Then, she claims she saw a glyph on my forehead."

"Glyph?"

"It's what their people have—magic symbols they can only see that they use to identify each other. Anyway, she believes I'm a Keeper and went back to her people to tell them that." Knick readjusted his position and went on. "I'm like, fuck, I have no idea what's going on. And then I get attacked by these angel-looking fucks and she just shows up out of nowhere to help me.

"Turns out, the Regent—their boss—wanted me dead for reasons we don't know and those angel-lookalikes were his loyalists sent to do her job. When they got back to their HQ, the Regent had run and the Order was in chaos."

"Keepers in chaos?" Jilk confirmed, jaw slack in disbelief.

"That's not the half of it," Slot mumbled and Jilk blushed again, remembering she was still clinging tightly.

"When you thought I was flaking, I was really running my ass off from these assassins. After you got hurt in Buschers, she showed up and chased them off. She was poisoned by one of her own and nearly died. After that, I said I'd go with her back to Keeper HQ to put this shit to bed."

"Whoa, whoa, wait a minute. You actually went to the

Keeper hideout?"

Knick nodded. "Yeah."

"No shit…" Jilk muttered, taken aback. He blew gray smoke out of his nose.

"Got no answers. Boss kicked me out. Traveled with a Bloodsworn to Moscow. Met a guy by the name of Roskolniv." Knick inhaled and the end of his rette crackled as it lit up. "Long story short, his dead girlfriend was killed by someone called Hermes, who was an associate of the ex-Regent. Hezara's looking up stuff on this Hermes guy somewhere and I'm lost in limbo."

"That's fucked up. How the hell are you involved again?"

"When Shade came to kill me, she said it was because my prophecy said I would bring a great advantage to the cogs. When she found out I was fallen, she thought that was it. But…nah, something's not right."

They all reflected on that idea while they finished their smokes. The hum of people in the distance waned as the lunch hour came to a close. Finally, Jilk spoke up.

"What are you going to do about all this, Coltin?"

Knick's eyebrows perked, index finger lazily picking at a snag in his thumb nail. When Jilk turned his gaze on him, he sighed out all the hot air building up inside him. He took one last drag on his rette and tossed it down the steps.

"I—"

"Knick…" a woman's voice whispered. His face contorted. "Knick…Knick Coltin."

"Knick?" Jilk asked. "What's that face you're making?"

"What the—" he started, confused, looking around, but her voice came again.

"Knick Coltin, listen to me."

"I said what are you going to do?" Jilk continued, but Knick was still looking for the source of the voice—the voice only he could here, the voice that had no body.

"Knick Coltin, you must hurry. Shade is in trouble. Asgard will fall," the voice said.

"What do you mean?" he asked.

"I mean you need a plan. You can't just sit around down here and wait, can you?" Jilk said.

"She needs you," she whispered. "Asgard will fall…"

Knick waited, but the presence felt gone as though the

spirit had entered his mind and left; the voice did not speak again. He shook his head, just to be sure, and then zeroed in on Jilk.

"You're right," he said. "I need to go." And he got up. He hurried down the steps and across the forum.

"Go?" Solo repeated as he, his sister, and his boss scrambled up and ran to catch up.

"Go where? Why?" Slot asked, snatching Knick back by the sleeve of his jacket.

"You're right," Knick said again. "This makes no fucking sense. I just...have a feeling she's in trouble. You know, with all this shit going down, I never should've left. It's like...the world is falling apart behind the scenes. I can't explain it. Look around you—shit seems normal. But something's...fucking crumbling and...and I need to go."

Knick tried to move again but Jilk pulled him back this time.

"Where are you going?"

"Didn't you hear me? Back to Asgard—back to the Keepers, I mean."

"Back to Shade."

"Yeah!"

"Do you even know where you're going?"

"Tonatti Haan. What do you care?"

"What, you taking the scenic route or something?" Jilk asked. Knick's brows creased.

"What?"

"Yeah. Probably you didn't know. It's kind of a Cogger secret. There's an express shaft from here to Gomorra—right between Tonatti and Rashrima Haan. You can be in Tonatti by midnight."

Knick hung his head in his hands for a moment, silently thanking the stars. He patted Jilk's shoulders.

"Thank you, man. Thank you," he muttered. "I appreciate it. Thank you."

"Sure. One hour." He pointed to the grand stairs. "Steps. One hour."

"I need to go *now*—"

"One hour." Jilk reiterated.

"45 minutes."

"Deal."

In the forty-five minutes that they were separated, Knick stopped by the ratty apartment he sometimes called home to shower, change his clothes, and pick up a couple of weapons. With a quick stop by a food stand, he stocked up on some meat buns, filled a couple water canisters, and stuffed a shoulder sack with the essentials. His faithful leather jacket with the red racing stripe came on, and it only took five minutes to make it back to the guild hall.

He found Jilk, Slot, and Solo showered, changed, and loading guns in the shade at the top of the stairs.

"What's all this?" Knick wanted to know.

"You think you're going by yourself?" Jilk asked. "Don't be stupid. The four of us are a team. We stick together. Besides, can't have my rookie stompin' Anshar without me."

"Are you sure?" he asked, feeling a little moved.

"We're family now, yeah?" Slot said with a smile.

"Besides, we let you do it alone once before and you came up empty-handed," Solo added. "This time, we got to make sure you get it done right."

Knick suppressed a smile, turned his back to them, and rubbed his wet hair.

"Yeah," he agreed.

Jilk stood up, smashed his clip into the .45s chamber, and shoved the pistol in the back of his pants. He motioned for them to follow with an "All right, let's go" and led them around the back of the guild house, passed a fenced industry yard full of sketchy affairs, and to a wooden ramp heading down into a pit.

They crossed a boardwalk to a landing platform where one man was slumped to one side, reading a magazine.

"Tace, we're going up," Jilk said. The man eyed the group suspiciously but didn't care enough to ask. He shrugged one shoulder, slammed his fist back on the call button, and they waited two minutes for the gears to grind to life and the creaky, metal-latticed doors to wrench open.

Jilk nodded and Solo, Slot, and Knick all climbed into the surprisingly spacious compartment; it was big enough to stand with room, and a bench on either side allowed them space to relax. Their boss tapped the metal frame as he climbed in, forced the doors closed with a sturdy heave, and then their carriage started moving.

"Sit back," he said. "It's a long ride up." He glanced over at Knick and grinned. "In the mean time, you can tell us about you and Gothic."

"Nothing to tell," Knick admitted, looking away.

"I call bullshit!" Slot exclaimed. Knick glared at her and she giggled.

"There isn't. You know Keepers don't fall in love."

"Bullshit," Solo mumbled. Knick gaped, feeling cornered. He checked Jilk; he was grinning.

"Let's have it, man. Or is it...there really isn't anything to tell?"

"Now you get it—"

"But you want there to be," he continued, "and she rejected you."

Knick narrowed his gaze on his boss. "That's not funny."

"C'mon, Knick. Who can you tell if not your best friends?" Slot encouraged playfully, but her grin was too conniving to be taken seriously.

"We...well, there's something there. It's just...I don't know. She resists, you know? That's the proof there's something there. I mean, not that I want there to be. Just... she's hot."

"Oh man," Jilk mused, "you've got it bad, huh?"

Knick shot him a look, but he had no rebuttal.

Otto Ferés's head snapped up when the second explosion rocked the fortress and he lolled in the darkness. The faraway booms reverberated through the walls as though distant bombs were dropping on the city. He turned his head this way and that, but his ears couldn't discern anything.

Were his eyes open? He didn't know anymore. The darkness was as thick as the black behind closed eyes. He listened longer and more thunderous bursts rattled the stones around him. He could almost make out... *Screaming?*

So it was time. He slowly unfolded his legs and arms from the fetal position, stretching out one numb limb after the other. His bones ached and his lips were peeling. He fumbled with a canister of water, wet his cottonmouth, and flexed his appendages to get the blood flowing.

He winced at the pain shooting up his right arm. He couldn't see it, but he could feel how swollen and tender it was. He imagined horrible red and purple bruising with yellowed skin around the swells, but couldn't see to confirm anything.

Otto carefully got onto his hands and knees, letting the right arm hang limp and be dragged along as he crawled down the narrow tunnel. He had no feelers and hit his head on brick more than once. *Funny how you plunge a man in total darkness, and any sense of direction he thought he had goes right out the window. We really are helpless, aren't we?* But Otto didn't care. He had a mission and he was going to get to her.

Suddenly, he felt the ceiling lift and knew he was getting closer, so he switched positions, slowly walking on his knees and allowing his hand to feel his way in the darkness. He brushed over webs and grime, spiders and hard balls that he didn't want to know what it was. As the wall rounded, he prepared for the jutting stone.

His knees spiked in pain with every shuffle forward, but he was driven by adrenaline, by the hope in his beating heart. *Isis*, he thought, moving faster. *Isis!*

He caught the corner of the stone with his chest and slumped down, rubbing the tender spot for a moment. Then, he scooted around to the other side and wrapped his arm across the top, bracing it with his side; it took some skilled maneuvering with strength he didn't really have, but he managed to pull it out.

Otto's eyes stung when the sudden beam of light invaded the dark corridor. He sat on the stone and blinked furiously, attempting to adjust, while the sounds of whispered commotion filtered up from the bottom of the room below. He glanced through the hole but couldn't see Isis. All he could see were women dressed in strange robes and body suits, rushing about, whispering furiously. There was strange equipment lining the curving walls of the cell.

"What is all this?" he whispered, trying to figure out what was going on.

The room itself was dimly lit with blue lamps and screens creating enough light to see. Otto was amazed that such low light penetrating darkness was enough to momentarily blind a person who had been trapped in it. He waited, watching what he could see, and wondering more and more at just what was happening above and below him.

"What is this place?"

The Kur marched with heavy footsteps lead by the sibling duo Kallo and Delia, two of the Kur's finest soldiers. Their dreadlocks bounced on their soldiers as they descended a spiral staircase into the lower depths of Asgard, dark skin hiding them in the shadows they passed under.

Their men followed them faithfully, wearing the same serious scowls that their leaders did. The tower shook and quivered and the screams from above penetrated even these deep layers. It was enough to rattle any man, but these few did not unravel.

"Delia," Kallo's deep voice began. She nodded.

"Yes," she agreed. Their silent communication had been developed when they were young. Others suspected telepathy, while some claimed intuition. No one was sure.

The forbidden door opened as the Kur approached.

"Is it really so serious?" Camilla, the Cleric, asked them.

"Orders from the Baron himself," Kallo told her. "Angels have infiltrated Asgard."

"We were ill-prepared for this attack," Delia continued. "Though we do not believe they could find their way to the Enoch's chamber, precaution prevails."

Camilla's head dropped and a heavy sigh left her lungs.

"Cleric," Kallo said. "We cannot let our arrogance destroy us. We believed Asgard impenetrable. Look at it now. Already, countless of the collective lie dead in the tower."

"All right," she agreed. "We will move the Enoch. There is much to do if we are to do this quickly. Please, we need your help."

And the twins entered the forbidden door to the chamber of the Enoch.

The chamber emptied out just as Isis had said. Otto scooted off of the stone and worked his way down the spiral stone staircase as fast as his numb legs could carry him. When he reached the bottom, he heaved against the wall. It took three tries before the slat slid away from the wall and more blue light filtered into the room.

Otto crawled out and stood up. The scene shocked him and he stumbled backward, tripping over the stone and hitting his head against the wall.

Every piece of machinery surrounding the cell had wires and tubes extending from their tops, suspended over the room and fed into a central point. It was a giant spider-like piece of machinery with long legs that hooked like a claw onto an oval pod on the ground. The wires descended into the pod, hooked into something, and tubes pumped various types of liquid to and from the thing within.

It was like a great spider tending to its precious egg.

As he got closer, he saw a machine extended over it with thin arms and needles spindling from it, poking the creature with spastic motions. A flickering light at the far end flashed dark blue.

Otto moved closer to the machine and both blushed and grimaced when he saw what was laid within. A pale-skinned, blond-haired girl was lying in water, naked and constantly poked and prodded with the tiny needles. Her limbs twitched, and he realized they were keeping atrophy from setting into her muscles. The tubes carried nutrients to her and took away the waste of a normal human being. He wondered what the other liquids were. Medications? Antibiotics? Then there was the lifeline monitor hooked up to her pulse.

The flashing came from a panel over her eyes where he could see tiny legs pulling the skin away from her eyeballs. He cringed inside.

"What have they done to you?" he whispered.

K-City was sometimes called the Dark City. It was lit entirely by neon lights lining buildings, signs, and blinking ads. It was a seedy realm for the nightstalker; the city that never sleeps, without time in its entirety. It also happened to house an exceptional collection of uniquely talented individuals. Specialists—that was the official title.

Hezara moved through the narrow streets and cramped quarters into the swarm district. She dipped in and out of blue, green, red, purple, and yellow glow, passed by plastic flaps with graffiti sprayed displays and blacked-out windows with open doors that looked like black holes. Bottom feeders of all kinds filtered around her; spikies, twists, hoops, loops, and razors. They all wore colorful plastic with glow-in-the-dark accessories and phosphorescent make-up. The rats—the non-fashionable lurkers—typically dressed in ratty black layers with stringy cuts ranging from full bloom wave to grease-ball limp.

The thumping bass from the clubs blended painfully with the electronic and automated vibrations from the rock cafes, but the noise worked for K-City and felt right. Hezara took a turn down a darker alley where the neons had trouble reaching under the overhang of roofs mashed so close together and took a left up another narrow space. She pushed on the third door she came to but it was locked.

Three knocks, pause, two quick knocks, pause, four quick—but then the door opened.

"Hezara." The man smiled from behind the crack. His black hair was shaggy onto his shoulders and his beard looked neglected. Those slanted eyes closed even more with his grin. She could see his shirt was open and that gorgeous body of his was still as appetizing as ever.

"Rook," she countered, resisting the smile trying to form on her lips. "Kede, Rook. Kede." It was a term popular in K-City to describe an impossibly attractive guy—like the airbrushed augments people paid billions for. He was au naturale. She remembered him from a time before he'd discovered his genetic gift; now, he played it up and wore it proudly.

"What kept you?"

She grinned.

"You owe me a favor, Rook."

"I do. Come in." And he stepped aside to let her pass; he locked the door behind her.

The foyer was black and cold and cramped, like the rest of the city. They climbed the steps up into the loft, which felt tilted to one side, and was cluttered with this specialist's specialty equipment. A fire blazed in a small hearth and a candle was burning down on the table. The bedroom was dark behind a curtain.

"Have a seat," he encouraged, eyes constantly lingering below her neck.

"I'll stand."

Rook's casual steps carried his body to hers and his arms wrapped around her waist. She turned away, but he buried his face in her neck, ran his lips across her skin to her ear and

222

nibbled the lobe, hot breath causing her skin to tingle.

"I missed you, Zara," he whispered huskily and she already felt his erection on her ass.

"Rook, this is business," she reminded him.

"It doesn't have to be." He traced the shape of her ear with his tongue, running over the many earrings; he never had cared about all of her jewelry. She believed it turned him on even more. Hezara pushed him back, keeping her arm stretched out to keep him at bay.

"It *is* business. And it's important," she insisted. His smirk didn't fade.

"Talk to me," he said, reaching out to take her arm. His fingertips glided, back and forth, over her skin.

"There's something I want you to look at."

"Yeah?" He kissed her fingers, her palm, her wrist.

"Rook!"

"Zara," he muttered, yanking her into him. He quickly closed his arms around her and kissed her. She made one single attempt to back out, but he wouldn't let her escape.

Hezara had him stripped forty-five seconds later.

Her robes dropped to the ground and she stepped out of them as he backed her through the curtain into his bedroom. They collapsed onto the stacked mattresses, lips and bodies locked in a passion they only experienced when together. He gripped her neck, holding her against him as his free hand explored the curves of her exotic body. She rose to meet his touch, his aggressive caresses, and lifted her leg to wrap around his thigh.

His mouth dropped to her neck and collarbone. He called her name over and over again—guttural, husky. She responded back with a pleading whisper.

"Rook…"

They tangled up in the sheets with animalistic sensuality, and even fell on the floor once. Their time together was a moment of raw love without understanding, without responsibility, just pure honesty. And when it was done, there was no illusion to be shattered.

Rook pulled some pajama pants on that sunk low on his hips as if they would fall off at any second. He lit a cigarette, brushed his hair back when he exhaled the smoke, and crossed over to her. He kissed her again, then gave her some space to get dressed. She chose one of his button-ups and a pair of boxer-briefs.

"I'm glad you're back, Zara," he reiterated.

"Rook, I came back because I need you to look at something for me." She went to her robes, fished out her satchel, and produced the heavy statuette. "I need you to try this."

He raised his dark, slender brows and cocked his jaw as he stared at her, smoke seeping out in a frozen moment.

"How long will you be staying this time?" Rook asked.

"Long enough. Now, about my trial."

"I wish you'd stay longer. I miss having you around. Remember when we went to Hygeia?"

"Of course," Hezara said with a smile, resisting the irritation rising to the surface as she recalled Rook liked to do this in his own time; perhaps, if she indulged him just a moment... "We were there—what was it?—six months?"

"The longest we've been in the same place together."

"Yes. We met that couple from Bloom—topsiders. They freaked out when they realized catha were allowed to walk free."

He laughed.

"Right, they tried to get off the island, didn't they?"

"Rook. My favor."

"You should stay with me Zara. We always had good times." He kept his eyes on hers, inhaling and exhaling smoke; they never strayed, even when he laughed.

"I wouldn't like your affairs, Rook."

"I wouldn't like yours, either, but we'd still have them."

"My trial—"

"We should go out while you're here. Don't you think?" His eyes narrowed on her. "Maybe get some sushi on Hamric. Then a club—oh, I know the perfect place." He grinded his cigarette butt into a nearby ashtray. "I was there last week— amazing atmosphere, good drugs."

"I came here for a favor, Rook, and you've been standing here for ten damn minutes avoiding me for spite, changing the subject every time without so much as glancing at this damn thing—"

"It's Asgard, one of the nine worlds of Norse mythology," he told her, lighting up another cigarette. Hezara stared at him, momentarily taken aback. "The tree is Yggdrasil—the world tree—supporting the nine realms of existence. That topmost world is Asgard, city of the gods."

"Rook," she whispered, stepping closer. "This is important. There's trouble in the Keeper Order. This statue is the twenty-five year old link between something that happened then and the terrible things going on now. Please. I need to know everything."

He evaluated her a moment and then nodded, holding the cigarette between his lips while he pulled on a shirt. Embers and ash sprinkled to the ground—to the dark rugs over the warped, wooden boarding. He took the statue to his desk and sat down, flicking on various table lamps of different colors and degrees of intensity; many types of looking glasses were hooked to mobile arms attached to the table. Papers, pens, bottled liquids, droppers, tracing paper pads in several sizes, and a hexton. He put his glasses on and began looking over the statue.

"Here, symbol of the Keepers," he said, pointing to the carving under the plain. "Why it's under...curious."

"Curious, why?" she asked, but he motioned for her to wait. She didn't mind him like this; when he was working, he was serious. She smiled and resisted tugging him off for another romp in the bedroom. She was one of the few who knew him like this—before he'd realized he was kede and flaunted it; personally, she found him most attractive this way, but decided telling him so would only delay her further.

"This statue isn't about Yggdrasil or the nine worlds. It's about Asgard. It's pointing directly to it. See the way the branches bend away from it? They're shrinking away in reverence. Or, fear."

"A man called Hermes sought to destroy it."

"Hermes? He was the messenger of the Greek gods. He was a guide. Also, a trickster. Stole the sun god's cattle the night he was born." Rook glanced up at her over the rim of his glasses. "How many newborns you know can pull that off?"

"I might know quite a few if I knew any gods."

He shrugged and went back to the trial. He did several tests that Hezara had never understood—material testing, dating, and various other scientific trials not yet possessing a simple synonym to describe it.

"It's very old. Centuries old," he told her. "But it hasn't passed through nearly enough hands to be this old. It must've been lost. Lost or…unneeded." His expression changed. "Why do you believe Hermes wanted to destroy it?"

"The woman who was hiding the statue said two men sought it: Hermes, to destroy it. Muriel, to keep it."

"That's it?"

"She's dead. The statue came with a letter."

"Can I see it?"

"Afraid not. The owner kept it."

Rook thought for a moment longer, staring off into space behind his glasses. He tilted his head up at her.

"How are you involved?"

"I was the deliverer. An old man held it for twenty-five years per instruction of the woman who sent it. She's been dead. She kept it secret all this time. Why deliver it now? Twenty-five years later?" Hezara folded her arms over her chest. "She said Hermes or Muriel would've killed her."

Rook went back to the statue, turning it over in his hands several times.

"The statue was sought for a reason, but I do not think Hermes would have destroyed it. Hermes was a trickster, but he was also a guide to the underworld. I think he would've kept this statue safe—hidden it."

"Why?"

"There's something terrifying about the way Yggdrasil responds to Asgard—as if something terrible were happening."

"You said the trees bent away in reverence."

"Or fear. After studying it more, I think it's the latter. See the way the trunk shrinks into itself?" He pointed with his pinky nail and Hezara bent in to get a closer look. "And the roots shrivel as though they're trembling. And do you see the temple? Valhalla—home of the gods. It's dark, as if dead. Asleep. Or…veiled. The bridge connecting Asgard to the nine worlds is broken—purposefully broken. I don't like that. It doesn't feel right."

"What does it mean?"

He tipped the statue up and showed her the Keeper symbol on the bottom.

"Symbols like this never go on the belly of an object. The

underside is representative of dissension, falling, chaos, and death. It's imprinted on Asgard. I think it means, 'Asgard falls', meaning it must fall, or will fall. Inevitable."

"And that means the Keepers will fall."

Rook pushed his tongue against his canines in uncomfortable revelation as he and the Bloodsworn stared at one another.

The state of the Keeper stronghold was quickly crumbling. Eros had received word that angels had broken through both side wells and were making their way up. The great defensive stand against them in the spiral had been futile.

"Fall back!" the Baron commanded, and the swarm of Kur moved up, higher into the tower. Eros backed away from the opening and a barricade of soldiers fell into his place, holding the line of angels still dragging away their comrades' corpses, still climbing over them to try to get to the Keepers.

Bartimaeus's shield kept the slugs from getting to them, but the screams from the collective began to rise above their heads and everyone knew the situation was far from uncontained. They were losing. The Keepers—invincible, having stood for thousands and thousands of years—were being defeated in their own sacred tower.

"Fall back!" Eros yelled again, forcing his way up through the crowd.

Sonia and Rexis moved up ahead of the soldiers to protect them. An explosion rocked the tower and chunks of the walls crashed to the ground.

"She's going to come down," Sonia whispered on shaky lips to her companion. Rexis turned an eye to her fearful gaze. "Asgard...will fall?"

"No," he said.

"The Keepers are dying."

"No!" he insisted. "Keep fighting, Sonia. We haven't lost yet."

The Kur above them began to holler and the Interim knew the angels had broken through on another level. Eros came up to them, eyes fixed upward.

"Baron!" a soldier cried out. "We've been cut off!"

Rexis looked at Sonia's sinking expression.

"Not yet," he reminded her, but her face told him she was beyond comfort. "Then, kill as many as you can."

She nodded.

Just then, from out of one of the hallways, a member of the collective came running up to them, screaming. The Baron and his Interim turned. His was clutching his face, torso twisting with the pain shooting through his nerves. Eros grabbed him and held him still, prying the monk's fingers from his face. A large slug was pulsing, hooked tight to his cheek.

"Rexis," Eros said, and the Interim stepped up and held onto the young scholar. Then, the Baron took hold of the slug and tore it off of his face, ripping a loud scream from the man's lungs when he did. Blood oozed in an outline of a deep, red burn down his face.

The monk stumbled out of Rexis's grip and his knees buckled, sending him to the ground. His hands shook an inch from his cheek as the stinging sensation caused his nerves to twitch. He lifted his gaze to the Baron, who crushed the vile slug in his fist.

"Your name?"

"Antion..."

"Antion, are you all right?"

The scholar's nod of confirmation was more like a violent twitch. Rexis helped the scholar to his shaky feet as the Baron continued.

"Antion, I need you to be brave. Find the High Counselor and bring him here. I do not think we can stay and we all must go together. Do you understand?" he asked and got another violent twitch in response. "Good." He motioned to a unit of Kur to come to him. "Accompany this scholar to the High Counselor and escort them both back here."

"Sir!"

The Kur turned to Antion, whose legs felt ready to melt under him. Rexis put a strong hand on his shoulder and gave him a firm nod. The scholar tried to smile but couldn't. With a deep inhale to steady himself, he turned and led the soldiers back down the hallway, following a very familiar path toward the High Study.

As they rounded a corner, trails of blood caused their blood to turn cold. Next came feet poking out from behind walls and arms reaching lifelessly through doorways. Bodies with large, black slugs attached to them were twitched over broken furniture and crumbled parts of ceiling and wall, crushed under objects, slumped against surfaces.

Antion could see some of their faces—the faces of men and women he knew. Their mouths were open, eyes wide, and every bit of their frozen expression spoke of utter agony and shock. Never in all of their lives had they ever imagined something like this could happen to them.

The coughing and sputtering of a dying man put them all to running.

"High Counselor!" Antion screamed, falling at his feet. Blood trickled down the old man's beard and the slug on his hand covered two long, bony fingers.

Through his tears, Antion managed to rip it off. He threw it down the hall and was horrified when it tried to leap at them again. A blade snatched it out of the air and pinned it to the wall. Antion glanced back at one of the Kur, easing out of the throw position.

"High Counselor, can you stand?" a Kur asked. The old man groaned and barely shook his head.

Antion glanced up at the soldiers with him in concern, wondering what they should do; he examined the High Counselor's face, tilting it left and right by the chin. Blood seeped from gashes on his head and his wrinkled skin captured it, holding it in red lines between folded flesh.

The footsteps of an assault team coming closer caused their hearts to pound loudly in the silence. It all happened so fast, Antion wasn't entirely sure what had given him the courage to act or how he had managed to dodge the spray. The angels opened fire on them and the Kur charged bravely ahead. In the flurry of stamping feet and flying bullets, Antion managed to hoist the High Counselor up by his armpits and drag him into the High Study. He locked the door, threw the bolts, and prayed the ancient wood would hold.

"I'm sorry, High Counselor," he sniffled, trying to hold back his tears, as he dragged the old man through the clutter and hid him in the back of the room. He dragged the desk to the wall to shelter them and ducked under it himself.

The pop-pop-pop of gunfire was much more prevalent than the shing-ska-skrrt of swords and knives. The dying shouts and yelps seemed to belong to familiar men—not the invaders. Antion buried his head in his knees and cried as quietly as he could, praying silently that they moved on. The High Counselor lifted a shaky hand and clasped the young scholar's forearm.

"Antion...was your name...wasn't it, lad?" he whispered, fighting for every word he choked out. The scholar nodded. "I thought...so. Nico's...boy. Sharp mind."

"Nico," Antion gasped. "He's in the dungeons. He'll be defenseless!" He leapt to his feet. "I have to go!"

"No!" the High Counselor cried, reaching out to stop him. His fingers brushed Antion's robes but the cloth slipped from his grasp. He lurched forward, whining in the back of his throat at the pain that wracked his body. He crawled, palms and weak arms dragging his limp frame over to the door where the young scholar was beginning to undo the latches.

The High Counselor snatched a fistful of Antion's robes and tugged, forcing the scholar's attention on him.

"It's too late!" the elder cried. "Antion," he pleaded, "it's too late..."

"But Nico wi—"

"The angels have t-taken...Asgard!" He gasped for breath, eyes fighting their desire to close. His muscles spasmed with the strain but he refused to let go of Antion's robe. "The scar on the wall... It is too late... Stay with a dying man. There is still something...I must teach you. Still something...left to learn. For you, Antion... It must be you now."

Though he did not understand, his heart wrenched at the sight of what once was a great man lying broken on the floor, begging. He ignored the tears falling out of his eyes and helped the High Counselor back into hiding, retrieving the chair cushions to make him more comfortable. The shallow breaths of a dying man were all that distracted him from the slaughter outside the High Study.

The High Counselor produced a book from his long, draping sleeve and Antion carefully took it.

"Sir?"

"Read...it..." he whispered and watched the scholar open up to the marked page. "Hurry!"

Gobol gritted his teeth as Shade pressed her palm hard to his wound and blood gushed between her fingers. She ripped at the long skirt that hung off the back of her pants, tearing long strips and crude patches.

"What were you thinking?" she demanded to know.

"I was told...I could learn more...about a relic if I came," he stammered, sucking air through clenched teeth at the pain.

"Who told you?"

"Sonia," he gasped, and Shade paused mid-tear. He suddenly knew, too. "You don't think..."

Her dark gaze flashed up at him and he closed his lips.

"There's too much blood," she muttered, and Gobol's heart throbbed in panic. "I'm going to remove my hand. Keep pressure there for a moment while I get these bandages in place," she instructed. He nodded quickly and covered her pale hand stained red. She gave him the comfort of a silent three-count and then pulled her hand away.

Gobol covered his own wound, fighting the urge to withdraw as the pain he inflicted on himself caused his arms to shake. He didn't have to fight long. Shade pulled off her top layer shirt and covered his hands with the bundle, and then he slid them from under it. The cloth pressed into the wound, quickly matting to his flesh as it sopped up the blood.

"Thank you for coming for me," he said, trying to retain some self-control.

"I need answers, Gobol. You're the last one with them."

His gray eyes looked sympathetically upon her and suddenly he knew that all of Nico's suspicions were true. Here, he had almost been assassinated for what he knew. How could the Order have fallen so profoundly, so quickly?

Shade motioned for him to hold the shirt in place and then she hoisted him up and dragged him to a curvature so that he could be propped up against it. She returned pressure to the blood-sopped rag, violet gaze twitching across his body and across the area around them; she was searching for something, for help, but there was nothing.

"Interim?" he asked, shaking breaths drawn with blatant breathing.

"The area is deserted. I'm afraid to move you. You're bleeding too much and we would have to go too far." She checked his expression but he only swallowed apprehensively. "I'll need to look for help—"

"Don't leave me," he interrupted her. "P-please. Not yet.

Ah... Not yet," he pleaded. She nodded so he knew that she wouldn't abandon him. "What do you want to know, Interim?"

"I want to know about the prophecy. *His* prophecy. You are the only one who knows what the Oracle really said. I need to hear it from your lips."

"Well," he started, "there were two prophecies uttered that day."

"Two?" she gasped. He nodded, feeling the taste of metal on his tongue.

"He comes, born with wings of heaven's light and darkness dim. In secret sins, he uncovers the truth of the pale hands and, marked a beast, the fallen angel flees and seeks the black and is welcomed into their selfish arms. He comes, ender of all things, to aid the shadows in the fight. His blackened wings will spread so far, they change the stars of both light and dark."

"Knick's...prophecy?" she asked, confused. "It's different."

"Yes," he agreed. "Tailored...so that you would kill him."

"Why? Nothing in the prophecy says he would act against us!"

"Because the Regent feared who he was." He narrowed his gaze on her. "You know...who he is...don't you, Shade?" He watched her firm eyes, unblinking, waver for only a second. "The one the Oracle spoke of a millennia ago."

"Can you say for sure?" she whispered.

"We know the One will walk the path of light and dark and that the ancient power is his to command. He has been called the ender of all things. That is why Muriel was afraid of Knick—that he was who he always feared."

"The One is not something we are supposed to fear."

"It is for Muriel—whose power would be gone."

"Muriel denies destiny, forsakes the Balance...all for this own power?" Shade balked.

"No one can truly know what is in his head. We have all speculated, all silently wondered." He coughed and felt the blood in his mouth. "The second prophecy," he continued, "came bearing the sacrificial glyph."

"And what did the Oracle say?"

"Only one thing: he has been seen...and True Sight has

awoken."

"What—"

"We don't know," he admitted. "Nico suspected the High Counselor did." He noticed Shade's face darken in agitation and suspected she'd already tried to pry the information out of the old man.

"What do you know about Malikiel? What do you know about Mesopotamia?"

"Nothing, nothing," he confessed. "Nothing but that they are well-guarded secrets."

"And the sacrificial road?"

"None know. I doubt even the High Counselor does." His last word was strained, eyes shut tight, as a clot of blood forced its way out of his throat. He coughed and blood splattered through his teeth and onto his robe.

Shade gathered up some of the torn pieces of her skirt and dabbed at his mouth and chin.

"Gobol," she began quietly, "you're going to go into shock. You're losing a lot of blood. I have nothing to help you, to prevent that from happening. You have to let me go find help."

The sad smile he gave her caused a knot in her heart to twist painfully.

"I still remember the day you were born as though it were yesterday," he whispered and her violet eyes widened in shock. None had ever talked about her past, not even Eros, as if it were taboo. Gobol knew he'd hooked her in. There was still something he had to say. "We all can feel a Keeper come into his power. You know the feeling…"

"The inheritance. Yes. I've felt it."

"Every Interim felt your birth…like a shuddering throughout our souls." He could tell she was confused by the deep slant in her brow. "We thought we had felt the One being born…but you had your own sign. That did not lessen the Regent's fear."

"Fear?"

"Three years later, a strong prophecy was uttered. The Oracle and the Enoch have never been so perfectly synced." He tried to smile but the blood on his mouth weakened the effect.

"Gobol," she hesitantly warned, unsure if she should be hearing this or not.

"The child born under the third sign will carry the power of the Old Ones, their unlocked secrets, and beneath this one's feet all faceless twins will gather in allegiance and, together, shall pave the way for the One, whom this child shall find, the ender of all things." He put his face a little closer to hers, gritted his teeth at the pain, and whispered, "There was one other born under the third sign..."

"Who?"

"Daedalus," he uttered.

With a heavy pang in her heart, Shade instantly recalled Daelus's words. *He was a man who died to protect an innocent girl from a prophecy the Regent greatly feared. He wanted her to live, and so he took her place; he brought the prophecy onto himself.* Shade shut her eyes tight. *He was deeply in love with her.*

"Daelus lost his brother when Daedalus sacrificed himself for you. At the time, we all thought he truly was the one the prophecy spoke of...and that we had lost our most promising Interim. He was very powerful. When it was discovered his twin brother was still alive and also had the gift, the loss didn't seem so great. Though Daelus isn't the Interim his brother was...he has power to show."

Shade's violet eyes opened angrily. After all this time and all that had happened, not an ounce of her could stand to hear Daelus talked of as though he were a lesser man. Gobol understood the warning in her eyes because he bowed his head in attempted repentance but was thrown into a coughing fit. More blood spattered his robe and Shade wiped it from his chin and mouth. He grabbed her wrist tightly, eyes desperately looking into hers.

"Shade, he knows now...he knows he made a mistake. He knows it's you... He knows..."

She looked from one wide eye to the other and back again, but she couldn't get Daelus's words out of her head.

"What have they done to you?" Otto whispered again. More importantly, how was he going to free her? He remembered her words, *do not hesitate* and *Otto, I beg you, please...hurry.* He immediately set to scrambling, looking from machine to machine to see if he could understand what any of them did.

The language... It was bizarre. Who in their right mind

could read this? Ever since the verbal unification nearly a millennia ago, unique tongues had all but died out except among small cliques, like the legendary Tribes of Typhi he'd been told about as a child.

Otto whirled around to face the machine. He was scared of button-mashing—that it would hurt her, that he would push the Doomsday button and fail her. He was going to manually disconnect everything. But how? He had one usable arm.

He started with the tubes—unhooking the feeding ones first. Liquid nutrients spilled onto the floor and sprayed the walls as it flung away. Then, the waste tubes, which mimicked the feeding tube display. He couldn't stop to think about how gross it was. He needed to figure out how to get the needle machine away from her.

His fingers curled around the arms of the apparatus and he cursed every time he got poked. He pulled hard, straining under the insistent gears of the contraption. His muscles flexed and his face nearly turned red, but finally the equipment gave up and lifted, on both sides, away from the body. The needles were still bicycling in a pricking rotation, but he would be able to lift her out without their interfering.

He came to her head and wondered how to safely pry the flashing box off her eyes. He ran his fingertips along the sides, searching for some type of release. His thumb brushed across a switch and the tiny winding of a gear withdrawing made him pause in wonder. He double-checked and saw the legs had lifted away from her eyes. His fingers slowly gripped the hanging instrument and he moved it away from her face.

Isis stared blankly up at him with crystalline green eyes and he thought he was going to cry. The lifeline monitor was still bleeping steadily and so he gently closed her lids for her and pulled out the final wire.

Otto...hurry... she begged. He dipped his arm into the water and sought her shoulder blades, pulling her up out of the water. He guided her head to his right shoulder, ignoring the tender flesh that protested her presence. He bent in at the knees, leaning his shoulders out to support her as he readjusted his grip. He gently pulled her left arm up around his neck and, as carefully as possible, slipped her further out of the pod. He bounced her higher onto him and then reached around her back, lifted her light weight out.

Water pooled onto the floor as she came free of the pod. Otto bounced her in his arms again until he had his arm under her rear and the rest of her body limp against his shoulder and chest. He hurried at a funny angle toward the hatch and carefully lowered her into it. With some strain, the slat closed shut and their presence dropped off the radar.

Nico was pacing back and forth in his cell, wondering what all the commotion above was about. He watched the fire-lit chandeliers swaying above, casting eerie shadows this way and that. One second, he was plunged into darkness, the next he was illuminated with dim light. The whole dungeon creaked dankly.

When the dungeon guardian left him unattended, Nico understood beyond a shadow of a doubt that something was terribly wrong. He found himself uttering his vows to serve and protect the Balance, recounting his favorite passages in the most interesting books he'd read, and even praying to whatever power created the universe to protect Asgard and the Keepers within.

The storm of feet on the stairs troubled his heart and he knew his prayers went unanswered. The angels burst into the dungeon and spread out. He cowered back into his cell, into the darkest part of it. The chandelier swung back and forth, and he was dipped in and out of light.

A few angels stopped in front of his cell, examining the darkness. Nico shut his eyes tight, and the chandelier swung back again. He heard the angels lift their weapons, fingers fondling the grips and triggers.

"I, Marcus Nico, swear on the Scales of the Great Justiciar, to serve no master but the Balance—"

Gunfire echoed in the cavernous room, filling the Keeper with two dozen bullets before they moved on. Nico slumped to the dungeon floor, mouth agape and eyes wide, and a trail of blood smeared the wall.

"Baron!" one of the Kur exclaimed. "Angels have flooded the arena! They're everywhere!"

Eros closed his eyes, feeling the tower. He forced time to slow down so that he could hear everything Asgard was trying to tell him. Gunfire—pop, pop! Swords—shing, kink! The crying...and the screaming. He couldn't shake the screaming. Then there was the tower whispering... Asgard was telling him it was done. Asgard was telling him to get out now.

He opened his eyes just in time to see the angels coming through the corridor he'd sent Antion and a unit of Kur to retrieve the High Counselor. So they had failed, too...

"Evacuate," the Baron told the men near him. "Give the order—we must evacuate."

"Baron," Sonia whispered.

"We have to get as many people out of here as we can."

"The angels have overtaken the tower," Rexis reminded him. "How many are still alive?"

The muscles beneath Eros's skin flexed in anger and the tiny cuts he'd obtained from using the Sword of Scars stung in pain. He nodded to the three Interim beside him.

"We must go up at least two floors. Take us there. I'll deal with these fools."

Eros flexed over the grip of his sword as his ordered Champions moved on. The glow of Vanguard on his blade seemed meaningless now. Donovan had betrayed them. Dimitri was lost. Vox was escaping with Basset. Shade was missing. They'd been cut off from Balthazar and Daelus.

The Baron's weapon lashed out angrily and the wounds on his body erupted just as violently. Dark red springs burst from bodies. With a flick of his wrist—just the swing of the sword—the Baron's will lashed out and his bidding was done. The Sword of Scars was an extension of its master's anger. The power within didn't need to place a cut into a chest or clash against another sword. All it needed was a target and its master's permission and it would kill.

But there was a price.

Eros cut new scars into himself with every swing, but he did not stop until every single Kur and collective was up the stairs and to the next level.

Kallo, Delia, and Camilla gaped at the empty chamber in front of them. Where once the Enoch had been, she was now gone.

"I don't understand," the Cleric whispered, shaking. "Where has she gone? Who? Who!"

"There was no way in or out," Delia reminded the Cleric,

clearly unnerved. "We would've seen."

"Search everywhere!" Kallo cried out, and the Enoch's attendants spread out.

"You won't find her," Camilla told them. "There is no way past us. This is a small sector. She is vanished…"

The twins exchanged glances, both thinking the same thing: the Oracle, too, was at risk. They grabbed Camilla by the shoulders and pulled her along, despite her protests, insisting there was nothing that could be done to find a missing girl.

They broke back out into the tunnels and climbed above the arena, startled when angels poured out of the underground channels.

"Climb, climb, climb!" Kallo rushed them, and the force moved higher.

They escaped down the corridor, running into more of heaven's sent. A battle immediately engaged while Kallo, Delia, and Camilla ducked into secret side passages and worked their way to the other side of the fortress. The twins' team filtered behind them, guarding their backs, and some rushed ahead to protect them from the front.

They took a stairwell, engaging enemies at every turn it seemed. The siblings and Cleric ducked through the firefight, hurrying to the other half of their prophesying duo in hopes they were not too late. When they breached the 4th floor, however, they found Bashyl's team dead in the corridor. Bashyl himself was headless not twenty yards from the Oracle's chamber.

"No," Camilla whispered, hoping denial would turn the clock back and prevent this from happening.

While she was frozen in fear, Kallo and Delia stomped down the corridor. Kallo pounded the door with his fist and it swung open with a loud bang.

The Oracle was gone.

Vines of thorns shot up through the ranks of angels, twisting around their appendages and yanking them this way and that. Some of the tendrils tightened like snakes around the angels' throats, puncturing their flesh and choking the life from them. The Sovereign of the Sword of Thorns turned vicious, casting spiked ropes to rip and tear every invader she saw.

The guns they grasped so tightly folded back and morphed as Rexis, Sovereign of the Sword of Steel, reshaped their precious weapons to be either utterly useless or extremely detrimental to the one wielding it. Together, the Interim succeeded in making a hole through the opposition so that the surviving collective and Kur could safely get to the next floor.

It was there they heard the deep and angry shouts of Balthazar and felt the static in the air from the electrical charges released from Daelus's weapon. The Sovereigns of the Sword of Earth and the Sword of Storms had managed to fight their way down to rejoin the group, but still...the angels kept coming.

How many did Heaven intend to sacrifice to be rid of the Keepers? Was the cost worth it to be rid of such an enemy?

"Sonia!" Balthazar exclaimed. His hulky arms tossed an angel clear across the room and he barreled through the ranks to them. "Where is Eros?"

"Bartimaeus is bringing the Kur and collective through and Eros is covering their retreat," she replied.

"We need to go up at least one more floor," Rexis momentarily piped in as he continued to fight the angels crowding them in. "Daelus!" he called to his comrade.

Daelus, in a single glance, was able to understand what was happening. They were moving up, protecting the people he could see cowered in the stairs of the spiral.

"Protect me!" he exclaimed, hopping from his vantage point down to where they were. "Give me some time!"

"How much time?" Balthazar asked.

"As much as you can give me," he replied, closing his eyes.

He held the sword vertical and directly in front of him and began concentrating, murmuring, tapping into that secret power. At first, he heard the steel on steel from his companions; he heard the lashing of thorny vines, the raw power of Balthazar's swings, the shrill twisting of metal, the rumble of the unsteady tower, the screaming of dying Keepers. Then, he heard nothing. He heard the soft call of forces whispering in his mind.

The sword was speaking with him and he with it. The bells on his wrist jingled in specific patterns until the fang of his blade began buzzing with electricity. A strange and unnatural wind began to blow and the air in the tower buzzed statically. Even the angels knew something terrible was happening and debated retreat.

"Get under Bartimaeus's shield," Daelus said quietly.

"But what about you?" Sonia asked, concerned.

"Do it."

And so she did. First Sonia, then Rexis, and finally Balthazar. They descended the steps and passed through the light barrier. Many angels attempted to come at Daelus, but the invisible shield of charged power sent thousands of volts through their bodies instantly and they dropped to the ground as charred and gaping corpses.

The power conducted through the sword and his own body soon became too much to contain. The Interim's hands flew out to his sides, stretched out, but the sword remained suspended in front of him. His scream was more like a roar.

And it brought down the sky.

Electricity so concentrated connected ceiling and floor in bright columns, catching angels in the flashes. All over the tower, their enemies were instantly cooked in the Storm Sovereign's anger.

From beneath the barrier, the Keepers gaped. Since when had Daelus been so powerful?

It took several moments for the energy surge to subside and Daelus to be released from the trance of the attack. The sword clattered to the floor and he collapsed onto one knee, bending over like a heavy branch.

"Daelus!" Sonia screamed, but he wasn't hearing her voice. He heard Shade's voice, calling his name. *Daelus!* she yelled. Her violet eyes flashed sharply. *I don't trust you.*

Sonia dropped to his side and gripped his shoulders, forcing him upright. He saw black hair and pale skin looking down at him. Her normal scowl was gone and, this time, her expression was soft. *Daelus... Are you all right? Can you hear me?*

"Sha...de..." he whispered. The woman in front of him gasped, as if taken aback.

"Daelus!" Sonia cried, rolling over her shock at his hallucination. Rexis and Balthazar came to them as Bartimaeus led the collective and Kur up through the spiral and toward the next level.

Daelus saw Shade lean toward him. He felt her lips and breath on his ear. *Wake up…Daedalus.* He blinked twice. Honey-brown hair and golden skin came into focus. Sonia leaned over him, worry etched in her expression.

"I'm okay," he insisted and they helped him to his feet. Rexis passed him his blade and Daelus gripped it tightly. He nodded once in thanks and the Interim followed the other Keepers.

Antion stared at the book long after he had read it. The implications were…great, to say the least. The story of King Malikiel and his connection to the Keepers was foreboding—a black stain on their legacy.

"Now," the High Counselor said quietly when he felt Antion had had long enough. "Give it to me."

Antion looked at the old man and handed it over willingly. Rip! The High Counselor tore a page out of the book, much to Antion's dismay. He jumped at the sound of the tear and his eyes widened in distress. Books were the collective's lives; to abuse one was a serious sin.

"Burn it," the High Counselor said, tossing the book back into the scholar's lap.

"What?" he balked.

"Burn it. If it gets into the wrong hands, the world is finished."

"But—"

"Burn it!" he cried.

Antion got to his knees and looked around, trying to find something to start a fire. There, on the wall—a torch. He grabbed it and attempted to light the book on fire. The ends crisped and the leather singed but the flames quickly went out.

"You need to start a fire," the old man told him.

"With what?"

"Look around you, lad," he said. "There's endless supply…"

"But High Counselor—"

"They are dead now, Antion… Burn it."

The scholar swallowed and began piling books. He followed the High Counselor's instructions to rip the pages out for better fuel. He used all but two torches on the walls to get a small bonfire going. And when it was nice and hot, he tossed the book onto the pile and watched as it burned.

The High Counselor dipped his finger into the blood at his temple several times as he drew a sigil onto the page he'd ripped out. When he was finished, he crumbled the page into his fist and sunk lower to the floor. Antion glanced back.

"Sir?"

"It's cold, Antion," he whispered. "I'm cold."

"...Sir?"

"Baron!" Camilla shrieked, racing through the corridor. Eros, who was at the back of the crowd moving up the spiral, turned and faced the Cleric and his two finest soldiers as they skipped over bodies on their way to him.

"Camilla, I'm glad you're safe," Eros said quietly, reaching out to catch her by the elbows, stopping her momentum. "Delia, Kallo," he began, looking beyond her, "where is the Enoch?"

"Gone," Kallo confessed. Eros looked to the Cleric in alarm and her sad nod confirmed it. "Vanished. And the Oracle—surrounded by bodies. Gone as well."

Eros bowed his head in silent anger. He took deep breaths, forcing himself to calm down. The hopelessness of their situation was beginning to sink in. He put an arm around Camilla and escorted her to the line of Kur and collective ascending the stairs.

"Go on," he encouraged her. "We have to leave Asgard."

"But Eros," she exhaled, "Asgard is our *home!* We can't leave!"

"Camilla," he shushed her.

"Are...are you sure?"

He nodded and she wept as she took to the stairs. Eros looked over at Kallo and Delia; they bowed their heads in repentance. When they looked up, the Baron did not seem enraged.

"More angels are coming. We need to move." He motioned for them to follow and then he pushed his way up the stairs.

On the next floor, the Keepers gathered, waiting for instruction. Eros moved to the center of the spiral and touched his hands to the great column. He muttered one word and a large glyph glowed brightly in the stone. A passageway opened up.

"Go," he ordered the Keepers. "Hurry."

One by one, the collective and Kur filtered into the secret passage. In the distance, they could hear more angels coming. Their hearts pounded, praying they were not caught. Some were sobbing, others breathing quickly in panic. Still, the Interim ushered them on, shoving those who moved too slowly. There was no time for dawdling.

"Baron," Balthazar warned, eyeing the corridors adjacent them. "They're coming."

Bartimaeus stepped forward.

"Get them out. I'll handle the angels," he told them.

Balthazar nodded and went to help push the remaining Keepers into the well; he was an excellent motivator.

Eros touched Bartimaeus's shoulder. "Join us when you can, my friend."

"Yes, Eros," he replied with a smile.

The Sovereign of the Sword of Suns raised his weapon and the bells on his wrist jingled. The light that flashed out of it burned deep into the eyes of the angels that appeared and they thrashed backward in agony.

But the angels kept coming.

At the apex of the tower, behind locked doors and in darkness, the angels crept through the dusty and secret room. There, in the center, the whirring of some peculiar machine brought them to a standstill. The sphere was orbited by rings, simultaneously spinning in opposite directions. On a half-ring, a tiny, winged ball twitched up and down, up and down, responsible for the whirring sound.

It looked like a strange hourglass of some kind, keeping track of time without the sand. It stood on the pedestal, all glimmering in gold, and as the angels drew nearer, it reacted as though it were living. It chirped and the winged ball dipped up and down quickly, like a heart monitor recording cardiac arrest.

"What is it?" 99-03-14 asked.

"I don't know," Captain 22-76-43 replied. He examined it a moment more and then motioned to his troops. "Get rid of it. All Keeper magic is to be destroyed."

Gunfire ricocheted off the object and its chirping became

angry screeching as it rotated violently. All in the room felt unsettled, taking a few steps back. Captain 22-76-43 reached into his utility belt and withdrew several tiny mites, tossing them onto the sphere. The mites latched on and began a series of beeps.

"Get down!" the captain ordered and everyone took cover.

The explosion rocked the tower as debris flew away from it. Then suddenly, everything stopped mid-motion. The angels peered over their barricades and watched the debris get sucked back into the core of the sphere.

"What the—"

A great shockwave was released, stretching for miles and miles. Deep underground, there was a pulse that shuddered the earth and every living creature felt it, stopped mid-motion in wonder. Then, the apex of the tower exploded with great fury, disintegrating everything near the blast. Chunks of stone were tossed across Tonatti Haan, smashing buildings and tearing chunks out of homes.

A shrill, piercing sound released from the shattered sphere, and every Keeper heard the call. It screamed in their ears, rattled their brains, and buried itself in their souls.

A thunderous wave of dark and invisible energy rocked down through Asgard, purging it. Chunks of the tower walls burst out as the wave traveled down. Angels were dispatched on every level, hearts instantly stopped when the energy touched them.

In the chaos, the High Counselor gathered the last of his energy and threw himself over Antion, shielding him from the blast. His heart stopped almost instantly.

As the walls and ceilings came down, Bartimaeus knew he had to protect Eros and the others. He reared back and threw his sword into the secret passage; it stuck fast to the wall. Even as he did this, he uttered the words and his bells jingled.

The power that left Bartimaeus shone brighter than any ethergy he had ever tapped before. Like a river, it flowed out of him to the sword and down the hidden well, covering the Keepers in its warm and protective barrier. The ethergy tugged at his vitals, ripping a scream from his throat.

"Bartimaeus!" Eros screamed from the doorway, lunging out toward his friend.

The Sovereign gathered his last bit of energy and

propelled it toward the Baron, knocking him back into the passage. The veins under his skin turned black with the strain and lack of oxygen, sweat drying up under the heat and pressure.

The shockwave hit the floor, collapsing the secret passageway and sucking the life out of the Interim. He fell against the crumbled stone at his feet, eyes drained white and lifeless.

Far beneath, the wave penetrated the earth to the depths of the tower, and Otto stared in shock up into the darkness. He felt the walls shaking. He held Isis tight and closed his eyes. He didn't see or feel the protective barrier rise up around them, but when the wave passed through them, they remained two of only three souls still alive in mighty Asgard fallen.

It had been two full hours since Knick, Slot, Solo, and Jilk had arrived in Gomorra. They'd stretched and ate as they walked, feeling insecure under the open sky. At first, they were quiet, always alert for angels, but the night was surprisingly quiet.

They kept off the roads, attempting to blend into the night. It was surprisingly cool out. Jilk, Slot, and Solo just kept looking up at the sky in surprise; they'd been in the mine their whole life. Knick kept looking around for angels, positive they'd catch his scent and come looking.

The scream that went through his head emptied out into a soul-shuddering feeling. He didn't even know what was happening until he felt Jilk and Solo picking him up off the ground and Slot's hand clamped tight over his mouth.

"What happened?" Jilk hissed. Knick stumbled to his feet, shaking his head; his black hair swished back and forth.

"Something's wrong… Something's really wrong…" he replied, gasping for air. The scream had taken his breath away.

"What is it?" Slot asked.

"We have to hurry. There's no time."

Knick broke into a sprint and the cogwheelers accompanying him were hot on his tail.

Hezara pulled her robes on and fixed the satchel over her shoulder.

"You don't have to leave so soon," Rook told her. She

glanced over her shoulder to where she'd left him on the bed. She admired his naked form behind a poker face and then looked away.

"This is more important than us, Rook."

"It doesn't have to be."

"It does."

Rook watched her put the statue in her satchel and buckle the leather flap closed.

"It's just a statue," he reminded her. "It doesn't mean anything."

"And if it does?" she wanted to know.

"Zara." He eyed her in disbelief. "It's just a statue."

Hezara finished dressing herself and faced her lover. She studied him a second, taking in the moment, memorizing his features; she had to take a mental snapshot, afraid this would become a memory she clung to.

"This is the last time I'll see you," she told him, adjusting her satchel across her shoulder.

"You said that last time," Rook replied with a smirk.

"I mean it this time."

"You said that last time, too."

Hezara turned around to hide her grin. Rook crawled off the bed and hugged her from behind. They stood that way almost a moment too long; Hezara broke away before she got tangled in his seductive web a third time that night. She backed toward the stairs and gave him a rare gift: her honest smile.

"Goodbye, Rook," she whispered.

"Don't be so serious." He smiled. "Bye, Zara."

And the exotic Bloodsworn exited into the darkness.

Shade's head jerked up and her violet eyes flared at the night sky. The call that went through her and Gobol's head unsettled them to the very core. Gobol's pale and clammy face contorted when he screamed in pain.

"Asgard," Shade exclaimed breathily. She tried to leap up but Gobol's weak fingers clung as tightly to her sleeve as he could manage.

"P-please," he begged, "please don't leave me."

She struggled against his grip but he held to her as though she were his lifeline. Finally, she submitted, with one last terrified glance to the horizon. She examined Gobol's haggard state. He'd lost an inordinate amount of blood.

Shade gripped his shivering hand tightly.

"You heard it, too," she whispered.

"Please…" Tears rolled down the side of his face. She bowed her head and nodded. She then leaned across him, hoping to transmit some body heat. His blood smeared across her chest and abdomen as she held him tightly.

Otto pushed past the debris in the darkness, dragging his body awkwardly as he attempted to haul Isis back to the secret hatch without her touching the ground. He'd propped her up against his body, using his left arm to move them.

When he'd made it over the chunks, he realized the hatch and part of the wall had caved in. Before them, bodies lay scattered in heaps of dust and chunks of stone. Otto propped himself up against the wall and hugged Isis close to him. Exhausted, he tilted his head back against the wall and closed his eyes.

The last brick of Asgard to fall echoed in the broken corridors and the tower fell to utter silence.

The underground hideaway was called Sanctuary, deep below the capital Rashrima Haan. It was a small, dimly lit chamber poorly furnished with ancient, wooden chairs gathered round a sturdy but old table. There were smaller rooms connecting off of it that held bed mats, tables and chairs, wash pits, laundry buckets and drying racks; a sick bay was the largest side chamber at the very back of the refuge.

Vox and Basset walked with weary and heavy footsteps toward the safe haven. They were damp from the cold and wet tunnel they'd walked miles and miles through. Their bellies were growling. Their heads were foggy. Their hearts ached.

Finally, a bit of light gleamed in the darkness and they rushed to the door cast in torchlight. Someone was already there! Vox drew her sword and kicked open the door, prepared to burn a thousand enemies to the ground in one angry swipe of her blade.

Dimitri looked up in shock, katana halfway out of the sheath. They stared at one another in shock. Basset's wife and daughters peered from behind their Interim savior and burst into tears when they saw Basset standing with the orange-haired woman.

"Daddy!" the girls cried in near unison.

"Robert!" his wife exclaimed, racing to her husband. He grasped her tightly, sobbing into her hair.

"Laura!" It was a whimper, mostly; his immense joy still bordered on the terrified and he grasped at her as though he still had cause to fear losing her. His two girls threw their arms around him and he hugged the eldest first. "Casey."

"Dad, we were so scared!" she told him. He then picked up his youngest girl and held her so tightly that Mirax themselves couldn't have ripped her away.

"Clara," he muttered into her cheek, kissing her tiny face so many times that his stubble scratched her skin until it was red.

As the family reunited in loving embraces, the Keepers put their weapons away.

"Dimitri!" Vox shouted, racing across the chamber. He opened his arms and held her with fierce longing. "I thought you were dead—when you didn't come back—I was scared—I thought—"

"Sh, sh," he hushed her, closing his eyes as he hid his face in her flame-like hair. "We were ambushed and I had to take other measures to get away from them. It was too close and I was unable to get back to Asgard." He tilted her chin up. "What's happened? Why are you here?"

"Dimitri," she whimpered. "Asgard is..."

"What?"

"It's fallen. The angels attacked—somehow. Eros forced me to go. I don't know what happened after." She tucked her face into his chest and cried again and he held her close. "I was so scared to lose you..."

He leaned back to look at her, cupping her cheek with one hand. "You won't," he told her. "You won't." He tenderly pressed his lips to hers, pulling her into his kiss with deceptively strong arms.

Dr. Basset's jaw felt slack as he watched them. The rumors

of Keepers said that love was forbidden. Yet here two were in a loving embrace. He watched Dimitri's hand slide down to Vox's stomach, pushing through her layered folds.

"Vox," he gasped. "You're...pregnant!"

The two Interim shot concerned glares in his direction.

"You can't tell anyone," she snapped. "Promise me."

"I p-promise," he replied, a little caught off guard. "How long?"

"Four months." She glanced up at Dimitri and then back to the doctor. "No one can know."

Part Six

"It is folly for a man to pray to the gods for that which
he has the power to obtain by himself."

Epicurus

Deep underground, they felt it—the Tribes of the ancient city. They cast their heads to the sky in silent prayers. The pulse of Asgard was a profound tremor in their souls. Then, they bowed their heads to the earth in honor and reverence, knowing the gong of the Keepers rang even deeper in the bottomless well of the earth. Through the many layers of earth and stone, the frozen, sleeping city felt a heartbeat thump throughout it and the sacred spell was broken.

There, at the black gates, the guardians awoke. And there, at the black gates, they stood waiting to open them.

The pair of crystalline green eyes slowly opened when she felt the trickle of water dripping on her temple and drizzling down her porcelain cheeks. The sounds of the storm reached her even underground. When her eyes focused, she saw another human body beneath hers.

Otto Ferés was lying lifelessly slumped against the wall, one arm still hooked protectively around her slender body; his other arm was swollen and the skin was a deep mixture of shiny red and purple patches. His chest rose and fell with shallow breaths.

Isis pushed herself up with all of her might, arms shaking at their first use, and gently touched his sallow cheek. It was the first time she'd ever seen anything with her real eyes. She was glad it was him.

"Otto," she whispered. "You did well."

The Enoch's bright, green gaze explored the room beyond their hidden hatch, at the rubble and the blown out wall, at the water dripping in from the cracks in the walls and ceiling.

"Mighty Asgard fallen," she said quietly to the silence.

The Enoch looked down at her body, at her pale skin, thin legs, and narrow frame. It was time to do something she'd never done before: stand. One hand's long fingers curled around the rough edges of the broken wall for support while the other pressed flat to the ground. Like a fawn, her skinny legs trembled and bowed as she pushed and pulled herself onto her feet.

Standing no more than five feet two inches, the Enoch of Asgard took her first step. The water was slick under her toes, rushing coolly in shallow streams around each appendage. Hard knots of debris pressed into her tender heels and the pads of her feet, pulling winces out of her throat.

Thunder rolled through the sky and a crack of lightning sounded far away. Isis's ears were filled with the sudden rushing of water as the light rain quickened into a torrent. She walked through the corridor, following the path she remembered taking Otto down. Back-tracking, she climbed the wooden stairs slowly, taking in every ounce of the destruction.

The rail to the stairs was snapped and splintered away. Part of the stairs had collapsed and she had to take care navigating around the hole. Her foot slipped once on the wet wood and a splinter shot up into her arch. Her sudden scream was a short burst quickly silenced as she lowered herself to her knees and cautiously crawled the rest of the way up.

At the top of the stairs, Isis took her time pulling the splinter out. She winced again as it came free, staring enthralled at the pearl of blood that suddenly appeared. It grew until it was too heavy and then dripped into the puddle under her foot, threading the water in red. She watched the liquids swirl until they blended together, feeling the cold pang of humanity setting in.

"I've broken all of the rules...haven't I, Kalha?"

Isis got to her feet again and limped until the pain was numb and she could walk normally again. When she finally reached her destination, she was both shocked and saddened. Half of the Abbey had caved in and now ran in a heaping pile of rubble down into the spiral's lobby.

She padded past the pews—the whole ones and the shattered ones—to stand at the top of the rocky hill. Rain was freely falling into the keep below her. More thunder rumbled and lightning lit up the dark clouds. The wind tugged at her blond hair and sent Goosebumps crawling up her naked flesh.

"Knick Coltin," the Enoch said into the rain. "I am waiting."

In the stillness of a side room in the Sanctuary, Dimitri and Vox sat across from one another on an old, animal skin cot; two torches brightened and warmed the room. The

Fire Sovereign dropped forward, forehead digging into the Water Sovereign's shoulder.

"What are we going to do?" she cried. He slid one arm around her back while the other hand held her arm, thumb stroking comfortingly. "What are we going to do? This baby was to be born in secret. How can we hide him now? What fate will he befall if there is no Asgard to shelter him?"

"We talked about this, love," Dimitri said quietly. "There is no guarantee he will be a Keeper. Perhaps, Asgard would never have been his home." He rested his cheek on her short, fiery hair. "Keepers do not have children with other Keepers. We don't know what he'll be. Possibly, the effects will negate one another and he'll be a normal human being."

Vox shut her eyes tight and tears slipped down her cheeks. The idea that, no matter what, her child could be homeless filled her with hopeless heartache. Dimitri rubbed her arm and hugged her close; his worry stemmed from the pregnancy itself.

"I'm so scared," she whispered. He kissed the top of her head hard, doing his best to keep his own emotions from flowing out. He was just as terrified as she was.

There was a single knock before Dr. Basset opened the door and entered. He gave a single, brief smile out of politeness for interrupting, and then cleared his throat. Vox sat up out of her lover's arms, swiping at the tears under her eyes.

"Thank you," he said, speaking directly to Dimitri, "for saving my family."

"How are they doing?" the Sovereign replied with a soft and gentle voice—a voice like water.

"They're okay. They're a bit confused." He hesitated. "We're all a little confused." He waited expectantly but Dimitri's expression and nod only confirmed he was as uninformed as the Bassets were. "How are you feeling, Vox?"

She looked up, mouth momentarily pursed with her shrug, but said nothing. Basset nodded.

"Before MAAR officially announced the positions were filled and all majors had to change, I was going to be a doctor. Now, it's been nearly twenty years since I had any practice, but I think I remember enough to do a simple exam…if you want."

Vox looked pleased as she and Dimitri nodded. Dimitri stepped back to let Dr. Basset in while Vox lay back on the cot.

"Have you been examined before?" he asked.

"Only to confirm the pregnancy," she admitted. Basset wrung his hands nervously, nodding out of habit. He slowly lifted her dress to expose her stomach.

"I apologize if anything makes you uncomfortable. Bear with me. You're my first official patient." He slowly began touching her stomach in various places. Sometimes, his fingers held tightly together pressed into her belly, and other times it was the heel of his palm. "Everything feels fine," he said, dropping his sentence like he was going to add to it, but he said nothing else and only continued the exam. His eyes flicked over to Dimitri and then up at Vox before returning to her belly. "This activity is unhealthy for a fetus," he reminded them, "and for the mommy."

No one said anything.

"I suspect if the Keepers knew of your pregnancy, they would not send you out into danger." He glanced at the parties in the room again. "Why is that?"

Dimitri sighed. "Keepers do not have children. Love is forbidden to spare attachment. That does not only include lovers, but children...family...even a friend one might be too scared to lose that they would forsake the Balance for the sake of that friend's life."

"Ah," Dr. Basset replied. "I see."

"We went against the Order's law," Dimitri confessed. "We fell in love and consummated it, and now we've made our beautiful creation a terrible burden."

Dr. Basset exhaled a deep breath of air as he stood up and began examining other parts of Vox—her breasts to make sure milk was forming properly and there were no unusual growths from the hormonal change, her throat and lymph nodes, and other various vitals for infection or abnormality.

"I'd like to check your blood pressure and urine," he said. "I'll go check the medical room to see if they have any supplies, all right?"

He got to his feet and motioned to Dimitri to follow him. They shut the door so Vox could have some quiet and walked wordlessly back to the medical bay. Once inside and digging through supplies, Dr. Basset eyed the Water Sovereign.

"Is there something wrong?" Dimitri asked and Basset shook his head.

"Not that I'm aware of. I wanted to ask you the same question. You seem…apprehensive?"

Dimitri sighed. "Vox worries about what will happen to the child once he's born. I worry about what will happen to her before he's born."

"What do you mean?"

"Never in our known history have Keepers mated with each other. We all know and suspect they've sought company with normal humans, but never with each other." He narrowed his gaze on the doctor. "You've seen Vox's power. I have a similar power. Will those powers negate one another or…"

"Or will it multiply," Basset finished for him.

"Yes." His expression was grim. "What if a combination of the powers—a swell of energies of that magnitude—could hurt her? Now, as the child grows stronger, or later…at birth, she—" He couldn't finish the thought. Dr. Basset crossed over to him and put a firm hand on his shoulder, perceiving the distress of a devoted husband and loving father.

"I will do everything I can to help her. I will do everything I can to catch a problem—if there is one—before it grows out of control. I'll give you as much time as I can."

Dimitri nodded in thanks but his brow was still wrinkled in worry. Dr. Basset went back to shifting through supplies until he found the tools he needed.

"Aha," he exclaimed. "It's primitive, but it'll work. Here, take this cup and have her urinate in it. I'll be there before too long to finish the examination."

Dimitri started for the door but stopped and looked back.

"Dr. Basset, the others don't know—can't know. Not yet." He cleared his throat. "Not until we decide what needs to be done."

Basset smiled from across the room.

"Don't worry," he told him. "I clearly remember the rules on doctor-patient confidentiality."

In spite of his exhaustion, in spite of the heavy rain, Knick Coltin's feet kept powering forward. Jilk, Slot, and Solo were lagging far behind, fatigued from walking all day and night. They didn't know what Knick knew: that they were close.

He tightened his leather jacket around him, the red racing stripe blending into the brown in the darkness. He pushed his fingers through his hair too heavy with water, ignoring the sopping, gathered strands as they smacked against his face. There was a tiny spark in the center of his chest that felt like a squirming ball of heat, tied to a string, tugging him along. He couldn't stop, driven.

Shade, he thought for the billionth time, but the closer to Asgard he came, the more anxious he was, the more he was afraid—no, *knew* something terrible had happened. Knick's quick pace suddenly turned into a run; he couldn't hear the shouts from his friends to "wait up" over the rain. He sprinted down the street and around the corner, sliding in the water. He caught himself with his fingertips and pushed his momentum forward.

The strange thing was that he didn't necessarily remember the way. Shade had kept the location of Asgard relatively secret. Somehow, he knew where to go, knew exactly the right steps to take to get back there. Maybe it was the voice in his head guiding him. Maybe Shade was, somehow.

Knick slid to a halt when he saw the boulder buried deep in the cracked street. All around him, destruction. The stones were smashed into buildings and roads; smaller rocks scattered over every surface like pebbles. He inched along in a dumbfounded stupor, wondering what the hell could've happened. That warning in his head flared up and he was moving again, unaware of the slap of his friends' shoes in the rain as they ran after him, calling out to him.

The stone wall's secret entrance to Asgard was now a gaping hole.

Knick slowly stumbled into the entry, gaze bouncing around the chunks of stone, splintered wood, torn tapestries, and dead bodies. Limbs reached out, buried under the trash, while eyes and mouths gaped up at him. Knick knelt next to one of the ashen monks, twisting his head. The slug still clung to his face, over his eye, and was now a hard and dead lump.

His blood ran cold. *How on earth did the angels find them?* he thought. The silver glimmer in his peripherals caused his head to snap up, transfixed on the spot at the top of the rockslide. A small woman stood naked with pale skin and long, blond hair. Her green eyes were clear and cool even at this distance. Knick slowly stood up.

"Welcome to Asgard, Knick Coltin," she said. Knick's eyes widened as he recognized the voice he'd heard in his head.

"You," he hissed.

"My name is Isis," she replied.

"I don't give a damn who you are!" he exclaimed. "What the fuck happened here?"

"The angels came, as the prophecy warned, and the Keepers were massacred. A thousand souls, butchered." Her eyes flashed with the haunting of a voice from the past. *"Lament them."*

A hard lump suddenly welled in Knick's throat. "Shade?" he barely choked out.

Isis shook her head. "She is not here."

Relief flooded him. It took him a moment to find the strength to react, but finally he climbed up the rocky slope and stood beside her, looking down at her.

"Eros?" he asked.

"There was a small handful that escaped. That much I saw before I woke up."

Knick scratched his beard. The clap-clap of shoes through the rain turned their attention to the foyer. Jilk, Slot, and Solo came around the corner, panting. Isis glanced up at Knick and then back to the strangers. They slowly walked into the building, jaws dropped in curious horror.

"All...dead..." Slot whispered. "Knick. Knick, what happened?"

"MAAR," he replied grimly. The cogwheelers exchanged glances.

"They're gone from this place. Asgard purged herself," Isis told them. "You are safe here."

That's when they noticed she was naked and the red set in their cheeks.

"Uh, Knick?" Jilk began. "I thought you said Gothic was...you know...taller?"

Knick rolled his eyes. "That's not her."

The cogwheelers joined them at the top of the slope and Isis led them deeper into the Abbey where the rain couldn't get them. The four newcomers made puddles and trails wherever they went, water dripping off them in droves. Slot shook herself like a dog, sprinkling everyone, including Isis. Her brother gave a light punch to her arm.

"Knock it off," he mumbled.

"Before anything else is said or asked," Isis began, "there is something I must ask of you." They all looked at her expectantly. "There is a very important man below us. He is in very bad condition."

"You go with her," Knick said to his friends. "There's something I have to check out."

"She's not here," Isis told him, even with his back to them, but Knick didn't stop. He disappeared down the rock slide and up the crumbling spiral.

Isis led the cogwheelers through the halls and down the ruined steps to where Otto was slumped over, unconscious.

"Wow, he's in bad shape," Jilk muttered as he and Solo knelt on either side of him; Slot began fishing inside of the backpack crumbled nearby. Jilk gently felt Otto's tender flesh, finding the broken bone in his shoulder almost instantly. "Broken," he announced. "He's emaciated. I can't believe how bad his condition is."

"It's my fault," Isis confessed. "Take him upstairs and I'll explain everything."

"Here," Slot said, throwing a t-shirt at her. "Put this on."

Isis slipped the white shirt over her head and it fell almost to her knees. It took all their hands to hoist Otto up in spite of how light he was due to their exceptional effort not to damage him any more than he already was. Isis was the guide, making sure they didn't stumble over any debris or put their foot in a hole. It took a full half hour to take him up to the Abbey where Slot made a bed out of the rest of the clothes in the pack; she ran her rough hands over the thin shirts and pants with care — a rare moment of femininity slipping through.

"Otto sacrificed much to save me," Isis began. "Some of those sacrifices were his choice. Some of them were mine. His body has degenerated to this state from of lack of sleep."

Everyone felt extremely uncomfortable.

"You mean...he's like this just from...losing sleep?" Solo asked hesitantly.

"Having a single bad night of sleep can set the mood for the entire day. Being tired, having headaches, feeling agitated... Imagine losing entire days, averaging merely hours in a whole week. Your body cannot heal, cannot rejuvenate.

You begin to live with the pain. Your appetite vanishes. Then, your body rejects food altogether. Your bones weaken, muscles eaten away. It is a terrible existence. Most people do not live as long as Otto has in this condition."

"You did this to him?" Jilk balked. "Lady, you're cruel."

"Please, help him," she said, not disagreeing with him.

Jilk nodded to Solo, who crouched over Otto and braced his body. Slot pinched his cheeks together to open his mouth, unbuckled her leather wristband, and slipped it between his teeth and over his tongue. She closed his mouth and, holding both ends of the bracelet, pulled it down to prevent him from spitting it out. When they were ready, Jilk fingered Otto's break until he knew exactly what the problem was, and then snapped his bone back into place.

Even in his unconscious state, the pain surged through him and his body jerked. Solo's muscles flexed as he held the frail boy down as best he could without injuring him even more and Slot kept the leather tight in his mouth until he stopped flailing and calmed down.

"Solo, find a good splint," Jilk instructed him. "Slot, get the bandages out of the pack so we can wrap him up." Both did as their boss told them while Isis's green eyes constantly watched Otto in never-ending sorrow and concern.

Upstairs, Knick was frantically searching, trying to find any sign of Shade as he fought to remember the way to her room. The passages were often blocked with bodies. Sometimes, he had to find another way around; other times, he had to clear them. He couldn't believe the carnage and destruction. Hundreds of brown-robed bodies, innocent-looking scholars and monk, lay twisted, bloody, broken, and terrified, frozen that way in death. The mighty bookcases were toppled or smashed, their shelves snapped and empty with books thousands of years old ripped apart and scattered like trash. Sturdy, thick walls were blown to bits.

The invincible, impenetrable, untouchable might of the Keepers was in ruins. It was like watching gods dethroned. No matter how much he hated them, refused to believe in them…he couldn't help but be impressed and awed by their might. Now, even if he wanted to believe in them, he couldn't. There was nothing left.

What would happen to the world now?

Knick somehow found his way to Shade's room. His heart ached when he saw the door smashed in. He tried to get in but it was jammed, splintered awkwardly into the frame. He kicked it hard until it gave way and cracked loudly, slamming into the room. He looked around frantically for Shade, but the room was empty. He crumbled onto the bed and put his head in his hands.

"Shit," he mumbled, feeling his heart pinch. He felt relieved somehow, even though he knew if Asgard was under attack, Shade wouldn't die lamely in her room; she would've been out there fighting with all of her strength.

Knick stood up and shoved his hands in his pockets, feeling the bell bracelet buried in the bandana. He rolled the bells between his fingers, feeling a wave of nausea in his gut at the thought that she'd given him her ability to defend herself.

"Fuck!" he screamed, kicking the bedside table right into the other wall. It fell over and rolled, smacking loudly when it hit. His earlier denial felt like sick karma now; all he wanted was to see her and know she was okay.

Back down in the Abbey, Isis met Knick at the top of the rockslide. They squared off for a moment before Knick pushed his fingers through his hair.

"You're the Oracle...aren't you?" he asked. She shook her head.

"I am the Enoch," she told him quietly. "The Oracle...that is exactly what we must discuss."

"Not here," he said. "I need to get you and Sleeping Beauty over there out of here. It isn't safe. Someone's bound to come looking."

"No one's coming," she reassured. "Otto and I cannot leave. We have to stay here and wait. She is coming."

"Who's coming?"

"Shade," she replied. "I will have something very important to tell her."

Knick's entire demeanor suddenly changed as his insides churned with hope. He glanced over at his friends watching him from the other side of the room, waiting. He stared down at Isis.

"We'll wait, too," he said. "You know, to make sure you two are all right."

Isis's smile was small but warm.

"There is much we need to talk about before she arrives, Knick Coltin."

When the rest of the Keeper refugees spilled into Sanctuary, Vox and Dimitri rushed to meet them. The monks and scholars, damaged and afraid, collapsed against the walls. Kur, some bloody beyond recognition, dropped their weapons, relinquishing the burden with the last ounce of their strength. Sonia, Rexis, and Balthazar steadily walked in with deep frowns in their brows.

Hope of good news dropped out of Vox and Dimitri like cinderblock-shoed villains in a deep lake.

"What happened?" Vox asked frantically. "Where are the others?"

"There are no others," Rexis answered grimly. For the first time since the Interim could remember, there was no musical jest in his tone; it was as flat and emotionless as the reflective eyes of an angel. Vox looked to Balthazar, who nodded. It was true.

"Then Asgard is gone?" Dimitri asked.

"It is gone," Sonia confirmed.

They were silent as the last of the refugees sprinkled in. Balthazar quietly closed and locked the door. Vox watched Dr. Basset roll up his sleeves in determination and cross to the nearest wounded.

"Girls," Basset said. "Come help your father. Can you do that for me?"

The frightened child, Clara, stared, unsure of what to do. The eldest, Casey, tied her hair back into a ponytail.

"What do you need, Dad?" she asked. He issued out instructions. His wife, Laura, also came to his side to help. When he had instructed her as well, the women spread to the next groups, taking note of injuries and what they might be able to do to fix it.

Clara crept up next to her father and stared down at the wounded man. He grimaced in pain as Basset set to work trying to peel off a slug from his arm. She took the man's free hand and held it tightly. He whimpered and clung to her desperately.

Vox turned back to her fellow Interim.

"What of the others? Eros and Daelus?" she wanted to

know. "I don't see them with you. Where are they? Where is Bartimaeus?"

Sonia, Rexis, and Balthazar exchanged glances.

"Eros went to look for Shade, and Daelus went after him," Sonia explained. "Bartimaeus..." She couldn't finish the sentence.

"Bartimaeus what?" Dimitri prompted.

"Bartimaeus is dead," Rexis finished.

Misery sunk into the Water and Fire Sovereign at the loss of their friend and the destruction of their home.

"Have we failed, then?" Sonia asked hollowly, examining her weapon. The word Vanguard glistened in the torchlight. "Champions of nothing."

Vox swallowed back the lump in her throat and put a firm hand on her exotic friend's shoulder.

"We are still Interim," she said firmly. She wanted to say something else, but the words wouldn't come. Instead, her silence was the speech, and the others listened just as quietly.

Sonia put her hand on Vox's shoulder. Each Interim in turn placed their hands on the shoulders near them until a unifying circle was formed. Even if that was all they had, they held it proudly.

The wind whipped coldly with an empty whistle across the plain of the abandoned Isahli. Shade stared down at the icy form of Ralph Gobol, frozen and dead. His face betrayed his final moments of pain. Her fingers curled around his arm and into his hand, the hand that still clung to hers.

She slowly released him.

In a fit of rage, her hand balled into a fist, flying at the plane wing Gobol was propped against. The shadow beneath her fist recognized her wrath and reacted, cushioning her blow and doubling the power behind it. The metal crunched under her fist, splitting in places, until a deep depression was left over.

She stood up, covered down the front in Gobol's blood. Her hands were red, stained and dried in the stuff. There was a storm in the distance, toward Tonatti Haan. There was a second storm—a storm of shadows—headed there as well.

"The Oracle is only one part of the Keeper's power,"

Isis told Knick as they walked toward the back of the Abbey. "I am the other part. It was seen that Asgard would fall long ago, and in order to keep us out of enemy hands, the Oracle and I agreed we must be separated."

"If it was foreseen, why was it allowed to happen?" Knick balked.

"A prophecy was uttered long ago by the Enoch—the only time in all of history that I have had a voice. Until now," she explained.

"I? Just how old are you?"

She frowned. "Not *I* as in myself. I am only one of many Enoch." Before he could ask, she continued, "I do not know how many there have been. Our minds bleed together. Was I the second? The third? The one-hundredth? Thousandth? No Enoch knows for sure which her number is. It is not important. No Enoch knows of itself." She paused and then added, "Except for me."

"Don't you remember anything before you were the Enoch?" he asked.

"There was never such a time," she replied. "I have always been the Enoch, a subconscious dreamweaver kin to the Oracle. We work in concert with one another. We are attuned. This, however, requires the Enoch to be entirely void of knowledge of herself. The Enoch understands itself as Sight, and Sight sees. Together, the Oracle and Enoch see beyond the veil.

"But because the Enoch is flesh and blood and bone, the Enoch can die. There, at the birth and death, the collective history is transferred from one to the other."

"You remember everything since the first Enoch?" he asked, a bit disbelieving. She stopped him just out of earshot of the others.

"Enoch are not given memories, Knick. We are given information. I see what is, what used to be, and what will be...but they are not memories. Not until the day I became aware of myself. That is when I met Otto in a dream...and the Oracle bid me save myself." She motioned to the sleeping man at the back of the room. "He was chosen, and he saved me, so that I could be here to speak with you. So that I could be here to guide Shade."

Knick studied her for a drawn out moment.

"Why are you telling me this? Shade said Keeper proceedings were for Keepers only."

"Because I need you to trust me," she replied. Then, with a small, wry smile, she continued. "Look around you, Knick. What Keepers? The ones fled to Sanctuary? Shadows of once great men. Can they protect the Balance with a handful of scholars and even fewer soldiers?"

Knick felt an odd prick of guilt. Isis walked back toward the overturned pulpit and stood at the top of the steps. He glanced at his friends; Slot shrugged and dropped into one of the pews. Her brother sat next to her. Knick and Jilk sat on the other side of the row.

"The poison of treachery clouds the Sight—that is, the Oracle and Enoch. There were many things we could not see," she admitted. "There were many things we merely glimpsed. Once I became aware of myself, I lost much of my ability to see what was already limited by the poison. What I know now was seen from before the poison was as strong, inherited information, and mere understanding of how the fates weave and the Paragon of Power operates."

"That's well and good, but what the hell does that have to do with me?" he asked. "The Regent wanting to kill me, Shade saving my life, this business about me being a Keeper—what the hell is all of this?"

"What I must tell you, Knick, is that you have a great thread in the weave. Strong. Unbreakable." She gazed on him sympathetically. "You were meant to come here just as Shade was meant to find you."

He shifted uncomfortably. "Bullshit."

"Choosing not to believe in fate does not make fate any less real. We do not make things true or false by believing it. Something cannot be turned into nothing because we'd rather it be that way; just the same, something cannot be created from nothing. Not now, not ever—not even in the black universe."

Knick gritted his teeth. "Go on…"

"You were branded long ago with the sigil of the ender of all things. Shade told you once: that you are the One."

"A Keeper." Knick stood up, getting angrier. "Look, I've done this before. I was an angel, a cogwheeler, and now they want to call me a Keeper. I'm not doing it—"

"Titles," Isis interrupted him. "Angel, cogwheeler,

Keeper…it doesn't matter. You are Knick Coltin," she said firmly. "One day, you can say that you were many things, and did many more. But in your life, you only ever served the will of two."

Knick sat down, elbows on his knees, and his forehead resting in the arches between his index fingers and thumbs. He peered up at Isis from under his other fingers.

"All right," he agreed. "I'll hear you out."

"Thank you," she said gently. She cleared her throat and her green eyes turned serious again. "There are forces at work that we cannot understand. Why Muriel has chosen to do what he has, the Oracle and I have only guessed. We know he is desperate for power—to keep it and to gain it. That is why he sees you as a threat: you can change that.

"Once Muriel abandoned the Order, the pieces were officially set and the game was put into motion. There is no escaping this now. I *am* sorry," she said quietly, "to all of you." She did not only address Knick; she spoke to the cogwheelers, too, also to Otto behind her, to Shade returning to Asgard, to the Keepers deep underground in Sanctuary, to the dead men around them. "The secret lies in Mesopotamia."

"Meso-what?" Slot asked, frowning. The others agreed with her confusion.

"Mesopotamia," Isis replied.

"Never heard of it," Knick said.

"No," she agreed. "You wouldn't have."

"What is it?" Jilk wanted to know.

"It is a place. A city."

"Is it in Anshar or Kishar?" Solo asked. Isis shook her head, letting him know the answer was neither. "Then where?"

"Not on any of your maps."

"Like an ancient civilization?" Knick asked.

"Very ancient," she replied with a smile. "The first."

Everyone was physically taken aback, sitting up straight or leaning back in surprise.

"No one knows where it is," she continued. "We will have to find it. *You*, Knick, must go there if you want to see this nightmare end."

"And…what will we find there?" he asked hesitantly, not even sure he still wanted to know.

"Tiamat."

"Tea mat?" he repeated in disbelief. "That hardly seems of earth-shattering importance." The others laughed. Isis only smiled and waited until they had calmed down.

"Tiamat," she said again. "When you meet it, you will not laugh."

"Well," Solo shifted, clearing the chuckles from his throat, "what is it?"

She only shrugged. "We have other concerns now." Her eyes returned to Knick's. "The Oracle has been taken. We must get it back."

"Who has it?" Knick frowned. Isis sunk to the ground and sat on the first step, pulling her knees up to her chest.

"I cannot answer you with any certainty. I know the Keepers did not take it with them when they escaped. The angels attacked us and it is likely that if any have it...it is them. I did not see any other presences in this place; but not seeing them in this poison does not mean they were not there. Some fate-lines changed greatly with the turn of events."

"Is this what you wanted to tell Shade?" he asked. Isis only stared at him. He sighed and pushed his fingers into his hair, head hanging in resignation. "All right," he muttered. "I got it." He looked up. "I'll get it."

Jilk and the others jumped to their feet.

"You'll get it? Are you out of your mind?" Jilk exclaimed.

"You're just gonna walk into Heaven and take the Oracle out?" Solo snapped. "You high or something?"

"I was an angel before," he reminded them. "I know where to go, what to do. I know how they work. I know the limits."

"Knick," Slot said quietly. Her face was pulled into a sad expression. "Knick, don't do this. You didn't leave the angels just to go back to them."

"I'm not going back to them," he told her. "I'm going in, getting the Oracle, and getting out. Got it?"

Jilk shook his head. "I don't like this, Knick."

"Don't worry," he muttered. "Black Tuesday doesn't have anything to worry about. I'm not going to go back to being an angel."

"I'm not saying this cause I'm worried about the cogs, man," Jilk exclaimed, "I'm worried 'cause you're my friend!"

Knick felt a little ashamed. He rubbed the side of his head and nodded.

"I know, man," he said quietly. Jilk's jaw clenched in agitation.

"All right. Guess we gotta clean you up. Hey, you two," he motioned to the siblings, "see if you can't find some angel swag in his size." Jilk turned back to Knick, slipping a knife out of his boot, barely resisting a small, half-smile. "Time to get rid of that grunge, man."

"Whoa, before you go crazy with that thing...let's see if we can't find a razor or something upstairs."

Jilk shrugged. "Suit yourself."

It took the boys more than forty-five minutes to find a man's room with shaving equipment. They set up a chair near a hole in the wall, attempting to let in as much natural light as possible, even in the dark and rainy weather, and then lit torches and stuck them close by. They set up the most intact mirror they could find in front of the chair, propping it against the wall, and Jilk snipped off Knick's long hair in thick chunks. Knick grimaced as he watched; he loved his hair. It wasn't so much the length, but the fact that he could have it. As an angel, he maintained a waxed head at all times. Growing it out was just another way to say "fuck you" to the man.

Jilk lathered Knick's head when the final bulk had been cut and ran the razor over his skin, shaving lines into his skull. To lighten the mood, he shaved strange styles that they were able to laugh about, but eventually every hair came off and he felt cold and naked. He ran his hand over his smooth, bald head; his skin felt like silk, wrinkly and soft.

Jilk handed him the blade. "Time for scruff."

Knick snatched the blade and soaped his face. With a heavy sigh, he shaved it off. After he washed his cheeks, jaw, and chin, he dabbed his face dry with a towel and then stared at himself in the mirror. He looked like a completely different man—a man he'd tried hard to forget.

Slot walked in and immediately fell back through the door with a loud shout of "whoa", knocking into her brother and nearly taking them both to the ground. Solo growled, wondering what the hell possessed her. They peeked inside and Solo jerked back with a grimace.

"Man," was all he said, unable to carry out the rest of his

sentence. Knick rolled his eyes.

"Yeah, yeah. You got the clothes?"

"Got 'em here," Slot said, handing them over. He quickly changed, feeling nauseous with the angel uniform back on.

"How do I look?" he mumbled, adjusting the tie.

"Like I'm gonna throw up," Jilk grunted, and they all walked back downstairs to the Abbey.

It took almost twenty minutes for Knick to find a working scrambler. He snapped it into the suit and strung it over his ear without putting the bud in. Slot exhaled two quick, hot breaths on a pair of silver frames and shined them for him. He gently took them and slipped them on.

The sight was frightening.

Knick glanced at the sad faces of his friends, at the crystalline eyes of Isis, and at the unconscious lump called Otto.

"Don't worry," Jilk said, slapping his friend on the arm and giving his shoulder a tight squeeze. "We'll protect them. Just be careful."

"Yeah," Knick replied, still working up the courage to leave. Solo grasped his other shoulder and Slot gave him a giant hug.

"I'm sorry, Knick," Isis whispered, walking him to the top of the slope.

"Tell—" he paused. "Never mind."

"Of all the things I remained to say to Shade, this is the most important."

Knick didn't really understand, but he nodded and slipped the scrambler in his ear. The loud screech registering his brainwaves inflicted such pain, his eyes nearly rolled back into his skull. He'd almost forgotten how badly it hurt to have the hive mind wriggling its way into his brain, or how much it would hurt to rip it out.

Isis reached out to touch him, but he held his arm out, keeping her away. He shook his head, warning her to stay back.

Then, he left for the quickest route to Rashrima Haan. To Heaven.

The black blur dropped out of the sky light a ball of black fire, crashing into the ground with a bright burst. Shade stood from the crouch-landing and put one foot forward, violet eyes locked on Eros. Daelus stood a few feet behind him. Thunder rumbled overhead.

"What's going on?" she asked. "Why did you pull me out of the sky?"

"Shade," he started toward her, but her demeanor was anything but friendly. He was frowning, concerned when he saw her state. "Where have you been? Why are you covered in blood?"

"Gobol is dead," she declared. "Assassinated. I couldn't save him. It's his blood."

"Shade…" Eros was sympathetic, voice soft.

"I sat with him," she told him quietly. "He was afraid to be left alone."

"Shade, Asgard is gone. There were few survivors." He took a step toward her again but her body flexed defensively. "Those still alive have fled to Sanctuary."

"What?" she hissed. "Who?"

"Mirax," he replied coolly. Her fists tightened; the muscles in her neck clenched. "The Oracle and Enoch are lost. Bartimaeus is dead."

She collapsed in disbelief, fighting a storm of anger and a swell of sorrow; one sent her adrenaline raging while the other slowed her heartbeat to a depressive sloth. Daelus immediately came to her side. Eros slowly crossed to her and knelt before her. He reached out and pulled her close, held her head against his shoulder; he hoped to transfer the pain out of her heart and into his. There were tears in her eyes, but none ever escaped.

"How?" she asked through clenched teeth. Eros gently ran his fingers through her hair.

"We believe the relic you were sent after was purposefully allowed to enter MAAR's hands. Donovon probably set the sibling stone in the tunnels for Mirax to find," Daelus replied. "We're not sure why."

She suddenly got to her feet and stomped away. Eros and Daelus rose.

"Where are you going?" Eros asked but she didn't reply. "Shade!" Eros called. "You bring a stranger into Asgard—an ex-angel—and we're attacked. Do you think that's a coincidence?"

"Are you blaming me?" she asked incredulously as she

spun to face him.

"No. Of course not. But before you run off again to find him, think about this," he implored. "He has betrayed us, Shade, just like I told you he would, like he's done to everything and everyone he's ever known." He inched closer to her as she stared at him, face blank like she didn't want to believe it. "He's betrayed you."

She suddenly frowned.

"I don't believe you," Shade said coldly. "For the same reasons, couldn't you accuse yourself? Invoking Vanguard gives you upmost authority. Then you are declared Regent, inheriting all of the Keepers, even beyond Vanguard? Stay away from me, Eros. Do not follow." Her violet eyes flared with her glare. "I'm warning you."

Eros put his head in his hands as she stormed off. Daelus stared a long time at Eros and his broken expression. He didn't understand quite how deeply Eros loved her, or even what kind of love it was, but he did understand there was something Eros was losing his grip on and that it pained him.

"Too many secrets," he whispered to himself. That was the real downfall of the Keepers. "Too many secrets."

Daelus took off after her, calling to her three times before she stopped. They were out of earshot of the Baron. She twirled to face him.

"Are you going to try to stop me, too?" she hissed. He shook his head as he got closer. Though she did not tense up defensively like she did with Eros, he felt no kindness in her. When he was face to face, he spoke.

"I know you're scared. You're confused. You're angry. We *all* are. Don't let that stop you from thinking of me...of Eros...of the others." He tried to smile but it didn't come out right. "We have met traitors, but...some of us would die first. You can believe in that."

Shade put her hand on his shoulder, sincere.

"Beware of Sonia. She sent Gobol to his death," she told him, and then turned.

Before she could get anywhere, Daelus put his arms across her chest and hugged her from behind. It was the first time he felt bigger than she was. He smelled her hair, her skin; though she'd fought, been covered in blood, and chilled in the weather, she still had the distinctive scent that was unmistakably her. Normally, it made his heart flutter. Now, it made him anxious.

"Let me come with you," he said softly. "I can help you. I can watch out for you. I don't know what you're expecting to find…or who you will go looking for, but I can help you." He shifted, adjusting his hold; his arms were crisscrossed in front of her, hands gripping her shoulders. She didn't fight him. "I know you don't trust me. I know you'd rather it was someone else—rather it was Rexis. But *I'm* here, and I believe in you…"

"Do you feel obligated to me?" she whispered, and there was a certain measure of hurt in her voice. "You shouldn't."

"Of everything I've ever felt, obligation was never one of those feelings," he assured her. She gently pulled out of his grasp and he let her go. He suddenly felt very empty, as if holding her had filled some hollow part of him.

"Then, go back to Sanctuary. Make sure Sonia cannot hurt anyone else." Her gaze wavered. "I will trust you with this."

He nodded, accepting her decision. "Be careful, Shade. I worry one day you won't come back, but I think you know what you're doing."

"At least one of us does," she replied, offering a rare and small smile that quickly faded. "For the Balance…"

"For the Balance," he agreed. She turned to depart, but stopped.

"I'm sorry about Daedalus," Shade said, causing his heart to skip a beat. And then she was gone—a black, shooting star.

The red hood was pulled tight as the Bloodsworn known as Hezara traveled through the more unfriendly parts of Howerton. She'd left K-City behind half-a-day before, and since then, she'd felt as though she was being followed. She was hoping the seedy nature would slow her stalkers down, but she still felt the eyes on her.

Hezara paused and looked down an alley to her right. If she remembered correctly, there was a Bloodsworn post in Howerton, merely a few blocks from where she was. With a quick glance around her, she started off down the alley, following her memory through the dark and narrow streets.

Howerton was a worker town, one of the thirteen famous labor camps of the Mine; like the others, it was established during the first settlement years of Kishar. A mere collection of tents had turned into tightly packed wooden constructs bound by black iron. Iron mongers and blacksmiths—that was the population of Howerton. It smelled of dirty water, smelted iron, and dogs. Seamy as a port city without the port and a lot quieter. Brothels were as plentiful as smithies, spread out among the population; mostly men inhabited Howerton. Only the strong and stupid women dared dwell in a labor camp; they were outnumbered 5 to 1.

The wooden shack was nondescript but a Bloodsworn always recognized the posts. She pushed through the creaky door into the dark room. There was a scrawny woman behind the counter, peering across the small space with turquoise eyes that glowed in the dark. Her stringy hair fell across pale scars worming across her face. She was terrifying to look at.

"Sworn," the woman purred, motioning Hezara over. "Taking up post or passing through?"

"I need you to do something for me," she replied, soothed by the woman's surprisingly kind voice.

"For a fellow Sworn, no favor is too great. How can I help you?"

Hezara leaned close so that she could whisper. She noticed the woman's muscles flex in her thin arms as she leaned down; the bulge was considerable. This woman was deceivingly formidable.

"I am delivering something very important...and I'm certain I am being followed. My package cannot fall into the wrong hands. I need your help."

The woman grinned, making a fist, showing off the blue and gnarly veins in her arms. Her sharp canines glinted in the filtered light.

The rain had reached Rashrima Haan by the time Knick stood before the gates of Heaven. They were not made of pearl. When the great gears silently cranked and the doors opened, Knick could see the street was not paved with gold. It was never paved with gold. It was a cold, white tower of plastic purposes.

The adopted identity he assumed—agent 89-03-211—was announced to Operations and he was ushered in the building. The only survivor, that's what they were saying. Luckily, he didn't have to worry about them recognizing him. Angels didn't see faces. One face bled right into another. The mental link to operations was enough to weed out spies and infiltrators; only angels could link to the hive mind without alarming the system to an intruder.

Knick took a deep breath, suppressing his fear at making that step across the threshold: the step of no return. The hive mind sensed emotions through various monitors—chemical, adrenaline, heartbeat, brain waves. That was the make-up of a human being. Patterns. And as soon as they broke a person down into chemical operations, it was easy to dehumanize them. Once dehumanized, control was imminent.

He stepped into the hallway and the doors closing behind him made a hollow gong of finality. There was a screech in his ear requesting his response. Knick touched his finger to the scrambler.

"Yes...Operations."

When the black star descended upon the ruins of Asgard, the furious form of the Sovereign of the Sword of Shadows manifested from the smoke and stalked through the entrance. Water dripped from the blasted overhangs and made ripples in the bloody pools gathered beneath the chalky dead.

The clutter of corpses sent shudders of ferocity through her pale body. The blood down the front of her was like a bright streak in the gray world around her, matching the glow of her violet eyes. And though the rain came down, it never seemed to touch her.

She glared at the rocky mound spilling out of the Abbey and then made her way up the steps, stopping at each level to inspect the dead. More and more bodies piled up until she found the wells of the spiral where the Keepers had made their final stand. Up a few more levels, she found the withered corpse of Bartimaeus and fell to her knees.

"Bartimaeus..." she whispered in disbelief. Though Eros had warned her, she had hardly accepted the truth of what he was saying. An Interim dead? Impossible. "Bartimaeus," she said again, closing his charred eyes. Black veins protruded on his leathery skin.

His corpse was warped by his own power. The magnitude of his spell had put his body under the strain. The forces he combated, the goal he attempted to accomplish: it was too great a task. Shade swallowed hard, gently touching her old friend's cheek before she stood. Would she suffer the same fate in this twisted world the Regent had left them in?

The shadows encroached around Shade, moving unnaturally with the invisible swells of her anger, and descended upon her, a black cloak that never touched her shoulders. Obediently, they answered her silent call, moved by her rage like a dark army waiting for an order to kill.

Her boots crunched through the debris for only a moment before the shadows gathered around her and she stepped through them, reappearing in the dungeon. It was dark. All the lights had gone out. Holes in the ceiling filtered in faint light from the destruction above ground, but it was barely enough to penetrate the blackness of the underground prison.

"Nico!" she screamed, stomping through the twisting rows of cells. The clutter of angel corpses confused her; could she take this as a sign of hope or a sign to despair? "Nico!"

She stopped in front of his cell. Shade could see the bloody holes in his chest and his lifeless eyes. She did this. She killed him. Her ideas had earned them no answers and sentenced him to death. A fire of rage welled up inside of her and the nethergy that sparked a smoky torch around her nearly drowned out the scream that escaped her lungs.

The bars across the door did nothing to keep her out. She went through them as though they weren't even there. Shade picked up Nico's mangled corpse and cradled it in her arms. He was weightless. She grunted at the pain in her own chest, carrying him out of the cell. She shadow-stepped again, reappearing in the Abbey, looking out to the rainy hole of the desecrated stronghold she once called home.

The despair overwhelmed her, sucking the last bit of energy from her limbs, and she fell to the ground. Shade yanked a rag free from the debris, closed Nico's eyes, and covered his body. Then she collapsed, head on his chest. It had been days since she slept and her rage had used up the last of the adrenaline keeping her going.

Her eyes closed.

Isis crept from the shadows at the back of the Abbey and crossed to her sleeping Interim. Jilk and the siblings inched behind her.

"Is she dead?" Slot asked. Isis shook her head.

"She is sleeping," she replied, kneeling at Shade's side. She stroked her hair from her face, reflecting on the tormented expression she wore even in sleep. "She will need her rest to do what she is going to do." Isis leaned down to her ear. "Rest well, Shade. I am watching over you."

The summons of the Priori was met with a chaos of footsteps in the massive hall the ex-Regent Muriel and his delegates commanded. While they gathered, Muriel sat in his center throne, looking older than he did before. His drooping eyes peered through slits as his forces gathered. Donovan was at the forefront, gleaming.

"All that are not in the field have gathered, your Excellency," the traitorous Interim told his master.

"Good," he muttered. When the noise of one hundred men gathering dissipated, Muriel pushed his own weight out of the great chair and his feet shuffled him to stand before the Priori. "Gentlemen…Asgard has fallen!"

A roar of victory sounded in the domed room, shaking the delegates to their bones with fear of what they'd only dreamed could be done. Muriel's viciously rotting smile spread across his wrinkled face, arms stretched to the ceiling with the rise of exclamation. Those same arms commanded silence and it was granted.

"In our time, we were unable to take more than necessary with us when we departed from dear Asgard. Now, we will return there, to reclaim the powers rightfully ours, and to destroy anything the faithless few may find useful."

This time, there was no excited roar.

One of the Priori spoke up. "But my liege," he began, "reports say Shade is there. Shade has returned to Asgard."

Muriel's arms lowered to his sides as he glared down at the man.

"And?" the ex-Regent demanded. It was another who answered.

"They say she is unpredictable. They say it is as if we knew nothing of the real power of the Interim."

Muriel's head snapped to another voice that spoke out.

"She's dangerous!" he exclaimed. Donovon gaped at the fear gripping the battalion.

"Are you cowards?" Donovon exclaimed. "One woman

against a hundred? You are the Priori, the High Regent's elite! She is just one pathetic bitch begging to die!"

"I will not go," someone said.

"I will not go," another agreed. Then, all around them, the voices rose as one, saying, I will not go. Donovon stormed up the ramp to the riser where the ex-Regent stood.

"My lord," he said, bowing his spiky head, utterly speechless against the defiance.

"If it were one or a few, I could make an example of them," Muriel said quietly, glaring down at his agents. "But I cannot punish all of my servants. There would be none left to fight for me."

"Then send me. I'll destroy her."

"I admire your courage, Donovon, courage we have seen before," the ex-Regent said, "but against the will of one-hundred men, I fear your bravery amounts to utter foolishness." He turned away from the Sovereign. "I never should have underestimated Shade," he said quietly. Then, with surprising volume, he announced, "Be at peace. We will not go," and stalked back to his throne.

Vox looked up at Dr. Basset as he entered the room, smiling. His sleeves were rolled up, shirt unbuttoned at the top. He looked tired and disheveled; his sleepless service to the injured Keepers had been going on for days and she could see in his eyes that he was utterly exhausted. And yet he was smiling with some mysterious discovery.

"You need to sleep, doctor," she said quietly. "You've done much for us, but you'll be of no use to anyone if you work yourself to death."

He waved it off as though it were unfounded concern.

"I was going to get a few hours," he said, "but I found something I thought you might like to see." He produced a wooden horn with a long flute and a round, concave end. "Or, to be more accurate, *hear*."

She frowned, confused, and he gently shut the door to give them privacy.

"Where's Dimitri?" he asked as he crossed to her.

"With the others," she replied. "We maintain a low profile to prevent rumors and suspicion from rooting out our secret."

He nodded and touched her belly. "Another time," he

assured her and handed her the horn so that she could feel it, examine it for herself.

"What is it?"

"It's called a Pinard Horn," he replied. "I suspect the world hasn't seen one for nearly a thousand years. They've long-since been considered barbaric and useless compared to the technologies we posses."

"What do you do with it?"

He took the horn from her and placed the end of the flute to her stomach. Then, he placed his ear to the cup at the end. The smile on his face told her he was listening to something amazing. Dr. Basset motioned for her to try, so she bent over as best she could and put her ear to it.

The sound of a heartbeat came through the horn and filled her to the brim with tears.

"My baby's heartbeat," she whispered, looking up at the doctor in shock. He nodded, still smiling. She put her greedy ear back to the horn, wanting to hear more and more. After a moment, she felt his hand on her shoulder.

"Do you mind if I listen for a moment?" he asked. "I promise I'll leave this with you so you can listen whenever you like."

She leaned back so he could take over. He pushed the horn around her belly, asking her to lie down after a moment, and finally stopped at the underside of her stomach. Then, he stood up straight and handed her the horn.

"Your baby's heart beat sounds fine," he assured her. Vox smiled, swiping at the tears on her lashes, and nodded.

"Thank you."

Dr. Basset nodded and quietly left the room, looking around at the sleeping refugees huddled around the room against the walls, against each other. There hadn't been enough blankets for everyone, and even fewer pillows. The soldiers and younger men had given the luxuries up to their elders, and only the severely injured were given beds.

As hard as he had thought life had been before his MAAR involvement, he'd never seen such torment. While having your freedom stripped and choices relatively made for you, he had been allowed to educate himself, marry the woman he loved, raise two girls in privilege, and live a peaceful life.

Little did he know at the time there were soldiers behind

the scenes fighting for him and his family. Now, they were lying on the ground, bleeding and starving and shivering under his care. For the first time, he had a true mission. Though he hated the pain it brought him when someone he was trying to help was unable to hold on to their life thread, he felt even more rewarded when someone pulled through.

Dr. Basset found his family in one of the back rooms. He smiled, motioning for his wife and youngest daughter not to get off the bed, but Laura did anyway.

"Sleep, Robert," she insisted. "You need your rest."

He smiled and kissed her, hugging her tight.

"This is all the rest I need," he said playfully. "Just a few hugs and I already feel rejuvenated."

Laura kissed her husband again.

"I'm so proud of you," she whispered. "Go on, lie down. I'll make sure nothing happens without someone nearby to help."

"If it gets bad..." he began.

"I'll wake you," she assured him. He nodded and curled up on the cot with his daughter, kissing her hair before his head touched the pillow.

He was asleep nearly instantly. Laura motioned to Casey, her eldest, and they snuck out of the room.

"We're never going home again, are we?" Casey asked, folding her thin arms under her breasts. Her mother shook her head. "I didn't think so. Clara keeps asking me, and I wasn't sure how to tell her...*what* to tell her."

Laura brushed her hair from her face and tucked a clump behind her ear. The subject clearly made her uncomfortable. She had done her best to distract herself with Robert's work so she didn't have to think about it.

"Mom," Casey continued, "what are we going do? Where are we going to go?"

"I don't know," Laura admitted, clearing the emotion out of her throat. "But as long as we stick together, we'll be okay. Okay?" She rubbed her daughter's arm, trying her best to smile. Casey nodded and followed her mother back toward the main room.

Laura admired her daughter's strength. Casey had managed to keep a brave face through everything that had happened. Even then, Laura resisted breaking down into sobs, but Casey hadn't an ounce of disturbance in her expression. That made her proud. She'd been so proud of her family throughout the entirety of this tragedy. From them, she was able to stay strong even when she had no idea what they were being strong for.

The cool breeze from the still-falling rain brushed Shade's face until her eyelids fluttered open. She looked up, eyes blurry and head groggy from sleep. There in the haze, she saw a glowing form of a nude young woman with long, blond hair and crystalline green eyes. She blinked, trying to raise her head, but pain momentarily overwhelmed her and she laid back down.

After counting out three breaths, she opened her eyes again. The woman was standing before her in a white t-shirt and there was no glow. Shade pushed herself up, ignoring the headache, and glanced around at the ruins.

"Welcome back," the girl said. "I have been waiting for you."

"How long have I been out?"

"Three days."

Shade frowned at her. "Three days?" she echoed.

"You were exhausted. It's understandable. You've been through so much."

"Not as much as these people here!" Shade exclaimed. "These people who are dead. This man," she angrily pointed at Nico's corpse, "not as much as him. Who are you? I know you. I know your voice."

"Yes," she agreed. "I am Isis, though we met long before now…back when you knew me only as the Enoch."

Shade's muscles slacked in surprise, anger instantly evaporating.

"It was your voice I heard in the tunnels," Shade said. "You sent me to Knick."

Isis nodded. "It was me," she confirmed, "though I sent you nowhere, I only bid you go to him. You were the one who sent yourself to him."

"How is that possible?"

"Shade," Isis said gently. "You have the potential to do much, much more than any Interim has dreamed of doing in thousands of years." She intercepted Shade's apprehension.

"You're unsure. After all, only a small sect of Keepers ever truly knew what the Enoch was. Please, do not be afraid. Please, do not waste time debating on trusting me. We are at an impasse in the weave and there is little time before one of many terrible fates—some worse than others—is chosen as our destiny."

Shade nodded and got to her feet, giving Nico's covered corpse one last regretful glance.

"How could this happen?" Shade wanted to know. "Why didn't you see this coming? Why didn't you warn us?"

"I did," Isis said. "The Enoch already prophesied the downfall of the Keepers over a thousand years ago. Once, this prophecy was treasured, looked for, honored, feared, respected. As the generations of leaders continued, some Regents hid it away, foolishly believing the time to have passed for such a downfall to occur.

"Beware the scar on the wall, the bloody king, for the bodies of the wall will crumble, the scales scattered," Isis quoted. "Do you remember it Shade? That part of the prophecy *you* fulfilled. Do you remember burning the glyph of the sacrificial road onto the wall?" The shocked and nauseous look on Shade's face told her she did. "Yes, you were warned. Unfortunately, you were deceived by treachery."

Isis turned, casting her sad eyes toward the ground.

"Shade, our Sight is clouded by the poison of treachery. I was only able to help you because I became aware of myself. Once I had been awakened, I was able to tap into the consciousness of the Keepers, but it limited my already limited Sight. Once, long ago, there was no veil the Sight couldn't pierce. But Muriel's poison has left us all in the dark."

"How did you...I mean, how were you able to..." But Shade's question wouldn't properly form.

"I led an outsider into Asgard and he saved me."

"Outsider? Could you not have depended on the Keepers?"

"The Keepers?" Isis asked, quirking one brow. "The Keepers who revere me as though I were some kind of god? It is easier for an outsider to come to the rescue of a woman he isn't entirely sure exists than it is for a zealot of the Balance to free the mystical dreamweaver they hold in such high esteem."

"Am I a zealot?" Shade asked.

"You have another destiny. Believe it or not, many people in this world have been called to play a part in the ending of all things—not just Keepers. Otto was called just as you have been called. Just as Knick has been called. As I have been called...and many more. Besides...I did not want to interfere in your thread too much; the fate lines are so fragile now. Too much tampering, and I could upset your weave. It is too important to alter."

She turned back to Shade, her eyes both serious and alarmed.

"As if the angels have not left us to an already terrible end, they destroyed a vital seal hidden away in Asgard, forcing events potentially avoided."

"What seal?"

"Hidden at the apex of the tower was a secret vessel called the King's Way. A time keeper, a lock, a key, a vassal, a guide, and a gong all in one. The King's Way was brought out of the ancient city when the doors were sealed and was the keeper of the towers of the Keepers throughout all of history. Though an object, it was an organic creation—a technology only understood by men long dead.

"It kept time, counting down...counting up..."

"To what?" Shade asked.

"To its death," Isis said darkly. "It kept the doors locked, the city sealed in frozen sleep. It is the key to breaking that seal. It is a vassal of the old king. A guide for the new king. A gong to awaken, to warn, to signal, to announce the coming."

"What are you talking about?"

"The King's Way was destroyed, and doing so awakened it. It understood the Keepers were in danger and that Asgard had been compromised. It purged the tower and sent a warning to all the servants of the Balance that they were in danger and must return home."

"I am home," Shade replied. "There's nothing here but death."

"No, not this place—this temporary house," Isis whispered. "To your real home...the real home of all Keepers. Consider this the rapture...when all Keepers are summoned to the birthplace. The King's Way has sent word to this place, warmed that frozen sleep and broken the seal; it has called out to it, readied it, awakened it. Now the journey must be made."

"A journey to where?"

"A journey we must all make, going the King's Way, to ancient and hidden Mesopotamia."

"Mesopotamia," Shade repeated, remembering the High Counselor's words. "King Malikiel." She spun around and ran hard.

"Shade!" Isis called, attempting to follow. She did not go two steps before Shade shadow-stepped and she was unable to go after her.

At the door to the High Study, Shade forced the door open, scattering the furniture and tomes that blocked the way.

"High Counselor!" she exclaimed, charging into the small study.

Torches still burned on the walls, illuminating the disheveled room. The desk had been dragged across the room, chairs fallen over, bookshelves with contents dumped, and a litter of knowledge hiding the floor. Shade saw the feet poking out from around the desk and hurried up to the second tier, coming around to the small alcove where two men were laying, dead or unconscious. The charred remains of many tomes caught her gaze and she feared the worst; in an hour of desperation, the book holding the answers had been destroyed.

Shade knelt next to the High Counselor but she could tell by the dried blood matted in his gray hair and beard and on his clothing coupled with his blanch complexion that he was dead. She bowed her head in reverence and a prayer to the Balance went through her mind. When she took his hand, she felt the crumbled piece of paper knotted in his palm.

She unfolded the old page and frowned at the blood-drawn sigil: Knick's glyph. *The One.* That was what the message beneath the drawing said. She lifted her gaze to the High Counselor and touched his hand. *Couldn't you have stayed alive long enough,* she thought, *to give me this message yourself?* Shade folded the page up and tucked it into one of her pant pockets.

Before she stood, she noticed the boy next to the High Counselor take a very shallow breath. She stepped across the High Counselor and turned the boy over, checking for a pulse. It was weak, but it was there. An ugly and wide scar started beside his right eye and curved over his cheek bone down to the corner of his lip.

Shade shuffled around the study, desperate to find some blankets. There were a few trapped under the High Counselor's toppled chair; she yanked them free and wrapped the young scholar up tight to keep him warm. She lifted him up, hugging him close.

"Come on," she hissed. "Stay alive."

Shade hoisted him up, finding him heavier than Nico had been, and carried him back down to the Abbey. Isis was waiting, and Shade saw more people hanging back in the shadows. When Isis saw what she carried, she frowned.

"He's alive," Shade told her. Isis motioned her toward the back where another boy was sleeping. She laid him near him, keeping him wrapped up. "He's in bad shape. His pulse is very shallow. I barely noticed he was alive."

The figures—three of them—stepped closer to her. She glanced up and paused, surprised, then tilted her head to the side. She knew them. She recognized them.

"You're Knick's friends," Shade said, slowly rising to her feet.

"So you're Gothic, huh?" Jilk asked. "You're Shade?"

Her head snapped to the Enoch.

"Where is he?" she demanded to know. Isis did not reply. "If they're here, that means he's here, too." She shifted her attention to the cogwheelers. "What are you doing here? Where is Knick?"

"We came here looking for you," Jilk explained.

"No," Slot corrected him, stepping forward. "He came looking for you. We came to protect him."

Solo put a protective hand on his sister's head, falling in place at her side. Jilk motioned back to her, ordering her to calm down. Though Shade had no idea why the distinction was important, she hardly cared.

"It's okay, Slot," Jilk said. "I don't think we have to worry." To Shade, he continued. "He's not here anymore. He moved on. We just stayed behind to watch out for these guys." He motioned to the unconscious men and the Enoch.

"Shade," Isis began carefully, "the Oracle is gone."

"Gone?" Shade repeated. "Who?"

"I assume the angels, but I cannot tell you with certainty."

"I can," she snapped, storming out of the Abbey. "Stay

here."

Shade followed the corridors to the Seer's Cell, noting the door had already been kicked in. A circle of bodies lay around the pedestal where the Oracle once perched. Cold water pooled around the bodies, but there were no openings in the cell for the rain to get in. She knelt and examined the corpses, fingers curling into fists as she found the blade wounds across their throats and through their chests.

"Shade?" Isis asked as she stormed back into the Abbey.

"Donovon," the Interim announced. "He must've come in during the chaos. He killed those men in the Seer's Cell. They had traces of aegis all over them."

Isis hung her head.

"Then I have sent Knick Coltin to his death," she said quietly.

"What do you mean? Where is he?"

"He's in Heaven," Solo piped up. Shade was slack-jawed in shock. "He went back to Heaven to get the Oracle as the only survivor of the attack on the Keepers."

"You sent him to the angels?" she bellowed, furious.

"There are many things I can only guess at," Isis defended herself. "I warned him I could not say with any certainty that the angels had the Oracle."

"You knew I was coming! Why didn't you wait for me?"

"The Oracle is precious! In the wrong hands, it is a powerful and dangerous weapon! The Oracle sacrificed itself for me. We must get it back. It is imperative if we are to go to Mesopotamia!"

Shade spun on her toes and began marching out of the Abbey.

"Where are you going?" Isis called after her.

"I'm going to get him before the angels destroy him."

"Don't go!" Isis exclaimed, much to everyone's surprise.

"What?" Shade snapped, turning enraged violet eyes on the Enoch. The cogwheelers took a step back, suddenly afraid of the Keeper. "What did you say to me?"

"You do not have your power," Isis reminded her. "Your bells are gone."

"Doesn't matter."

"All you have is a single piece of steel against the nest of angels!"

"It doesn't matter!"

"Do not go, Shade," Isis reiterated. "Do not go...unless you love him. If you do not love him, you will fail." She watched Shade's expression falter in her hesitancy and then harden again.

"I'm going," she said seriously, marching out of the Abbey and down the rocky slope.

"Was that a confession?" Jilk whispered. "I'm a little unclear on that. I mean," he looked at his friends, "she wouldn't go unless she loved him, right? Or would she?"

"She doesn't seem the type to scare easy," Solo muttered.

"Right?" Jilk agreed. Slot rolled her eyes.

Isis bowed her head and closed her eyes, inhaling the sense of things and organizing it in her brain. The game was officially in motion, and now they had to wait.

The summons to Operations had taken days to be initiated. One did not simply hop an elevator up to the boss. In the mean time, he'd gone about standard post-operation procedures: filing reports, psychological and physical evaluation, et cetera. That was behind him now. Now, Knick was before the great tomb.

The door did not whiz away; it phased out—solid, two meters thick trianium ghosted until Knick was able to pass through it as though its density was that of air. The chamber of the hive mind was not located at the peak of Heaven, but rather in the depths of its basement. The descent to that level included twelve scans and just as many sanitation cubes; he was lowered through two sets of blast doors and his identity confirmed at seven checkpoints. He was disarmed at the first and it was reconfirmed over and over again until he stood at the phasers and stepped into the room.

The chamber was called the Nest. He'd only ever been there once, and it was still as chilling the second time as it had been the first. When he stepped through the doors, they solidified behind him and he was blasted by a disinfectant spray. The room was lit with ceraphin runners in the ceiling between the bar-work and by side panels, leaving much in the dimness to protect the organic machinery.

The hive mind was a network of black wires, cables, and tubes connecting the super-computer to power generators hidden behind the massive walls. The gray motherboard resembled a gigantic brain installed in the floor and all of the black tendrils of neural activity wormed away from it, dripping with lubricants to keep it from overheating. Some of it, Knick was sure, was ooze produced by the mind itself.

Parasites, as they were called, constantly snaked over the brain, each with a different duty; some sucked up the tallow blobs to prevent the brain from drowning in the fluids while others made constant reparations, replacements, and upgrades, while some chewed away at and vacuumed up the hardened liniment clots.

The brain itself was moist and sleek with a unique type of metal: sylimar. Sylimar was spongy, self-humidifying, and capable of breathing. When touched, it hardened in self-defense, becoming as impenetrable as trianium. The intelligence of such a substance made Knick uneasy; not to mention, the deep ridges spidering around the cables made it look exactly like a human brain. He could even see it pulsing, reacting to the quadroton dump of information, exabytes processed every second.

Operations was a collaboration of twelve men, if they could still be called men, plugged into the cerebrum. To Knick, it looked as if they were eternally being absorbed by the hive mind. They were seated around the bolted ring that encased the mind, but they were sinking into it. The sylimar had grown around their legs and up their torsos, pulsing and pumping as though feeding off of the humans. It connected directly to their neural wiring and the mind's own neural tubes had speared their flesh and wound through their bodies, wrapping around them and connecting them to the machine. Jelly-like lubricants slimed over their augmented bodies. Their arms hung in the cables above their heads; their faces were covered with white sheets changed daily, stained with the grease constantly absorbed and sweated. Knick had never seen their faces. He was positive he didn't want to. The sheets, he knew, were in-part to protect their plasmacoded, photosensitive eyes, and in-part to hide the utter absence of humanity.

The final part of Operations was the spokesman called Centrum. Hooked into the heart of a massive machine four stories above the hive mind, a part-man, part-cyborg normally remained inside the machine; when there were visitors, such as now, he was moved out of the well of the machine like the cuckoo in a clock and left suspended over the room by the cables sunken into his skin.

Knick refused to flinch when the great, electronic eye of Centrum opened and stared down at him; the half of his face where the other eye should be was covered with a black patch stitched into his pale skin. His voice was cybertronic, cold, empty, and pitched a little high.

"Agent 89-03-211, you are the only surviving member of the attack battalion 9X1-Gv5578, target: Keeper Headquarters located quadrant 997-A in Tonatti Haan. Verify."

"Yes, Operations," Knick replied mechanically.

"Scenario indeterminate. Verify."

"I was thrown from the tower during an explosion. I was knocked unconscious. When I awoke, I investigated the field. All targets dead. All allies dead."

"Communications disrupted. Battlefield analysis terminated. Report viable. Zero articles returned to hive. Verify."

"Nothing was retrieved from the remains. The tower was in ruins."

"Artifacts: verify."

"None."

"Repository: verify."

"Destroyed."

"Oracle: verify."

"Gone."

There was a long silence in the machine. Knick suddenly felt very confused. He thought the angels had taken into possession the Oracle. Why was Centrum asking him about it? Was it a test?

"Operations," Knick asked, voice echoing in the cavernous room. The brain behind Centrum pulsed and glistened with sweat, reacting to some information flux that he could neither access nor guess at. "Do we not possess the Oracle?"

"Units to retrieve target. Verify."

"A retrieval unit post-purge was not issued?" he asked.

"Negative."

There was another long pause and Knick did his best to keep calm. Machines did not think. AIs' processed information faster than a human being could breathe. The silence could only mean the hive mind was conferring data that wasn't adding up. The only thing that would fail to add up in Heaven would be Knick himself.

Sonia whipped around when Daelus threw open the door. He registered the startled look change to confusion and then to fear when he cleared the distance between them, grabbed her by her throat, and slammed her against the wall.

"What—" she barely choked out.

"Did you betray us, Sonia?" he growled. Her head twitched out a "no" but that only made him squeeze tighter. She clawed at his hand desperately. "Your resistance to Shade was a result of your allegiance to the Regent?"

"No!" she gasped, choking. She went for her weapon but Daelus roughly pinned her arm to the wall and rammed his knee into her blade so that she couldn't try to wriggle it out with her other hand.

"Why did you send Gobol into a trap?" he barked.

"Trap?" she rasped. "What trap?" She kept clawing but Daelus barely noticed her nails raking across his skin. "I was asked to inform Gobol about a relic development in Isali." She started kicking, trying to get air. "A development I was told Eros wanted investigated!"

Daelus eased up on her throat and she gasped, sucking in deep breaths.

"Who told you?" he asked, suddenly afraid.

"Rexis," she gasped. Daelus snarled and leaned onto her.

"You're lying?" he hissed. She shook her head, struggling to breathe again.

"No!"

In disbelief, he dropped her and took a step back. Sonia collapsed against the wall, holding her own throat as she took ragged breaths.

"What the hell...is going...on...?" she panted but Daelus could barely respond. She looked up at him and recoiled at his expression. "Daelus?" There was fear in her voice.

He spun around and swished out of the room, heading down the hall to where Eros had told him he'd be. Once in the privacy of the room, he swallowed the lump in his throat. Before he could even get it out, Eros read his face and immediately came to his side.

"What's happened?" Eros demanded to know.

"The other traitor," he whispered around the grapefruit lodged in his windpipe. "I know who it is."

"Who?"

"Rexis."

Eros's brow pulled together in a deep frown. "Are you sure?"

"He bade Sonia send Gobol to Isali on your order to investigate a development. Shade said it was a trap. He had access to the delegates. He moved easily through Asgard. As Shade's biggest supporter, he was above suspicion."

The deeply disturbed expression on Eros's face reflected Daelus's own. The Baron gave a curt nod and then brushed past him. Daelus followed, his heart sinking like a stone in his chest. They found Rexis in the main hall. He started to smile when he saw them coming but it faded fast and he nodded in understanding. He turned his back to them.

"This isn't how I wanted it to go down, Eros," Rexis said.

"How exactly did you intend for it to go down? When you were standing over our corpses?" Eros asked. Rexis looked off to the side and Daelus could see the frown on his face behind his wild, dark red hair. "Either way, you gave quite the performance. I never would have guessed you could betray us."

"It wasn't a performance," Rexis rebutted, turning to face them. "I never wanted any of this to happen. Unfortunately, it was necessary."

"Necessary?" Daelus balked. "Thousands of lives were *necessary?*" He was silenced by the rise of Eros's hand.

"How could you align yourself with Muriel?" Eros asked.

"Tch, Muriel," Rexis hissed, turning into a slow pace. "He and I share the same interests...for now."

"For now?"

"The destruction of the Keepers. That is what we want. Regrettably, Muriel plans to rebuild them once they're dead...remake them in his image, ey." His shoulders slumped. "I'm afraid that's as far as we go together. I'll have to kill him then."

By then, the other Interim had joined them in the hallway, listening with hurt and angry expressions to the news another friend had betrayed them. The collective and Kur still in the room looked utterly broken by the dissention.

"Rexis, why?" Vox pleaded. "You swore to *serve* the Balance!"

"Who bade me take that vow?" Rexis asked. "Keepers! Who swears to uphold the Balance? Keepers! Not Keepers of the Balance... Keepers of Deception! Of Power! Of Secrets!"

Eros and Daelus exchanged glances and Rexis continued.

"Muriel came to me, ey. He told me I had potential...that I had a taste for blood. Like any Keeper at the time, I was honored to be summoned to a higher calling by the Regent. I had no need for thoughts of loyalty to one sect or the other. We were all on the same side, weren't we? I was wrong.

"Muriel told me of all the deception in the Order. He told me every sorry tale." He turned his steely gaze to the Baron's right-hand commander. "Even yours, Daelus. He suspected I was pliable enough to deem him as some type of savior, but I saw he was a part of it as well—the biggest part. He was a filthy snake! But he was right in one thing: the Keepers had to be destroyed to be purified."

"We were family, Rex," Dimitri muttered.

"We were," Rexis agreed.

"You would do this to your family?" Eros asked. "And to your best friend?"

The burnt-orange eyes of Rexis reflected the torch light as he turned his head toward Eros. His brows were pulled tight in confusion, lips parted in disbelief.

"Shade?" he whispered. "No. No, I could never hurt Shade. That's why I lured her out of Asgard—to protect her. I knew she was seeking answers; when Shade is looking for something, it can never hide from her. She is unrelenting." He pursed his lips a second. "I suspect she is why Muriel recruited me. He wants to destroy her. He intended I help him do that. But I will never let him have her."

"You have dishonored everything she stands for," Sonia suddenly exclaimed. "Shade always carried the mission in her heart even if she did not carry Keeper law."

"Your friendship is over," Balthazar told him. "Shade holds no allegiance to cowards and traitors."

Rexis snarled in anger. "You're wrong!" he exclaimed. "She'll understand. She will."

Eros bowed his head. Daelus knew he was regretting everything that had happened, that he was feeling responsible for this dissention. Then, Eros lifted his head and he wore the cool expression of the Baron once more.

"Rexis, Sovereign of the Sword of Steel, resign your blade and bells. You have been found guilty of treason and are under arrest by the authority of the Baron of the Keepers of the Balance."

"You know I can't do that," Rexis said calmly.

"Then we will make you." He nodded to the other Interim, who each drew their blades and approached their quarry. Kallo and Delia also stood, gripping their swords tightly.

Rexis kicked up one of the discarded Kur weapons, much to everyone's surprise. Only he did not bear it as a weapon; instead, he held the pike toward him. There was a small smile that played out on his lips before his bells jingled and he gently touched the steel tip of the pike.

Rexis disappeared and the weapon clattered to the ground.

"Shit," Eros cursed.

Centrum's head suddenly dislodged, interrupting the quiet pulsing of the hive mind. The head wound down to Knick, attached to a long, ribbed hose. The cybernetic eye stared invasively and the rest of his mutilated and patched head made his stomach feel queasy. He had believed Centrum to be human enough not to have his head detach and snake around.

"You are Agent 89-03-211. Verify."

"I am," he replied without hesitation.

"Report to Tartarus. Confirm identity with the Halo. Verify."

"Understood, Operations," Knick said and the head recoiled. Once it clicked onto its body, Centrum was retracted and sealed back inside the machine.

Knick turned to the doors, trying not to sweat, and felt a little relieved when they phased out. He exited up through the ascending tunnel and was locked inside the elevator that would transport him out of the well of the hive mind. There was just one problem: he could not confirm his identity at the Halo.

He would not be able to escape Heaven.

Solo put a cold, wet rag against Antion's scar, wincing at the pus welling under infection. His eyes flitted between the patient and his sister, who was huddled on one of the pews. Granted, it was freezing; the relentless rain had taken the temperature down several notches, and the sun going down had knocked a few more degrees off the thermometer.

Still, did Jilk have to be the one to warm her up? The boss had cleared his throat and sat down next to her, offering his arms. She accepted, cuddling against his chest; he wrapped the folds of his jacket around her, holding her tight. All it took was once, Solo knew, and then it was over. Solo didn't care if Jilk was his boss and his friend; he'd probably have to kick his ass and wouldn't mind doing it to protect his sister's honor. She'd cuddled him back in Thebes, so what? She was just happy he'd come out of the coma. Jilk needed to learn the difference between flirting and friendship, that's what he thought.

He glanced over to Isis who was kneeling by Otto, shivering; her crystalline green eyes were focused on the night sky in the open ceiling beyond the Abbey.

"Are you cold?" Jilk asked, getting up. He took her Knick's leather jacket and helped her put it on. It relieved Solo only a moment because just after, Jilk returned to Slot's side and they were back to cuddling.

He continued nursing Antion's wound, checking for a pulse here and there, making sure it hadn't disappeared.

Isis suddenly sat up straight, torso twisting as she looked behind her. Otto groaned. She crawled over to him, leaning over his emaciated form.

"Otto," she whispered. He groaned again, head rolling. Her green eyes shot Solo a pleading gaze. "Help me prop him up."

Solo obliged, gently hoisting Otto up by his shoulders. He rotated him around and leaned him against the wall. Isis slipped in, placing her hand on his cheek.

"Otto," she said as though beckoning him out of sleep. He opened his eyes.

"Isis…"

She smiled warmly. "Yes, Otto."

"Isis," he said again, tears misting his baby blues.

"Yes, Otto," she replied. With his good arm, he reached up

and gently touched her cheek. "You were so brave, Otto. You did everything I asked of you and you saved my life. Thank you."

His thumb stroked her cheek and the skin under her eyes, running over the faint indentions where her lids had been peeled away from her eyeballs. The tears ran down his cheeks and, for the first time in months, he felt no pain.

"I'm so glad," he whispered, voice hoarse. She held his hand against her cheek.

"How do you feel, Otto?"

"Like I was finally able to sleep..."

"You've been asleep almost a full week," she told him. "You'll be able to sleep more soon. Right now, I need you to eat something for me. Will you eat something for me?"

"Yes, I'll try," he rasped. Isis looked over to Solo, and that's when Otto first noticed there were other people with them. "Who are you?" he croaked, alarmed.

"They're friends, Otto. Don't worry. You're safe." She leaned closer to his face, knowing he was more worried about her than himself. "I'm safe," she assured him. "While you were sleeping, they watched over us."

Otto nodded and Solo got up, crossed to his pack, and dug around for something to eat. He pulled out a canister of water and a meat bun. Otto drank the water first, managing a few sips taken in intervals. Next, Isis pinched off pieces of the meat bun and fed him small bites. It took him a long time to get each piece down and longer still before he was ready for another one, but Isis managed to feed him half of the bun before she accepted Otto was unable to take anymore.

"I can't move my arm," Otto mumbled sleepily.

"Do you remember anything before you fell asleep?" Isis asked.

"Some. It's all...broken up...in patches, coming in and out..."

"You broke your arm," Solo told him, peeling back the bandages to check the wound. "It was pretty bad but somehow you avoided infection. We set it and splinted it. It should be healing okay, though you might need a mender."

Solo fixed the bandages and gave Isis and Otto some room. She pulled a blanket up against him, tucking it around his waist and chest and arms.

"Are you warm enough?" she asked.

"Isis," he whispered. "Am I dreaming again?"

"No, Otto. This is all very real."

"It's real?"

"Yes."

"You watched over me all this time?"

"I did," she said. "And I will never leave you."

He pulled her to him and hugged her as tightly as his weak arm could manage, crying into her soft hair. She wrapped her arms around his head and held him tenderly.

"You've been so brave, Otto," she soothed, gently combing her fingers through his hair. "I cannot thank you enough."

Deep underground in the Nest, Centrum suddenly opened his cybernetic eye.

"Sir," the voice echoed in the chamber. Centrum's response was a loud screech that vibrated the coils hooked to the hive mind. "There's a Keeper at the door. Target Dreadknight. How should we proceed?"

There was a long pause as Operations conferred. The brain quivered with excitement and Centrum was barely able to contain itself as it delivered the response.

"We have her now," Centrum screamed. "Let her in."

The great doors of Heaven cranked open, spilling light into the dark street, illuminating the deadly figure standing before the gates; the corpses of slaughtered guards littered the property as far as the angels could see. The dried blood down her front was covered with fresh blood. Her long, black hair blew with her ripped skirt in the wind, contrasting with her pale skin. But those violet eyes glowed viciously with the glyph on her forehead and her right fist gripped the menacing sword she wielded.

Shade took a step forward, not even hesitating when the Enoch's words flashed through her mind. *Do not go if you do not love him.* Love or not, she didn't know. She did know that she would tear down all of Heaven until she found him.

The doors slammed behind her with an uneasy, finite clang. She did not look back. The long hallway that stretched in front of her was lined with rows of angels, shoulder to shoulder, two men deep. They smiled behind their silver lenses, and, all at once, ripped their weapons from the polyspace film attached to their Nightwalkers.

Shade darted forward, making quick cuts to the first row. Ruptured arteries splattered blood all over the stark white walls and floor. By then, the others had prepared themselves thoroughly and were not as easy to assassinate. Her sword clanged against the metal bars of the Nightwalkers, between the folds of mace heads, and parried off the bodies of other blades. She dodged the deadly swing of morning stars, ducking under sweeping arms and jumping away from swooping blows.

When Shade reached the end of the hallway, lumps of bloody corpses were like a candy trail leading up to her.

"Did you think a few angels would stop me?" Shade screamed.

She followed the corridors to the next room, avoiding the traps in the hallways as angels appeared out of concealed passages, blending into their white surroundings. Sometimes, they looked like nothing more than a smiling head on the wall. The Sovereign brought her blade up so quickly, she left streaking lines that ruined any chance of sneaking up on her.

"Why has she not used the battle-ether of the Dionysian artifact?" the hive mind asked itself, barely a whisper in the machine.

"Perhaps she cannot use it," the mind answered itself in another quiet voice.

"Perhaps she feels she does not need to," another voice suggested.

"She would not fight for the thrill of fighting when she is on a mission."

"What mission? Verify."

Shade's statistics registered from remote scans and monitors squealed past each of the hive mind's twelve pairs of plasmacoded eyes. They could see it—she was far too focused for a woman bent on rampage.

"Verified," a voice answered.

"Then she cannot use the battle-ether. Scrimmage assessment."

A flux of information whirled through the hive mind, reliving every encounter they'd had with the Keeper code-named Dreadknight. Of all thermal, optic, laser, and cybernetic scans, the common elements were pulled from the images and collated into categories that helped them narrow the field even further. Only one item was missing from her standard repertoire: a bracelet of bells.

Operations immediately analyzed the bracelet, coming up with many theories on its purposes. Yet to be a hypothesis proven, they accepted the most logical conclusion: the bells emitted a special frequency that the sword responded to.

"She cannot use the battle-ether," the hive mind declared.

"Verified," the other voices said at once. Centrum nodded and sent a loud screech through every scrambler in Heaven, excitedly delivering this new piece of information.

The next room was larger than what she'd seen so far. It was empty and poorly lit, as if somehow she was hindered in the low light. She stomped to the center, knowing it was a trap, and therefore was not alarmed when she heard the uniform marching of angels moving into place to surround her.

She wished, at that moment, that she had her bells. She could really use the nethergy of the Shadow Sword right about then. Squeezing the handle, she worked her fist around it, stabilizing her grip. She'd faced numbers like this before, she reminded herself, ignoring the tiny facts that she had been able to command the nethergy in those fights.

The first wave did not catch her off-guard, and she fought with utter grace. The Shadow Sword rang darkly with each parry and blow. Never once did they manage to take the offensive, and when the last of the first wave fell in a heap, she realized they had been merely testing her. Her breathing was normal, as though she hadn't exerted an ounce of energy. Her arms hung strong at her sides, not even close to tired. In spite of her calm state, she had suffered minor injuries under the swell of enemies. Small cuts on her arms and legs were not so great that the adrenaline coursing through her could not make them painless.

Shade's violet eyes scanned from one end of the ambush to the other. *What are you waiting for?* she wondered. *What do you know?* Suddenly, she felt a pull in the sword. Her gaze flicked down at it, muscles tense and ready to respond. She felt the pull again. It was drawing something out of her. She could feel the blood flowing in her veins, drawing down as if flowing out of her body and into the sword.

Impossible, she thought. She'd only ever felt this kind of feeling when she used the nethergy of the sword. Shade looked up, at the silver-eyed faces gleaming at her. The shadows encroached on the ambush. That's when she heard it—their wraith-like voices whispering to her.

"I understand," she said quietly, standing straight out of her battle stance.

The angels suddenly flexed on guard, wondering what she was doing. Shade stalked toward the nearest one, like a great, black cat. And then, without warning, she broke into a run, and then dove for his feet. The angel started to take a step back, ready to meet her weapon as she came out of the roll, but she dropped straight into the floor, passing into his shadow as a person into a pool.

And she was gone.

Shade stood up straight, feeling the darkness whipping around her like a violent wind, only the air was still as death. She looked around, vision warped at the edges in this shadow realm. Beside her stood a tall, black silhouette; it was faceless and still. There were dozens like him, clustered and surrounding her. For every angel there had been, there was a blank-faced shadow man now in his place. And on the ground, these shadowmen casted images of their physical selves; she saw silver-eyed angels looking this way and that, wondering what kind of trick she'd pulled.

She walked to the back of the ambush and stood face to face with one of the shadowmen. Her eyes told him what he needed to do and he nodded sluggishly, obedient to only her orders.

He suddenly melted down into the ground, snaking up the legs of his angel counterpart. The man did not realize what was happening until he felt the wispy fingers around his throat, squeezing so tight that he couldn't breathe. The black head came up, indentions where eyes should be blacker than the rest of him. The angel tried to scream, but it was a mere gurgle; his windpipe collapsed and the angel slumped to the ground, dead. The shadow fell, too, returning to the dark place it roamed.

Shade nodded to it and the shadowman was released from his rooted place beneath the dead man's feet. Their hollow whispers sunk into her spirit, melding with her. She went to another one, pressed into him; she slipped out of the floor at her target's feet. Her blade raked across his ankles and he yelped, falling to the floor. Her pale hand shot out of the shadow and caught his face, holding it up while she pulled her sword across his throat. As his friends turned to help him, they saw Shade disappear into the floor again and the body slump, blood pooling beneath him.

That was the moment Shade realized she was more than just a Sovereign of a sword. The shadows heard her, answered her, obeyed her! She glanced around at this dark realm, wondering why she had not been able to use it before. Perhaps, until now, her need had not been great enough.

Without speaking, she gave orders to the shadowmen around her. They nodded sluggishly. Shade then began sprinting toward a center spot where the world was blackest. She jumped straight into it...

And fell from the ceiling into the physical realm once more. Her scream unnerved her enemies and threw them into cries of their own as they charged toward her. Her long, black hair whipped with her twirling movements as she threw herself into their ranks, twisting and bending with practiced moments.

The lights suddenly dimmed, as if drowning in the swelling darkness, and the shadows squirmed out of their flat spaces. They rose out of the floor and walls like black sand and fog. The angels screamed again, but this time in fear as their own projected silhouettes turned on them. And with a dark army at her call, the room was matted in thick, slick red.

But not all of it was enemy blood. Shade gritted her teeth, feeling the sting of larger wounds: a gash across her back and a deep cut in her right thigh; she had been stabbed in her other leg and the weapon had found muscle to dig into. She ripped more of her skirt off and bent to tie it as a bandage. Before she could, however, one of the shadows knelt in front of her.

His smoky hand glided over the hole and it felt cool and silky. Then suddenly his fingers plunged into the wound and she grunted behind her teeth. The shadowman's hand burned her skin, razing the tissue closed; the pain piqued with her growl and then he withdrew. Though it throbbed, the bleeding had slowed. The shadowman stood up as his comrades melted back into the ground, and then he, too, disappeared.

The door that she encountered refused to open. Her jaw clenched, teeth grating in anger. Her fist banged twice, palm flattening on the third blow.

"Open," she commanded. The shadows obeyed her and the door was pried apart, bending and snapping against the machines that did not agree with their opening.

She swept through the hallways, this time without confrontation. She suspected they were gathering to lay another trap, doubling the size of the force. Now that she could use the nethergy, and more, they had a reason to stop smiling.

In the next room she came to, employees were scattering across the floor, crying out in helplessness as they stumbled around each other and slid across the waxed floor. Shade's arm flew across a desk, holding the secretary there by her throat.

"Where is he?" she hissed. "Where is the Asgard survivor?"

"Upstairs," the woman whimpered. "At the Halo!"

"How do I get there?"

"The elevator will—" but she winced when Shade squeezed tighter. "There are stairs and risers! The 175th floor!"

Shade dropped her and moved past her. The crowd parted as though she were a walking plague, not stopping their flight even when she was beyond them. An automated voice announced, "Intruder alert in Sector 9. Code Red. All personnel proceed to the nearest evacuation route in a calm and orderly fashion. Panic Vaults are now open." The message repeated over and over. None proceeded calmly, however, and the bloody footprints left behind by the Keeper caused all the more panic in the great, white tower.

Outside Heaven, Rashrima Haan was a quiet, capital hub. None could have suspected what was happening in the tower as they went about their evening in peace and tranquility. That was until a great shriek emanated from the white tower and red lights began flashing, sirens wailing in cadence with the trouble internally. That horrific cry came from none other than the hive mind as it wailed in frustration and fear.

The fact that the Dreadknight could command the very

shadows around her was enough to terrify the hive mind into base survival instincts. It was surrounded in the stuff, the shadows, and no matter how hard it tried to brighten them away, there was always a nook or cranny somewhere that was filled with darkness. Most of those nooks and crannies were in the brain of the hive mind itself.

The city was suddenly locked down and alert, forces sweeping through the streets as far as Luftwafa in the south, Ca'arimiriel in the north, Kaiwi in the west, and Vandenberg in the east. Enforcers, unsure of what they were looking for, were ordered into the street and to attention. News crews near independent of MAAR rallied outside of the walls of Heaven's property, broadcasting to every console and vidscreen connected to the livenet.

In the bowels of the Regent's refuge, Muriel gaped at the screen being held in front of him. The delegates behind him shook with fear. The carnage played out in the streets and lawn of Mirax's headquarters was unmistakably Keeper deeds.

To their own undoing, a media hacker managed to siphon a 12 second clip of internal footage. The long, black hair and violet eyes were inimitable.

"What have I unleashed?" the ex-Regent whispered. Donovon's icy gaze was transfixed on the clip of his arch-nemesis constantly replaying as newscasters speculated and reported and gargled awestruck.

"Oh shit," Donovon muttered, gripped by the glare in her eyes.

Suddenly, behind them the Oracle began to glow. Wraith-like voices hissed and churned with the water. The circulet and Priori shrank away from it, afraid of what was happening.

"Sir!" Kallo yelled as he and his sister Delia burst into Sanctuary, returned from their rounds. He was holding a datapad with a scrawling news report that he thrust in the Baron's hands.

Eros and Daelus both looked at the broadcast with mild interest that quickly turned to utter shock.

"What is it?" Vox wanted to know. The other Interim crowded closer, worried by the alarm splayed on their leaders' faces.

"Shade has attacked Heaven," Eros announced, looking up from the pad, unable to fathom the situation.

"What?" Dimitri exclaimed.

"That goes against everything we as Keepers strove to protect," Sonia reminded them. "Against the Balance!"

"Shade, what have you done?" Eros whispered.

With the rain pouring harder than before, Isis suddenly got to her feet, feeling the tingling sensation in her fingertips. Otto and the cogwheelers looked up, wondering at her strange behavior. She walked out of the Abbey and down the rubble slope until she stood under the falling rain.

Isis tilted her head up to the sky. The sensation had spread up her arms, a cool feeling in her limbs. It branched out in a flurry when it hit her shoulders, racing through her many networks. Through her chest, filling the deep pockets within, and down her sides, weaving through her stomach, and spiking down into her pelvis it spread. It shot into her legs and down her feet until it reached her toes. The sensation through her neck forced her head back further and it climbed up into her jaw, circulated through her lips, burrowed over her cheekbones and into her ears. It lit up the optics in her eye sockets and then finished its course as it plugged and overcame her brain.

"Isis?" Jilk yelled at the top of the slope. She slowly turned to face the cogwheelers. They flinched back.

"What's happening?" Otto called from behind them, still too weak to get up. None had the voice to answer him.

Isis was misting a black aura and her eyes were ten times a darker shade of green. The indentations around her eyes were black. She looked charged, full to the brim with energy.

"I can feel it," she whispered. "I can feel you, Shade."

She closed her eyes for only a second and then tilted her head back again. She was lighter than air, just as she had been when she was still the Sight, as if she was still floating, beyond existence. She couldn't feel the clothes anymore, not the t-shirt or Knick's jacket. Isis wasn't even sure her feet were still on the ground; she felt no rubble beneath her toes. She felt no rain against her skin. Her arms hovered at her sides like plants in water. Her hair brushed her face, her shoulders and chest, her arms, and back.

An ancient tongue vibrated through her throat. Isis could hear it...she could hear Shade's heartbeat, the flux of the power of the Sovereign of the Sword of Shadows, and the voice of the Oracle.

She suddenly cried out. Otto pushed himself up, sometimes crawling, sometimes shuffling hunched over until he stood with the cogwheelers. Solo had to hold him up to witness the happening.

The Enoch could now see everything clearly.

The march of the Dreadknight left the tower of Mirax in utter ruin. It had come to the attention of Operations that it would be better to cut their losses against one Keeper and merely strive to maintain the order of Anshar. Their assembled findings generally concluded an uprising would proceed this disastrous attack.

"We have outposts all over Anshar," the hive mind told itself. "We are in no danger of losing the war."

The argument raged. It was the first time the hive mind had disagreed so adamantly with itself. Of course, it was a night for firsts. Since when had the Keepers had such power? Since when had they been the target of a direct attack.

"She is weakening. We can kill her."

"We can," the rest of the voices agreed.

Centrum's great voice rose into the scramblers of the angels connected to the hive.

"Kill her!" he screeched.

Knick stared up at the Halo, somewhat resigned to his fate. He had removed the scrambler the moment he'd reached the Halo and proceeded to kill every angel that attempted to relieve him of his free will. The scientists were allowed to escape—those who didn't attempt to subdue him. Then, he sealed the doors and wracked his brain for a plan, but every idea dead-ended. He felt trapped.

The attack on Heaven wasn't known to him until the alarms started wailing. He wondered if they were for him. So he killed a few angels inside their sanctum. Big fucking deal. At this point, they would be knocking down the door any minute. That's what he thought. But he'd been waiting for hours and wondered what they were hesitating for.

Were they trying to protect the integrity of the Halo? His gaze flicked over it in wonder and a type of sickened awe. It represented everything he loathed. Knick pulled the bandana out of his jacket and ran his thumb across it.

"Idiot," he cursed himself. "Are you an idiot? Coming back here after it was so hard to get away... Fucking moron." He thought of all the reasons he'd risk it all on such a stupid endeavor but he could only see Shade's face.

There was something at the door. He felt chills go up his back when it wrenched open. It wasn't supposed to open. He'd jammed it. It was going to have to be blasted or melted. He turned around to face what was coming to him, feeling more uneasy than he thought he'd feel.

Covered nearly head to toe in blood stood the Sovereign of the Sword of Shadows. Her long, black hair had come undone and was tangled around her ripped and wounded body, but her violet eyes were bright with life and energy.

"Knick," she gritted.

"Shade?" he asked, astounded. He shook his head, he even pinched himself and bit his tongue, praying he hadn't resigned himself to death so profoundly that he was seeing things.

"We need to go," she told him. "I've worn out my welcome."

"What have you—? How did you—"

"I don't know. I just did."

"Why?"

"To bring you back."

Shade swallowed the taste of copper in her mouth. He stepped closer to her and reached out to touch her face. He smeared the blood across her cheeks in an effort to wipe it away but there was just too much. He never thought he'd see her again.

"What about the Balance? Didn't you fuck that up by coming in here?"

"Yeah," she agreed. "But I didn't think about it at the time."

Knick couldn't stop himself from grinning. *Take that, Zara,* he thought. He hugged her much to her surprise. She didn't hug him back, he noticed. Her arms were stiff, as if stuck, braced at her sides. Her sword was clutched so tightly, her fingers were trembling. But her head slumped against his shoulder in acceptance.

That's when Knick knew everything was going to be okay. He squeezed tighter and she grunted so he eased up.

"Lead the way," he said as he stepped out of the hug. "I'll be a good princess and follow the knight out of the tower."

Shade narrowed her gaze on him, annoyed. Then she noticed the Halo. The bright blue sphere rotated like a helix, projecting a great image. Thousands of numbers raced across a complex ordering of information that dwarfed the room.

"What is it?" she whispered, nodding in its direction. Knick twisted at the torso.

"The Halo," he replied. "It's a record of every angel that ever existed and that exists today. All of these numbers are all of the men under the hive mind. Only Operations can fully understand what we're looking at. Operations assigns the numbers once the man is brought forth." He glanced back at her. "Women cannot be angels."

"Why?"

"They can't be mind-controlled. Their emotions break the bond with the hive mind under the right conditions. Those factors cannot be broken down into chemical understanding and therefore they cannot be dehumanized. Honestly," he mused, "the thought of someone trying to control *you*…"

There was a loud bang in the corridors outside the chamber. She spun around, ready.

"Is there a way out of here aside from the front door?" she asked.

He put his fingers to his forehead, desperately trying to remember everything he knew about the tower, about what he had seen upon returning. No good. He glanced around, grasping at everything he laid his eyes on in vain hope. Nothing.

"Wait a minute," he muttered, eyeing the magnifying glass pane at the top of the catwalks. "The lens—it's a back-up generator to power the Halo in case of failure. It connects to three different grid bulbs."

Shade nodded. "Get up there. Get it open."

"What about you?'

But he heard the angels in the hallway. They appeared before his feet could move. He watched momentarily as they filled the space, blocking the exit with layers and layers of bodies. Shade sunk into a battle stance, sword raised high.

"Knick, go," she commanded. One of the angels stepped forward.

"There is nowhere to go. We will kill the fallen angel after we have killed you," he said.

"You won't touch him!" she cried and a column of nethergy shot out of the ground, spearing the man who had spoken up and eating up his essence in seconds. He collapsed no more than a heap of bone. "How many of you do I have to kill to get the message through?" Without looking back, she yelled, "Knick, *go!*"

His feet started moving that time and he ran to the back, taking the phaseporter up to the higher levels. He didn't let himself watch the carnage unfolding beneath his feet; every glimpse he granted himself gripped his chest with fear. Though she slaughtered every angel that came at her, she was wearing down.

He wondered how many hours of fighting she'd endured? He wondered how many wounds she had, and how much blood smeared on that graceful form belonged to her.

Instead of getting stuck in these thoughts, he climbed the catwalks as fast as he could until he reached the lens. He pushed and tugged but it was sealed in the wall. It had to be at least ten inches thick, possibly more. It was impossible to tell. He tried punching it, but that only embarrassed him with bloody, cracked knuckles. He braced himself and tried kicking it a few times, but it was impervious. The Nightwalker dagger he'd confiscated from an angel he killed was useless against it.

Knick groped around on the catwalks, desperate for something. A loose beam, a forgotten wrench—anything. But Heaven was too methodical for such an important room to go unrepaired. Clutter, too, was against the will of the hive mind. A machine required an absolute measure of order. But what the hell could break glass this thick?

"Wait a second," he mumbled, touching on a long-shot of an idea.

Knick hopped down the catwalks until he was level with the peak of the Halo. He kicked at the thick cable streaming from the machine, finding the one directly connected to the power supply. Next, he ripped smaller cables from the Halo and dragged them up to the lens, using their magnetic hinge to stick them to the plate ring around it. Electricity sparked and buzzed along the glass, crackling and hissing and popping. It wouldn't be enough, he knew, but it would help compromise it.

He glanced down below and regretted it instantly. He could barely tell what was going on or differentiate one body from the next.

Hurrying, Knick went to the broadcasting panel at the wall, forced it open, and tugged at the wires, pulling some out and reconnecting others. Next, he ripped the scrambler cord out of his shirt and hooked it into the panel. Then, he went back to the Halo and to the large coil.

"Operations!" he screamed, commanding the full attention of the hive mind. Then, he began hacking away at the cable with the knife and bashing the connectors with the handle.

A loud screech surged through the scramblers the angels wore, and also through the speaker in the chamber. It wasn't enough. He kept hacking, working through the ear-shattering sound that blasted through. Finally, the cable was unhinged and a spray of electricity whipped out. Somehow, he dodged it. Then, the crippling cry squealed so loudly that the compromised lens cracked. Knick fought through the paralyzing sound, catching glimpses of the fight below. The angels mostly collapsed in agony, unable to withstand the shriek of the angry hive mind nor capable of deciphering the information in the cry.

Knick knew why: because there was no information. There was only rage.

Shade stumbled, somehow keeping on her feet. Anyone that came at her, she slapped their attack away with her sword, but it was a heavy and tortured battle. They all were stumbling in agony, unsure of whether they were to keep fighting or suffer together.

He ripped the scrambler out of the wall and the noise suddenly stopped for them. The angels still twisted in pain. Shade looked up at Knick, both panting with the exertion. He hauled himself up to the lens and ripped the cables away. With one quick kick, the glass shattered out.

The angels suddenly got to their feet, recovering from the scream that must have finally stopped. Shade's feet slid back, knees starting to give way.

"Shade!" Knick exclaimed.

Just as the angels charged, the Keeper shadow-stepped and reappeared at Knick's side. Before he knew what was happening, he was being forced out of the window and was freefalling in the cold night air with her arms tight around him.

"Shade?" he cried in a panic. Her eyes were calm, lips barely moving as she whispered something. He felt the strangest sensation in his body. He frantically searched for something to stop their fall but there was only blackness—an unnatural blackness rising up to meet them.

And when they passed into the great shadow, they did not come out the other side.

The Enoch suddenly fell out of the power flux and dropped onto her hands and knees. Her head snapped up, hair flying with the movement.

"They're here!" she announced.

Just then, two bodies fell out of the shadows of the Abbey, rolling across the floor. Shade's long, black hair twisted around them, tangled.

"Knick!" Solo exclaimed; the cogwheelers ran to help their friend. He was already on his feet and helping Shade to hers. The group recoiled at the sight of her.

"We have to get out of here," Knick said. "We have to get back to the Mine."

Otto took a quick survey as he helped Isis back up the rubble. The number was 8. Masha had told him that one day, when the shadow was in trouble, they would go to her. The number was 8. He took a quick count. Eight.

"You're the shadow?" Otto asked Shade. She looked up at him with hard, strong eyes surrounded by weak and bloody tissue.

"She is," Isis confirmed.

"Then I know the way. Come on, hurry!"

Solo ran to the back and hoisted Antion up while Knick and Jilk helped Shade down the slide. Slot supported her brother's load down the hill and then kept ahead of the group with her fists at the ready. When they hit the alley, they heard the commotion out on the streets. Hanging back, they observed, wondering what the hell the enforcers were doing patrolling.

Otto recognized one of them and flinched when they made eye contact. Mr. Fischer jogged over to the alley.

"Otto?" he gasped. "What happened to you? Where've you been?" He noticed those with him, the injured and the bloody. Shade glared up at him, twitching, with eyes ready to kill. "What...happened?"

"Mr. Fischer, sir," Otto croaked. "My friends and I are in danger. We have to get to Masha right now."

"Masha?" he repeated. "But why?"

"Please. I can't explain." And Otto really couldn't. He had no idea what was going on. He was following orders given by dreams turned reality, yet nothing had been explained.

"They're looking for you," Fischer said to Shade. "You're the one they're desperate to find. You and your friend here. But you...you've damaged the tower into unspeakable rage. They're desperate to find you."

Shade's eyes were wild. And though she could barely stand, barely keep her head up, he was afraid of the primal nature of those eyes. Slot stepped in front of the group threateningly, but Fischer held his hands up in surrender.

"I have no intention of turning you over to the demons I hate. But it won't be easy getting across the street. Once they spot you, you're finished."

The Shadow Sword scraped across the ground as the Sovereign brought it to bearing.

"I will kill them if they try," she hissed.

"Like that?" he said gently. Her feral gaze widened as though she dared them to come for her. He turned and stared across the alley. "It's a short run across. There are only five men close enough to stop you—three on the left, two on the right. But once you get to Masha's you'll have nowhere else to go and more men will be on their way."

"Hey, Fischer!" one of the other enforcers called. "You find something?"

"Just a couple of frightened stragglers!" he yelled back, then whispered, "What will you do then?"

"It'll be okay," Otto assured him. "Trust me."

Fischer nodded and motioned Isis and Otto out. He pulled Solo carrying Antion out first then nudged Slot along. She hesitated, wanting to protect her friends, but Jilk shook his head and silently bid her go. She obeyed.

"Get across the street," he told them, then glanced back at the others. "I'll distract them then you head across. Start running the moment they catch on to you. I'll cover you, and it should give you enough time to get across the street."

And then he disappeared with the others, explaining about how they were scared and one of them was hurt and they just needed shelter. Masha can help, that's what he said, and they all knew it was true. After a few moments, Knick and Jilk agreed it was time to go and began inching out of the alley. They managed to hit the street before something began barking at them.

As ordered by Fischer, they ducked low and began running.

"Hey, stop!" someone yelled. "Hold it ri—"

A pulse beam whizzed through his throat before he could finish the command. The team was shocked initially and Fischer managed to kill another one before they returned fire. He ducked behind one of the closer enforcers and took out the second closest to him. The third on the other side shot out his meat shield and Fischer got him back.

Knick, Jilk, and Shade ducked into *The Dark Mermaid* just as back-up arrived to investigate. Fischer was gunned down on the spot.

"What's going on here?" Masha exclaimed as she stomped from the back of her shop. The moment she laid eyes on Isis, her face paled and she stumbled against the bar. "It's you. You've finally come!" She counted the people in the room. "It is time."

Masha jammed a button under the bar and reinforced barricades sealed the door and window.

"Follow me," she said, sweeping into the back.

They followed her into a cramped space where she pulled the shelves aside and banged out a hidden passage. Lifting the boards away and using her thumb print to unlock the door, she hurried down a long, narrow, and rough corridor to an even tinier room. In the floor was a rusted hatch. She twisted the valve and the pressure locks hissed when they released. She yanked it open and motioned them inside.

"Where does this go?" Jilk asked.

"To the Mine," she replied, "to our sister sanctum, *The*

Bright Mermaid. They are friends of *her*," she pointed to Isis, "and will help you. You must hurry. It won't be long now."

Slot climbed down first and helped Isis and Otto into the steep and sloping tunnel. Solo handed Antion down, and then climbed down himself. Jilk went in after and helped lower Shade inside.

"Aren't you coming?" Knick asked halfway down the ladder when Masha went to close the vault.

"I must seal it," she replied, afraid. "Now go. It's time."

Knick dropped the rest of the way as she slammed the hatch closed and twisted the valve. A loud siren penetrated even the ground, hurrying them along in the blackness. The ground began shaking as they stumbled, and then a violent tremor knocked them down the tunnel, rolling until they hit a drop-off and fell straight down into the blackness.

"Shade!" Knick exclaimed, feeling her body limp in his arms. "*Shade!*"

"Get up!" a familiar voice called out to them. Two pairs of blue eyes shone in the pitch.

"Lethan?" Knick coughed. "How did you—?"

"No time!" he hissed. "Get up! I will lead you. Now come."

Another tremor knocked them around as the Krueh-jin scout and his lehn companion tugged them along. Directly above ground, a smoldering plot of embers popped and snapped where *The Dark Mermaid* used to be, and the tunnel to Kishar had collapsed in the bombing.

Hezara was halfway to Thebes, just hitting Skiba. In the middle of the night, it was a ghost town and she wasn't surprised to find the streets deserted and dim. Quietly, she shifted from spotlight to spotlight, wondering if keeping herself in the open would do any good in a place that spooked.

The feeling that someone had been following her was even more prevalent than before and she'd had a cold, creeping sensation on her spine since that morning.

Hezara frowned, glancing back. The street was empty, as

expected; still, she'd been sure someone was following her. She put her foot forward and stepped out of the spotlight. The hard arms of an assassin reached out, grabbing her throat and head and tossing her to the ground. She tried to react with Nabari magic, but was not fast enough. Her attacker kicked her hand away and then kicked her face. The toes of his boot caught the chain connecting her nose and earring and ripped them both out. She yelled, twisted onto her stomach, and held her face in pain.

The boots came close and a cold hand gripped her bald head, lifting her up effortlessly. His spiky, blond hair and light blue eyes were menacing.

"Who...are you...?" she mumbled, feeling warm liquid dripping down the side of her head and over her lip. She could taste the blood in her mouth and felt the sting of pain from the cut on her lip.

"You were traveling around with a man called Knick Coltin. You carried a package. Give it to me."

"I delivered it," she rasped. He smacked her hard and she was sure he knocked some teeth loose.

"The package wasn't with Roskolniv, only some fucking letter. Give it to me," he persisted.

"I don't have it."

"Hand it over and I'll be merciful."

She spat in his face. "I will never help you," she whispered. "Long live...the Keepers..."

At first he glared, and then he grinned. "The Keepers are dead," he mumbled.

The shing of a weapon being drawn caused her to twitch. Then she felt it plunge into her back, eyes widening in shock. Then the icy sensation began to spread from her toes to her legs and knees, traveling up her body. She winced, looking down. Her body was being frozen. She could already feel her blood flow start to slow.

The man smiled at her, showing his teeth. Hezara tried to kick but her legs were frozen. Panicking, her eyes glared wildly at her assailant as the ice comppletely encased her. Her heart froze over long before her face and terrified eyes.

Donovon dropped her to the ground, reveling in the crunch. Then, he bent to wretch her satchel from her frosty drapes. When he dug inside, he found only empty boxes,

Nabari marbles, and miscellaneous documents. With a scream, he flung the memorabilia into the street and stalked off, disappearing into the black fog of transportation.

A picture fluttered to the ground. There were two people in the photo. One was a woman, smiling, with short, blond hair and henna tattoos on her neck and arms; she had several piercings on her ears and one on her nose. She was leaning against a black-haired man with slanted eyes and a five-o-clock shadow; he, too, was smiling and had his arm around her.

The couple looked happy, as though they lived in another lifetime.

[The Order of the Keepers]

The Order//The Order of the Keepers is the utmost neutral force with one goal in mind: to protect the Balance. The Order exists under a strict hierarchy, with the Regent at the head and twenty-six delegates that act as his council. His personal representative is the Consular. Beneath the Regent are the three Primordials; they are the High Counselor, the Baron, and the Cleric. The High Counselor, the scholar, is head of the collective and Oracle, bearing five priests as consultants. The Baron, the military leader, controls the Interim and the Kur, who are managed by seven generals. And the Cleric, the healer, oversees the naga and the Enoch.

The Collective//A group of monks split into two sects. The first, and the majority, is the scholars that spend day after day in the libraries researching the prophecies. The second is a very small group called the savants that tend to the Oracle, recording all information the Oracle bestows. The savants pass that information to the scholars, who research everything pertaining to the prophecy. The scholars pass their research to the High Counselor, who, aided by his priests, sifts through the research, discarding irrelevant information and organizing the rest to present to the Regent, who will use the research to interpret the prophecy's meaning with the guidance of his delegates.

The Oracle//An unknown force of fate seen through a scrying pool. It reveals glyphs and murmurs prophecy. The Oracle can be invoked but usually only speaks when it wants to. The Oracle is one of two equal parts and forms a synergistic bond with the Enoch. The Oracle resides in a very private chamber called the Seer's Cell; only the savants, the Primordials, and the Regent are allowed to enter.

The Interim and Kur//The Interim is a small sect of elite warriors chosen by the Balance to wield the aegises, weapons of power. They answer to the Baron and the Regent only. The

Kur are the military force who performs everything from small, covert missions to large-scale assaults.

The Naga and Enoch//The naga are the attendants of the Enoch, a very small group that is comprised entirely of females. The Enoch is the dreamweaver and the other half of the Oracle. The naga, the Cleric, and the Regent are the only ones allowed to enter the Enoch's chamber.

Priori//The Regent's personal bodyguards; an individual is called a Prior. They are promoted into the position from the Kur and their command is transferred from the Baron to the Regent.

Elysium//A period of one month out of the year when the collective are not allowed to use the Oracle or the Enoch. It is believed that fate and the future is like a delicate spider web; when the spider web is poked and prodded too much, it breaks. The Keepers declare Elysium as a time when none are allowed to interfere with that delicate web and tamper with fate, allowing the threads to strengthen and fall as they may. It had never before been broken until Ralph Gobol accidentally discovered the prophecy concerning the new glyph. Emergency states of Elysium have been called before, but only in the most strenuous of times when the fate lines are very thin and tangled.

Vanguard//A state of emergency that gives the Baron and his Interim supreme power over all Keeper proceedings, resources, and persons, including the Regent, to solve a problem or problems. Vanguard may only be invoked by the Baron and only under extreme duress. Once the problem is resolved, Vanguard ends and power is immediately restored to the respective authorities.

Circulet//The official assembly of the Regent and his closest delegates, named for the semi-circle arrangement of the thrones.

Ether//Pure energy with mystical properties. Ethergy is positive ether that adds energy to the world; its counterpart is nethergy, the negative ether that takes energy out of it.

[Angels]

The Nest//A chamber in the deepest sub-layer of Heaven that houses Operations.

Operations// A collaboration of three parts. The first is a complex computer motherboard and processor composed of both organic and synthetic material called the cerebrum. The second is twelve men, part-human and part-cyborg, plugged into the cerebrum. Finally, there is Centrum, the mostly-cyborg spokesman who issues the orders to the angels.

Hive Mind//The Operations network that every angel is neurally connected to.

Halo//The DNA archive of every angel, past and present.

[Cogwheelers]

Street Gun//Cogwheeler field operative. There are seven types; the most common are cogger, gunny, heavy, and techy, and the rare ones are sammy, firebug, and longsights.

Cogger//The leader of a cogwheeler cell and tactics master.

Gunny//Weapons specialist is the official job description but that's just code for "uses lots of guns". Gunnies are the most common type of Street Gun.

Heavy//Brute force. Once the gun clips are empty, a Heavy will go straight into a fistfight, utilizing everything they can as a weapon until they are taken out.

Techy//Tech experts, typically hackers.

Sammy//Slang for samurai, which is slang for melee weapons expert. Sammies are rare in that it takes a rare individual to bring a sword to a gun fight and walk away still breathing.

Firebug//Demolitions expert with a penchant for flame-throwers, though there's little need for explosives in the mine, and flamethrowers in tight spaces (like most spaces found underground) typically cause unnecessary collateral damage.

Longsights//Sniper. This type of Street Gun is so rare that each sniper wears his title like a name.

[Other]

Krueh-jin//Gypsy nomads who shine their eyes to see in the dark and hunt with creatures called lunalehn. They inhabit the Grey, constantly scavenging for lost treasures, artifacts, and relics. Their survival depends on trade so thievery is punishable by death.

Bloodsworn//The dark messengers of Lotus Maze who, for a pretty price, transport letters, packages, verbal messages, and much more back and forth between Anshar, Kishar, and even the coal mines near the core. They have outposts in nearly every city where their agents can report. Whoever is given the letter and payment delivers the package; whatever payment the Sworn accepts is fully his, so being paid with items as well as currency is not uncommon.

ACKNOWLEDGEMENTS

First and foremost, thank you to my family for always encouraging me to write, even when it felt like it bordered on the bored listener dying to escape my never-ending informationals outlining in great detail my many story ideas. Thank you for your love, your support, and your willingness to let an overactive imagination run rampant. And thank you Dad for always calling out of the blue to ask me if I've written anymore on my story.

Thank you Fonzi for asking "when are you going to write the next part?" Without you, *Mesopotamia//Tiamat* would be a 25-page short story lost somewhere on my hard drive. Thank you Hugh for inspiring me to write this story. Thank you Robert for spending what little free time you had editing my manuscript.

Thank you to GRV Mortifer for providing the perfect soundtrack to write to.

A very special thank you to "Sill". You have spent countless hours at the most random times, night or day, helping me work through scenes, solve problems, and find the answers to my many questions. Thank you for your patience and perseverance when I was being unacceptably difficult. Without you, my works would undoubtedly remain unfinished.

About the Author

Ashley's first great fictional loves were Star Wars, EverQuest, and Nexus Prime. Her greatest passions in life are writing and video games. She has been writing fantasy and science fiction since she was a child and gaming nearly as long, accumulating many obnoxious "in my day, in the snow, uphill both ways" stories of the gamer equivalent. She is obsessed with jesters and tricksters, has wanted to be a Jedi Knight since she was four years old, and is terrified of xenomorphs.

About the Cover Artist

Oksana Kharitonova, also known as Aira Gitt, is an amazing artist from Russia who studied CG and illustration on her own, and draws every single day. Her artwork can be viewed and commissioned at airagitt.deviantart.com and airagitt.tumblr.com.

Working with Oksana was a great experience. She is so talented, was easy to talk to, and focused on capturing my vision. I honestly can't say enough kind things about her.

About Mesopotamia//Tiamat

Mesopotamia//Tiamat was originally a short story written in 2008 as an experiment in writing styles, intended to feel like a blur of action rather than fleshed out prose. When it became a short story series, the storytelling method evolved again and again until it became the novel it is today.

While the bulk of Mesopotamia//Tiamat is fictional, much of the content concerning Mesopotamia and its mythology is based on the historical cradle of civilization and ancient Mesopotamian religion.